P. J. Tracy lives in the US. *Want to Play?* is her first novel.

Want to Play?

P. J. TRACY

PENGUIN BOOKS

PENGUIN BOOKS

Published by the Penguin Group
Penguin Books Ltd, 80 Strand, London WC2R ORL, England
Penguin Group (USA) Inc., 375 Hudson Street, New York, New York 10014, USA
Penguin Books Australia Ltd, 250 Camberwell Road, Camberwell, Victoria 3124, Australia
Penguin Books Canada Ltd, 10 Alcorn Avenue, Toronto, Ontario, Canada M4V 3B2
Penguin Books India (P) Ltd, 11 Community Centre, Panchsheel Park, New Delhi – 110 017, India
Penguin Books (NZ) Ltd, CNR Rosedale and Airborne Roads, Albany, Auckland, New Zealand
Penguin Books (South Africa) (Pty) Ltd, 24 Sturdee Avenue, Rosebank 2196, South Africa

Penguin Books Ltd, Registered Offices: 80 Strand, London WC2R ORL, England

www.penguin.com

First published in the United States of America as *Monkeewrench* by G. P. Putnam's Sons 2003
First published in Great Britain as *Want to Play?* by Michael Joseph 2003
Published in Penguin Books 2004
1

Set in Monotype Garamond
Typeset by Rowland Phototypesetting Ltd, Bury St Edmunds, Suffolk
Printed in Great Britain by Clays Ltd, St Ives plc

ISBN: 978-0-141-04983-0

www.greenpenguin.co.uk

For Edie and Don Hepler

We remember

I

The brandy had been absolutely essential. It always was on Sunday nights, when Sister Ignatius took it upon herself to cook and serve Father Newberry a 'proper meal.' In this part of Wisconsin that usually translated to hamburger cooked in canned cream soup.

The shape varied with the good sister's whims – sometimes meatballs, sometimes meat loaf, and on one memorable occasion, rolled tubes that looked disturbingly like a casserole of severed penises – but the basic ingredients and the resulting indigestion were always the same.

Father Newberry had learned long ago that antacids couldn't touch it. Only the brandy helped, blessing him with a quick sleep where he passed the time in happy oblivion while his stomach fought the demons of Sister Ignatius's kindness.

On this particular Sunday night the demons had been multiple. In some sort of aspiring gourmet fit the sister had baked meat loaf in God only knew how many different kinds of canned soups. When he'd asked her to name the ingredients of this daring culinary experiment, she'd tittered like a schoolgirl and locked her lips with an imaginary key.

'Ah, a secret recipe.' He had smiled at her rosy face, greatly fearing that clam chowder lurked somewhere in the ocean of oily liquid in which the meat loaf had drowned.

And so it was that the juice glass had been filled with brandy for an unprecedented second time, and Father Newberry had fallen fast asleep in the recliner facing the television. When he next opened his eyes, the screen was a snowfield of jittery flakes hissing static, and the clock face read five A.M.

When he went to turn off the lamp by the window, he saw the frosty car in the church lot and recognized it immediately. It was a Ford Falcon of indeterminate age, dying slowly of the cancerous rust that devoured old cars in a state that salted roads as liberally as they salted food.

In a moment of weakness, he wished he could just sneak off to his warm bed and pretend he'd never seen it. His only sin was in the wish, however, for he was already moving toward the door, tugging his cardigan close around his abused belly before stepping out into the dark chill of an October morning.

The church was old and almost Protestant in its plainness, for these rural Wisconsin Catholics eyed all things magnificent with deep suspicion. The Blessed Virgin wore the gleam of plastic and bore an unsaintly resemblance to the mannequin in the window of Frieda's House of Fashion on Main Street, and the only stained glass window was oddly placed on the north side, where the sun could never set it afire with brilliant color that might offend.

A dour place in a dour parish in a dour state, thought Father Newberry, missing the California of his youth, nearly forty years gone now, speculating again that all bad priests were sent to Wisconsin.

John and Mary Kleinfeldt were kneeling in a middle pew, heads resting on folded hands, utterly still in a devotion the Father had always thought almost obsessive. It was not unusual for the aging couple to visit the church during off-hours – sometimes he thought they preferred solitude to the company of fellow parishioners they believed corrupt with sin. But to the best of his knowledge, they had never come so early.

It did not bode well for a rapid return to the cozy rectory, and Father Newberry was loath to ask what trouble had brought them here this time, since he already knew the answer.

He sighed and moved slowly down the aisle, reluctantly propelled by a sense of duty and a good heart. 'Good morning, John. Good morning, Mary,' he would say. 'What troubles you today?' And then they would tell him they had discovered yet another homosexual in his congregation – a man whose lashes were too long or a woman whose voice was too deep, for this was proof enough for them.

It wasn't simply homophobia; it was a zealous crusade against what they called the 'abhorrent, unnatural offense to God's eye,' and listening to their self-righteous accusations always left him feeling sad and somehow soiled.

Please let it be something else this time, Lord, he prayed as he drew near the middle pew. I have, after all, already endured the penance of good Sister Ignatius's meat loaf.

And indeed it was something else. What was troubling John and Mary Kleinfeldt this morning was not the suspected presence of homosexuals in the parish, but the indisputable presence of small, tidy bullet holes in the backs of their skulls.

2

It wasn't the first homicide in Kingsford County since Sheriff Michael Halloran had pinned on his star five years ago. Scatter a few thousand people over the northern Wisconsin countryside, arm a good half of them with hunting rifles and skinning knives, throw a hundred bars into the mix, and eventually some of them are going to end up killing each other. That's just the way it was.

It didn't happen very often, and for the most part they were the kind of killings people up here could get their heads around: bar fights, domestics, and the occasional suspicious hunting accident, like when Harry Patrowski said he shot his mother through the kitchen window because he thought she was a deer.

But an old couple gunned down in a church? Now that was something else, something senseless and evil that wasn't supposed to happen in a little town where kids played outside after dark, nobody locked their doors, and corn wagons still lumbered down Main Street on their way to the feed mill. Hell, half the people in the county thought smoking a joint meant lighting your elbow on fire, and you still had to drive ninety miles south and east to Green Bay just to see an 'R' movie.

This murder was going to change everything.

Four of the five squad cars on third watch were

already in St Luke's parking lot by the time Halloran arrived at six A.M.

Great, he thought. I've got one car left on the road patrolling over eight hundred square miles of county. He saw Doc Hanson's ugly blue station wagon sandwiched between two of the squads, and off in a corner, an ancient Ford Falcon in an ominous rectangle of yellow crime-scene tape.

Deputy Bonar Carlson walked out of the church and waited on the top step, tugging at a belt that had no hope of ever again making it up to his belly button.

'Bonar, that holster hangs much lower you're going to have to kneel if you ever need to get at your weapon.'

'And I'd still beat you at the draw,' Bonar grinned, which was true. 'Man, you're ugly this early. Good thing you don't work the third. You'd scare the other boys.'

'Just tell me you've solved this already so I can go back home to bed.'

'Way I figure, Father Newberry did it. Forty years of listening to confessions and sniffing incense and then one day, poor bastard just snaps and shoots two of his parishioners in the back of the head.'

'I'm going to tell him you said that.'

Bonar stuffed his fat hands into his jacket pockets and snorted a frosty exhale, serious now. 'He didn't hear anything, didn't see anything. Fell asleep in front of the TV after dinner, didn't even know Kleinfeldts were here until he looked out the window at five A.M. and saw their car. Went over to see if he could help, found the bodies, dialed 911, end of story.'

'Neighbors?'

'We're working on it.'

'So what's your take on it?'

It wasn't an idle question. Bonar might look and talk and act like another good old Wisconsin boy, but there were some scary processing chips in that head of his. He could take one look at a crime scene and tell you things the state forensics boys would never find with all their fancy equipment.

He and Bonar had both done a year-long stint in Milwaukee right out of the academy before hustling back home and jumping into county uniforms. They'd seen a lot in that city they were still trying to forget, but they'd learned a lot, too.

Bonar sucked at the inside of his cheek for a minute, thick eyebrows working like a pair of caterpillars. 'Actually, it looks like a hit, which makes about as much sense as the padre doing it. I don't know. My gut tells me psycho, but it seems too clean for that.' He pushed open the heavy wooden doors.

A lifetime of conditioning made Halloran's hand twitch as he passed the font of holy water, but it was only a twitch, the last contraction of a dying thing.

Father Newberry was sitting in a back pew, motionless, tiny, old. Halloran touched his shoulder as he walked up the aisle, felt the answering brush of dry fingertips on his.

Two deputies were stringing yellow crime-scene tape from pew to pew in a terrible parody of the white satin ribbon draped for a wedding. Two others were on their hands and knees with flashlights, searching the floor.

Doc Hanson was crouched sideways in the narrow space between the Kleinfeldts and the pew in front of them, eyes and hands busy with the dead, oblivious to the living. Nobody talked. The church was absolutely silent.

Halloran circled the scene slowly, letting it imprint on his mind. There was something wrong with it; something a little off-kilter about the bodies, dancing at the edge of his consciousness, just out of reach.

'Just from the rigor, four hours, give or take,' Doc Hanson said without being asked, without looking up. 'I'll check the temps when I'm ready to move them. Harris, give me one of your bags. I got a hair here.'

Long gone, Halloran thought, moving out of the way, back down the aisle toward Father Newberry. Whoever did this could be in New York by now, or California, or next door.

'So everybody hated them.'

'I didn't say that, Mikey.'

'Father, meaning no offense, but could you not call me Mikey when I'm on the job?'

'Sorry. It slipped out.' Father Newberry smiled at the one man on this earth he could truly and freely admit he loved like a son in a very human way. Michael Vincent Halloran was broad and tall and very imposing indeed with a gun on his hip and a badge on his chest, but the priest still saw Mikey the altar boy, dark and intense in this land of bland and blond, tailing him through those years before puberty when the priesthood had still been a magnet.

'Okay, then who were their friends?'

The priest sighed. 'They had no friends.'

'You're not helping, Father.'

'No, I suppose I'm not.' Father Newberry frowned at the yellow crime-scene tape around the pews ahead, framing the centerpiece of John and Mary Kleinfeldt. Doc Hanson was rummaging in his bag now, bumping John Kleinfeldt's body, grabbing it by the shoulder when it started to tip over. Father Newberry closed his eyes.

Halloran tried again. 'You said they tried to get several parishioners removed from the congregation because they believed they were homosexual. I'll need a list of those people.'

'But none of them took it seriously. I can't think of one who was really upset, the accusations were so preposterous.'

'So none of them are really gay?'

Father Newberry hesitated again. 'Not to my knowledge.'

'I'll need the list anyway, Father. You have a file on the Kleinfeldts? Next of kin, that sort of thing?'

'In the church office, but they had no family.'

'No kids?'

Father Newberry looked down at his hands, at the shiny spots on the knees of his pants that marked him as a professional supplicant, thinking that this was the gray area; that dreaded place where the obligations to the secular and spiritual worlds clashed in a terrible way. He sorted through his memory for what he could say, setting aside what he could not. 'I believe they had a child, but they refused to speak of him. Or her. I don't even know if the child was son or daughter.'

'Still alive?'

'I don't know that either. I'm sorry.'

'It's all right. Anything else you can tell me about them?'

The priest frowned, mentally ticking off the pathetically few scraps of information he possessed about the Kleinfeldts. 'They were retired, of course, at their age. Both in their seventies, as I recall. Very devout, in their own way more than God's, I'm sorry to say. And very solitary. I don't think they trusted a living soul, including me, and I always thought that was very sad. I suppose that isn't an uncommon trait among the wealthy.'

Halloran looked doubtfully at the shabbily dressed corpses. 'Land poor?'

Father Newberry shook his head. 'They tithed a precise ten percent. December thirty-first every year they'd send a check and a financial statement from their accountant to prove it was exactly ten percent, as if I would question it.'

Halloran grunted. 'Weird.'

'They were . . . unusual people.'

'So what were they worth?'

The priest looked up, found his memory on the ceiling. 'Over seven million, I believe, but that was last year. It would be considerably more now.'

Behind them the church door opened and closed and a wave of cold moved up the aisle, Bonar in its wake. He stopped next to Halloran. 'We got nothing from the neighbors. State forensics is just pulling in.' His eyes narrowed on Halloran's face. 'What? You got something?'

'Motive, maybe. Father tells me they were worth millions.'

Bonar glanced up the aisle at the bodies. 'No way.'

'It isn't exactly a motive, Mike,' the priest interjected. 'Unless you consider me a suspect. They left everything to the church.'

Bonar elbowed Halloran. 'I told you the padre did it.'

Father Newberry almost smiled; stopped it just in time. 'Lutherans,' he muttered instead.

Up in the front of the church Doc Hanson stood abruptly. 'Oh *shit*.' He shot a quick, guilty glance back at Father Newberry. 'Sorry, Father. Mike, you want to come and take a look at this?'

Beneath the black coat that Doc Hanson had started to unbutton, Mary Kleinfeldt's once-white blouse was saturated with the red-brown of coagulating blood. The smell of it filled the pew.

'She was shot in the chest, too?' Halloran asked.

Doc Hanson shook his head. 'Not unless they brought along a cannon. Head hole looks like a .22, and this is way too much blood for anything that small.' He unbuttoned the soggy blouse and opened it. The two deputies watching both took a quick step backward.

'Jesus,' one of them whispered. 'Looks like someone started a do-it-yourself autopsy.'

Mary Kleinfeldt's slip and bra had been sliced in half and peeled to each side, exposing blue-veined skin that had never seen the sun. A vertical gash ran down the center of her chest, exposing the sternum. Another gash ran horizontally, so deep that the lower half of her breasts hung inside out.

Halloran stared at the old woman's chest and felt a new kind of fear he couldn't put a name to yet. 'That's not an autopsy incision,' he said softly. 'It's a cross.'

3

Grace MacBride lived in the Merriam Park neighborhood of St Paul, on a block of tall, narrow houses that remembered the Roaring Twenties. Her backyard was very small, and the solid wood fence around it was very high. Mitch said it was like being in a shoebox with the lid off, but then Mitch had always had a problem with the small closed spaces that were Grace's salvation.

The tree was the real reason she'd bought the place. It wasn't much of a tree, by Mitch's suburban standards, with a fat squat trunk and gnarled limbs that grew sideways instead of up, as if the sky were weighing them down. But it was a magnolia, by God, and that was a rare thing in Minnesota. A precious thing.

Mitch had been quick to point out the cramped lot, the nearby fire station, the hard-pack rectangle of earth the realtor had dubbed a backyard; but he'd been trying to talk her out of buying the house then, trying to lure her to the Minneapolis suburb where he and Diane lived in a neighborhood of sprawling lawns so perfectly trimmed and edged they looked like they were screaming.

'You could surround yourself with space there,' he'd told her; 'a couple of empty acres where you could see someone coming in plenty of time.'

But Grace had only smiled and said, 'This place has a magnolia.'

'Not for long,' he'd replied. 'If it is a magnolia, it'll be dead in a year.'

That had been five years ago, and Grace had never once believed the tree would die, even though it appeared to attempt suicide on an annual basis. Every fall it dropped crisping leaves in a single, noisy shower, as if it just didn't have the strength to hang on to them any longer. But every spring the bud clusters swelled and burst and tiny green fingers waved at new blue sky in a silly fit of optimism. The tree was a survivor, just like she was.

This morning it was drooping in the dry air of autumn, threatening to drop its leaves in the next heartbeat, and she had the hose running at the base of its trunk.

She and Charlie sat on the two Adirondack chairs facing the tree, listening to the trickle of water, watching morning happen. Grace was mummified in a long terry robe; Charlie was naked.

'You've got to stop pissing on it. It's too much ammonia.' Her voice was layered with the faint trace of a southern accent corrupted by the cold, brittle cadence of the north.

Charlie turned his head and watched with rapt attention as Grace sipped from her cup.

'Forget it. It's caffeinated.'

Charlie sighed and looked away. He was a mess of a dog, a concoction slapped together by a blind Frankenstein. The size and bulk of a shepherd, the wiry coat of a terrier, the long, floppy ears of a hound, and a totally hairless stump of a tail that something had chewed off long before she'd met him. Charlie was a survivor, too.

Grace moved in the chair, felt the gun slide to one side of the robe's oversized pocket, and grabbed it before it could clunk against the wood chair.

The holster is not a fashion accessory. It is a safety necessity. Keep your firearm in its holster whenever you're carrying, and never, ever *carry a gun in your pocket, are you hearing me, class?*

Well, yes, Grace had certainly heard him, but you had to take some small chances every now and then; otherwise caution became paranoia and it ruled your life. Sitting in her own backyard in her bathrobe was one of those things that seemed worth the risk. Not that she would have tried it unarmed – she wasn't that stupid.

'Well, this has been nice, but I've got to get to work.'

Charlie whined once and shifted his haunches in the chair like an old man in a hair coat.

'Please don't get up. I'll see myself out.'

It took her five minutes to dress. Jeans, T-shirt, a black canvas duster that took all kinds of weather down to zero, and of course, the English riding boots. Those who knew she'd never been on a horse in her life thought it was a fashion affectation. Only five people in the world knew differently.

Well, maybe six.

On the drive to work, she passed a cluster of police cars nosed up to the curb on the river parkway.

Dead jogger by the river, she thought automatically.

It was one of those exceptional years when the autumn colors along the Mississippi River almost stopped your heart. The low foliage of sumac flamed red, the maples glowed in ethereal shades of rose and orange, and the fragile leaves of quaking aspens shimmered like gold lamé on a drag queen.

Detective Leo Magozzi had been walking a beat the last time the colors had been this intense, so full of himself he'd barely noticed anything around him – which explained a lot about the mess he'd made of his life – but for some reason, he had noticed the leaves that fall.

Watercolors wouldn't do it, he thought as he drove along West River Boulevard. You had to have oils for something like this.

Ahead he saw the flashing turret lights of at least eight patrol cars and the Bureau of Criminal Apprehension Crime Scene Unit van. No news vans yet, thank God, but he'd bet his pension they'd be here within the sweep of his second hand.

A young, baby-faced cop was directing traffic while keeping a wary eye on a small knot of gawkers that stood shivering in the morning chill, hoping to catch a glimpse of someone else's misfortune. Magozzi was surprised there weren't more of them – murder in Minneapolis was always big news, but in this neighborhood, it was *really* big news.

He eased the car up to the curb, got out, and showed his badge to Baby Cop, who actually moved his lips trying to sound out the name.

'Good morning, Detective . . . Mago-zee?'

'Ma-go-tsee. Tsee. Like in tsetse fly.'

'Oh. Like a what?'

'Never mind. Is Detective Rolseth here?'

'Rolseth . . . shorter guy, light hair?'

'Sounds about right.' Magozzi had to give Baby Cop

diplomacy points for leaving out some of the more colorful terms he'd heard used to describe his partner, like 'paunch' and 'receding hairline.' The kid maybe wasn't the brightest bulb on the tree, but he might have a future as chief of police.

Baby Cop jabbed a finger toward the row of huge, expensive old houses perched high above the street on sloping, manicured lawns. 'He took some of the guys to do a door-to-door before people started leaving for work.'

Magozzi nodded, then stepped over the yellow crime-scene tape and crunched through the litter of fallen leaves, shoving his bare hands deeper into the pockets of his trench coat against the chill of the river wind.

BCA techs were fanning out over the strip of grass between the boulevard and the riverbank, marking the perimeter, walking the grid. He nodded greetings to the few he knew as he passed, then headed toward the edge of the river embankment where a tall, lanky man in an olive green coat was crouched over a body. Although his back was toward Magozzi, the black hair gave away the man's identity as surely as the sloped shoulders that seemed to apologize for excessive stature.

'Anantanand Rambachan.' Magozzi loved wrapping his tongue around this guy's name. It was like eating a cream puff.

Dr Rambachan turned his head and welcomed Magozzi to the crime scene with a toothy, white smile. 'Detective! Your Hindi accent is excellent this morning!' His dark, hooded eyes crinkled with mischief. 'And look at this! You are so pretty! You must be on the hunt.'

'Huh?'

'You have lost weight, your muscles are more toned . . . which means you have finally grown weary of the solitary life and are now seeking the companionship of the fairer sex.'

'Department physical's coming up next month.'

'Or it could be that.'

Magozzi crouched down to take a quick visual inventory of the body. The victim was young, barely twenties, wearing nylon jogging pants and a faded sweatshirt. His still, waxen face was expressionless and his open eyes were filmy with the cataracts of death.

'See here?' Rambachan pointed to a small, dark hole just above the left brow. 'Tiny hole.' He stated the obvious. He always did. 'Very clean. And either excellent marksmanship or a lucky mistake for our shooter. Very unlucky for our friend.'

'Twenty-two?'

'Oh yes, very likely.'

Magozzi sighed and looked out over the river. The sunlight had broken through the low veil of clouds, creating sparkling prisms in the icy mist that rose from the water. 'Cold this morning.'

'Oh. Oh! I have recently learned from a book my wife gave me that the proper response to that statement is: "Could be worse."'

Magozzi picked up an evidence bag and peered at the driver's license inside. 'Oh yeah? What book is that?'

Rambachan's brow wrinkled. 'It is a linguistics book. I believe the title is *How to Talk Minnesotan*. You have heard of it?'

Magozzi almost smiled. 'Any more personal effects?'

'Just the license and the twenty-dollar bill. But there is something else, something very strange. I have never seen such a thing. Take a look at this.' Rambachan slipped gloved fingers between the corpse's lips and pried open the jaw.

Magozzi squinted and leaned forward, close enough to smell it, then sat back on his haunches. 'Son of a bitch.'

4

At about the time Detective Magozzi was rubbing noses with the dead jogger, Grace MacBride was turning her big black Range Rover onto Washington Avenue and heading for the warehouse district.

From her first day here Grace had pegged Minneapolis as a prissy city, an aspiring lady with her skirts held ankle-high to avoid the prairie mud. It had an underbelly, of course – the hookers and johns, the porn shops, the junior-high kids cruising for a hit of black tar or Ecstasy – but you really had to look to find it, and that it existed at all never failed to shock the stalwart Lutheran populace into action. It was one of the few cities in the country, Grace thought, where the self-righteous still thought you could shame the sleaze into redemption.

Washington Avenue, once the province of the homeless and dealers, had long since been scolded into submission. Old warehouses wore new windows and sandblasted brick; seedy diners had been polished and transformed into sparkling oases of nouvelle cuisine; and only the bad people, the very bad people like Grace, ever smoked on the street.

She parked in front of a small warehouse with a decidedly pink cast to the old brick, got out, and looked down the block.

Annie was just coming around the corner, sending a

smile on ahead. She was wearing a bright red wool cape that flapped open as she walked. The hood clashed nicely with her hennaed hair, Grace thought. She was wearing it short this year, in a flapper's bob. A ruler-straight row of bangs rode high on her forehead over unnaturally green eyes.

'You look like Little Red Riding Hood.'

Annie laughed. '*Big* Red Riding Hood, sugar.' Her voice was cane-syrup sweet, remembering Mississippi. 'You like?' She turned in a tight circle, a glorious scarlet hippo in a pirouette.

'I like. How was your weekend?'

'Oh, you know. Sex, drugs, rock and roll. Same old, same old. How about you?'

Grace keyed open an innocuous door that was unmarked save for the relatively fresh coat of paint Annie derisively called Martha Stewart Green. 'I worked a little.'

'Hmph.' Annie walked through the door into a ground-floor garage, empty except for a brand-new mountain bike and a mud-splattered Harley hog. 'A little. What would that be? Ten, twelve hours a day?'

'Something like that.'

Annie clucked her tongue. 'You need a life, honey. You never go out. It's not healthy.'

'Not my thing, Annie. You know that.'

'I met this really nice guy I could set you up with . . .'

'Last time you set me up it didn't exactly work out.'

Annie rolled her eyes. 'Grace. You pulled your *gun* on him. He still won't talk to me.' She sighed as they walked toward the freight elevator on the far wall, the click of their heels echoing in the cavernous space. 'We could go clubbing together after work tonight, maybe snag a couple of young farm boys if you put a bag over that ugly mug of yours.' She inserted a key card that started the throaty growl of machinery overhead, then turned and gave Grace her usual morning once-over. The look was that of an exasperated mother, silently disapproving the mystifying raiment of a rebellious child.

To Annie Belinsky, a day without sequins was hardly worth living; a day without makeup was unthinkable. To have Grace's Black Irish palette and refuse to paint it was surely a mortal sin. She reached over and lifted a thick black wave off her friend's shoulder, then let it drop in disgust. 'It drives me nuts that that stuff just grows out of your head like that. When you die I'm going to scalp you and make myself a wig out of that hair. It's just wasted on you anyway.'

'Keeps my head warm.' Grace smiled.

'That is so Cro-Magnon. Hey, get a load of this.' She lifted the flaps of her cape and revealed neck-to-ankle rows of lime green suede fringe, which explained the new contacts. Annie's eyes always matched her outfit. 'Fat Annie is going to break some hearts today.'

'You break hearts in burlap.'

'This is true.' She sighed and stared at the dented elevator door. A lopsided, cartoonish stencil of a monkey's face leered back at her. 'How the hell could Roadrunner have screwed this up? He uses a T-square to line up the tops of his socks and he can't level a friggin' stencil.'

Grace cocked her head at the monkey. 'I don't know

why he didn't just laser-print a decal with the real logo. This thing looks . . .'

'Maniacal?'

'Exactly. Maniacal.'

Harley looked more like a Hell's Angel than any Hell's Angel Grace had ever seen – enormous, solid, tattooed, bearded, and intimidating. He was waiting to lift the elevator gate for them, a donut clenched in his teeth, a trail of powdered sugar leading back across the wooden floorboards of the second-floor loft. 'Angels rising.' He grinned around the donut, little powdery pieces falling to his chest.

'Cretin.' Annie pushed past him.

'Hey, I opened the gate, didn't I?'

Grace gave him a commiserative pat on the cheek as she headed for the jumbled maze of desks and computer equipment in the center of the otherwise empty loft space. She lifted a hand in greeting to Roadrunner, a beanstalk of a man in a yellow Lycra warm-up suit doing yoga stretches in a far corner.

'Grace, Annie, thank God. Voices of reason. Harley's still pushing for a chop and dice.'

'Like I said, cretin,' Annie grumbled, tossing her briefcase on her desk and glaring at a white bakery box resting on the slab of Harley's right arm. 'I *told* you not to bring that crap in anymore, Harley.' She continued to stare at the box. 'Got any lemon custard in there?'

He pushed the box in her direction. 'Don't I always?'

'Prick.' She snatched the lemon custard Danish.

Harley plucked out a bismarck and talked around his first bite. 'You know, I've been giving this a lot of thought. About killing this last guy? It's gotta be messy, don't you think, Grace?'

'Nope.' She hung her duster on a coat tree by her desk. The gun was properly in its holster now, riding low under her left arm. The black straps disappeared against the black T-shirt.

Harley plopped his bulk down in her chair and beamed up at her. 'You look absolutely ravishing this morning. Downright beatific. Madonna-esque.'

'Which Madonna?'

'Whichever one you want.'

'Don't try to butter me up, Harley. We're doing this guy just like the others.'

'No changes,' Annie agreed.

'Okay, I expected this. You're women, naturally squeamish creatures, but you're just not thinking this through. This is the guy who started it all. If it wasn't for him, we wouldn't have had to kill the rest of them. If we're punishing anyone with a violent death, it should be him.'

'Maybe if we'd killed him first,' Roadrunner piped up in mid-stretch, 'but we didn't. To tell you the truth, I'm so tired of this whole thing, I'd be just as happy if we didn't have to kill another one at all.'

'Are you out of your friggin' mind?' Harley bellowed. 'We *have* to kill him.'

'Duh.'

'*Horribly*. Maybe with a chainsaw.'

Annie glowered at him. 'You know what scares me, Harley? Your pervasive enthusiasm for this kind of thing.'

'Hey, what can I say? I love my work.'

Grace nudged Harley out of her chair and sat down. 'A .22 to the head, just like the rest of them.'

'Come *on*,' Harley complained.

'Forget it,' Annie said. 'You're outvoted.'

Harley threw up his hands. 'You're all a bunch of pussies.'

'It has to make sense, Harley. We have to stick to the pattern,' Grace said.

'Mitch ought to have a vote. Where the hell is he?'

'Airport,' Grace reminded him. 'And even if he voted with you, that would still be three against two.'

'Goddamn pussies . . . oh, man . . .' He was watching Annie take off her cape, getting his first glimpse of quivering lime green fringe. 'Oh, man.' He repeated, staring at her, pulling at the collar of his T-shirt. 'Would you look at that stuff *move*? That's gotta be sexual harassment.'

'Are we done? Can I do it?' Roadrunner was rising to his full height after touching his toes. It was like watching a stork unfold.

'Go for it,' Grace told him, watching as the man's preposterously long legs and arms found their rhythm and propelled him over to his computer. There was a support beam just in front of his work station, six and a half feet above the floor. Roadrunner had to duck.

5

Sheriff Michael Halloran watched as Danny Peltier pulled the twelve-gauge out of the cruiser's trunk rack and checked the load.

'What the hell are you doing, Danny?'

'Inspecting arms, sir.'

Danny was fresh out of officer certification school, and although the phrase 'eager beaver' came to mind, it was woefully inadequate. For at least a year he would clean his unfired weapon two or three times a week, polish his badge and boots nightly, and iron creases in his pants that would cut lemons. But that would wear off eventually, and soon enough he'd start to look like the rest of them.

Halloran watched him, sipping too-hot coffee from a cup, trying to shake the feeling that he was forgetting something.

'Doesn't look like this weapon's been fired in some time, sir.'

'Not since crowd control at the high-school homecoming dance.'

Danny's head jerked around to look at him. The grin, when it finally came, spread slowly across his face, moving all his freckles. 'I guess you're a kidder, aren't you, Sheriff?'

'I guess I am. Mount up, Danny. It's a fair drive.'

'Yes, sir.'

There were over a dozen cruisers in the lot this morning, exhaling exhaust into the morning chill. This was a rare thing in a county that kept only eight patrols on the roads at any given time. Most of the third-watch deputies would pull a double shift today, canvassing the members of Father Newberry's parish, interrogating the faithful for a hint of madness.

Halloran was wondering how he was going to squeeze the overtime out of an already pinched budget when Sharon Mueller rapped angrily on his window with a gloved knuckle.

He looked out at a pair of fierce brown eyes in a cold-reddened face and wondered what had tripped her trigger today. Not that he'd grow any older waiting to find out. The concept of stoic silence eluded her completely. She was short-tempered, painfully straightforward, and had a tongue that could slash a grown man to ribbons. Last year she'd cut her brown hair very short. Around the office they called her the rabid elf.

Still, for reasons he couldn't begin to explain, Sharon was one of the many things that made Halloran glad he wasn't bound to the dogma of confession anymore. If he'd ever once looked at her without having impure thoughts, he couldn't remember the occasion.

She rattled a piece of paper at him when he rolled down the window and bent down to get in his face. He smelled soap. 'Simons put fifteen people on my list, scattered all over the damn place. At this rate I'm going to spend more time on the road than questioning people.'

'Good morning, Sharon.'

'Everybody else gets a block of people in one tight

area, which makes perfect sense, but me he sends to all four corners of the county, and if that isn't gender discrimination I don't know what is, and aside from the fact that I resent it, it's just plain stupid . . .'

'I told him to do that.'

That took her back a little. 'Huh?'

'You're the best interrogator I've got. I told Simons to give you the ones the Kleinfeldts tried to have banned from the congregation. I know they're scattered and I'm sorry about that, but if there's anyone in this county with even half a reason to want them dead, they're on your list.'

Sharon blinked at him. 'Oh.'

'You all right with that?'

'Sure, Mike . . .'

Danny was instinctively careful, waiting until they were out of the lot and on the county road before he asked his question. That was a good sign, Halloran thought. The kid might make a fair deputy, given time. 'Seriously? Sharon Mueller's your best interrogator?'

'She is that. Works child protection, mostly, and if you can get a six-year-old to tell you her daddy's climbing into bed with her every night, you can get an adult to tell you almost anything.'

'Oh.' A single syllable, and then silence.

'Sometimes the job sucks, Danny.'

'Yeah, I guess.'

Highway 29 flattened out and stretched for about five miles before it climbed a ridge on the edge of the state forest, and that was where the wind always hit you. As far as Halloran was concerned, it was about the ugliest piece of land in the county, especially this time of year: treeless and flat with the cornfields cut to dead brown stubble, as if something big had come along and sucked all the life out of the earth. He punched the cruise up to seventy and kept his eyes on the center line.

'Going to have an early snow,' Danny murmured, as if there were finally enough miles behind Halloran's mention of incest to make talking safe again. It was still a touchy subject in this part of the country, and not all the media blitzes and public awareness campaigns in the world would change that. Some people – good people, mostly – just didn't want to believe such things happened.

'How can you tell?'

'Highway Department's two weeks late putting up the snow fence along here. Almost a sure-fire guarantee we'll have an early blizzard.'

'Just what we need,' Halloran said, and that was enough small talk. 'You know what we're looking for out here, Danny?'

'Yes, sir. Information.'

'That's right. Paperwork, mostly. Anything at all that'll tell us something about the Kleinfeldts. Phone records, credit card receipts, legal papers, like that.' He slowed the car at Steiger's House of Cheese and Video and turned right onto a narrow strip of washboard gravel. 'The more we know about the victims, the better chance we have figuring out who might have wanted them dead.'

Danny unwrapped a stick of Juicy Fruit, folded it in thirds, and pushed it into his mouth. 'Diaries, journals . . .'

'They're good.'

'. . . calendars . . .'

'Anything.' *Something*, he added mentally, because a dead end loomed large. 'Forensics didn't get anything useful from the church, and Doc Hanson said that all he got from the bodies was nightmares.'

'We got a usable slug, though, right?'

'The one out of the missus is still in pretty decent shape, but there were no hits in the database, so it doesn't count for squat without the weapon. So right now we've got no witnesses, no physical evidence to speak of, and only one more thing to look for to shine some light on this thing.'

'Motive,' Danny said without hesitation, and for the second time that morning, Halloran smiled. The kid was going to do all right.

There was a gate at the end of the Kleinfeldts' driveway, with a padlock that glinted in the cold sun, a taunting reminder. 'Damnit, damnit, *damnit*.' He banged his hand on the wheel.

'Sir?'

'I forgot the keys.'

'Some of the guys say you're real good with a pick.'

But apparently he wasn't that good. In the end he'd said the hell with it and taken the bolt cutters to the chain.

It wasn't much of a house, for someone sitting on seven million dollars. Just a boxy, two-story farmhouse, unchanged, as far as he could tell, from when the Tikalskys raised Holsteins and children here.

Halloran had gone to Calumet High School with Roman, their youngest, and the day after that boy graduated they'd turned the house over to Countryside Realty and moved to Arizona.

Smart people, he thought, tugging up the fur collar of his jacket and still feeling the promise of winter crawl down his neck. The Kleinfeldts bought the house three months later, according to Nancy Ann Kopetke at Countryside, who had apparently been knocked over with a feather when they paid the asking price without a twitch. The idea of Nancy Ann Kopetke, three bills if she was a pound, being knocked over with anything smaller than an eighteen-wheeler had given him the only other smile of the morning.

He climbed the front porch with Danny, eyed the heavy plate of a good dead bolt, but still tried the knob. Stupid, of course. You didn't padlock your driveway and leave your house wide open.

'Should I try the back, Sheriff?' Danny was almost on the toes of his spit-shined shoes, eager to get into the house, find the clue and solve the crime.

'Go ahead. I'll try running the picks through this one.'

For all the good it'll do, his thoughts grumbled a sullen accompaniment to the strangely merry sound of Danny trotting around the house through a crackling carpet of dried leaves. He'd played with this kind of dead bolt before and knew damn well that it was far beyond his meager skills. Still he went down into a crouch and started fooling with it, going through the motions, just as he was doing with the whole investigation.

The minute he'd seen that cross carved into Mary Kleinfeldt's chest, he'd had the bad feeling that this was probably one of those crimes that would haunt his old age. From that point on it had just been a matter of how much of his budget and how many of his resources he would use up before the county commissioners shut him down. Unless there were clues inside this house with big red arrows pointing to them, there was no way he could justify keeping the whole department committed.

He gave up on the lock, pushed against his knees, and felt a crick he swore hadn't been there yesterday. He rapped once against the door just to feel the weight of it, and frowned. One of those heavy metal numbers you usually saw only in the city. Hinges on the inside. Weird. Unless Danny worked miracles and found a way in through the back, they were going to have to break some glass here, because there was no way he was going to drive all the way back to town for the keys.

He glanced down the porch at the old-fashioned six-over-six windows, thinking they'd have to break some hundred-year-old woodwork, too, and that was a shame. He reached inside his jacket for the package of Pall Malls in his shirt pocket. The cellophane wrapper crackled in the silence.

The house muffled the sound of the shotgun blast, as much as such a thing can be muffled. It was still loud enough, or maybe just so unexpected, that Halloran jumped backward away from the door, heart pounding. Instinct kicked in before thought, dropping him to a crouch, 9mm already in his hand. *See that, Bonar?* he thought crazily. *How's that for a quick draw?*

Before the thought was finished he was down the steps, off the porch, still crouched but running now, below the windows, around the house to the back corner. He stopped with his shoulder pressed against steel siding, gasping in silent, shallow breaths, listening so hard he could hear dried cornstalks rustling in the back field.

Goddamnit, where are you, Danny?

The part of the backyard he could see was treeless, lifeless; nothing but brown, close-cropped grass stretching a good hundred yards to the corn. He stooped, shot his head out to look around the corner, and jerked it back. Nothing. No bushes, no trees, no place for a shooter to hide, just a shallow cement stoop at the back door. He hugged the house and crept toward it.

A few minutes later he found the first bloody pieces of Danny Peltier spattered all over the small mudroom. He walked a little farther into the house and found the rest of him, and almost wished that he hadn't.

Bonar found Halloran an hour later in the middle of the Kleinfeldts' backyard. He'd dragged a kitchen chair out there and was sitting hunched over with his arms across his thighs, staring at the house.

Bonar dropped to a squat next to him and started pulling out blades of dried grass. 'Warming up,' he said.

Halloran nodded. 'Sun feels good.'

'You okay?'

'I just had to get out of there for a minute.'

'I hear you.' He held out a ballpoint pen stuck in a pack of Pall Malls. 'Found these on the porch. Yours, or do we have to print them?'

Halloran patted his pocket, then reached for the cigarettes and tapped one out. 'Must have dropped them when I heard the shot.' He lit one, drew on it deeply, then leaned back in the chair with a long exhale. 'You ever out here when we were in high school? When Tikalskys owned this place?'

'Nah. Different bus route.'

'Used to be a lot of trees in this yard back then.'

'Yeah?'

Halloran nodded. 'Bunch of apples, couple oaks, biggest cottonwood I ever saw stood right over there, with a big old tractor tire hanging from a rope as thick as my arm.'

'Huh. Storm damage, maybe. They had those straight-line winds out here six, seven years ago, remember?'

'Yeah, maybe.' Halloran thought about it for a while. 'Wouldn't think a wind would strip a place this clean. You could hardly see the house for the bushes; those droopy things with the white flowers . . .'

'Bridal wreath, generic name, spirea.'

Halloran looked at him. 'Where do you get this stuff?'

Bonar found a blade of dried grass long enough to stick between his teeth. 'I am a man of great and varied and mostly useless knowledge. What's your point?'

'All the hiding places are gone. They got rid of them.'

Bonar spit out the grass and looked around, eyebrows and brain working. 'Fits, I guess. You see the stockpile of guns in there?'

'Some of it.'

'Seventeen of them so far, just on the first floor. Do you know how weird that is? I mean, these people were *old*. You got Polident and bifocals and a .44 Magnum all in the same drawer. Survivalist books and magazines all over the damn place. And the rig they used to set up that shotgun? That thing's so high-tech even Harris is spooked. He's got the boys on their hands and knees, moving by inches, looking for more trip wires. These people were seriously paranoid.'

'Maybe money does that.'

Bonar shook his head. 'I don't think so.'

'Me neither.' Halloran took another drag, pitched his cigarette, then stood up. 'The thing is, they had every entrance to this house locked up tighter than a drum, and then the back door, they just leave wide open.'

'Where the shotgun was set up.'

'Yeah. They were expecting someone.'

'Oh, man, this one is going to be a pip.' Bonar shook his big head, grunted his way to his feet, looked over at his old friend. 'You look like shit.'

Halloran's eyes were fixed on the empty gurney waiting outside the back door, Danny Peltier's last ride. 'I forgot the keys, Bonar.'

'I know, buddy.' Bonar's sigh sounded like the corn.

6

Mitchell Cross arrived at the warehouse shortly before noon, parked his black Mercedes in the downstairs garage, and rode the freight elevator up to the loft. The morning had been a disaster.

He'd spent half an hour waiting for Diane in the virtual parking lot at airport arrivals, dodging parking police who were ticketing every car that idled at the curb for longer than two seconds. Then Bob Greenberg caught him on the cellular on the way back, snippy and self-righteous about the SKUD thing, almost threatening outright to pull the Schoolhouse Games account. Only the Lowry Tunnel had saved him, cutting the transmission just before Mitch lost his temper.

They spent fifteen minutes in that black wormhole, blocked by God knew what on the other side. Volume congestion, they called it. Mitch called it too many goddamned people with too many goddamned cars.

Diane's fretting turned to whining after the first five minutes, and then in the middle of a diatribe about carbon monoxide poisoning, she had actually stuck her head out the window and screamed at a pickup truck full of blaze-orange hunters to shut their motor off. Jesus. Sometimes he thought the woman had a death wish.

He'd been so angry he hadn't even gotten out of the car at the house, just dropped her off and pulled away.

He'd caught a glimpse of her in the rearview mirror, just standing there in the driveway with her hands full of luggage, looking wounded and small.

The elevator workings clunked above him and the cage jerked to a stop. He looked at the loft through the latticework of wood and released a long breath, thinking, *Home.*

'Hey, Mitch!'

Annie saw him first, but only because she was over by the coffeemakers, away from her computer. The rest of them were huddled around Roadrunner's monitor like bad witches making a poison brew, utterly oblivious.

'Come on out of there, honey. You look like caged Armani.'

'Hi, Annie.' He joined her at a wall counter that held four coffeemakers and the large white bakery box.

'Damn, you look good.' Fat Annie tucked all her chins and gave him one of those slow, seductive smiles that made most men forget she was carrying an extra hundred pounds. 'Half-expected you to stay home and celebrate today. Diane's got to be floating.'

Mitch shrugged. 'More tired than anything. Maybe we'll crack some champagne tonight. What's everybody working on?' He lifted the lid of the white box and peered inside, hoping for something not quite lethal, like a bagel.

'Mitch, you scruffy sack of shit, get over here! We're killing the last son of a bitch, is what we're doing,' Harley bellowed. 'Securing an Ivy League education for your kids.'

'I don't have any kids.'

'I know that, but I'm an eternal optimist. I keep

thinking that one of these days you might get it up. Jesus. Did you pay money for that tie?'

Grace felt Mitch's hand on her shoulder and glanced up at the little white clouds on a field of blue. 'That's a Hermès tie and I gave it to him last Christmas.'

'You gave him a Hermès tie and I got a goddamned keychain?'

'She gave you an Italian stiletto, you dumbshit,' Annie said.

Harley thought a minute. 'Oh yeah. So what cheap prick gave me a keychain?'

Roadrunner leaned back in his chair, exasperated. 'Do you kids want to go play somewhere else so I can get this done?'

'Is it really the last one?' Mitch asked.

Grace nodded. 'The big two-oh. And we've had over three hundred hits on the test site so far. Over half of them preordered the game.'

'We're going to need more than that to replace the Schoolhouse account. Greenberg called this morning.'

'What's his problem this time?' Harley asked.

'Oddly enough, he doesn't think the company that designs his software for children should be producing a CD-ROM game about serial killers.'

'It is not a game about serial killers,' Grace reminded him. 'It's a game about *catching* serial killers.'

'Grace, the damn thing is called *Serial Killer*.'

'*Serial Killer Detective*,' a chorus of four corrected him.

'Apparently the distinction is lost on him. And me, frankly.'

Harley grabbed Mitch by the arm. 'You and Greenberg have both been pushing paper too long. Come on, partner. I'm going to show you this thing, it's friggin' brilliant.' He rolled an extra chair in front of a desk that looked like it had been sacked by vandals. 'Sit down, buddy.' He shoved aside stacks of file folders, printouts, and biker magazines, exposing four purring hard drives and a 21-inch monitor.

Mitch balked, but in the end, when Harley wanted you in a chair, you sat. 'I've seen this –'

'You saw the text files, not the game,' Annie said. 'For Christ's sake you own twenty percent of this thing and you've never even played it.'

'I don't want to play it. I was the dissenting vote, remember? As far as I'm concerned, the whole concept is sick.'

'That's because you don't get it,' Grace snapped. 'You *never* got it.'

The comment stung, but Mitch kept his mouth shut.

'Well, he's going to get it now.' Harley's large fingers started dancing over the keys with surprising agility. The monitor went black for a moment, then snapped back to life. Huge, shadowed block letters began to materialize, then seemed to jump off the screen:

MONKEEWRENCH SOFTWARE DEVELOPMENT
Throw a MONKEEWRENCH into the works

'Okay, okay!' Harley was almost quivering with excitement as the screen went black again. 'Check this out!'

Thousands of sparkling red pixels started to materialize on the screen, bonding together into giant, red, scrawled letters.

'You like the font on that or what? I did it – I call it my serial killer font.'

Mitch shuddered. 'Oh, good Christ.'

'Okay, here comes the good part. We're entering the game now. First thing that comes up is a digital photo of the murder scene.'

Mitch watched in horror as a picture of a dead jogger appeared on the screen. 'Jesus Christ! Did you have to use real people? I thought this was going to be animated!'

'Nah, this is better. Much more realistic. Looks just like a police photo, doesn't it? Except this is *art*.' Harley stabbed a thick finger toward the screen. 'Check out how I used the shadows from that tree to enhance the negative space. Really pulls your eye toward the subject, doesn't it?'

'But . . . aw . . . aw, God.' Mitch grimaced at Roadrunner. 'It's *you*?'

Roadrunner leaned back in his chair far enough to see Harley's monitor. 'God, I'm good.' He grinned. 'I look so dead. Hey, Harley, skip to murder two.' He winked at Mitch. 'That's my best performance.'

'Performance my ass,' Harley snorted. 'Everyone knows the real genius here is the photographer.' He was working his magic with the mouse now, nodding enthusiastically at Mitch. 'Roadrunner's right, though. Number two's a great one. Probably the best, although I can't take credit for the creativity, much as I'd like to. This one was Grace's idea.' Harley punched a few keys and a new photo appeared.

Mitch leaned forward and squinted at the image. Roadrunner – well, Roadrunner dressed as a prostitute – was draped over the wings of an enormous stone angel, looking quite dead. 'What the hell . . . ?'

'Neat, huh? I really got some incredible backlighting here . . .'

'It's grotesque. Where did you take this?'

'Lakewood Cemetery.'

'That statue's *huge*. How could anybody hoist a dead body up there?'

Harley nodded in approval. 'Good question, Grasshopper. That's something you've gotta figure out, because it'll give you a clue.'

Mitch cocked his head, more curious now than repulsed, relaxing just a little. 'Actually, it's not so bad. I was expecting more gore.'

Harley beamed. 'See? Tasteful, isn't it?'

'There's just a little spot of blood, right there . . . looks like she was shot.'

'Right. And when you click on it, you get a nice close-up of the brain matter splattered on the . . .'

Mitch pinched his eyes shut. Harley gave him a gentle punch to the arm that nearly knocked him off his chair. 'Kidding. You get the ME report. Cause of death: a single .22 caliber bullet to the brain; and when you punch on another part of the body you get info about other stuff – any defensive cuts, ligature marks, blood type and chemistry, time of death . . .'

'What's that?' Mitch pointed to a shadowy smear on the concrete at the base of the statue's pedestal.

'That's a footprint. Click on that and you get a pull-down menu of the police workup. Rubberized sole, jogging shoe, Reebok, men's size 11 . . .'

Mitch cocked his head. 'Hmm. So you figure it's a man . . .'

'Or a really large woman, or a smaller woman wearing men's shoes . . .'

'No way the killer is a woman. A woman wouldn't have the physical strength to hoist a body up there. It's gotta be a man.'

'Maybe, maybe not. You gotta figure it out.'

'So then what? How do you solve it?'

'There's a list of five hundred possible suspects in the game's databank. It lists their stats, stuff like occupation, hobbies, DOB, where they live, criminal records, shit like that. Every crime scene has a lot of clues, but some of them are really hard to find, and only a few of them help you eliminate some of the suspects in the databank.'

'How?'

'There's a million ways. We didn't actually use this, because it's too simple, but say for instance you found a clue that proves the killer was right-handed. Then you eliminate all the left-handed people on the suspect list.'

'Oh-h-h.' Mitch's eyebrows went up. 'That's cool.'

Grace and Annie exchanged a glance, then silently rolled their chairs a little closer to Harley's station. Mitch never noticed.

'Anyhow,' Harley continued, 'since the murders are all committed by the same perp, the deeper into the game you get, the more suspects you eliminate and the more you learn about him. Or her. Our killer has fifty-seven profile characteristics. Identify two of those characteristics, plus find the right clues and eliminate the right suspects from the list, and then, and only then, will the program move you from the first murder to the second.'

Mitch was nodding. 'And then you get a few more clues about the killer from the second murder, and you eliminate a few more suspects . . .'

'There you go. You're getting it.'

Mitch leaned forward and pointed at the screen. 'What's that?'

'Gotta click it to find out, buddy.'

Mitch's right index finger was poised over the mouse when he heard Grace chuckle softly behind him and say, 'Gotcha.'

Mitch jerked his hand away from the mouse and spun in his chair. They were all there: Grace, Annie, Roadrunner; so close he couldn't believe they'd gotten there without him noticing. And they were all grinning. 'What?'

'You're playing. You're playing the game, Mitch,' Roadrunner needled him.

'I'm not playing. I'm just trying to get a handle on this thing. And I really don't have any more time for this.'

The others watched as he got up in a huff and headed for the glass-block wall that divided his office from the rest of the loft. He turned at the last minute. 'Grace, you got a minute?'

'Sure.'

'And, Harley?'

'Yeah, buddy?'

'This thing on my computer?'

Harley grinned. 'Always has been.'

Grace followed Mitch into his office and dropped into the client chair. She watched as he went through his arrival ritual.

Suitcoat on the wooden hanger, button top button.

'How was Diane's flight?'

'Long.'

Suitcoat in the closet, closet door closed.

'She called me from LA last night.'

'She told me. Said you talked for half an hour.'

Cross the room to the desk, unfasten cuff links, drop them in the center compartment of the center drawer.

Grace watched him, smiling to herself. 'She was funny. Giddy. Still high from the show.'

'Well, she made a pile of money. Sold out every painting in the first hour or so. Again.'

'She's our star. Does she know we put the game on-line this week?'

Roll up sleeves, three turns each, sit down.

'She knows. Why?'

'I don't know. She didn't mention it. Seemed a little strange.'

Mitch grunted softly. 'There's nothing more either one of us could say at this point. It's out there now. Too late to stop it.'

Wet-dry out of a pack, wipe desktop.

'It's just a game, Mitch.'

'Would I be stating the obvious if I said murder isn't a game?'

Grace blew out a short, exasperated puff of air. 'This from a man who created *Time Warrior*.'

'That was different. The Time Warrior is a good guy fighting evil . . .'

'So's this. Good detective, evil serial killer.'

'. . . and the Warrior uses an atom shifter. No blood, no guts . . .'

'Oh, I get it. Murder is okay as long as it isn't messy.'

'No, damnit, it's more than that. For one thing the Time Warrior is fighting a *war*. He's a *soldier*.'

'Oh-h. Murder is okay as long as it isn't messy, and as long as you wear a uniform and couch that murder in the paper-thin cloth of patriotism . . .'

'Goddamnit, Grace, don't start this again.'

'You started it.'

'It's totally off the point, which is exactly where you wanted to be. So you muddy the waters with an esoteric argument; Bob Greenberg's argument, for God's sake, which is not to say there aren't a lot of Bob Greenbergs out there who are going to think we're all a little twisted for putting out something like this. But the real point is that when he called the whole concept sick today, all I could think of was, buddy, you don't know the half of it.'

Grace pretended he hadn't said that.

He moved a pencil cup an inch to the right. 'So what is it? I've been wondering ever since you came up with the idea. Catharsis? Empowerment?'

She pretended he hadn't said that, either. She simply crossed a jeans-clad leg and looked over at the side wall, away from him. One of Diane's first paintings hung there; a quiet abstract with a lot of white space. 'Can I ask you a question?'

He gave her his eyes, and they gave her everything else.

'What would happen if you ever wiped the desk first?'

He smiled his first genuine smile of the day. 'Armageddon.'

She smiled back, a little wickedly, he thought, but not soon enough to save himself. He shouldn't have said that thing about catharsis. He shouldn't have alluded to that at all, and now she was going to punish him.

'No one's going to find out, Mitch.'

He sighed and decided to play straight man. 'Find out what?'

'About the Speedo thing.'

'Oh, God. Grace, for heaven's sake, this is not about that.'

'Come on, Mitch. You nearly passed out when you read it in the text file.'

'It surprised me, that's all. I hadn't thought about it in years.' He shook his head a little, eyes closed. 'Christ. I can't believe you put that in there.'

Grace shrugged happily. 'I needed a clue.'

'Uh huh. And the one and only clue you could think of was a necklace with "Speedo" engraved on it.'

'You loved that necklace. It looked just like dog tags, which went perfectly with your Army Surplus Grunge couture, I might add. You laughed till you cried when you opened it, and you wore it all the time.'

'Under my clothes, if you remember, so no one would ever see it. And I had to wear it. It was a gift. I didn't want to hurt your feelings. Did you know that damn thing turned my chest green?'

It *had* turned his chest green, and still he wouldn't take it off, just because she had given it to him. 'I thought you'd get a kick out of seeing it in the game.'

'Oh, really? You thought I'd get a kick out of being reminded of one of the most humiliating experiences of my life?'

Grace looked positively merry. 'Hey, you were a babe. You still have the pictures?'

'No, I do not still have the pictures, and would you please keep your voice down? Do you have any idea of what kind of flak I'd get from those guys out there if they found out . . .'

'That you modeled Speedos?'

'It was a one-time thing. I needed the money. And they were not Speedos.'

'They were tiny. Really tiny.' She grinned, waiting for the blush to start creeping up his neck, for his eyes to start blinking rapidly the way they always did when she teased him about something, but he surprised her.

'You're bringing it all up again, Grace,' he said, his expression deadly serious. 'I never thought you'd want to do that.'

And then Grace was the one who blinked.

7

That night Grace watched from the stove as Charlie climbed slowly up onto the kitchen chair, carefully placing his massive paws to avoid tipping it over. It had taken him a long time and many toenail-scrabbling falls to the linoleum to teach himself the trick, and Grace thought that in doggy terms, Charlie was probably a genius.

Once he had all four paws centered on the slippery wood seat, he turned by inches until his stub of a tail brushed the chair back, then sat down with an audible sigh.

'You are a brilliant animal.' Grace smiled at him. Charlie smiled back, letting his tongue fall out.

She had no idea why the dog insisted on sitting in chairs, but she understood panic when she saw it, and the first night she'd brought him home from the alley where she'd found him, Charlie had panicked when she'd tried to keep him off the furniture. He hadn't lain on the floor with his head in his paws, whining pathetically; he'd *danced* on his hind feet, howling in terror, as if the floor were writhing with monsters, and height was his only salvation.

Full-grown then, but obviously weak from near starvation, she'd had to help him up into a chair, acting first and thinking only later that the strange dog could easily have turned on her with flashing teeth.

But Charlie hadn't done that. Once she had him safely above whatever nightmares lived on her floor, he'd only whined softly and licked her face, over and over, making Grace laugh, and then strangely, making her cry.

'Which was more than all those silly psychiatrists were able to do,' she told Charlie, as if he'd been privy to her mental reminiscing. He cocked his head at her, then nudged the heavy ceramic bowl on the table in front of him, politely reminding her that supper was late.

It was lamb stew tonight. Grace took hers without kibble.

After supper Charlie headed for the couch and Grace headed for the long, narrow room sandwiched between the kitchen and dining room. A pantry, originally, the realtor had told her, back in the early part of the century when the house was young.

It was the first room Grace had remodeled, stripping the floors and refinishing the wood, replacing the one existing window with stained glass in deep, impenetrable colors. You couldn't see the bars on the outside of the window anymore, and no one could see in, either.

There was a desk-high counter on one wall where computers hummed twenty-four hours a day, and barely enough floor space for a rolling chair that Grace rode up and down the length of the counter.

'You can't possibly work in here.' Mitch had been horrified when he'd seen it. 'This isn't an office; it's a coffin.' But it was the one place in the world where Grace felt almost safe.

She walked to the big IBM that was networked to all the office computers. 'Come on, come on.' She spun the ball on the mouse to bring the computer out of suspend mode, and waited impatiently, fingers poised over the keyboard.

She'd been struggling with a stubborn command line for the last murder all day at the office and had finally visualized the solution during dinner. She could hardly wait to test it.

She heard the familiar muffled sounds of the hard drive examining itself, then finally, the soft crackle of the monitor coming to life. She'd imposed a digital photo of Charlie on her desktop, long tongue lolling, eyes half closed as if he were smiling around a secret. It always made her smile.

She reached for the function key that would call up the programming file for *Serial Killer Detective*, but never had a chance to push it. She frowned when the screen suddenly went black, then froze as the scrawled red message appeared on her screen.

WANT TO PLAY A GAME?

She straightened slowly, her eyes glued to the words on the monitor that simply shouldn't be there; not unless she'd called up the game file, and even then, not until she'd moved to the second screen.

Glitch, she thought. It has to be a glitch. But even knowing that, for a moment she still felt that old fear tiptoeing up her spine, prickling at the back of her neck, paralyzing her.

The past ten years vanished in an instant, leaving the younger Grace that still lived in her mind huddled in a dark closet, trembling uncontrollably, being very, very quiet.

8

Alena Vershovsky walked in mincing steps, teetering on the highest heels she'd ever worn, constricted by the tight dress. In this deathly quiet place she could actually hear the sequins rubbing against one another, snicking like the scales of a snake scraping across grains of desert sand.

'Sequins make *noise*,' she whispered, lips parted in delight.

'Yes they do. Aren't they wonderful?'

Alena nodded happily, then held up her fingers to look at them again. As dark as it was, she could still see the red enamel gleam of the long press-on nails, making it look like someone else's hands were dangling at the ends of her wrists.

Oh, how she loved this. Never had she dressed in such a way, and with good reason. Her parents would have killed her. But this was the first night of her life away from home; a night for breaking rules and taking chances with a stranger who was going to change her life.

She'd always known that fate would find her, that she wouldn't have to go looking for it like ordinary people. Let the plain girls settle for the trinity of boredom – education, marriage, children – Alena was better than that, more beautiful than that, and soon everyone would know it.

Alena shivered as a gust of wind hit her. She hoped she wouldn't have to take off the dress – it wasn't much protection from the cold, but at least it was something. She also hoped there wouldn't be any sex involved. She'd heard that photographers sometimes tried to have sex with their models before they were stars. But it didn't really matter, she supposed. She'd had sex for worse reasons before.

'Here we are.'

Alena stopped and looked up at the huge sculpture and immediately understood the heavy, garish makeup, the fishnet hose and the revealing dress. She could see now what the photographer envisioned for the first photograph in her portfolio: a whore transported on the wings of an angel. A striking image – a mesmerizing photograph – and not so very far from the truth after all.

The climb was difficult, especially when she had to worry about the stone snagging the stockings or scraping her brand-new nails, but eventually she managed to position herself across one of the cold, massive wings. 'Is this all right?'

'Almost perfect. I'm just going to climb up and clip your hair back. It's beautiful, did you know that?'

Alena smiled. Of course she knew that.

'But it's blocking part of that million-dollar face. We certainly can't have that.'

The fingers were soft on her cheek as they tucked her hair behind her ear, and they lingered there a moment. *'You're going to be very famous, Alena.'*

And even though that had been the whole point, when Alena felt the cold circle of metal that didn't feel like a hair clip at all, thoughts of fame disintegrated in an instant. She thought of her mother, saw her warm, gentle face, and then she felt the wing of the angel shift powerfully beneath her, and start to lift her up.

9

Sheriff Michael Halloran pushed his chair back from his desk and rubbed his eyes with the heels of his hands. When he opened them again, he saw Sharon Mueller standing in his office doorway.

'Those things'll kill your eyes.' She nodded toward the green-shaded lamp on his desk.

'It's a reading lamp. I've been reading.'

'It's too dark in here for reading.' She reached for the wall switch, dropped her hand when he shook his head. She was wearing her heavy jacket, collar pulled up around her ears because her hair was too short to do the job.

'You coming or going?' Halloran asked. 'And if you're going, what're you still doing here? It's almost midnight.'

'Stuff on the Kleinfeldts. Don't worry. I'm off the clock.'

'I'm not worried, and you're not off the clock.'

She wandered into the office and started touching things – furniture, books, the cord for the blinds Halloran never pulled over the big window. He'd known a lot of women who did that whenever they entered someone else's environment, as if they could gather information through their fingertips. She stopped directly in front of his desk. 'How's your hand?'

'What do you mean?'

'Bonar said you put it through a wall at Kleinfeldts' this afternoon.'

'I was annoyed.' And he was annoyed now, too. 'I asked you what you were doing here so late.'

She looked at him for a minute, then sat down in a chair facing his desk. 'I've been looking at all the interviews from today. Mine and everybody else's.'

'Did Simons tell you to do that?'

'No, but it needed doing.' She tossed a thick file folder onto his desk. Several sheets of paper were stapled to the front cover. 'Individual reports are inside. That's a list of all the parishioners, all checked off except a couple – one guy was in the hospital, another couple was visiting their daughter in Nebraska, like that. No red flags anywhere.'

'You talked to everybody they tried getting banned from the church?'

'Oh yeah. Twenty-three of them, can you believe that? Four are actually gay, in case you're interested.'

'They told you that?'

'Hell, no. But they are.'

Halloran glanced down at the list and saw names he'd known his whole life. Sharon had marked the ones the Kleinfeldts had accused of homosexuality with a yellow highlighter. When he caught himself wondering which ones were actually gay, he set the list aside. 'But no red flags.'

Sharon shrugged. 'Not really. Oh, a lot of them were pissed; a few of them even tried beating the Kleinfeldts at their own game – getting *them* kicked out of the church for bearing false witness or something like that. But it turns out the Catholics will forgive you for breaking one of the Ten Commandments. You can still be a card-carrying Pope dope. On the other hand, practice a sexual preference in the privacy of your own home with a consenting adult and you're out of there. Jerks.' She blew out a long, exasperated sigh. 'Anyway, after the first few accusations, nobody paid much attention anymore. I mean, the Kleinfeldts thought Mrs Wickers was gay. The woman is eighty-three years old and totally around the bend, doesn't have a clue what a homosexual is, let alone if she might be one. Her kids are bitter about it – hell, a lot of the twenty-three are – but none of them are homicidal. Trust me.'

'I do.'

'Okay. I also checked in with VICAP and NCIC. We've got the only creative thoracic carver in the country at the moment. At least with a religious theme. There's a guy in Omaha doing breasts, but he's just chopping them off, and if you were talking genitalia, even faces, they've got a wide assortment . . .' Suddenly she pressed her lips together and stared hard at a point on the wall behind his head. 'There's stuff going on out there you wouldn't believe, Halloran, you know?'

She looked at him, stood up, then sat down again. 'You look bad. You need to go home.'

'So do you. Good night, Sharon.' He pulled a stack of papers into the pool of light and started reading again.

'You want to talk about it?'

'About what?'

'Danny.'

'Christ, no.' He kept reading.

'Well, I do.'

'Then go do it somewhere else.'

'It wasn't your fault, Mike.'

'I am not one of your abuse cases, Sharon, and I don't need analysis from a kid with a penny-ante U of W psych degree, so give it a rest.'

'You're doing the mea culpa Catholic thing. It's stupid.'

'Fuck you, Sharon, goddamnit.'

'Well, that might help, but I don't think you're ready for it yet. Never heard you say the F-word before.'

Halloran looked at this nice young Wisconsin woman who dealt with sexual abuse of children almost every day of her life, and yet couldn't bring herself to say the F-word. 'Get out of here,' he said wearily. 'Go home. Leave me alone.'

She sat there quietly for a moment, staring at the stacks of papers on his desk. 'What are you looking for?'

'Go.'

'Can't do it. I love this place. The buzzing fluorescent lights, the lingering smell of sweat, the sexual harassment – I can't get enough.'

Halloran pushed his chair a few inches back from his desk and looked at her. 'Tell me what I've got to do to get rid of you.'

'What are all those?' She nodded at the stacks of papers.

Halloran sighed. 'Stuff we pulled out of a home office at Kleinfeldts'. Paid bills, some receipts, tax returns, mostly.'

'That's it?'

'That's it.'

'Bank statements, correspondence . . . ?'

Halloran shook his head. 'Nothing. They paid cash for everything. I ran a credit check this afternoon when we came up empty at the house, and these people simply did not exist in any databank in the country.'

'That's impossible.'

'That's what I would have said before today, but I'm running out of rocks to turn over. DMV didn't even have anything, and that really frosts me. As far as I can tell, the Kleinfeldts have been driving in my county for the past ten years without a driver's license.'

Sharon was really interested now. She was leaning forward, eyeing the papers on his desk trying to read upside down. 'They were really hiding.'

'They really were.'

'And whoever they were hiding from obviously found them.'

'Unless you ascribe to Commissioner Heimke's theory that it was either a gangland slaying or a nomadic psycho.'

'You're kidding.'

'I kid you not.' He thumbed through a packet of papers on top of one of the stacks: a five-year-old tax return. 'Anyway, if you're nixing disgruntled parishioners, I've got to find somebody else who at least knew these people enough to want them dead, and there certainly isn't anyone in this county that qualifies. They might as well have been hermits.'

'So you're getting their old addresses from tax returns.'

'That's what I thought I was doing, but the copies only go back ten years, just as long as they've lived here.

So I called the IRS to request previous addresses and got some song and dance about privileged information and special dispensation, and when I threatened warrant the little snip on the other end said good luck on the journey through Federal court, he'd talk to me in about fifty years.'

'Jerks,' Sharon muttered, getting up and heading for the door.

'I thought the Catholics were the jerks.'

'It's a big category. There's room for everybody. Give me a minute.'

'To what?' He followed her out into the main office, squinting in the sudden brightness, noticing for the first time the persistent buzz of the overhead fluorescents. He looked around at all the empty desks. 'Where are Cleaton and Billings?'

'Downstairs.' Sharon settled into her chair, grabbed the phone, and punched in a number from memory. 'Melissa's on dispatch tonight. Nobody works up here when Melissa's on dispatch. Haven't you ever been here for the third?'

'Not that I can remember.' Halloran dropped into Cleaton's chair at the desk next to Sharon's and called up a mental image of Melissa Kemke, the Marilyn Monroe lookalike who was the deputy manning dispatch tonight. 'They don't harass her, do they?'

Sharon snorted. 'Not unless they have a death wish. They just like to look at her. She thinks it's funny.'

'She does?'

'Of course.'

Of course? He was missing something about women. Again. 'Who are you calling at this hour anyway?'

‘A guy who never sleeps . . . Jimmy? Sharon. Listen, we’re looking for previous addresses on the Kleinfeldts, you heard about them? Yeah, well, we’re getting stonewalled by your people. Some sort of special dispensation shit . . .’ She listened silently for a moment, then said, ‘You can do that? Bonzai.’

She hung up and spun her chair to face Halloran.

‘You got a mole in the IRS?’ he asked.

She ignored the question. ‘Apparently it’s possible to keep your addresses off the form under special circumstances. Witness protection, stalkers, stuff like that. That’s probably what the Kleinfeldts did, and addresses like that aren’t accessible, even by subpoena. IRS keeps them locked down. Now under the circumstances, since they’re dead and all, we might be able to get them after we jump through about a thousand hoops at the Federal level, like your guy said, but that could take months.’

‘Damnit.’

‘Anyway, he’s gonna call back. Shouldn’t take long.’

Halloran blinked at her. ‘He’s going to get the addresses? Now?’

‘Sure.’

‘Isn’t that against the law?’

‘Oh yeah, but Jimmy’s a pretty decent hacker. He can hook up to the database from his home computer and make it look like the contact came from Timbuktu. They’ll never figure it out. He’s the guy they call when someone else tries to do it.’

‘Jimmy must owe you big time.’

Sharon shrugged. ‘Sort of. I sleep with him every now and then.’

Halloran just sat there and tried not to look surprised.

Sharon said, 'That's a pretty good poker face, Mike.'

'Thanks. I'm working hard at it.' Nice Wisconsin women might not say the F-word, but apparently they could do it.

'Just because you're a monk doesn't mean the rest of the world . . .' The phone rang and she snatched it off the hook. 'Yeah, Jimmy.' She listened for a time, then said, 'No kidding. How many? Huh. Okay. Thanks. No, I do not owe you, you four-sided fool.' She hung up and went over to the fax machine. 'He's sending a list.'

Right on cue, the machine hummed and started to kick out a page. Sharon tipped her head to read the lines as they appeared. 'These were some strange ducks,' she murmured. 'Kleinfeldt isn't their real name, for one thing.'

Halloran raised his brows and waited.

'Looks like they had . . . Jesus . . . they changed their name every time they moved, and these people moved a lot.' She handed the first page to Halloran and started reading the second as it scrolled out of the machine. 'Okay. This looks like the first joint return, almost forty years ago in Atlanta. They were the Bradfords then. Stayed in Atlanta for four years, then moved to New York City, stayed there twelve years, then they turn up in Chicago as the Sandfords . . . Huh. Only nine months there, then they start hopping all over the place.' She passed Halloran page two and started reading the third. 'Mauers in Dallas, the Beamises in Denver, the Chitterings in California, off the books for a year, maybe out of the country, then they land here as the Kleinfeldts.'

'And they've been here for ten years.'

'Right. Must have been a good safe house.'

Halloran grunted. 'For a while.' He took the last sheet from her and sat up a little straighter, energized. 'This is great, Sharon. Thanks. Now go home, get some rest.' He took a look at Cleaton's phone, thought maybe he should be wearing rubber gloves before he touched it, then said the hell with it and dragged it toward him across the desk.

'Who are you calling?'

'The locals at all these old addresses.'

She sighed and slipped out of her jacket, then readjusted her shoulder holster. 'It's a long list. Give me half.'

'You've done enough . . .'

'Gimme.' She wiggled her fingers at him.

'You're going to take some grief for being here alone with me this late.'

'No problem. I'll just tell them I was trying to sleep my way to the top of the Kingsford County Sheriff's Department.'

'You don't have to go that far. Tonight I'd give this job away.'

Sharon smiled. 'The job wasn't exactly what I wanted.'

Halloran watched her punching numbers on her own phone, thinking that he would never understand women.

After an hour working the phones, making enemies of sleeping law officers all across the country, Halloran finally caught a break.

'Chitterings? Hell, yes, I remember them.'

The minute Halloran had mentioned the name to the California detective, the sleep had gone out of his voice. Halloran could almost imagine him jerking up in bed. He covered the mouthpiece and said to Sharon, 'Got something.'

'Damn explosions could have taken out the whole neighborhood if the houses hadn't been so far apart,' the detective went on.

'Explosions?'

'Yeah. What happened was somebody turned on all the gas in the house, dumped the pilots, then torched it. Blew like a son of a bitch, then burned right to the ground before FD even made it to the scene. Santa Anas that night, you know. Fire rules the world when there's a Santa Ana wind blowing.'

Halloran was scribbling furiously on the back of an envelope. 'What about the Chitterings?'

'Well, that's the weird part,' the detective said. 'They had a little guest house out by the pool. Said they were sleeping there that night, for no good reason I ever heard. And that's about all I'm going to give until you tell me what you're working.'

'Double homicide.'

'No shit. The Chitterings?'

'I guess. Only they called themselves the Kleinfeldts here.'

'Huh. Might have guessed. You know I worked that case for about a week, but before I could really get into it they just disappeared. Poof. Sent me a note, if you can believe that. Sent me a goddamned note saying the fire was their fault, some kind of bullshit about trying to fix the hot water heater.'

‘Is that possible?’

‘Hell, no, it isn’t possible. Arson confirmed accelerants, kerosene, in five different locations in the house, and you know what the Chitterings said? Lamps. Friggin’ kerosene lamps. Bullshit is what I said, but my chief is clicking his heels because we can clear a case, and so he shuts me down cold.’

‘I hear you,’ Halloran said.

‘So they bought it, huh?’

‘Looks that way.’

‘Listen. Department doesn’t have a file here, since according to the vics there was no crime, but I’ve still got my notes. Keep ’em at home. I’ll fax them out to you in the morning if you let me know what you dig up. Damn case has been driving me nuts for years.’

Halloran agreed, gave him the fax number, then hung up and filled in Sharon. When he finished, she leaned back in her chair and whistled softly. ‘Man, that was twelve years ago, and they were still scared. This has got to be some serious vendetta.’

He pressed the heels of his hands into his eyes and thought that if he didn’t move soon, he’d fall asleep where he sat. ‘You get anything?’

‘Zilch in Dallas. Chicago is a maybe. The on-duty guy thought he remembered some hullabaloo about a Sandford family – that’s the name they were using there – that went down years ago, just before he joined up. Sandford’s not exactly a unique name, though, so it could be nothing. Said he’d have someone dig through the archives tomorrow.’

She yawned and raised her arms in a stretch that showed Halloran a little more than he thought he should see of what was under her uniform shirt. 'I'm whipped.'

'I seem to remember telling you to go home a long time ago.'

'Yeah, well, I seem to remember telling you the same thing.' She gave him a glance. 'You look worse than I do.'

'Always did.'

She smiled a little, stood, pulled on her jacket, reached in to settle her shoulder holster properly, then zipped up. 'Feels good, doesn't it?'

'What?'

'Getting the first date out of the way.' She pulled a dark watch cap over her head, flattening a fringe of brown against her forehead. 'Next time we can sleep together.'

Well, that certainly woke him up.

10

The dead jogger by the river had been the lead story on all the stations in Minneapolis, which was almost a miracle, Detective Leo Magozzi thought, being that it was the middle of football season.

On orders from the chief, he and his partner, Gino Rolseth, had worked the case all day, shunting last week's murder of a Hmong teenage girl over to Gangs. Gino hadn't liked that. 'You know how much this sucks, Leo?' he'd complained bitterly on their way out of the chief's office. 'We get pulled off one murder and slapped on another, and don't tell me it isn't politics when the one we're pulled off of is a Hmong gang member and the one we get put on just happens to be a nice white boy in his first year at the seminary.'

The nice white boy had a set of very nice white parents that he and Gino destroyed in the few seconds it took to say, 'We are so sorry to tell you that your son is dead.'

After they'd asked the questions they had to ask, they waited until friends of the parents arrived to take their place in the new and terrible solitude, and then they walked away from the dead-eyed, emotional ruins that had been parents before their arrival. Funny. The mother of the Hmong girl had looked just the same.

Gino hadn't been much good after that. He always took the kids hard, and Leo sent him home early so he could look at his own kids and touch them and talk to them while all the time he'd be thinking, *Thank God, thank God.*

Magozzi didn't have any kids to talk to, or any god to thank, for that matter, so he stayed at the station until eight o'clock, making calls, sifting through interviews and the preliminary forensics report, trying to find a lead that would hint at either a motive or a suspect on the dead jogger. So far, he'd come up empty. Jonathan Blanchard was almost a caricature of a model citizen: a 4.0 seminary student who was putting himself through school working twenty hours a week – Christ, he volunteered at a homeless shelter on Wednesdays and Saturdays. Unless he was running drugs or laundering mob money out of the soup kitchen's back door, they were looking at a dead end.

Frustrated and melancholy, Magozzi had finally given up for the night and gone home to his modest stucco on the edge of uptown Minneapolis. He ate a microwave dinner, sorted his mail, then escaped up a rickety second-floor ladder into his attic studio to paint.

Before the divorce, he'd painted in the garage, slapping mosquitoes in the summer and standing in a circle of space heaters in the winter that doubled their electric bill. The day Heather moved out, taking her aversion to turpentine and chemical sensitivity to anything she didn't buy at the Lancôme counter with her, he'd dragged all the paraphernalia inside and set up in the living room. For two months he painted there, just because he could, and only hauled everything up to the attic when his Froot Loops started to taste like mineral spirits.

He took a deep, calming breath as he popped up through the hatch, savoring the warm tang of turpentine and oil paints that saturated the air. Now this was real aromatherapy.

It was almost two o'clock in the morning by the time he washed his brushes and crawled into bed, exhausted. The fall landscape was still just blocks of color, a mess really; but it would shape up nicely, he thought as he drifted off to sleep.

The bedside phone shrilled him awake at a little after four. For a millisecond, he fantasized about drawing his 9mm and silencing the phone forever, but the fantasy dissolved and he reached for the receiver, wondering if at any time in the history of the telecommunicating world had an early-morning phone call brought good news. He doubted it. Good news could always wait, but for some reason, bad news never could. 'Magozzi here.'

'Get your ass over to Lakewood Cemetery, Leo,' Gino said over the phone. 'We got a real sparkler this time. BCA's on their way.'

'Shit.'

'Shit is right, my friend.'

Magozzi moaned, tossing his warm covers aside and cringing at the rush of frigid air he hoped would shock him into consciousness. 'Why the hell do you sound like you've been up for an hour already?'

'Whaddaya think? I been up half the night with the Accident.' He was talking about his six-month-old son, a surprise arrival thirteen years after the last one.

Magozzi let out a long-suffering sigh. 'You got coffee?'

'I got coffee – my sainted wife is loading up the thermos as we speak. And bring your parka. It's frigging freezing.'

Half an hour later, Magozzi and Gino were standing in Lakewood Cemetery, staring up in shocked silence at an enormous stone statue of an angel with massive wings extended. A dead girl was draped over one wing, arms and legs dangling on either side, her face partially obscured by a curtain of blood-stained blond hair. She wore a red dress, net nylons, and stiletto heels.

Crime scene had set up bright white lights on tall aluminum tripods to illuminate the gruesome tableau and the whole effect was surreal. Magozzi couldn't quite shake the feeling that he'd been transported to the set of a Kubrick film. Or a B horror flick.

He looked over at a row of crumbling grave markers backlit by the kliegs and saw little tendrils of mist curling on the ground around them.

He blinked a couple times, trying to dispel the image. Then he realized that it was real fog, and sometimes in real cemeteries, real fog crept along the ground the same way it did in the movies.

Gino took a gulp of coffee. 'Christ. This looks like some cult bullshit to me.'

Jimmy Grimm from BCA forensics was making a meticulous circuit around the pedestal of the grave marker, tweezing up minuscule pieces of evidence and bagging them.

Anantanand Rambachan stood off to one side, waiting for Jimmy to finish. He gave the detectives a melancholy nod. No banter this morning.

Magozzi looked back up at the body. 'She's young,' he said quietly. 'Just a kid.'

Gino took a closer look. Not much older than Helen, he thought, then pushed that thought right out of his mind. His fourteen-year-old daughter didn't belong in the same mind where images of dead girls were floating. 'Christ,' he muttered again.

Magozzi moved in a little closer, examining the dark drip marks down the angel's side. 'Who found her?'

Grateful for the distraction, Gino nodded toward a pair of bedraggled-looking college boys wearing U of M letter jackets. A uniform was interviewing the lanky, blond one while the shorter, dark kid dry-heaved on his hands and knees.

Magozzi clucked his tongue, genuinely sorry for the kids. How many years would it take before the nightmares stopped for them? Maybe never. 'Let's go talk to them so we can send the poor bastards home.'

As they approached, the officer turned and gave them a grateful look. 'They're all yours.' He leaned forward and spoke confidentially. 'You want some advice? Talk to the blond kid, name's Jeff Rasmussen. The other one's still drunk as a skunk and as you might have noticed, he pukes every time you ask him a question.'

Gino moved in on Jeff Rasmussen, while Magozzi hung back and watched. Sometimes body language told a better story than words.

Jeff bobbed his head up and down nervously when Gino introduced himself. He had glittery, pale blue eyes shot through with red that kept darting toward the statue. His friend looked up miserably and tried to focus without much success.

'You want to tell us what happened, Jeff?'

Jeff bobbed his head again. 'Sure. Sure. Yeah.' Very nervous. Very wired. 'We were at the hockey game . . . then after, we went out for a couple drinks . . . they have three-for-ones at Chelsea's on Mondays. So we stayed until bar close – we were a little lit, you know? Hitched a ride with a friend – he had a twelve-pack in the trunk – so we drove around and told him to stop here. He chickened out, but he gave us a couple beers and . . . well . . .' He paused and his face flushed bright red. 'Is that trespassing?'

Gino nodded.

Jeff seemed to fold in on himself. 'Jesus, my parents'll kill me . . .'

'Let's not worry about the trespassing now, Jeff. At least you weren't driving drunk.'

'No, no! I'd never do that, I don't even have a car . . .'

Gino cleared his throat impatiently. 'Tell me what you saw when you got here.'

Jeff swallowed hard. 'Well . . . we didn't see anything. It was empty, you know? Late. So we walked around for a while, looking for the Angel so we could do the Dare.'

'What dare?'

'The Angel of Death Dare.' His eyes shifted back and forth between the two detectives. 'You know . . . the Dare?'

Gino and Magozzi both shook their heads.

'Oh. Well, there's this ghost story, legend, whatever. Says this guy buried here was some dark priest or something for a Satanic cult. He bought the angel for his grave marker and told his followers that he'd put a curse on it – if you held the angel's hands and looked into her face, you'd see the way you would die.'

Magozzi turned and looked up at the blank, stone eyes of the angel, then at the dead girl's limp form, wondering if she'd looked into the angel's eyes before she died.

'Anyhow,' Jeff continued, 'we found the angel . . . at first we thought it was a joke or something. Like a doll? It was just too weird, I mean, this is Minneapolis, right? But then we saw the blood and then . . . well, Kurt.' He jabbed a thumb in the puking kid's direction. 'Kurt had a cell phone and we called you guys.'

'That's it?'

Jeff looked thoughtful for a moment. 'Yeah. That's it.'

'You didn't see anything? Didn't hear anything?'

'Nope. Just a bunch of tombstones. There was nobody else here.' His eyes wandered to the body again.

'So it was just you two in the cemetery, you're sure about that?'

Jeff looked at Gino again, and his eyes sprang wide in panic. 'Jesus, you don't think . . . oh shit, you don't think *we* did this, do you?'

Gino pulled out a card and handed it to the kid. 'You think of anything else, you call this number, okay?'

'Yeah. Yeah.'

Magozzi and Gino walked back to the statue in silence. Rambachan was up there with the girl now, but Jimmy Grimm was walking toward them, his round, ruddy face solemn. 'Didn't get shit, guys,' he said in a gloomy voice. 'A couple hairs, probably the vic's, couple bags of trace from the surrounding area, just for good measure, even though they're contaminated as hell. No personal effects. Rambachan says it's another .22.'

'Too goddamned many of those on the street,' Gino muttered.

'Tell me about it.' Jimmy chewed on his lower lip while he pondered the scene before him. 'It's very clean, guys. Almost looks like a pro job, but then this girl is most likely a hooker, and who's gonna spend the money to hit a hooker? Weirdest goddamn thing I've seen in twenty years and I've seen it all. You want her down yet, Anant?'

Rambachan was crouched on the pedestal, peering into the girl's upside-down face with a high-intensity penlight. 'A moment, please, Mr Grimm.'

Jimmy shook his head. 'A year I been working with that guy, and he still calls me Mr Grimm. Makes me feel like a fairy tale.'

'Maybe she knew something. Maybe posing her on the statue was a warning,' Gino said.

'Oh, I think she posed herself on the statue before she was shot,' Jimmy said. 'Which is even weirder. Check out the blood splatters. You got drip marks down the statue's side and a whole lotta daisy-shaped blood splatters on the pedestal, a "crown" effect. Perpendicular impact, high height, high velocity. Which meant that she was probably already on top of the statue when she was shot. If she'd been killed somewhere else and hauled up there, there'd be different kinds of splatters and they wouldn't be so consistent. And maybe not as much blood, depending on how long she'd been dead. God, I hate this job. I'm gonna take early retirement and start day-trading or something.'

'We're all just janitors,' Gino mumbled. 'Cleaning up somebody else's messes.'

'They don't call me "The Grimm Reaper" for nothing,' Jimmy said cheerlessly.

11

Mitch had made breakfast, his marital equivalent of half a dozen Hail Marys. He started plating the food when he heard the back door open and close.

'What's this?' Diane breezed into the kitchen on a current of fresh air. Her cheeks were pink from her morning run, her blond ponytail damp when she pulled back the Gore-Tex hood. She looked like an ad for a health club.

He smiled at her. 'Penance.'

'I didn't even hear you come in last night.'

'I slept in the den. It was very late. I didn't want to wake you.'

'Hmm.' She was trotting in place to cool off, running shoes squeaking on the tile. 'Do I have time for a shower?'

'Sorry.'

He carried the plates through the dining room he preferred, out to the glass sun porch, Diane's favorite room in the house. It was a large space made small by a jungle of ferns and palms and flowering plants that all looked healthier than he felt. The air was heavy and humid and smelled of damp earth. Mitch hated that smell.

'Oh, this is lovely, Mitchell.' Diane settled at the wrought-iron table and admired her plate. A spinach omelet in fluted puff pastry, iced pears with grated

Reggiano, a single fanned strawberry. 'You must have done something truly awful. Are we going to have sex, too?'

He must have looked startled, because she smiled a little as she tucked a pear into her mouth and held out her cup. 'Half, please.'

'How's the new painting coming along?'

'Badly. If I don't have any luck today, I may pull it from the show.'

'Oh. Sorry.'

'Don't be silly. It's not your fault, now is it? And one painting more or less isn't going to make any difference to the gallery. This is really extraordinary. Nutmeg?'

'Right.' He laid his fork upside down on the edge of his plate, cue to a nonexistent waiter. He wasn't hungry at all; still a little off-balance from her sex remark.

'I can't place the cheese.'

'Five cheeses, actually.'

Silver scraped china as she chased down the last bite of her omelet. 'You are so good at this. You really should come out of the closet and cook for your friends.'

His cup clattered into the saucer. 'Why do you do that?'

She looked up, all innocence. 'Do what?'

'Call them *my* friends. They're *our* friends, not just mine.'

'Oh. Did I say that? I didn't mean anything by it. It's just that you spend so much more time with them . . .' Her voice and gaze drifted until she focused on his plate. 'You aren't going to let that go to waste, are you?'

He stared at her for a moment, almost irritated

enough to pursue the issue if it weren't so damn hot in this room; so damn *close*. When she glanced at his face, her own crumpled instantly. My God. What had he looked like? What had she seen?

'Please,' he said quickly. 'Help yourself. I ate while I was cooking.' He wanted to run, out of the room, out of the house, but he made himself sit there and smile until her mouth curved in a tentative answer, and then he watched in silence as she polished off both breakfasts. It was amazing, really. She had an almost frightening appetite, and yet remained in perfect physical condition, never gaining or losing a single pound.

Use that. Give her something. You owe her that much.

'I don't know how you do it, Diane.' He added another smile for good measure. 'If I told Annie what you ate this morning she'd have you killed.'

She laughed out loud, almost frightening him. She never did that. 'Maybe Annie should start running. You all should, for that matter. It's not healthy being cooped up in that loft all day, just sitting in front of those silly computer screens.'

'We take an occasional break. Roadrunner bikes and does his yoga, Grace lifts weights . . .'

'Does she? I didn't know that.'

'Maybe that's because you hardly see her anymore.'

'I try to keep in touch. I called her the minute the show was over in Los Angeles, didn't I? We had a wonderful chat.'

'So call her more often. Come into the city for lunch. She'd love that.'

'You're right. That's precisely what I should do, right after this show is over.' She sipped at her coffee and opened the newspaper he'd left neatly folded to the left of her place. 'Hmm. Market took a tumble yesterday.'

Mitch pushed back his chair. Time to leave.

'Oh dear.'

'What?'

'I certainly don't need to read that sort of thing with my morning coffee.'

'What sort of thing?'

She passed him the paper with a disgusted flick of her wrist. 'There simply are no good newspapers anymore. They're all like tabloids, reporting every single grisly detail . . .'

She may have continued talking, but if so, Mitch didn't hear her. He'd started to read the article that had dared to offend, eyes darting back and forth, then freezing suddenly while all the blood drained from his face.

'It's horrible, isn't it?'

He blinked at her, confused for a moment, then remembered to nod. 'Yes. Horrible.'

'Well, I'm off to the shower.' She popped out of her chair and paused long enough to kiss the top of his head. 'Thanks for the breakfast, darling. It was wonderful.'

Mitch refolded the paper carefully, running a thumbnail along the crease. 'My pleasure,' he murmured, but by that time, Diane was already in the shower.

12

The Monkeewrench loft space was cavernous and silent, still asleep like most of the city. The sun was just beginning to creep over the eastern horizon and its weak light struggled to penetrate the bank of windows on the far wall.

In the dark maze of desks in the center of the room, a computer monitor hissed to life – an eerie blue window glowing brightly in the gloom. Slowly, letter by letter, red pixels coalesced on the screen and a message materialized:

WANT TO PLAY A GAME?

Down on the ground floor, the freight elevator rumbled and groaned, then wheezed to a stop at the loft. Roadrunner emerged, walked over to the computer monitor, read the message, and frowned. He tapped a few keys, but the message remained and his frown deepened. He tapped a few more keys, then shrugged and headed for the coffeemakers.

As he started grinding beans, he gazed out the windows at the awakening city below. In the distance the Mississippi River flowed sluggishly, as if it were practicing for its winter hibernation in ice, and even the first wave of commuters was moving more slowly on this frosty morning. Winter was a state of mind in

Minneapolis, and it always started long before the first snows flew.

He began the meticulous work of leveling tablespoons of fresh coffee and carefully depositing them into a new filter. He was so intent, so focused on his chore that he never saw the massive figure creeping silently, stealthily, toward him through the shadows.

'BEEP, BEEP!'

Roadrunner twitched convulsively and sent coffee grounds flying. 'God*damnit*, Harley, that was Jamaican Blue!'

'Heads up, little buddy.' Harley shrugged off his battered leather bike jacket and tossed it on the back of his chair.

Roadrunner started scooping up coffee grounds with angry sweeping motions. 'Where the hell were you, anyhow? I thought the place was empty.'

'I was taking a leak. And you gotta loosen up a little. You got a spooky little ritualistic thing going on with that coffeemaker. Every time you get within five feet of it, you enter a fugue state. It worries me.' He glanced over at the monitor where the red message still glowed. 'You working on Grace's computer?'

Roadrunner looked over his shoulder. 'Do I look suicidal? It was up when I got here. Check it out. I can't get it to clear.'

Harley punched a few keys with sausage fingers, grunted, then gave up with a shrug. 'Another glitch.' He blinked in surprise when the letters disappeared abruptly. 'Gone now. Grace must have been transferring data from home. Guess what?'

'Your dick fell off.'

'You stay up all night thinking of that, you asshole? Listen to me. I checked the site this morning. Almost six hundred hits, over five hundred preorders for the CD-ROM. Some of them are ordering two, three copies. We are gonna be filthy, stinking rich.'

An hour later Annie and Grace were at their respective computer stations, clattering out lines of arcane programming language that the computer would eventually translate into the twentieth murder scenario. Harley was loading a CD into the boom box on the counter while Roadrunner circled around him, snapping impromptu mug shots of him with a digital camera.

'What the hell are you doing with my camera?'

'Just seeing how you look pixeled. We need to take care of the photo shoot today so I can start integrating it.'

Harley shook his head. 'I'm not going to be the dead guy.'

'It has to be you. I've already been the dead guy three times. And it has to be a man.'

Grace lifted her eyes as the freight elevator rumbled up from the parking garage. 'Ask Mitch.'

Annie snorted. 'Right. You'd have to drug him first. What the hell is this music?'

Grace listened for a moment, then grimaced. 'ZZ Top. Harley, take it off.'

'ZZ Top happens to be a seminal band of the 1980s, you cretins.' He collapsed under the weight of Grace's gaze. 'All right, all right, but no more classical. That stuff puts me to sleep.'

Harley settled for instrumental jazz, then went back to his chair and swiveled to prop his jackbooted feet up on Roadrunner's pristine desk. 'You know what I'm going to do with my share of the money?'

'Get your feet off my desk.'

'I'm going to buy a really nice place in the Cayman Islands. Or maybe the Bahamas. Grass roof, nice stretch of beach, big hammock under a palm tree. And chicks in thongs with huge tits. You guys can come down and visit whenever you want. *Mi casa, su casa.*'

Grace rolled her eyes. 'I can't wait.'

'Harley, if you don't get your feet off my desk . . .'

Harley gave Roadrunner a toothy grin and swung his feet back down to the floor. 'How 'bout you, Grace? What are you gonna do with the loot?'

She shrugged. 'I don't know. Maybe get an underground bunker in the Idaho panhandle, start stockpiling weapons, get a few cabana boys in thongs with huge . . .'

They were all laughing when the elevator gate slid up into its moorings. Mitch walked into the room, a newspaper clenched tightly in his right fist.

Grace waved him over. 'Come on, Mitch. Smile for the camera. You have to be the dead guy for number twenty . . . Jesus. What's the matter with you?'

Everyone looked up and an ugly hush fell over the room. Mitch was not looking good. His face had a decidedly unhealthy gray cast, he was wearing a polo shirt and chinos instead of a suit, and his hair was uncombed. For anyone else, this would be the equivalent of going out in public naked.

He laid the newspaper down on Grace's desk. 'Has anyone seen a paper?'

'Not since '92,' Harley said. 'What's up?'

'Just read it.' He pointed to the article, then stood to

one side as the others crowded around Grace's desk to read over her shoulders.

Grace started to read aloud. '"The body of a young woman was discovered early this morning . . ."' She stopped abruptly.

'Oh my God,' Annie whispered.

They all read in silence for a moment, frozen in position. Harley was the first to look away. 'Jesus Christ on a crutch.' He took the few steps to his desk and sat down very slowly. Annie and Roadrunner did the same, and then they were all sitting, looking at their hands or their monitors or at anything except each other. Only Mitch remained standing, the evil messenger.

'Maybe it's a coincidence,' Roadrunner mumbled.

'Oh, right,' Annie snapped. 'People are flopping dead girls over that statue all the time. Oh, Jesus God, this can't be happening.'

'It just said she was *on* the statue, not on *top* of it,' Roadrunner insisted desperately. 'Maybe they found her on the pedestal. Maybe it was a drug thing, or a gang thing. For Christ's sake we don't know what goes on in that cemetery, it could have been *anything* . . .'

'Roadrunner.' Harley's voice was uncharacteristically gentle. 'We have to find out. We have to call the cops. Right now.'

'And tell them what?' Mitch asked, his eyes on Grace. She was still staring at the newspaper, her face absolutely expressionless.

'I don't know. That maybe there's some freak out there who liked one of our murder scenes so much he decided to do it for real, I guess.'

Roadrunner's eyes slid sideways to his monitor,

where the number of hits on the game site kept climbing as he watched.

'If that's what's happening, he's one of our players,' he said. 'He's got to be.'

Grace's hand reached for the phone, then just rested there.

'Grace?' Mitch asked softly. 'You want me to do it?'

13

Magozzi was watching Gino inhale a Tupperware container of sausage-stuffed manicotti. As a forkload hit his lips, a big, gooey blob of garlicky ricotta slid out of the pasta tube and splatted on the front of his white shirt.

'Shit.' Gino went to work with a napkin.

'You look like a backhoe when you eat,' Magozzi said pleasantly.

Gino refused to take the bait. 'Yeah? Well, you would too if you were eating Angela's homemade pasta.'

Magozzi's mouth watered until he looked down at his own lunch – a bruised banana, an apple, and a flattened turkey sandwich on low-calorie bread that tasted like particleboard. His stomach rumbled loudly.

'Jesus, I heard that all the way over here,' Gino said through a mouthful. 'Eat something, for Christ's sake. You want some of this?'

'Can't.'

Gino wiped marinara sauce off his smile. 'You know what your problem is? Mid-life crisis. Male menopause. Man reaches that hump halfway through his life all of a sudden he wants to be a high schooler. So he loses weight, starts jogging or some such stupid bullshit, and before you know it he's driving around in a friggin' Miata convertible trying to pick up jailbait.'

Magozzi looked pointedly at the extra thirty pounds

Gino was carrying in his gut. 'Yeah, well, when you end up in the hospital next month for a triple bypass, just remember this day.'

He smiled and smacked his lips. 'Don't knock yourself out sending flowers or anything. Save the money for Angela when I croak.'

Gloria, a substantial black woman who favored bright shades of orange, clomped into the room on platform heels, waving a fistful of pink phone message slips. 'You guys owe me big time, running interference like this while you're feeding your faces.' She slapped the stack of messages on Magozzi's desk. 'Nothing much. Mostly cranks and reporters. Speaking of which, we've got every single television station and newspaper in the tristate area setting up camp on the front steps. Chief Malcherson wants to know how they got this.' She laid down a copy of the *Star Tribune* with a grainy photo of the dead girl on the angel statue above the fold. A banner headline read *Angel of Death?*

'Long lens,' Magozzi said. 'Press didn't get through the lines when we were there.'

'Anyway,' Gloria continued, 'the old man is between heart attacks and wants to talk to you ASAP about a press conference.'

Malcherson was the extremely hypertensive chief of the Special Investigation Division of MPD; Magozzi suspected he was locked up in his office at the moment, mainlining Valium.

Gino threw down his fork in disgust. 'Press conference? What for? So we can stand in front of the cameras and say we don't know shit?'

'That's Malcherson's job,' Gloria said. 'Don't steal

his thunder. Missing Persons called; no matches on the girl, so Rambo What-the-hell's-his-name is sending the prints to AFIS.'

'Rambachan. Anantanand Rambachan. He doesn't like it when you call him Rambo,' Magozzi said.

'Whatever. And you got a call waiting on line two, Leo.'

'I'm in the middle of lunch.'

She looked down at the pathetic pile of food on his desk and snorted derisively. 'Right. Anyhow, it's a woman who says she knows something about the statue murder and she wants to talk to the detective in charge. *Demands* to talk to the detective in charge or she's going to sue somebody. Or maybe she said "shoot somebody," I didn't catch the last part.'

'Great.' Magozzi snatched his phone.

The cold wind hit Grace the minute she stepped out the warehouse door. She hunched her shoulders and flipped up the canvas collar of her duster, almost relishing the discomfort. Something else to hold against a world that only pretended to make sense for a while, before slipping right back into chaotic insanity.

She kept telling herself it wasn't so bad for her. She'd never relinquished the conviction that there was horror around every corner, that the turn of every calendar page promised catastrophe, and if it didn't hit you one day, it would catch up with you the next. The secret to survival was accepting that simple fact, and preparing for it.

But the others . . . the others couldn't live like that. They, like most people, had to believe that the world was basically a good place; that bad things were an aberration. Life was simply too hard otherwise. Which was why, she thought, Pollyannas sometimes got their throats cut.

Grace was the last one of the group who should have called the cops, let alone come out here to wait for them. She knew that as well as anyone else, and yet nothing would have stopped her. It was the control thing, she supposed. She had to run everything. 'Don't hurt them, honey,' Annie had said to her on the way out, only half-kidding.

It wasn't that Grace hated cops, exactly. She just had a better understanding than most that they were basically useless creatures, constricted by laws and politics and public opinion and, too much of the time, general stupidity. She wouldn't hurt them, but she wasn't going to genuflect either.

'Come on, come on,' she muttered impatiently, toes tapping, eyes busy as she scanned the lunchtime traffic. Every now and then a real truck with a real load passed in a cloud of diesel fumes, heading for one of the few remaining real warehouses down the block; but for the most part Hondas and Toyotas owned this part of Washington Avenue. Eventually, she supposed, they would force the trucks out altogether. God forbid particulate contamination of someone's radicchio at one of the sidewalk cafés that kept springing up like weeds.

She started to pace, twenty steps north of the green door, twenty steps away from, so acutely aware of every detail of her surroundings that the sheer quantity of information bombarding her brain was almost painful.

She memorized every face she passed, noted every car and truck, even analyzed the sudden, lumbering takeoff of a pigeon that was, in its own way, an alarm. She hated it out here. It was exhausting.

On her tenth circle past the green door she finally saw it, nosing around the corner two blocks down: a brown, nondescript late-model sedan that screamed UNMARKED POLICE CAR.

Inside the car, Magozzi turned onto Washington and passed a few unremarkable warehouses that looked like faded building blocks from a giant's play set. Gino squinted out the window, looking for numbers, but most of the buildings were unmarked. 'You need a damn GPS to find an address down here.'

'She said she'd wait for us on the street.'

Gino pointed to a small cluster of men milling around a semi that was backed up to a loading dock, chuffing puffs of white exhaust from the tailpipe. 'Does she look like a Teamster?'

'She sounded like one on the phone.'

'You think she was yanking your chain?'

Magozzi shrugged. 'I don't know. Maybe. Hard to tell.'

Gino shivered a little and turned up the heater fan on the dashboard. 'God, it's cold. Not even Halloween and it's twenty-five frigging degrees.'

They drove another block and spotted a tall woman in a black duster standing in front of a green door, a tangle of dark hair stirring in the wind. She dipped her chin at them in what Magozzi supposed was a signal, if you thought every human being on the planet was watching you, waiting for a sign.

'Doesn't look like a Teamster,' Gino mused happily. 'Not one bit.'

But she had the attitude. Magozzi saw it in her stance, in the cool blue gaze that flayed them alive while they were still strapped in their seats, helpless. God, he hated beautiful women.

He pulled over and slammed the car into park, meeting her eyes through the dusty windshield. *Tough*, he thought in the first instant, and then he looked a little closer and found a surprise. *And afraid.*

So this was Grace MacBride. Not what he'd expected at all.

Grace had typed them both before they got out of the car. Good cop, bad cop. The tall one with the quick, dark eyes was the bad cop, certainly the Detective Magozzi she'd talked to on the phone, and the only surprise was that he looked as Italian as his name. His partner was shorter, broader, and looked too much like a nice guy to actually be one. They both wore obligatory ill-fitting sport coats to accommodate their belt holsters, but Grace looked to the shirts beneath for the summary of their lives.

Magozzi was single, or more likely divorced, at his age. Late thirties, she guessed. A man alone, at any rate, who actually believed permanent press meant what it said.

His partner had a doting wife who spoiled him with homemade lunches he used to decorate the JCPenney shirt she had ironed so carefully. The expensive silk floral tie spoke of a fashion-conscious teenage daughter who would certainly be horrified to see him wearing it with tweed.

'Thank you for coming.' She kept her hands in her

pockets and her eyes on theirs. 'I'm Grace MacBride.'

'Detective Magozzi . . .'

'I know, Detective. I recognize your voice from the phone.' She almost smiled at the slight tightening around his eyes. Cops didn't like to be interrupted. Especially by a woman.

'. . . and this is my partner, Detective Rolseth.'

The short one gave her a deceptively harmless smile as he asked, 'You got a permit to carry that thing?'

Surprise, surprise, she thought. The vapid-looking one is paying attention. No way he should have been able to see her shoulder holster under the heavy duster. Not unless he was looking for it.

'Upstairs in my bag.'

'No kidding.' The smile remained fixed. 'You carry all the time, or just when you're about to meet a couple of cops?'

'All the time.'

'Huh. You mind me asking the caliber?'

Grace lifted one side of the duster and showed the Sig Sauer. The detective's eyes softened briefly in a look usually reserved for lovers. Leave it to a cop to get mushy over a gun, she thought.

'A Sig, huh? Impressive. Nine-millimeter?'

'That's right. Not a .22, Detective. That is what killed the girl in the cemetery, isn't it?'

To their credit, neither man batted an eye. Magozzi even affected nonchalance, shoving his hands in his coat pockets and looking away from her, down the street, as if her knowing the caliber of the murder weapon had no significance at all. 'You said you had some information on that homicide.'

'I said I might. I'm not sure.'

His right brow shifted upward a notch. 'You *might*? You're not sure? Funny. Sounded on the phone like London was burning.'

Magozzi could have sworn that none of her facial muscles moved, and yet something in her face conveyed instant disdain, as if he'd behaved very badly, and she'd expected nothing better.

'What I *might* have to show you is proprietary information, Detective Magozzi, and if it isn't relevant, I won't show it to you at all.'

He struggled to keep his tone even. 'Really. And just when are you going to decide if it's relevant?'

'I'm not. You are.' She pulled a chain bristling with plastic cards from a deep pocket. 'Come with me.' She turned immediately, inserted a green plastic key card into a slot next to the door, and led the way inside.

She walked fast, boot heels clacking sharply on cement as she crossed the garage toward the elevator. Gino and Magozzi moved slower. Gino was watching a black duster flapping around long jeans-clad legs; Magozzi was looking around, seeing money in the empty space. People paid a healthy sum for secure parking places in this city, and there were at least twenty empty slots down here.

Gino nudged him with an elbow and spoke softly. 'I'd say you two are running about neck and neck for the Miss Congeniality award.'

'Shut up, Gino.'

'Hey, don't try so hard. You already got my vote.' His eyes found the monkey stencil when they stopped in front of the elevator door. He looked at Grace with a surprised smile. 'You're Monkeewrench?'

She nodded.

'No kidding. My daughter *loves* your games! Wait till I tell her I was here.'

She almost smiled. Magozzi waited for her face to crack and clatter in pieces to the cement floor.

'Children's games and educational software are our bread and butter,' she was saying, and Magozzi frowned, trying to place the accent. Some of the consonants were soft, but the pattern of speech was East Coast rapid-fire, as if she didn't want to talk very long and had to get the words out as quickly as possible. 'But we've been working on a new project . . . that's why I called you.' She slipped another plastic card – a blue one this time – into a slot and the doors of the elevator slid open. She lifted the heavy inner gate effortlessly with one hand.

'We?' Magozzi asked as they all stepped inside.

'I have four partners. They're waiting upstairs.'

When the elevator ground to a halt, Grace lifted the gate onto a bright, open loft striped with sunlight. Computer stations were clustered in the center of the huge space in no apparent order, and fat black electrical cables snaked across the wooden floor. A somber group of people – three men and a heavyset woman – looked up as they entered.

'These are my partners,' Grace said, and Magozzi waited for the tiresome formality of introductions. Women always did that, even when you went to arrest them. Introduced you to everyone in the room while you were slapping on the cuffs, as if you'd dropped by for tea or something. But Grace MacBride surprised him, making a beeline for the desk of a tattooed, pony-tailed man who looked like he belonged on Wide World of Wrestling, essentially ignoring the Ichabod Crane lookalike, the yuppie type in a polo shirt, and the incredibly fat woman who nonetheless made Magozzi's heart thump a little harder.

'Harley, pull up number two,' Grace directed the muscle-bound guy in the ponytail. 'Gentlemen?'

Magozzi and Gino joined her behind the man's chair. It was like cozying up to a redwood. The rest of the people in the room kept their distance and their silence for the moment, which was just fine with Magozzi.

'What are we looking at?' He frowned over the man's massive shoulder at a blank monitor.

'Just wait,' she said, and in the next instant a photograph filled the screen.

Magozzi and Gino both bent closer, squinting at a wide-angle shot of that morning's Jane Doe when she was still draped over the angel statue in Lakewood Cemetery. The strange thing was that there were no cops in the picture, no gawkers, no crime-scene tape . . . just the body and the statue.

'Who took this shot?' Gino asked.

'I did.' The man called Harley rolled his chair to one side to give them a closer look, but neither cop needed it. They both took a step backward, eyes on Harley.

'Looks like you got there long before we did,' Gino said carefully.

'Is that what this morning's crime scene looked like?' Grace MacBride asked.

Magozzi ignored her. It didn't look like the crime

scene. It *was* the crime scene. 'The kids who found the body said they never left it until the first responders arrived,' he said, still looking at Harley. 'They called 911 on a cell. Which means you were there before anybody . . . with the possible exception of the killer.'

'Oh, for God's sake,' Harley muttered. 'I am not your killer, and that is not the crime scene.'

'We were there, sir.' Gino's voice was tight. 'And obviously, so were you. Now when exactly did you take that picture?'

Harley threw up his hands. 'Christ, I don't know. When was it, Roadrunner?'

Magozzi's head jerked left when Ichabod Crane piped up, 'A couple weeks ago. Anyway, I can't remember the date . . . Oh, wait a minute. It was Columbus Day, remember, Harley? You had to loan me twenty because the banks were closed –'

'Wait a minute.' Magozzi interrupted. 'Just wait a minute. You took that shot a couple *weeks* ago?'

'I don't think so.' Gino was looking at the picture again, shaking his head.

'We were all there,' the heavyset woman said. 'Two weeks ago. All except Mitch.'

'That's right,' Grace said.

'I didn't *want* to be there,' the yuppie type muttered, 'but I remember which night it was . . .'

'All *right*.' Magozzi took a breath, looked from one to the other, his gaze finally settling on Grace. 'Let's hear it.'

'It's a staged photograph.'

'Excuse me?' Gino was confused, belligerent now.

'It's a game, darlin'.' The big woman got up from her

chair and walked over to a coffeemaker on a counter, about twenty yards of peacock blue silk swishing around her. Neither detective could take his eyes off her. '*Serial Killer Detective*, SKUD for short. Our new computer game.'

'Perfect,' Gino muttered. 'A game about serial killers. How uplifting.'

'Honey, we feed the market; we don't create it,' Annie drawled. 'It's like Clue with more dead people, that's all. Anyway, the player catches the killer by finding the clues in a series of crime-scene photos. That one's murder number two. Take a closer look. That's Roadrunner up there on that angel.'

Magozzi and Gino looked at the beanpole in Lycra, then back at the picture again. They both saw it at the same time, the details they'd missed at first glance because the general image was so close. The red dress, the long blond hair, the stiletto heels . . . they were all perfect. But their Jane Doe had had tiny hands with red lacquered nails. The hands in this photo were large and sinewy and obviously male. And the feet . . . the feet were huge. As was the protruding Adam's apple.

Gino glanced down at Roadrunner's size four teens, then up at his neck. 'Jesus,' he whispered. 'It *is* him.'

Magozzi continued to stare at the picture, his mind racing, his blood pressure rising. The damn thing was part of a *game*. He had to struggle to focus on what Grace MacBride was saying.

'. . . most of the murder scenarios in the game are pretty ordinary. But the setting for this one was so unique that the odds against a coincidence seemed . . .'

'Astronomical,' Magozzi said, turning his head to look at her.

'Yes.'

He looked at the fat woman. 'You said it was a new game.'

'Brand-new. It hasn't been released yet.'

'So the only people who have seen this photo are in this room.'

Harley snorted and spun his chair around. 'You think we'd call you if one of us was the killer?'

'Maybe,' Magozzi said evenly.

Grace MacBride walked over to Roadrunner's desk and laid her hand on his shoulder. 'How many?' she asked quietly.

Roadrunner looked up at her. 'Five hundred eighty-seven.' He glanced over at Gino, then at Magozzi. 'We put the game on our local test website over a week ago. As of this morning, we've had 587 hits on that site –'

'*What?*' Gino exploded. 'This thing's on the Internet?!'

'We shut it down!' Roadrunner was defensive. 'Right after we saw the paper this morning.'

'Which means that only 587 people besides us have seen these photos,' Grace MacBride interjected.

'*Only?!*' Gino bellowed.

Grace leveled her gaze on Gino. 'I don't know what you're so upset about. A few hours ago you had an infinite number of suspects. We've just narrowed the field for you, down to 587.'

'Plus five,' Magozzi said pointedly, looking at each of them in turn, Grace MacBride last. 'And if you don't know what Detective Rolseth is upset about, then you obviously haven't considered that if you hadn't put this game on the web, a very young woman might still be alive.' He paused for a moment to let that sink in, then felt his mind screech to a halt as something Annie had said finally registered. 'Wait a minute. You said this was the second photo. What was the first?'

Harley turned back to his keyboard and started typing. 'I'll pull it up, but it's not nearly as dramatic as number two. Here it is.' He rolled his chair to the side to give the detectives a closer look. 'Number one. Nothing special. Just a jogger by the river.'

Magozzi heard Grace MacBride catch her breath next to him, wondered briefly what that was about, then was immediately distracted by the photo on Harley's monitor.

He and Gino stared at it for a long time, both faces devoid of emotion. Magozzi was remembering yesterday morning, kneeling next to the body of the jogger across from Rambachan, watching gloved fingers pry open the dead mouth, smelling childhood candy in a corpse. 'What's wrong with his mouth?' he asked.

Harley brightened a little. 'That's a clue. All you do is click on it.' He started to reach for the mouse, but Magozzi's words stopped him cold.

'Tell me it's not a piece of red licorice.'

Harley turned his head slowly to look at him. 'How'd you know that?' he asked, but before the words were out of his mouth he knew. They all knew, but the guy in the polo shirt had to hear it out loud.

'A jogger was murdered?' he asked weakly.

Gino said, 'Yesterday morning. Don't any of you people watch the news?'

'And he had a piece of red licorice in his mouth,' Magozzi added. 'And that *wasn't* on the news.'

The silence lasted only a few seconds, as long as it took them all to absorb the reality of what had already happened, and the chilling possibility of what might lie ahead.

'Oh Lord,' Annie finally whispered. 'Oh Lord in heaven. He's playing the game. He's doing them all.'

Magozzi felt his chest tighten. 'How many is "all"?'

'Twenty,' Mitch said flatly, fumbling behind him for a chair, then sagging into it. 'There's a total of twenty in the game.'

'Jesus, Mary, and Joseph,' Gino whispered.

Roadrunner flapped his arms, frustrated. 'No, no, no, you don't understand how this works! Yes, there are twenty murders in the game, but no one's seen anything past murder seven.'

'How do you know that?' asked Magozzi.

Roadrunner sighed impatiently. 'Because I monitor this thing 24-7, that's how. You have to solve one level before you can proceed to the next and none of the players on the site have gotten past murder seven. Some of them haven't gotten that far.'

'Oh, well, that's a relief,' Gino said. 'Here I thought we were going to have a bunch of bodies cluttering up the city. Turns out we've only got five more to go.'

Magozzi was longing for a chair. A recliner, preferably, and maybe a few beers, and certainly a world where people didn't kill each other for fun. 'I assume you've got some kind of a registration list for the players who signed onto your test site.'

'Sure. Name, address, phone number, e-mail.' Annie

pushed away from the counter and swished over to the one computer in the loft that looked like a human being might run it. The desk was deeply polished butternut, free of clutter, with a porcelain pot that held an artful arrangement of silk flowers precisely the same peacock blue as her dress. Magozzi wondered if she changed the flowers daily to match her wardrobe. 'I'll show you a list, for all the good it will do.'

'And why's that?' Gino asked, closing in on her desk.

'A lot of the entries are pure fabrication.' She pointed to a name on her monitor, hypnotizing Gino with a white lacquered nail sprinkled with blue sparkles. 'Take a look at this one. Claude Balls, and he lives on Wildcat's Revenge Avenue.'

'That is so old,' Roadrunner complained.

'Tell me about it. People have no imagination anymore.'

Gino leaned over Annie's shoulder for a better look. 'Your computer doesn't catch things like that?'

Annie's plump right shoulder rotated in an amazingly sensual shrug. Gino nearly had a heart attack. 'Registration of any kind became an exercise in futility a long time ago. Most programs only require that certain fields be filled in; they don't cross-check to make sure the entries are legit. And why would you? Are you going to refuse potential buyers access to the site, just because they want some privacy?'

'So there's no way you can find out Claude Balls's real name.'

Annie smiled a little. 'I didn't say that. In theory, it's pretty simple. Just trace back from where he signed onto the site, then get the membership records from his Internet service provider.'

Magozzi addressed his shoes because he didn't want to look at the Monkeewrench partners. Not right now. If he told them what he needed and saw the slightest flicker of hesitation cross the face of any one of them, he thought perhaps he might pull out his gun and shoot them. 'I want a copy of that registration list. I also want copies of every murder scenario in the game, especially the staged crime-scene photos. Now am I going to have a problem getting this stuff from you people without a warrant?'

'Of course not,' he heard Grace MacBride say. Her voice was shaking. She was standing perfectly erect, motionless, a tall, beautiful woman with a gun under her arm, and yet for some reason she looked totally helpless to Magozzi in that moment.

'The man on the riverboat,' she said to Harley. 'Print it.' And then she turned to Magozzi. 'That's the third murder. You've got to stop it.'

14

Magozzi was sitting alone in Mitch Cross's office, phone hooked in his shoulder, drumming his fingers on a desk that looked sterile enough for surgery.

While Muzak bastardized the Beatles in his ear, he examined the room for evidence that a human being actually worked here, and found none. Not a single scrap of paper littered either the desk or the credenza behind it, which held a computer that looked new and unused. He could see his reflection in the dark monitor screen, and not a speck of dust. He slid open the top desk drawer an inch, saw uniformly sharpened pencils nesting in a neat row, points aligned, and a flat box of wet wipes.

The walls were white and empty, except for a single abstract painting that did absolutely nothing for Magozzi. No color, no life, just a few black blobs on a lot of wasted canvas that filled him with the childish urge to find some colored markers and try his hand at graffiti.

A copy of the crime-scene photo of murder number three lay perfectly centered on the desk in front of him. It was only a serendipitous act of placement – he'd tossed it there when he sat down – but it bothered him that the thing had seemed to position itself in perfect harmony with the obsessive-compulsive surroundings.

He moved the photo until it was slightly crooked, and immediately felt better.

Crime-scene number three was the kind of childishly naughty image a teenage kid would dream up: a pudgy, middle-aged man sitting on a toilet with his pants puddled around his ankles and a bullet hole in his head. Magozzi decided it was probably the brainchild of the big tattooed guy, a case of arrested development if ever he saw one.

According to the SKUD game, the third victim was found in the restroom of a paddleboat during an evening party cruise on a river. He supposed there were even better places to lay a trap for a killer, but this one suited Magozzi just fine.

He'd been on one of the paddle wheelers years ago, a dinner cruise down the St Croix River back in the days when he and Heather did such things together. It had been bigger than he'd expected – three decks and seating for five hundred – and a lot less romantic. The interior decks were single, vast rooms with no private spaces where romantic – or homicidal – fantasies could be indulged. The restrooms were right out in the open, with access in plain view. If he had to, he figured they could cover a boat with just twelve officers, four per deck, although he was hoping for an even better scenario. Cancel the charter, fill the boat with cops in their best civvies, and let the bastard come.

The Muzak switched from Beatles to Mancini and Magozzi glanced at his watch impatiently. It had taken five minutes to find out that only a few of the great paddle-boats were still on the river this late in the year, and that only one – the *Nicollet* – was chartered for a party cruise tonight. Getting the rest of the information he needed was taking a lot longer than it should have.

The music clicked off abruptly and Mr Tiersval, the president of the paddleboat company, came back on the line. 'Detective Magozzi?'

'Still here.'

'I'm sorry for the delay. We have . . . a bit of a situation here.' The man's voice was strained to the breaking point. 'Tonight's charter is the Hammond wedding reception.'

It took Magozzi a beat. 'As in Foster Hammond?'

'Yes.'

'Jesus.'

If there was royalty in Minneapolis, Foster and Char Hammond were it. A near monopoly on Great Lakes shipping had filled the family coffers back at the turn of the century. Now they owned half of downtown Minneapolis if the rumors were true, and had more political influence than all the voters in the state put together.

'There's no way the Hammonds would agree to cancel this event, Detective. They've been planning it for over a year, and the guest list reads like a Who's Who of Minnesota. I checked with our lawyers to see if there was anything I could do, but apparently the legal ramifications of canceling the charter are considerably more severe than having a man killed on one of our boats, if you can believe that.'

Magozzi believed it.

'If I were to refuse to honor the Hammonds' contract, they can, and most certainly will, sue the line into bankruptcy. On the other hand' – and now a bitter sarcasm crept into his voice – 'if we forewarn the passengers about the potential for danger and they still choose to board, the law holds us blameless if one of them dies.'

Magozzi nodded to himself. Sometimes the law was a bitch.

'Can't the police order us to cancel the charter?'

Magozzi smiled a little. 'Not in this country. Not without an Emergency Powers declaration from the governor, and all we're working with here is a suspicion of something that might happen, not a clear and present danger.'

'Maybe the mayor could help you with that. He's on the guest list.'

Magozzi covered his eyes with his hand.

'I want you to know that if it were up to me, Detective, I would haul that boat out of the water myself and the hell with lawsuits.'

'I believe you, Mr Tiersval.' It was always something of a surprise for Magozzi to find genuinely decent people at the top of any corporate ladder. He'd probably watched *Erin Brockovich* too many times.

'I called the Hammonds and explained the situation briefly. They agreed to give you a hearing if you can get over there within the next thirty minutes. Do you need the address?'

Magozzi didn't. Everyone in the city knew who lived in the big stone mansion on Lake of the Isles.

Gino walked in just as he was hanging up the phone. He looked exactly one donut fatter than when Magozzi had left him out in the loft ten minutes earlier.

'You broke bread with them,' he accused him, pointing to his chin.

Gino dragged his hand across crags and whiskers and white powder fell to Mitch Cross's immaculate gray carpet. 'I'd break bread with Satan if it was a sugar donut. They made us hard copies of the game and registration info for every player who signed onto the website. Didn't even have to ask twice. General MacBride had the printers going before I could open my mouth, and now we got two boxes out there stuffed with paper. You have any luck nailing down a boat?'

'Yeah, and it was all bad. I'll tell you about it in the car.'

When the elevator door slid shut on the detectives, Grace looked away toward the windows and concentrated on the pale strips of light an anemic sun painted on the floor. She wasn't quite ready to meet the eyes of her friends, not just yet.

People were dying because of her. Again.

Mitch collapsed into a chair next to her. Outwardly, he appeared calm, but hysteria emanated from him like a toxic aura. 'We are screwed,' he finally announced.

The comment barely registered in Grace's mind, but Annie was quick to respond with a scowl. 'That's a nice attitude, Mitch.'

Mitch raised his eyes to look at her. 'What do you think is going to happen to Monkeewrench when this thing blows wide open?'

That comment registered in Grace's mind and she turned to look at him. 'What are you saying, Mitch?'

she asked carefully, knowing full well she was opening Pandora's box.

Mitch blew out a breath and raked his fingers through his hair. 'I'm saying that Greenberg was pissed off just because we were creating a game about serial killers. When he finds out we're responsible for a rash of copycat murders, Schoolhouse, along with about fifty percent of Monkeewrench's income, is going to be a happy memory.'

Grace recoiled and stared at her old friend as if he were an unpleasant stranger. 'I can't believe I just heard you say that.'

Mitch scrubbed his unshaven face with his hands. 'What? I'm the only one who's worried? I'm talking about the future of our company, Grace. This is not a minor setback, this is a disaster.'

'For God's sake, Mitch, people are dying out there because of this game!'

'Which I didn't want to do in the first place, remember?' he almost shouted, and then he saw the look on her face and would have given his life to take the words back.

Your fault, Grace. Your fault then, and your fault now.

15

Magozzi felt like Chicken Little in the Twilight Zone. He and Gino had just told a roomful of people that the sky was falling, and all they did was sit there with small, condescending smiles that seemed to make allowances for his stupidity.

They were sitting on a plum settee in a room Magozzi figured was about a foot too short for regulation basketball. Char and Foster Hammond sat directly across from them, looking tan, fit, and composed, flanked by the twenty-eight members of the wedding party, plus the groom's parents.

'Well, Detectives, we certainly appreciate your concern.' Foster Hammond gave them a practiced, gracious smile. For a minute Magozzi thought he was going to pat him on the head for being a well-intentioned, if ill-advised, public servant. 'But I doubt very much that this . . . individual would attempt such a thing at this particular event. It would be sheer insanity.'

'He's a psychopathic killer, Mr Hammond,' Gino blurted out. 'Sheer insanity goes with the territory.'

Magozzi looked around the room, measuring faces for some sort of normal human reaction. Nothing. Not one eye flickered at the phrase 'psychopathic killer.' Even the bride and groom looked cool and aloof, insulated by upbringing and money from common, nasty things like homicide.

Hammond gave him an elegant shrug. 'I've no doubt about that, Detective Rolseth, but unless he's very anxious to be apprehended, I don't think we'll be seeing him this evening. This event has been highly publicized over the past few months, much to our dismay, I might add, and there will be media present. On the periphery, of course.'

Of course, Magozzi thought. God forbid the reception be sullied by the obvious presence of people who worked for a living.

'It took me months to get those devils to agree to stay on the sidelines. The bane of my existence.' Hammond was still speaking, a little more animated now. 'And what a spectacularly ironic twist! All that unwelcome publicity mandated that we take the most stringent security measures, given the stature of some of our guests. And thank God we did.'

'The power of the press,' Gino said with sarcasm that was totally lost on everyone present but his partner.

Foster Hammond paused to take a dainty sip from a crystal tumbler and when he looked up again, his expression was deadly serious. 'This really is a dreadful turn of events, Detectives. Pointless, brutal killings in our beautiful city.'

'It is, sir,' Magozzi agreed, wondering if Hammond believed there were other kinds of murders besides pointless, brutal ones. 'That's why we're here, trying to prevent another one.'

Hammond nodded emphatically. 'And I'm sure you're doing a fine job, which is why I've always been a generous sponsor of the Minneapolis law enforcement community. And you *will* let me know if there's anything I can do to help.'

Anything but cancel his daughter's wedding reception, was the clear implication. People like Foster Hammond and family heard only what they wanted to hear, cooperated only if it fit into their agenda. It was time to be a sycophant, trade compliments and convince the King that preventing this murder fit into the agenda. Anything else would be a waste of time.

In the end, they settled for a modest contingent of officers on board, as long as they were suitably attired. Hammond had even agreed to a warning announcement after the ceremony, and again at the entrance to the paddleboat landing.

Magozzi had been watching Tammy Hammond, the bride-to-be, when he said this, and caught a disturbing flicker of perverse excitement in those cool blue eyes.

The entire drive back to City Hall, Magozzi and Gino were shaking their heads, trying to make sense of what had just happened back at Hammond Manor.

'I haven't been snubbed like that since ninth grade,' Gino said.

'What did you do in ninth grade?'

'Asked Sally Corcoran to the prom. She was the most popular girl in the senior class.'

'That was stupid,' Magozzi offered genially.

'Hammond scares the shit out of me, you know? He reminds me of a mongoose. Just when you think you've slithered around and got him by the balls, you realize he's already got you by the neck.'

'Very poetic, Gino.'

'Thanks. I'll put it in my journal,' he said dispiritedly. 'Jesus, I always wanted to believe people like that are real, real as you and me and Joe Pig Farmer down the road. Never mind the gossip, the rumors, the bad press . . . You ignore that because you want them to be just folks.'

'Everybody wants to believe that.'

'And why? Because they run the show and you want to believe that the people running the show have your best interests in mind.'

Magozzi stopped at a red light and looked over at Gino. 'And you don't think Foster Hammond has our best interests in mind?'

Gino stared at him for a moment, then burst into laughter.

16

The room was an olfactory museum of hundreds of meetings just like this one. Fast food, sweat, and the now-forbidden cigarette smoke – all these smells and more seeped from the plaster walls and rose from the uneven waves of the warped wooden floor.

Which is as it should be, Magozzi thought. Rooms where cops gather should smell like bad food and frustrated men and women and late nights and pisser cases, because smell was memory, and lingering smells were a memorial; sometimes the only one a crime victim got.

Magozzi looked over his audience from his perch on the front desk. Patrol Sergeant Eaton Freedman was in a crisp uniform custom-tailored to wrap itself around the three hundred pounds of coal-black muscle packed into his six feet nine inches. The rest of them – eight detectives besides him and Gino – wore low-end off-the-rack slacks and sport coats. Nobody wore their good suits on the job. You never knew what you might have to kneel in, or crawl through.

Chief Malcherson was another matter. The offal he was sometimes forced to crawl through was almost entirely political, and required a different uniform – designer suits and silk ties and shirts so starched the collars left a red necklace of abrasion around his throat. He had a thicket of white-blond hair that looked good on camera, and a bloodhound face that didn't.

He was standing in a front corner now, intentionally setting himself apart from the men and women under his command, his expression more hangdog than usual. Today's suit was a dark charcoal, double-breasted, suitable for mourning.

It wasn't a designated task force. Not yet. Task forces were long-term, and Magozzi was praying this thing wouldn't come to that. What he needed right now was manpower, and the chief had been disturbed enough by the murders to give it to him. Or maybe it was the media that really frightened him. Either way, now that Magozzi had laid out the Monkeewrench connection and passed out copies of the SKUD game photos, everyone else in the room was disturbed, too. Apparently the idea of murder as a game was universally chilling.

'Any questions so far?' he asked.

Nine heads lifted at the same time. The amazing synchronized head-raising team.

'This is unbelievable.'

The other amazing heads turned to look at Louise Washington, the department's showcase detective. Half Hispanic, half black, a woman and a lesbian to boot, she satisfied multiple minority groups. That she was damned good at her job seemed incidental to everyone except the cops who worked with her.

'Bleep,' Gino blatted from his place next to the door. 'That was not in the form of a question.'

'Isn't this unbelievable?' Louise corrected herself, which was the signal for Chief Malcherson to straighten up in his corner and pretend to take charge.

'There is no cause for levity here. And no excuse for it. Two innocent young people are dead, and we have a psychopath roaming the streets of our city.'

Gino wiped his mouth with a beefy hand while the amazing heads dropped in unison and pretended to study the photos on their desks. The chief was well-intentioned, but he'd been off the streets for a long time and tended to talk like an old Humphrey Bogart movie. Magozzi broke in before someone blew it and laughed out loud.

'Okay, listen up. Whoever this actor is, he took down two in less than twenty-four hours, so we've got no breathing time here. The first two murders followed the game murders almost exactly and he's doing them in order. If this guy stays true to form, we know where the third one is supposed to go down; when is another matter. Could be tonight, could be this weekend. Everyone got photo number three?'

There was a rustle of papers and then a voice called out from the back of the room, 'Hey, that guy's sitting on a toilet, right?'

Magozzi looked back at Johnny McLaren sprawled all over a seat in the back row. He was the youngest detective on the force; bright red hair, sunny disposition, serious gambling problem.

'Can't get anything past you, Johnny. According to the game, murder three takes place during a party on a riverboat – a paddle wheeler, specifically. Normally we've got a few of those running on both the Saint Croix and the Mississippi, lunch, dinner, party cruises during high season, leaf tours through October, but we caught a big break this week. The only one running before the weekend is the *Nicollet*. They've got a wedding reception going tonight.'

'Bunch of fools,' Louise muttered. 'It's going down to the teens tonight. Nothing like wearing a parka over your wedding gown.'

'Too bad we can't just shut it down,' Patrol Sergeant Freedman said, and heads turned to look at him. James Earl Jones lived in Freedman's voice box, and the man couldn't say two words without commanding the complete attention of anyone within listening range.

'Nice going, Freedman,' Gino spoke up. 'A black man advocating a police state. Let me get on the horn to the NAACP, see if we can't get you nominated for an Image award.'

Freedman grinned at him. 'Hey, I'm all for a police state. I just want to run it.' And then to Magozzi, 'You boys reach out to the family?'

Magozzi nodded. 'Yeah, and that's the bad news. The blushing bride is Tammy Hammond.'

'Oh shit,' Louise Washington said. 'The Hammond wedding? As in Foster and Char Hammond?'

'None other. And let me tell you, these people have the entire "A" list on their speed dial. By the time Gino and I got to their place, Chief Malcherson had had calls from the mayor, four council members, the attorney general, and Senator Washburn.' Chief Malcherson confirmed this with a miserable nod. 'The message was pretty clear. Under no circumstances are we to in any way disrupt the Hammond wedding reception.'

'Wait a minute.' Tinker Lewis waved a hefty, tweed-coated arm from the back. He had sad brown eyes and a hairline that had receded halfway to Australia. Ten years in Homicide and he was still one of the gentlest men Magozzi knew. 'We're supposed to just sit by and watch this thing go down?'

'They don't think anything's going to go down,' Magozzi said, 'and they might be right. There's another charter Saturday night – some 3M exec's retirement party – and if I were the killer, that's the one I'd pick. No security, as compared to Argo covering tonight's cruise.'

'Argo? Red Chilton's bunch?'

Magozzi nodded. All but the youngest in the room had worked with Red Chilton back when he was in Homicide, wearing cheap sport coats and driving five-year-old cars like the rest of them. Seven years ago he'd taken early retirement and started Argo Security with some of the best ex-cops in law enforcement. Now he was wearing Italian suits and driving a Porsche.

'There are some pretty high-profilers invited tonight. The mayor, for one, couple of state congressmen, some film people. Hammond contracted with Argo a long time ago for this, and Red's bringing damn near his whole roster. There'll be twenty of them on site tonight, all armed, funneled gate, metal detectors, the whole nine yards. Hammond did agree to a "small, very discreet police presence," but that's it. It isn't going to be our show.'

Tinker grunted. 'So what do we get?'

'Couple of squads and uniforms in the lot, six people on board dressed as guests. Gino talked to Red, brought him up to speed so his people don't take down our people and vice versa.'

'So we'll have thirty armed people and a paddleboat,'

Freedman said. 'Hell, we could point that thing south and probably take Louisiana.'

Louise Washington was shaking her head. 'Our boy's never going to show tonight.'

'Maybe not, but if he does, this is our best shot at taking the guy down. This is the only murder in the game in a contained environment. The next one, for instance, takes place at the Mall of America, and I don't even want to think about how we'd cover that.

'Freedman, you and McLaren are heading up the detail. Gino will give you the rest of your roster when we're finished here. Reception starts at seven, Red's expecting you at the boat landing at five. Take a good look at his security arrangements. You see any holes, check back in and we'll find a way to fill them. Any questions?'

'Yeah, I got a question,' McLaren said. 'Is anyone telling the people coming to this thing there might be a little murder problem?'

'Oh yeah.' Magozzi stared at the back wall and remembered that glitter of excitement in Tammy Hammond's eyes. 'Hammond's going to make an announcement after the ceremony, and Red's people will do the same at the gate for anyone who skipped the church scene, but I don't think it's going to keep anyone away, not with all the security in place. Chief already called the politicos he knew, and they're still coming, and the rest of them . . . I don't know . . . I get the feeling they're getting off on it a little.'

Louise made a face. 'Rich people are totally weird.'

Magozzi glanced at his watch and hurried along. 'Anyway, that's the setup at the boat. In the meantime, some of the rest of you are going to be working the list of people who registered to play the game on the test site. We need to cross-check with public records and narrow it down so we don't have to knock on over five hundred doors. Some of the addresses are going to be bogus –'

'Like the killer's, for instance,' Louise snorted.

'Maybe. Maybe not. This guy's a gamer, remember. He *wants* to play. Putting his real name and address on that list, looking us in the eye when we go to interview . . . that kind of thing has to be worth big points, so pay real close attention to the possibles. Eliminate the seniors, kids under ten, quadriplegics . . . anybody else, look at hard. Once we get it honed down, we'll hit the streets for the locals.'

'Forget the out-of-towners?' Freedman asked.

Magozzi shook his head. 'Absolutely not. Some guy from Singapore could be sitting in the downtown Hyatt playing on his laptop. These murders were bang-bang, two nights in a row. Could very well be an out-of-towner making his mark before he heads home. Check every name on the list, and I mean every single one. Call whoever you have to, any*where* you have to. Do what you can by computer and phone; if you run across a possible out-of-state, or even out-of-the-country, pass it on to Gino, and he'll deal with asking the locals for an on-site. Chief gave us open overtime on this, so anyone who wants to pull a double tonight, talk to Gino when we're through here. He'll set you up.'

'What about the idiots that put this game out there in the first place?' Tinker Lewis grumbled.

'We're going to look at them.' Magozzi hopped off

the desk and handed a single sheet of paper to Tommy Espinoza, a slight, twitchy man in the front row wearing a corduroy jacket over denim. He had his Latin father's dark coloring, his Swedish mother's blue eyes, and a pear-shaped belly that belonged to Chee-tos. Technically he was a detective, but in actuality, he never saw the streets. As the resident computer genius, he was far too valuable at the keyboard to risk outside the building.

'Those are the stats on the five Monkeewrench partners, Tommy. Put together profiles on all of them ASAP. Before you leave tonight.'

'You think one of them's good for it?'

'In my gut, no. They're equal partners, and if this game goes in the dumper, they've each got a lot to lose. But they're on the list. Anybody with access to the game is on the list, and they sure as hell have access.'

'Did you ask any of these people if they had alibis?' Louise asked.

'Yeah,' Gino said. 'We learned that in our mail-order detective course. Every one of them was alone during both murders. Cross is the only one who's married, but his wife was in LA when the jogger bought it, and he was alone at the office until late last night, so she can't place him for either one.'

Espinoza glanced at the five names, then looked up at Magozzi. 'You're kidding, right? Roadrunner?'

'That's the name on his license,' Gino put in.

'No shit?'

'No shit.'

Espinoza looked down at the names again, head shaking. 'And Harley Davidson? Tell me these are not the names they were born with.'

'You tell us, Tommy. By the way, McLaren, Freedman, you've got MDL blowups of these people in your handout. Special eye out for any of them tonight. They're not on the guest list. Gino?'

'I'm done.'

'Chief?' He looked over at Chief Malcherson, who was still standing in exactly the same spot, deep into the cool-as-a-cucumber routine that fooled absolutely no one. His cheeks were too red, his eyes as busy as his body was still. Magozzi figured he'd blow a vessel in about five minutes. 'Anything you want to add?'

'Just that we've got a lot of media downstairs. They're all over this angel thing. Avoid them if you can, refer them to me, Magozzi, or Rolseth if you can't. I don't want to hear a lot of "no comments" on the news tonight. Sounds bad.'

17

You wouldn't know it to look at me, thought Wilbur Daniels, but in my heart, *this* is the man I have always been. A wild man. A risk-taker. A sexual adventurer, willing to try anything once, desperate to taste the thrills of the bizarre, the exotic, the near-perverted, if someone would only ask.

And finally, someone had.

Within the past ten minutes, Wilbur had decided that there was indeed a god, and that occasionally he smiled on paunchy, middle-aged men with lives as colorless as the few remaining wisps on their otherwise bald pates.

There was pain involved, of course. These flabby legs that had spent the last twenty years in the cubbyhole of a desk were not used to the demands of this demeaning position. An under-used, flaccid quadricep was pinching, convulsing, threatening to knot, and yet he would not wish for the cramping to stop; would not move an inch to ease the pain that only seemed to heighten this sinful pleasure. *If the gang could see me now*, he sang in his mind, imagining the shock and revulsion on the faces of those who thought they knew him. The image pleased him, and an unmanly giggle bubbled from his lips. He apologized immediately, only to be told that one should never apologize for finding joy, no matter how dark the deed that created it. Oh, yes. Oh, God, that was so true.

In the next second he bit down on his own hand to stifle a cry of ecstasy, and for a fleeting moment, wondered how he would later explain the wound. But then he was asked to assume a new, deliciously naughty position, and he forgot his hand, and the cramp in his thigh, and the whole of his miserable life at a sensation so intense he doubted that his heart would survive the experience.

The gun didn't frighten him when it appeared. Well, all right; it did, a little, but that was part of it, wasn't it? Didn't the omnipresent specter of death always intensify the pleasures one extracted from life? And it was certainly intensifying this one.

As the barrel pressed against his temple in the ultimate threat, he felt a corresponding surge of pleasure so exquisite he thought he might explode.

And then, to a degree, he did.

Patrol Sergeant Eaton Freedman fastened his belt holster and shrugged into a pin-striped suitcoat that had been too tight before he tried to stuff a gun under it. You'd have to be blind not to see the bulge, but most people who looked at Eaton Freedman never saw the details, just a really big black man.

Detective Johnny McLaren rapped on the door frame of Freedman's office. 'Stop preening, Freedman, we gotta go . . . ooh. Sharp.'

Freedman looked critically at McLaren's maroon polyester blazer. 'You get that at Goodwill?'

McLaren looked indignant. 'Damn right. Five bucks.'

'We're supposed to dress like wedding guests.'

'Hey, I wore this to *my* wedding.'

'Which explains your divorce. Besides, it clashes with your hair.'

'What a team. No one will notice us, no way. A big, black linebacker and a carrot-top Mick. What was Magozzi thinking, picking the two of us?'

Freedman's laughter rumbled like thunder. 'You don't know?'

''Cause we're the sharpest, best guys on the force?'

'How about because we both live ten minutes away and could get to our good duds faster than anybody else?'

McLaren looked crestfallen.

'*And* because we're the sharpest, best guys on the force,' Freedman added.

'That's what I thought. Let's go. You get any prettier the groom'll dump the bride and marry you.'

When Freedman and McLaren nosed the unmarked up to the *Nicollet*'s access gate a half hour later, two bruisers in black suits came out of nowhere and flanked the doors. Freedman rolled down his window and looked up at a guy with no neck and a shaved head. 'Berg, you son of a bitch, what happened to your hair, man?'

The guy's face remained expressionless. 'Women kept pulling on it in the throes of passion, so I shaved it off. Get out of there, Freedman, so I can frisk your fat black ass.'

'In your dreams, you fish-belly Swede.' Freedman grinned, and then in a stage whisper to McLaren, 'I had this guy walkin' the Hennepin patrol a while back. He wanted me the first time he saw me. Was about to file sek-shu-al harassment when Red Chilton up and hired him away from us.'

Berg ducked down and filled the window opening with his head, looking skeptically at McLaren's slight form. 'I don't know about you new cops. You all look little.'

'Yeah, but we got bigger guns,' McLaren said, touching a finger to his forehead. 'Johnny McLaren.'

'Hey, Fritz, come on around here and meet Patrol Sergeant Eaton Freedman and Johnny McLaren.'

The second bruiser bent to look inside the car, nodded once, then retreated.

'Well, there's a Chatty Kathy,' Freedman rumbled.

'He was ATF for a dozen years,' Berg said. 'And as you know those guys are a little short on conversational skills. I'll do my best to keep him from shooting you by accident.'

'That would be good.' McLaren's eyes followed the man as he hulked around the car suspiciously, probably looking for bombs or biological weapons or contraband cigarettes. 'Man, he looks grim.'

'That's why we put him up front,' Berg said. 'Makes our clients feel real secure. The guy's a puff ball, though. Raises cocker spaniel puppies.'

'He probably eats them.'

Berg laughed and rolled his hand at someone in the guard booth by the gate, and two hundred square feet of cyclone fence unlatched and started to hum open. 'Red's on board, waiting for you. Some doin's tonight, huh?'

'Might be,' Freedman agreed. 'This the only access?'

'For cars, yeah. We check everybody against the guest list here, and sweep them before they get through.' He raised a handheld metal detector.

'Mayor's going to love that,' McLaren said.

'Him, I'm doing personally. Always thought he was a shifty bastard. Good to see you again, Freedman.'

'You, too, Anton.'

McLaren waited until they'd pulled through the gate into the parking lot before whispering, *'Anton?'*

'Don't go there,' Freedman told him.

The *Nicollet* rested at dockside, about ten times larger than anything McLaren had expected, three stacked decks gleaming white against dark gray clouds that were starting to shred in the middle. They'd be gone by dark, the weatherman had said, and clear skies would send the temperatures plummeting. Hell of a night to be on a riverboat.

'Bitchin' cold already,' Freedman grumbled, picking up the pace. 'There's Red. You ever met him?'

'Nope.' McLaren looked at the man striding toward them across the parking lot. He'd expected a bulky, Minnesota homegrown kind of guy, but Chilton looked more like Clark Gable in his prime, right down to the little dark mustache and the million-dollar smile.

'Lookin' good, Red.' Freedman gave him back a smile and pumped his hand. 'Johnny McLaren, meet the fool who sold out the noble profession of public service for a measly few hundred grand a year.'

'It's always an honor to meet a man with real brains,' Johnny said warmly as he shook his hand. 'Especially when they saddle me with a guy like Freedman.'

Red gave a hearty laugh. 'Pleasure to meet you, Johnny McLaren. You got a taste of gate security coming in, right?'

'Looks tight,' Freedman said.

Red nodded. 'It is, but all that does is control vehicle

traffic.' He waved at the parking lot, which bled into adjoining riverfront property with no obstructions. 'Anybody could walk in, so the real security is at the two gangplanks. I'll have four men at each of them, and everybody gets swept again. No one boards with hardware unless they've got one of these.' He handed Freedman and McLaren lapel pins with the Argo logo. 'How many people have you got coming?'

'We'll have a couple squads and uniforms in the lot. Only six plainclothes on board, including us,' Freedman said.

Red dug in his pocket and came up with four more pins, handed them to Freedman. 'We already checked out the boat. I assume you'll be doing a walk-through of your own.'

'Right.'

'Okay. We can double up checking in the crew and waitstaff and caterers; they should be showing up anytime now and there's going to be a lot of them, plus the musicians, some asshole bunch called the Whipped Nipples.'

'No shit?' McLaren asked. 'The Whipped Nipples?'

Freedman stared at him. 'It scares me that you know who that is.'

'Are you kidding? They're incredible. All strings. Cello, bass, violins, dulcimer, some native instruments you never saw from countries you never heard of. You're going to like this, Freedman.'

'I am not going to like this because I do not like their name.'

Red grinned. 'Neither did Foster Hammond. Paid 'em extra not to display it or say it.'

Freedman gave his big head a what's-the-world-coming-to shake. 'Don't know why anyone would want a name like that.'

'One of my boys told me they're a bunch of faggots – for real. You take that wherever you want to go.'

McLaren shook his finger at him. 'That was not politically correct.'

Red grinned at him. 'Can't get anything past you, McLaren.'

'That's the second time somebody said that to me today.'

'Well then, it must be true and we're all in good hands. Now on board we've got three cans. Six, actually. A men's and women's on each deck. Rolseth said you'd want your people to cover those, but I'll leave one man stationary in each of those areas just as backup. You think of anything else you need, let me know.'

Freedman nodded. 'Thanks, Red. Appreciate your cooperation.'

'Cooperation, hell. Somebody gets blown away on this tugboat, doesn't hurt to have the MPD around to share the blame. Why don't you two come aboard and I'll introduce you to Captain Magnusson. A real character, that guy. He'll give you the nickel tour and then we can discuss tonight's plan over tea and petits fours.'

'I'd prefer a scotch,' Johnny said.

'Yeah, wouldn't we all? This detail has been giving me nightmares for six months in the form of Foster Hammond. Didn't think it could get any worse. How wrong I was. And so for our troubles, we get tea and petits fours. Not their job to feed us, of course, but as a courtesy . . .'

'You were serious about the tea and petits fours?' Freedman asked incredulously.

Red shook his head sadly. 'There's one thing I never joke about and that's food. Stick with the pink ones – got a nice framboise custard in the middle. So just between the three of us, you really think this crazy s.o.b. is going to show tonight?'

Freedman shrugged. 'If he does, we get all the credit.'

'Sixty-forty. I just bought a place in Boca Raton, so I could use the extra business. Property taxes are killing me.'

Captain Magnusson was on the foredeck, standing by helplessly as he watched his ship being taken over by a lot of armed men in suits. He was a weathered-looking old man with ruddy, freckled cheeks and tufts of reddish gray hair poking out from beneath his cap.

'They pick him for the job based on appearance alone?' McLaren wondered aloud.

'You could almost believe it,' Red agreed.

'Hey, another redhead, could be one of your relatives, McLaren,' Freedman teased his partner.

'Not a chance. He's Viking stock, you can tell by the paunch.'

Freedman looked over at McLaren's own paunch. 'So you're a Viking now?'

'This is not a paunch. This is a Guinness gut, Freedman. You get a paunch from too much damn lutefisk.'

'Nobody gets a paunch from lutefisk. It's an emetic.'

'You had it before?'

'Hell no. But my mother-in-law makes it every damn

Christmas. Makes the whole house smell like a three-day-old corpse.' He let out a long, low whistle as they boarded the gangplank. 'Nice-looking boat.'

'That she is,' Red said, waving to the captain. 'Permission to board, Captain?'

Magnusson actually smiled. 'Aye!'

'So how do they get that paddle to move anyhow?' McLaren asked.

'Squirrels.'

'Good. I'll tell the little sons of bitches that are eating the insulation in my attic that they should get a job.'

18

Roadrunner kept his eyes front, focused on the asphalt a few feet ahead of his bike, alert for a new crack in the tar that could bite the narrow racing tire and send him careening into the traffic on his left.

He felt the burn in his thighs and calves from pedaling hard up the hill by the river, but it didn't hurt enough yet. He should have done it twice, maybe three times or four, until the pain blossomed and the world turned orange and all the noise in his head abruptly, blessedly, stopped.

'Watch where you're going, asshole!'

He'd strayed over the yellow line that separated the bike lane from traffic, and was only inches from the sleek black finish of a late-model Mercedes. He turned his head slowly, put his light eyes on the red-faced man glaring at him from behind the wheel, and left them there. He kept pedaling to keep adjacent to the sedan, just looking at the man and nowhere else while bike and car moved side by side at twenty miles an hour down Washington Avenue.

A wave of uncertainty rippled across the anger in the man's face, moving the little pockets of flesh under his eyes. He jerked his head front, then back at Roadrunner, then front again. 'Crazy son of a bitch,' he muttered, powering up the passenger window and increasing his speed, trying to pull away.

Roadrunner pumped harder and came abreast, kept his eyes on the man, his face empty as they sailed through the green light at Portland Avenue. He downshifted to first gear to make it harder, almost smiled when he felt the burn in his thighs brighten and saw the uncertainty in the man's face turn to fear.

Quit staring at me, you skinny freak, you hear me? Quit staring or by God I'll make you sorry . . .

The voice in his head was so loud, so clear, it erased the years between then and now and slammed Roadrunner's eyes shut so he wouldn't see the hammer coming down, over and over.

When he opened them again the Mercedes was long gone and he was stopped at a red light, straddling his bike, breathing hard, staring down at the crooked, lumpy fingers of a hand that looked like a bunch of carelessly tossed Pick-Up Sticks. 'It's all right.' His whisper was lost in the noise of cars and whistles and the grinding gears of a city bus. 'It's all right now.'

He turned right and headed down toward the Hennepin Avenue bridge, saw the sluggish, autumn flow of the Mississippi slipping beneath the concrete and steel on its journey south. The water looked gray here, which seemed odd to Roadrunner because it had been so blue earlier. Of course that had been downriver at the paddleboat landing, and maybe the clouds hadn't rolled in yet – he couldn't remember.

It was almost six o'clock by the time Grace pulled into her short driveway and butted the Range Rover's nose up to the garage door. Less than an hour of daylight left; no time to take Charlie for his daily run down to the park on the next block. She wondered how she was going to explain it to him.

She keyed a code into a pad on her visor and watched the steel-clad door rise in front of her. Inside the small garage a bank of overhead floods turned on automatically and filled the space with light. There were no shadows, and there were no hiding places.

'Be a lot cheaper if you just let me put the track for these lights on one of those crossbeams, miss. Hanging them up in the peak is going to be a bitch.'

Stupid man. He'd never thought that if you hung the lights below the crossbeams, the space above would be dark, and that someone could hide up there, crouched on a two-by-six, ready to pounce.

She'd been very restrained, and hadn't told him what an idiot he was; she'd just smiled and asked him very politely to hurry with the garage; she had a lot of other electrical work for him to do before she could move in.

Once the Range Rover was safely in the garage with the door closed behind her, she pushed another button on the visor and turned off the floodlights. There was only one window in the small building – a narrow one by the side door that admitted a slice of the fading light from outside. Other than that, the darkness was almost absolute.

Drawing her weapon before she got out of the car was so much a part of her routine that Grace never thought about it. In the five years she had lived in this house, she had never once stepped out of the garage without the 9mm in her right hand, held close to her side in a rare gesture of consideration for neighbors who might not understand.

She made her way to the side door, looked out the narrow window at the patch of yard between the garage and her house, then pressed six numbers on a keypad next to the door and heard the heavy clunk of a releasing latch. She stepped outside and stopped for a moment, holding her breath, listening, watching, every sense alert for something out of place. She heard the swoosh of a passing car stirring up dry leaves on the street; the bass throb of a sound system somewhere down the block; the muted chitter of sparrows settling for the night. Nothing unusual. Nothing wrong.

Finally satisfied, she pulled the small door closed behind her and heard the soft beep of the alarm system signaling activation. Nineteen quick steps on a strip of concrete that led from the garage to the front door, eyes busy, palm sweating on the textured grip of the 9mm, and then she was there, slipping the red card into the slot, opening the heavy front door, stepping inside and closing it quickly behind her. She released the breath she'd been holding as Charlie came to her on his belly, head down in submission, the stub that remembered a tail trying to sweep the floor.

'My man.' She smiled, holstering the gun before she went down on her knees to hug the wire-coated wonder. 'Sorry I'm late.'

The dog punished her with a spate of furious face-licking, then bounded away down the short central hall back to the kitchen. There were a few seconds of toe-nails scrabbling for purchase on linoleum, then Charlie returned at a dangerous gallop, leash in his mouth.

'Sorry, fella. There isn't enough time.'

Charlie looked at her for a moment, then slowly

opened his mouth and let the leash fall to the floor.

'It'll be dark soon,' she explained.

The dog gave her his best crestfallen expression.

Grace sucked in air through her teeth. 'No walks after dark. We made a deal, remember?'

The scruffy, gnawed-off tail wiggled.

'Nope. Can't do it. I'm sorry. I'm really sorry.'

He never begged. Never whined. Never questioned, because whatever life Charlie had had before her had beaten those things out of him. He simply collapsed on the Oriental runner and put his head on his paws, nose nudging the discarded leash. Grace couldn't stand it.

'You are a disgraceful manipulator.'

The stub moved, just a little.

'We'd have to run all the way down there.'

The dog sat up quickly.

'And we couldn't stay long.'

Charlie opened his mouth in a wonderful smile and his tongue fell out.

Grace bent to hook the leash to his heavy collar, feeling the excited quiver beneath her fingers and, stranger still, the seldom-used muscles at the corners of her mouth turning up. 'We make each other smile, don't we, boy?'

And what a wondrous thing that was for them both.

They literally ran the short block to the little park, Grace's duster flapping in time with Charlie's ears, her boots clicking hard on the concrete sidewalk.

The last feeble light of a cold sun flickered between the closely set houses as they ran, flashing in Grace's peripheral vision with the distracting jerkiness of an old silent movie.

The neighborhood was quieting with the onset of cold and the dinner hour. Only two cars passed them on the way: a '93 teal Ford Tempo with a young girl at the wheel, license number 907 Michael-David-Charlie; and a '99 red Chevy Blazer, two occupants, license number 415 Tango-Foxtrot-Zulu.

They're just people, Grace told herself. Just normal, average people heading home after a workday, and if they slowed a little when they saw her, if they looked a little too long out their windows, it was only because they weren't used to seeing someone walk their dog at a dead run.

Still, she watched the cars until their taillights disappeared down the street, and she would hold the plate numbers in her phenomenal memory for days, perhaps longer. She couldn't help it.

It wasn't much of a park. A small square of closely cropped grass, a few red oaks with crispy leaves clinging to naked branches, a rusty swing set, a pair of weathered teeter-totters, and a sandbox used more by neighborhood cats than children. Charlie loved it. Grace tolerated it because it was a relatively open space with a clear view in any direction, and because it was almost always deserted.

Off the leash Charlie ran hard for the first tree, lifted his leg and left his mark, then ran for the next. He hit each tree at least twice before trotting back, tongue lolling, to where Grace waited for him by the teeter-totters, her back pressed against the firm trunk of the largest oak, her eyes as busy as the dog's legs had been.

'Finished?' she asked him.

Charlie looked startled by such a ridiculous suggestion and bounded away immediately to begin the tree circuit all over again. His paws shuffling fallen leaves into a new order was the only immediate sound that broke the breathless stillness of dusk in this quiet neighborhood. Life probably existed within the small houses that lined the streets around the park, but you'd never know it from the outside. Yards were empty, windows were closed, the city bears were snug in their dens.

She tensed at the sudden slam of a door a few houses down, relaxed when she saw a definite kid shape run across the street and into the other side of the park. He ducked around a broad tree trunk and disappeared, and Grace imagined a nine- or ten-year-old reprobate coming out to sneak a smoke.

Charlie suspected something more sinister and was at her side in an instant, pressing hard against her legs, his wet nose burying itself in her cold palm. He didn't like sudden noises or sudden movement, unless he was making them.

'My hero,' she whispered down at him, stroking his bony head. 'Relax. It's just a kid.' She started to hook the leash to Charlie's collar for the run home, but then the door slammed again and her head jerked up to see three more shapes racing across the street after the first. These were bulkier, obviously older kids, and there was something wrong about the way they moved; something stealthy and predatory that made Grace go still and watchful.

'Goddamn it, you little prick, you're going to get it this time!'

The enraged shout from across the park sent the

poor dog down to his belly, nails furrowing the dirt as he clawed his way between Grace's legs and the trunk of the oak.

Little bastards, Grace thought, down on her knees instantly, stroking the trembling dog, murmuring reassurance. 'It's okay, boy. It's okay. They're just kids. Loud kids. But they won't hurt you. I wouldn't let them. No one will ever hurt you again. You hear me, Charlie?'

His tongue swiped her cheek in a hot wash that chilled immediately in the cold air, but he still trembled. Grace kept stroking him, fastening the leash by touch as she watched the three older kids cruise the far side of the park. It took them only moments to find the first one and drag him from behind the tree.

'No-o . . .'

It was a single word of desperation; a kid's voice carrying an adult fear, cut off by the muffled thud of a fist hitting a soft body part. Grace rose slowly to her feet, eyes narrowing as they focused on the scuffle fifty yards away.

Two of the older kids were holding the arms of the small one while a third danced in and out like a boxer, taking punches at his belly. Maybe the little kid had it coming; she didn't know; but the basic rules of fair play were being violated here, and Grace just hated that.

'Stay,' she told Charlie – a totally unnecessary command considering that the dog was still flattened against the ground like a doggy pancake. She did it more for his pride than anything else.

There was little light left to reflect on the figure in the long dark coat striding across the park; and even if there had been, the three older boys probably wouldn't have seen her coming. They were too intent on the task at hand. To them it simply seemed that one moment they were alone, and the next there was a quiet, even voice just a few feet away saying, 'Stop.'

Startled, the kid throwing the punches jerked upright and spun on the balls of his feet to face her. He was maybe fourteen, fifteen at most, with stringy blond hair, a narrow angry face, and acne eruptions that shouted puberty.

Testosterone overload, Grace thought, her eyes flicking briefly to his two companions, who looked so similar they might all have been brothers. The three wore multi-pocketed baggy pants, the kind that sagged well south of a belt line, and cheap overshirts that hung down to their knees. Wannabe Scandinavian gang-bangers. Clothes too thin to hide a gun.

The little one they held pinned by his arms was the only one wearing a coat, and Grace suspected that if he ever took it off he'd never see it again. You didn't get lambskin jackets like that at Kmart, or even Wilson's Leather. Obviously the kid lifted at the best places. He was as black as the others were white, which was surprising. You didn't see the two races mingling much in the city, in peace or war.

He was folded over from the last punch he'd taken to the belly, and when he looked up she saw a baby-smooth face that should have been on a swing set instead of taking a beating. His eyes and nose were streaming, but his little jaw jutted defiantly, and he didn't make a sound.

'Who the fuck are you?' The puncher's small pale

eyes made a disdainful sweep of her body that was intended to intimidate.

Grace sighed. It had been a long day, and she was too tired for this. 'Let the kid go.'

'Oh, yeah, right, sure we will. Get the fuck outta here, bitch, before we start on you.'

Brothers two and three jerked on the black kid's arms simultaneously, as if they were one organism instead of two, chiming in with their own colorful suggestions. 'Fuck her.'

'Yeah, fuck her. Hey. Maybe we should really fuck her.' Nervous giggle.

'Yeah, teach the white bitch a lesson.'

The white bitch. Grace shook her head, deciding not to point out that they, too, were white. I'm getting old, she thought. I no longer understand the insults of young people.

The puncher hunched his shoulders and dropped his head, looking up from beneath lowered brows. 'You like getting fucked, lady? You like it in the ass? That your problem? Your old man don't give it to you in the ass like you like it, so you come over here looking for it?'

They were a year or two away from being truly dangerous, as long as they weren't carrying. They could have blades, of course, and she was ready for that, but she didn't think so. When they were this underdeveloped, weapons always came out early.

'I told you to let the kid go,' Grace said.

He took a step toward her and stopped, squinting in the near-darkness, something flickering in his eyes when he got a good look at her. 'Oh, yeah, you did, didn't you? Well, I'll tell you what. You get down on your knees and suck my dick and maybe I'll think about it.'

It was probably poor manners to smile, but Grace couldn't help it. 'You are a disgusting little beast, aren't you?'

'Whaddya mean, "little"?' he snarled, and that made Grace laugh out loud. Funny, the things that set people off.

He took another quick step toward her, started to raise his arm, then screamed at an electric bolt of pain that started in his right trapezoid and shot down to his fingers.

Grace dropped her hand back to her side and calmly watched the would-be boxer scramble backward, clutching his shoulder, face screwed up in a furious effort not to cry. 'Jesus Christ! What the fuck did you do that for? Who the fuck are you? Get the fuck away from me!'

Grace pouted. 'What. No more romance?'

'You bitch. You motherfucking bitch what did you do to me I can't feel my motherfucking arm!'

'What'd she do, Frank? What'd she do?'

'I'll show you.' She took a step toward the other two, who exchanged an alarmed glance over the black kid's head, then dropped his arms and quickly backed away.

'Your ass is dead, bitch!' one of them hissed at her, trying to swagger as he scurried backward. 'You are one dead motherfucker.'

'Uh-huh.'

She didn't chase them, exactly. She just walked after

them at an unhurried pace, finally stopping when she got to the curb, reminding herself that they were only kids, and you weren't supposed to frighten children.

She watched them disappear into a crumbling stucco across the street, and then said out loud, 'Don't come up behind me.' She turned to see the black kid frozen in mid-stride, a few feet away.

'You weren't supposed to hear me.' Crestfallen.

'Well, I did.'

A full lower lip jutted. 'No one hears me. I'm the black shadow. I'm quiet as night. I'm the best.'

'You are good,' Grace gave him. 'But I'm better.' She started walking back toward the tree where she'd left Charlie. A loose sole flopped on the kid's left tennis shoe as he trotted beside her. 'You should have lifted a new pair of sneakers when you got the jacket. That's what gave you away.'

'The jacket's mine.'

'Sure it is.'

'Good leather lasts a long time. Sneakers don't. Those, I lifted. Show me what you did to Frank, huh?'

She lengthened her stride. 'Go home, kid.'

'Oh, right. Me and the blond brothers alone in the house after you made them look like pussies? Ain't gonna happen. I'll wait till Helen gets home.'

Grace stopped, took a breath, then looked down at him. 'You live with those kids?'

He jerked his head toward the stucco that had swallowed Dumb, Dumber, and Dumbest. 'Foster home.' He shrugged.

One of Grace's eyebrows shifted up a notch. 'An integrated foster home?'

'Not enough black people signing up. Don't you listen to the news? So sometimes the brothers get lucky, and sometimes we get Little Rock.'

'What do you know about Little Rock?'

'I read about it.'

'Oh yeah? How old are you?'

'Nine. Almost ten.'

Going on a hundred, Grace thought, and started walking again. It was almost full dark now, and she wanted desperately to be home. The kid stuck like glue.

'Where do you think you're going?' she asked him without stopping.

'I'm just walking.'

'This Helen, is she your foster mom?'

'Yeah.'

'You like her?'

'She's okay. At least she keeps the other three from killing me, when she's around.'

'So where is she?'

'Work. Gets home at seven-thirty.'

Up ahead, Grace saw Charlie's nose peek around the trunk of the tree. 'You've got about half an hour to walk, then.'

'About. Hey, is that a dog?'

Grace's arm shot out to block the kid's chest. 'He scares easy.'

'Oh.' The kid went down on his knees and stretched out one arm, pink palm up. 'C'mere, boy, c'mere.'

Charlie flattened his head onto the ground and tried to disappear.

'Jeez, what happened to him?'

'He came that way.'

The kid cocked his head and studied the dog for a minute. 'That's really sad.'

Grace gave him a sidelong glance, considering. It was her opinion that anyone who could empathize with the suffering of an animal might not be totally irredeemable.

She made a small gesture with her hand that Charlie considered for a long moment before rising and moving cautiously toward them, head down in fearful submission.

'Wow,' the kid whispered, staying stock-still. 'He's scared to death, and he still comes. You're some alpha dog.'

'Where do you get this stuff?'

'I read, I told you.'

'Nine-year-old kids aren't supposed to read. They're supposed to sit in front of violent video games, frying their brains.'

The kid's teeth shone an unreal white in the dark. 'I'm a rebel.'

'I guess.' She watched Charlie inching closer, his trust in Grace doing noble battle with his fear of strangers. 'Come on, Charlie, it's all right.'

But Charlie was having none of it. He stopped dead and sat down, worried eyes jerking back and forth between the woman who represented safety and the apparently terrifying visage of a four-foot-tall boy.

'I guess that's as close . . .' she started to say, but before she could finish the sentence the kid was on his back on the ground. 'What are you doing?'

'Exposing my belly,' he whispered up at her. 'Total submission pose. Nonthreatening.'

'Ah.'

'That guy who went up to Alaska and lived with the wolves? He said this is what the outside wolves have to do to get accepted into the pack. How come you carry a gun?'

Grace sighed and looked down the dark street, thinking she must really be slipping if a fat cop and a little kid pegged her in one day. When she looked back, Charlie was standing over the boy, washing his face with his long sloppy tongue, his hind end wagging like crazy.

'Hey, Charlie, you good ole boy, you,' the kid giggled, squirming now, trying to dodge the lashing tongue. 'That old wolf man, he sure knew what he was talking about, huh?'

Grace folded her arms and looked on, her expression faintly disgusted. Charlie was all over the kid now, licking, whining, the stump of his tail beating the world, generally making a fool of himself. There was no dignity in this. Worse yet, it was distracting. A car seemed to appear out of nowhere, cruising slowly by the park. She hadn't even heard it coming.

'Charlie!' A little panic in the voice as she watched the car pass, then turn into the driveway next to the stucco house. A woman got out, reached back in for a bag of groceries. Grace exhaled. 'It's time to go home.'

With obvious reluctance, Charlie moved obediently to her side and the kid got up, brushing dried leaves off his pants. 'We were just playing. Dog like that needs a boy. If you like, I could come over after school sometimes, keep him company till you got home.'

'No thanks.' Grace jerked her head toward his house. 'Your salvation just arrived.'

The kid glanced over at the car, and when he looked back, Grace and Charlie were already walking away. 'Wait a minute! You didn't show me that thing you did to Frank yet!'

Grace shook her head without turning around.

'Come on, lady, have a heart! Thing like that could save my little black ass, you know!' he shouted after her.

She kept walking.

'Trouble with some people is they just don't get what it means to be afraid all the time!' An angry shout now; frustrated.

That stopped her. She took a breath, let it out, then turned around and walked back. He stood his ground, looking up with the whites of his eyes showing. Defiant and wet, all at the same time.

'Listen, kid . . .'

'My name's Jackson.'

She ran her tongue over the inside of her left cheek, considering. 'You're too short for the hold I put on Frank, got it? But I could show you something else . . .'

19

Freedman and McLaren were thorough. They did one walk through the boat with Captain Magnusson, then another on their own, double-checking the three sets of restrooms, the food service areas, even the tiny cabin where the captain kept a book, a recliner, and a spare uniform hanging on a wall hook.

'Not a lot of space in here,' Freedman had told him, trying to maneuver his bulk through the doorway.

'All I need,' the captain had replied, eyes twinkling. 'Now the wife, she needs a living room, a dining room, a family room, a breakfast nook, just room after room, God knows why, but me? Give me a chair and book and maybe a little TV and I'm in heaven. I've often thought if men *really* ran the world like the women claim, all the houses would be eight by ten and we'd have a lot more room in the suburbs.'

By the time crew and caterers arrived at six Freedman and McLaren had their squads and uniforms posted in the lot, helping Chilton's men screen the arrivals, and the other plainclothes officers briefed and stationed on board.

At 6:30 they stopped at the bar in the center-deck salon before going back outside in the cold. They begged a couple of bottles of water from the young man polishing glasses, then drank them while they watched the caterer's staff put finishing touches on white linen tables crowded with crystal and silver and fresh flowers. A fussy, hawk-nosed woman in a dark suit was following them about, occasionally moving a glass or a piece of silver an inch this way or that.

'We're ready,' McLaren said.

'Couldn't be any readier,' Freedman agreed, his eyes taking in the two plainclothes officers by the restrooms, then following three of Chilton's men as they paced the salon's circumference like caged animals. 'Damn boat's like an armed camp.'

'Too much hoopla,' McLaren said. 'He's not gonna show up here tonight.'

'Nope. Which means we're going to have to do this all over again Saturday.'

'I got Gopher tickets Saturday. They're playing Wisconsin.'

Freedman clucked his tongue in sympathy.

The two of them each took a gangway once the guests started to arrive, watching Chilton's people run the sweeps, eyeballing every single person who boarded. A colossal waste of time, Freedman thought, shivering in his wool suitcoat, watching a parade of the state's rich and richer pass through a phalanx of armed men with metal detectors as if they did it every day. Maybe they did. How would he know?

When the boat finally cast off and moved out into the river, he and McLaren started making the rounds they had worked out, alternating levels inside and out. Cold as it was, after a few circuits Freedman began to feel more comfortable outside than in. You put a six-foot-nine black man in a cheap suit on a boat with a bunch of Fortune 500 white people, and pretty soon some ditzy broad wearing his year's salary around her neck is going to ask him to refill the water carafe. It had happened four times in the first fifteen minutes, and his patience was wearing about as thin as his self-esteem.

'Hey, Freedman.' Johnny McLaren was coming out the center-deck salon doors as he was heading in. 'I was just coming to get you . . . What's the matter with you?'

'People keep asking me to get them drinks, that's what's the matter with me.'

'Assholes. Fuck 'em.' He pulled Freedman inside and started weaving through tables toward the dance floor. The Whipped Nipples were on this deck, playing something that sounded like a classical waltz with a salsa beat. Freedman might have liked it if they hadn't had such a stupid name.

'I'm not dancing with you, McLaren. You're too short.'

'Play nice, Freedman. I'm taking you to the trough. Hammond had the caterers set up a buffet for us security types back in the kitchen.'

'Yeah?'

'Yeah. Not a bratwurst on it, just caviar and lobster and shit like that, but it ain't bad.'

Captain Magnusson was making his own obligatory rounds through the salon, smiling, answering questions, looking captainesque. Freedman wondered who was steering the boat. 'Everything as it should be, Detectives?' he asked as they passed him.

'Shipshape,' McLaren answered with a little salute, staring at a wet pink splotch on the captain's collar.

'Pink champagne,' the old man confided, dabbing

at it with a snowy handkerchief. 'I had an unfortunate collision with a lovely young woman and an overfilled glass.'

'Too bad.'

'Not at all. It was really quite invigorating. She ran smack-dab into me. Full-front.' He had a wicked little grin for an old man. 'I was just on my way to put this in a sink of cold water and change into a new one. See you later, gentlemen.'

Freedman and McLaren watched him walk toward the forward door of the salon as they continued past the dance floor toward the food service area.

They both stopped at the same time.

'McLaren?'

'Yeah.'

'The restrooms are in the back.'

'Yeah.'

'He went forward.'

'Right. Toward his cabin.'

'So where's he going to soak his shirt?'

McLaren closed his eyes, saw the tiny cabin with its single chair and book and narrow closet door – only the spare uniform was hanging on a hook on the wall, and why would he put it there if he had a closet to hang it in? 'Shit,' he exhaled softly, and then they were both moving as fast as they could without actually breaking into a run, weaving through the tables, breaking apart a cluster of giggling bridesmaids at the door, then outside to the bitter cold of the deck, right turn, and then they both started to run, the little Mick and the big black man, up toward the captain's cabin.

*

Tommy Espinoza's shift had ended three hours ago, but he was still at his desk, slurping cold coffee and hammering out commands on the computer keyboard. His eyes were raw from eleven hours at the monitor, but that's why God made Visine.

He reached into the orange plastic jack-o'-lantern that grinned on the corner of his desk and fished out a mini Snickers bar. 'Come on, come on . . .' He raked his fingers through his black hair, waiting for his computer to talk to him; it finally did, in the language of a shrill alarm.

'Damnit,' he muttered, his fingers busy on the keyboard again.

'Got anything for me, Tommy?' Magozzi was standing in the doorway, a battered leather satchel slung over his shoulder.

Tommy never looked up from the screen, he just waved Magozzi over. 'Check this out, Leo. I'm running across the damnedest thing with these Monkeewrench folks.'

By the time Freedman and McLaren burst into Captain Magnusson's cabin, the old man had already opened the sliding door to his private head and was scrambling backward. The recliner caught him by the backs of his knees and he collapsed into it, his eyes wide, his breath coming in short little puffs. McLaren went to him while Freedman took the first look.

It was the tiniest of rooms, everything reduced to the smallest possible size the way it is on all boats. Tiny stainless steel sink, tiny mirror, a shower stall Freedman would have been hard-pressed to squeeze into. Only the toilet seat was full-size; so was the man sitting on it. He was wearing a suit, but he was naked from the waist down, pants puddled around his ankles, fat white knees spread wide, shirttails dangling between flabby thighs. His head was propped against the back wall as if he were only resting, but this one had been a messy kill. Trails of blood had coursed down from the bullet hole in his forehead, spreading on either side of his nose, filling the lines around the mouth, sliding down his neck to stain the collar of his white shirt.

Freedman had seen enough gunshot victims to know that this one hadn't died right away. There had been some heartbeats left to account for that much blood pumping out of the relatively small hole.

He stepped aside so McLaren could see inside the narrow doorway.

'Aw, Jesus.' McLaren exhaled in a rush. 'I don't believe this. Captain? When's the last time you used the head?'

Captain Magnusson looked up at him from his chair, blinking rapidly. 'Oh dear. Um, yesterday, I think. No, wait. We didn't go out yesterday. The day before, I guess.'

Freedman and McLaren turned back to the dead man.

'Blood's dry,' Freedman remarked. 'Didn't happen on our watch.'

'Which means he was in here when we checked the cabin earlier.'

Freedman's big head went up and down solemnly. 'Worse yet.'

*

Magozzi and Espinoza were now hunched in front of his computer screen, looking equally baffled.

'It's unbelievable,' Tommy was saying. 'I've never seen firewalls like this before in my life.'

'You can't dig up anything on them?'

'For the past ten years, I can get you anything you want. Tax returns, medical records, financial statements, hell, I can just about tell you when any one of 'em took a crap. But before that, nada.' Tommy flopped back in his chair. 'No employment records, no school records, not even birth records. For all practical purposes, none of these people existed until ten years ago.'

'That's impossible.'

'Apparently not. At first blush, I'd say these people erased themselves.'

'You can do that?'

Tommy shrugged, grabbed a potato chip from the open bag on his desk, stuffed it in his mouth, and talked around it. 'Theoretically, sure. Almost everything's computerized now. And if it's on a computer, it can be deleted. But it's not as easy as it sounds. Your average hacker can't just sit down with his laptop and a six-pack and erase his history. You'd have to be friggin' brilliant to break through some of the firewalls, especially the ones the Feds set up, like for the IRS and the SSA. I'm telling you, this is unreal.'

Magozzi grunted. 'Witness Protection?'

'No way. The Feebs aren't this good. Their trails I can follow in my sleep. If this is Monkeewrench work, Witness Protection should be hiring *them*.'

Magozzi scratched at the day's worth of stubble on his chin, mulling over this new wrinkle. 'So they changed their names and got themselves new identities.'

Tommy shoved another potato chip into his mouth. 'Makes sense. Where else do you get names like Harley Davidson and Roadrunner? So the hundred-dollar question is, why would five ordinary people go to the trouble of totally obliterating their pasts?'

Magozzi didn't even have to think about it. 'Criminal activity.'

'That's what I was thinking. Maybe they're better suspects than you thought.'

Magozzi reached for a potato chip. The fat pill was in his mouth before he realized what he was doing. God, it tasted good. 'A team of five serial killers acting together? Man, we should be so lucky. We could buy Japan with the movie rights.'

'Yeah. They were probably just bank robbers, or international terrorists. Ten years ago they saw the computer revolution coming and decided there was more money in software.'

'There you go.' Magozzi rubbed his eyes, trying to push away the headache that was blossoming behind them. 'Are we at a dead end here?'

'Not necessarily.' Tommy rolled his neck to release the kinks. 'I've still got some things I want to try, and even if I come up dry, computerization isn't total yet; not by a long sight. We've still got a lot of paper trails lying around if you're old enough to remember where to look. It just takes a really long time, doing it the old-fashioned way. You want me to keep at it?'

'With all my heart.' Magozzi turned his back on the evil potato chip bag and headed for the door. 'By the way, how are they fixed financially? Are they going to go under if this game doesn't make it to market?'

Tommy looked at him as if he were crazy. 'Are you kidding? The company did over ten million last year, and it wasn't the first time. Lowest net worth on any of the partners' – he pulled a single sheet out from under the potato chip bag and glanced at it – 'is four million. That's Annie Belinsky. Woman's got a clothes budget you wouldn't believe.'

Magozzi stared at him. 'They're rich?'

'Well, yeah . . .' A cell phone chirped and Tommy started pawing through the mess of printouts on his desk. 'Damnit, where'd I'd put that thing?'

'It's mine,' Magozzi said, pulling his cell phone out of his coat pocket. 'Get me hard copies on whatever you find, will you, Tommy? And while you're at it, see what you can dig up on Grace MacBride's permit to carry.' He flipped open his phone. 'Magozzi.'

Tommy watched as Magozzi listened to the voice on the other end. The blood suddenly seemed to drain from his face and in the next second, he was running out the door.

20

The town of Calumet, Wisconsin, hadn't received this much media attention since Elton Gerber's six-hundred-fifty-seven-pound pumpkin had fallen off the back of his truck on the way to the Great Pumpkin Contest in 1993. But even then, they'd missed the real story.

The TV news had covered it tongue-in-cheek, since the pumpkin had been the only casualty, and not one reporter ever connected that shattered pumpkin with the bullet Elton put in the roof of his mouth two weeks later. The grand prize that year had been $15,000, just enough to cover the balloon payment due on Elton's farm, and there was no doubt he would have won it. His closest competitor weighed in at a paltry five-hundred-thirty pounds.

Not a tongue-in-cheek story, Sheriff Mike Halloran thought. More like an American tragedy, and the media missed the point. And they were missing it this time, too.

The thump of rotors from somewhere outside barely penetrated his consciousness. He was used to the news helicopters now; used to the vans with their satellite-dish hats cruising the streets of his town, stopping anyone who looked mournful enough or frightened enough to deliver a titillating sound bite; used to the clamor of reporters from the front steps of the building whenever a deputy tried to get outside to his car.

According to the autopsy report, John and Mary Kleinfeldt had died between midnight and one A.M. Monday morning. Less than eight hours later it was a lead story on every channel in Wisconsin, as interchangeable anchor people reported the small-town tragedy of '. . . a God-fearing elderly couple savagely murdered while at their prayers in church.'

There was no mention of the bloody crosses carved into their chests – so far Halloran had managed to keep that little gruesome detail under wraps – but even without it, the story was irresistible to reporters, and mesmerizing to the public. The idea of someone shooting the elderly was bad enough; stage the crime in the supposed sanctuary of a church and you added outrage to the horror, and maybe a little fear. Bad news, great ratings.

Later that morning Deputy Danny Peltier's death hit the airwaves as a bulletin, less than half an hour after it happened, while Halloran was still standing over the ruin of his body, looking for the poor kid's freckles, weeping like a girl. By sunset Monday print reporters and TV news crews had increased the population of Calumet by at least a hundred, and now, a full day later, they were all still here.

But they were missing the story, every one of them; missing the tragedy beneath the tragedy, the crime beneath the crime. None of them knew that Danny Peltier, freckled and fresh and heartbreakingly innocent, had died because Sheriff Michael Halloran had forgotten the key to the Kleinfeldts' front door.

'Mike?'

Before he looked up, he cleared his face of whatever expression had been there, and raised dispassionate eyes to where Bonar stood in the doorway.

'Hey, Bonar.'

His old friend walked closer and scowled at him, looking like an angry Jonathan Winters. 'You look like shit, buddy.'

'Thanks.' Halloran set aside one of the tilting towers of paperwork on his desk, pulled a cigarette from his pocket and lit up.

Bonar sat down and waved a beefy hand at the smoke wafting toward him across the desk. 'I could arrest you for smoking in a public building, you know.'

Halloran nodded and took another pull off his cigarette. He hadn't had one in his office in years, and couldn't remember the last time smoking had tasted this good. Pleasure enhanced by the illicit nature of the act. No wonder people committed crimes. 'I'm celebrating. I've cracked the case.'

Bonar gave him the once-over, taking in the uniform that looked slept in, the circles under his eyes that were almost as dark as his hair. 'You don't look like you're celebrating. Besides, that is such bullshit. *I* solved the case. The kid did it. I told you that right from the start.'

'You did not. You told me Father Newberry did it.'

'That was just wishful thinking, and it was also before I knew the Kleinfeldts had actually reproduced. Minute you told me that I pegged the kid, and you know it. Hated to give up the padre, though. It was so perfect. Crosses carved in the chests, big inheritance for the church . . . I mean, you had to love the old guy as a suspect.' He leaned forward and poked around the paper clutter on the desk. 'You got any food in here?'

'Nope.'

Bonar sighed unhappily and leaned back, lacing his fingers across his expansive belly. His brown uniform shirt gaped between buttons that were hanging on for dear life. 'So angels came down and told you the kid did it, long after I told you the kid did it, may I point out, but such insight, my friend, is useless. We don't know who or where the kid is, what he looks like, how old he is . . .'

Halloran smiled a little. This was good. Talking about the case with Bonar, focusing on that and nothing else – it was a straight line he could stand on for as long as it lasted. 'The kid was born in Atlanta. Thirty-one years ago.'

'Oh yeah? You had a vision? What?'

'Tax returns. First ones we had were thirty-some years ago, back when the Kleinfeldts were the Bradfords. They weren't rich then. Newly married, probably, just starting out, low enough on the income ladder to deduct medical expenses. Big ones for that day and age, their fourth year in Atlanta. I figured maternity expenses.'

Bonar straightened a little in his chair as his interest piqued.

'So I called county records down there, asked for Baby Bradfords for that year, and there it was. Baby Bradford born to Martin and Emily Bradford, October 23, 1969.'

Bonar seemed to hold his breath for a moment. 'Wait a minute. The Kleinfeldts were killed on October 23.'

Halloran nodded grimly. 'Happy birthday, baby.'

'Damn. DOB, DOD. The kid really *did* do it.'

Halloran took a last drag and then dropped his cigarette into an empty Coke can. 'Too bad you're not the district attorney. That guy's a hardnose. Wants fingerprints, witnesses, you know, the kind of forensic evidence we don't have? The kid didn't even inherit.'

Bonar shook his head. 'Doesn't matter. You don't carve up your parents' bodies just because you want the money. He had something else going, and we aren't going to like looking at it.' He blew his cheeks out in a long sigh, pushed himself wearily out of the chair, and walked over to the window.

Helmut Krueger's farm was across the road, and he watched a line of Holsteins filing from the pasture toward the barn for evening milking, thinking that maybe he should have been a farmer. Cows hardly ever killed their parents. 'You run the kid's name through the computer yet?'

'Got a problem with that. No name on the birth certificate.'

'Huh?'

'The lady clerk I talked to said it wasn't all that unusual. The certificate's filed on the date of birth, and some parents just don't have a name ready. Unless they call it in after they decide, it just stays blank. But the name of the hospital was there, and they gave me the name of the family doctor.'

'You talk to him?' Bonar asked.

Halloran shook his head.

'Don't tell me. He's dead.'

'Alive and golfing. His wife said she'd have him call back tonight.'

Bonar nodded, looked out the window again. 'So we're on our way.'

'Maybe. You want to catch a bite before the doc calls? I gave his wife my cell number so we could get out of here.'

Bonar turned and looked at him, a tired, massive silhouette blocking the last of the day's light from the window. 'I'll meet you at your place. I've got to stop at the grocery first.'

'We can go to the café.'

'It's the twenty-fourth, Mike.'

'I know that . . . ' Halloran started to say, and then stopped abruptly. 'Oh, shit. Bonar, I totally forgot. I'm sorry, man.'

'No sweat.' Bonar had a sad, silly grin that forgave everything. 'We're getting too many October dead people, you know that?'

'That is the truth.'

But you shouldn't have forgotten *that* dead person, Halloran thought a half hour later when he pulled into his driveway. He sat in the car for a moment and rode out the guilt, almost wishing he still believed just so he could go to confession and be forgiven.

Technically, Bonar was a bachelor, but in all the ways that mattered, he'd been widowed since the October blizzard of '87, when his high-school sweetheart had gone off the road and buried the nose of her father's pickup in Haggerty's swamp. Thirty-seven inches of snow had fallen over the next forty-eight hours, but the road past Haggerty's was seldom traveled, so it was four days before the county snowplow finally got to it and found the frozen, unpretty remains of Ellen Hendricks.

She hadn't died right away, and that had been the worst of it, since she used the time to write Bonar a letter that wound all around the borders of a Standard Oil road map of Wisconsin. She'd been hurting, and she'd been cold, but there was no fear in that letter, just a dead certainty that Bonar would find her. She talked about their upcoming wedding, the three kids they were going to have, the two-seater Thunderbird that Bonar absolutely positively had to trade in because there was no room for children, and toward the end, when the pencil lines were starting to waver, she scolded him gently for taking so long.

She wrote her last words on October twenty-fourth, and every year since Halloran and Bonar had spent that evening together, eating, drinking, and not talking about things that might have been. The tradition had become more a part of their friendship than a conscious tribute to a girl who had died a long time ago, but in some way they never tried to understand, the date remained important. He shouldn't have forgotten it.

'Yeah, well, you shouldn't have forgotten the Kleinfeldts' goddamned keys, either,' he said aloud, and then he banged on the steering wheel until the side of his hand hurt.

Hundred-year-old elms shaded the single acre that remained of his great-grandfather's farm. He'd kept up the house and yard, but the old Dutch Colonial looked like an interloper in this new subdivision of tacky ramblers and split-levels. The house was much too large for a man living alone, but four generations of Hallorans had been raised in it, and he couldn't make himself let it go.

He got out of the car and walked across the lawn to the front door, tugging the open flaps of his jacket closed. The wind had picked up since he'd left the sheriff's office just a few moments before, and dried leaves skittered and swirled away from his boots, heading for Florida if they had any sense. You could almost smell the coming winter, and Halloran remembered Danny's prediction of an early snow yesterday, while he had been driving the young deputy to his death.

He walked into the small entryway and heard his snowy childhood boots hitting the floor, and then his mother's voice, silent for ten years now, reminding him to close the door, what did he think he was doing? Trying to heat the whole outdoors? In a gesture of defiance a decade too late, he left the door ajar for Bonar, wondering why most of his memories were of winter, as if he'd lived thirty-three years in a place with no other season.

He hung his heavy jacket in the front closet, then placed his belt clip and gun on the shelf above.

'How dumb is this?' Bonar had asked the first time he'd seen him do it. 'I'm a drug-crazed burglar, okay? And here you go, leaving your piece right here in the front closet so I can pick it up on my way in and shoot you in the gut when you come stumbling down the stairs in your skivvies.'

But Emma Halloran would never permit firearms beyond the entryway of her house. Not her husband's fifty-year-old Winchester, and certainly not her son's department-issue 9mm. Ten years she'd been in the ground, and Halloran still couldn't make himself walk past that front closet wearing his gun.

There was a bottle of Dewar's in the refrigerator, a criminal offense according to Bonar, but Halloran liked it cold.

He poured healthy shots in two glasses that had once held grape jelly, then sipped out of one as he examined the contents of the freezer. He pushed aside a stack of frozen dinners and found treasure in a rectangle of butcher paper covered with frost.

'Honey, I'm home!' Bonar called from the front door, slamming it hard behind him. He stomped down the hall into the kitchen and dropped two grocery bags on the counter. Halloran looked skeptically at the greenery poking out of the top.

'You brought flowers?'

'That's romaine lettuce, you numbnuts. You got anchovies?'

'Are you crazy?'

'That's what I thought.' Bonar started unloading the bags. 'Never fear. Got the anchovies, got the garlic, got a sad and limp bunch of green beans here that are going to need life support . . . '

'I got Ralph.'

Bonar sucked in a breath and looked at him. Ralph had been the last Angus Albert Swenson had raised before he sold his farm and moved to Arizona. They'd bought the young steer together, feeding him out on corn and beer for the last two months of its life. 'I thought we polished him off last time.'

Halloran nodded toward the white package in the sink, then handed Bonar his Dewar's in a jelly jar. 'I saved the tenderloin.'

'Praise Jesus.' Bonar clinked his glass, downed his shot, and winced. 'Man, how many times I gotta tell you? Cold mutes the flavor. You can't keep this stuff in the fridge, and you sure as hell shouldn't be drinking it out of old jars with cartoons all over them. Who is this? The Martian?'

Halloran peered at the dark figure on his friend's glass. A lot of the paint had worn away over the years, but part of the helmet was still identifiable. 'Damn. I wanted the Martian.'

Bonar snorted as he refilled his glass, then started to rub a clove of garlic around a wooden bowl Halloran had always thought was supposed to hold fruit. 'Nuke Ralph on defrost for about three minutes, turn the oven as high as it will go, and get me out that big cast-iron skillet.'

'I thought we'd just grill him outside.'

'Well, you were wrong. We're going to sear him on high heat and then finish him in the oven. Then I'll add wine to the skillet drippings, reduce it to a glaze, throw in some morel mushrooms, and voilà.'

Halloran rummaged in the silverware drawer for steak knives. 'You're kidding, right?'

'Of course I'm kidding. You ever try to buy morels at Jerry's Super Valu?'

'In the old days you would have stuck this thing on a stick and held it over a blowtorch. I wish you'd quit watching that cooking channel.'

'Can't help it. Those guys are the twenty-first-century clowns. Like Gallagher without the watermelon, remember him?'

'The guy with a sledgehammer.'

'He's the one. God, I loved that guy. Is he dead?'

Halloran drained his glass and refilled it. 'Probably. Everyone else is.'

Bonar was silent for a moment, and then started to chuckle. The Dewar's was working.

By the time Halloran's cell phone chirped Ralph was a bloody memory on chipped white dishes and the kitchen was trashed. 'Here we go,' he said, flipping open the phone, wishing he'd had a little less to drink, trying to remember all the questions he'd wanted to ask the doctor. 'Hello?'

A man's cultured voice soared through space and into his ear, slow and rich with southern heat. 'Good evening. Dr LeRoux, returning the call of Sheriff Michael Halloran.'

Good evening. Jesus, did people actually talk like that? He didn't know what it was – the accent, maybe – but something about talking to southerners always made Halloran feel like a country rube, a farmer's son, which he was; and an uneducated fool, which he was not.

'This is Mike Halloran. Thank you for returning my call, Dr LeRoux. If you'll hang up, sir, I'll call you right back on my dime.'

'As you wish.' There was an abrupt click.

Halloran folded up the cellular and went for the phone on the wall.

'What's he sound like?' Bonar asked.

'Like Colonel Sanders with an attitude. Hello, Dr

LeRoux. Mike Halloran again. I'm the sheriff of Kingsford County up here in Wisconsin, and I'm trying to locate the heir of some patients you tended to years ago –'

'Martin and Emily Bradford,' South interrupted North. 'My wife told me.'

'That was over thirty years ago, Doctor. You remember them?'

'Vividly.'

Halloran waited a moment for him to volunteer more information, but there was only silence on the line. 'You have an impressive memory, sir. You must have had hundreds of patients since then –'

'I don't talk about my patients, Sheriff, no matter how long it has been since I've treated them. As a law enforcement officer, you should know that.'

'The Bradfords died earlier this week, Doctor. Confidentiality no longer applies. I'll be happy to fax you copies of the death certificates, but I was hoping you'd be willing to take my word and save us some time.'

The doctor's sigh traveled over the wires. 'What precisely did you need to know, Sheriff?'

'We understand there was a child.'

'Yes.' Something new in the voice. Sadness? Regret?

'We're trying to locate that child.' Halloran glanced at Bonar, then punched on the speakerphone.

'I'm afraid I can't help you, Sheriff.' The doctor's drawl filled the kitchen. 'I delivered the child, I treated Mrs Bradford and the child after the birth, and then I never saw them again. Or heard from them.'

Halloran's shoulders slumped in disappointment. 'Doctor, we're at a dead end here. Your county's birth certificate was never completed. No name, no sex. We don't even know if it was a girl or a boy.'

'Neither do I.'

Halloran was stunned into silence. 'Excuse me?'

'The child was a hermaphrodite, Sheriff. And unless someone intervened on behalf of that poor creature, I doubt that he or she knows its own gender to this day. I tried to get Social Services involved down here immediately after the birth, and I have always suspected that those good intentions were responsible for the Bradfords' sudden disappearance from the Atlanta area.'

'Hermaphrodite,' Halloran repeated numbly, exchanging a glance with Bonar, who looked positively stupefied.

Doctor LeRoux sighed impatiently. 'Asexual, or more precisely, duality of gender. There are variations of physical manifestation within certain parameters. In the case of the Bradford baby, testes and penis were partially internalized but nonetheless complete. The vaginal configuration was present but deformed, and whether or not the ovaries were functional was indeterminate.'

'My God.'

The doctor went on, warming to his subject. 'It's a rare occurrence – I can't remember the statistics offhand – but even that long ago, it didn't have to be a lifelong tragedy. When the genitalia and internal organs of both sexes are present, as they were in the Bradford baby, the parents simply choose the gender of their child based on the physical viability of the organs. The surgery to implement that choice is really quite simple.'

'And which did the Bradfords choose?' Halloran asked, and the doctor snapped back immediately.

'They chose a living hell for their child, and for that, I hope they now find themselves in the same location.'

'I don't understand.'

'Those . . . *people*,' the doctor sputtered, 'called their own child – and I'm quoting here, because I will never forget the phrase they used – "an offense to the eye of God. An abomination." They believed its birth was divine punishment for some imagined sin, and that to interfere would somehow compound the sin and . . .' He stopped and took an audible breath. 'At any rate, in the short time they were under my care, the parents chose neither name nor gender for their child, and I tell you, Sheriff, even all these years later, my thoughts are haunted by what that child's life must have been like. Can you imagine? *They wouldn't even give it a name . . .*'

Someone in the background was talking urgently to the doctor, his wife, probably, but Halloran couldn't make out the words. 'Is there something wrong, Doctor?' He heard a dark chuckle.

'Atrial fibrillation, high blood pressure, a slight valve defect. At my age any number of things are wrong, Sheriff, and my wife worries about all of them. Tell me one thing, if you will, before we close this conversation.'

'Anything I can, Doctor.'

'In my part of the country, it is not generally within the purview of law enforcement to track down missing heirs. There is a crime involved, is there not?'

Halloran looked at Bonar, saw him nod. 'Homicide.'

'Really.'

'The Bradfords – actually they called themselves the

Kleinfeldts while they lived here – were murdered early Monday morning.' And then, because the doctor had been forthcoming, and much more human than Halloran had expected, he gave him what he knew he'd want to hear. 'They were shot to death in church, while they were praying.'

'Ah.' It was more of a breath than a word, and there was the sound of satisfaction in it. 'I see. Thank you, Sheriff Halloran. Thank you very kindly for that information.'

The disconnect was loud on the speaker.

Halloran went over to the table and sat down with Bonar. Neither one of them said anything for a minute, then Bonar leaned back in his chair, tugging his belt away from his belly. 'I got an idea,' he said. 'What say we just close this thing down and say the Kleinfeldts died from natural causes.'

21

Magozzi had never been in a war zone, but figured it couldn't look this bad or no one would have stayed to fight the damn thing.

The access road to the riverboat landing was clogged with emergency vehicles, news vans, and an amazing array of upscale SUVs and sleek sedans, some of them abandoned with doors open and engines running. News helicopters hovered overhead, sweeping the ground below with their big floods, rotors beating the cold night air with the rhythmic whomp of a war movie soundtrack.

There were people everywhere: uniforms, plain-clothes, crime scene, and a lot of tense-looking civilians milling about, the more determined ones barging through the brush on either side of the vehicle check-point to get to the landing.

Magozzi maneuvered the Ford through the maze of people and vehicles and stopped at the booth Chilton's men had set up. Through the windshield he saw the MPD uniforms and Red Chilton's crew fighting a losing battle as they tried to keep civilians and the media out of the parking lot. The barriers had kept the news vans from driving in, but reporters and cameramen with handhelds were all over the place, shouting into their mikes to be heard over one another as they broadcast live back to their stations, interrupting regular programming for a special report.

Barring an alien invasion from Mars, the Hammond wedding reception itself probably would have topped the ten-o'clock news. Throw in a murder and top billing was guaranteed. And in this news-junkie state, Magozzi guessed over eighty percent of the population was watching the circus live right now. And one of those eighty percent was probably the killer himself.

A man in a tux with a face like a contract killer rapped on his window. Magozzi saw an Argo pin making a hole in his thousand-dollar lapel. He rolled down the window and badged him, then jerked his thumb over his shoulder. 'Who belongs to all the cars?'

'Relatives, friends, who knows,' the man said with a sour expression. 'Everybody on that goddamned canoe's had a cell phone pressed to their ear since they found the body. That big Lexus back there?'

'Yeah, I saw it.'

'Came in like a tank, clipped one of our guys in the knee when he tried to stop it. Mother of some kid in the wedding party, and we'd have had to shoot her to keep her from getting through.'

'Red won't let you shoot people?'

The guy actually smiled, but it didn't do much to soften his face. He still looked like a contract killer.

Magozzi parked between two squads and shut off the car. Fifty feet away the paddle wheeler was spitting out an occasional already-interviewed guest, tidbits tossed to a piranha press. Stunned by the turn their party had taken, blinded by the camera lights, the rich and powerful looked weak and strangely vulnerable in their couture gowns and black-tie tuxes. Most stood like sheep under the onslaught of shouted questions, but one older, bejeweled woman Magozzi thought looked familiar was having none of it. When the pushy female reporter from Channel Ten entered her space, the woman shoved her hard, right onto her pushy little ass.

Magozzi finally placed the woman as the mother of the groom. 'Good for you, lady,' Magozzi murmured with a dark smile, pleased that someone had finally done what he'd wanted to do for years.

He hadn't taken two steps away from the car before the mob smelled fresh meat and turned on him. He raised a hand to protect his eyes from the lights of a dozen cameras, and winced at the sudden noise of shouted questions. There were too many to sort them out, and he was just about to stick his elbows out and barrel through, the hell with the department's long-standing policy to always accommodate the press, when the blond from Channel Ten charged toward him, waving her porta-mike like a broadsword to clear a path.

She was too good-looking, too hungry for an anchor spot, and she had a tabloid mind-set that didn't mesh well with Channel Ten's bland, kid-oriented newscasts. Magozzi saw her leaving for another market within the year, and as far as he was concerned, it wouldn't be soon enough. She was rude, aggressive, had a nasty habit of quoting out of context, and besides, she hadn't pronounced his name correctly once.

'Detective Ma-go-zee?' she yelled so loudly it startled the other reporters into silence.

Magozzi saw several disapproving glances in the crowd. As a rule, the Minnesota media was remarkably well behaved. They'd all talk at once, they'd ask stupid, insensitive questions like, *How did you feel when you learned your six-year-old was shot by her brother?*, and sometimes, like now, they even shouted, but only so loud. He'd always wondered if there were some kind of silent agreement on a maximum decibel level so no reporter would ever cross the border from eager to rude. If there was, the blond had just exceeded it.

'You bellowed?' he asked, taking some small pleasure in the angry flash of her eyes as a titter spread through the crowd.

'Detective Ma-go-zee . . .' she started again.

'That's *Magozzi*. Ma-go-tse.'

'Right. Kristin Keller, Channel Ten News. Detective, can you confirm that the man shot on the *Nicollet* tonight was using the restroom at the time he was murdered?'

Indelicate bitch, Magozzi thought. And definitely not a home-grown girl. Your proper Minnesotan never made public reference to bodily functions, no matter how vague.

'I just got here, Ms Keller. I can't confirm anything at this point. Excuse me.' He started to ease through the crowd toward the gangplank, but swore he could feel her hot breath on his neck.

'Was this another Monkeewrench killing?' she shouted from behind him.

Oh shit. He stopped and turned around, saw her sly smile.

'Our sources tell us that the murder last night in Lakewood Cemetery was identical to one in a computer game created by Monkeewrench, a local software company. Do you have any comment on that, Detective?'

'Not at this time.'

Hawkins from the *St Paul Pioneer Press* spoke up. 'Come on, Leo. We've had calls trickling in all day about that cemetery murder, from other people who were playing that game on the net. They all said that murder was right on, and now we're hearing that this killing could be a match for another one in the same game.'

'We've gotten the same calls,' Magozzi said.

'So the police department *is* aware of the connection between these killings and the game?'

'We are aware of some similarities, and we are investigating.'

'There were twenty murders in that game . . .' Kristin Keller called out, and then her very own news chopper moved in overhead, drowning her out. 'Get that fucking thing out of here!' Magozzi heard her scream as he hurried through the crowd toward the gangplank.

McLaren met him on the main deck. 'It's really going to hit the fan now, isn't it?' he said dryly.

'Yeah, and we're going to get splattered big time.'

It had taken a murder to do it, but someone had finally upstaged Foster Hammond, and he had not been happy about it. The *possibility* of a murder at his daughter's wedding reception might have given him a cheap thrill, but he'd lost his sense of humor when MPD had crashed the party en force.

The social event of the year was now a crime scene, the bride was inconsolable, twenty-five grand worth of food was going to end up in steam trays at a downtown homeless shelter, and Hammond's illustrious guests had all been corralled into one salon for interviews, 'like common criminals,' he'd sputtered to Magozzi.

Magozzi was still patting himself on the back for holding his tongue throughout Hammond's tirade, but when the bastard started talking about police incompetence he'd excused himself before he said something really inappropriate, like 'I told you so, you stupid, arrogant prick.'

Now he was fifty yards away from the controlled mayhem that reigned on the *Nicollet,* staring into the inky black water of the Mississippi, wondering how the hell they were going to catch a cipher who lived in a cyberworld and killed in this one.

He looked up across the river and saw a million hiding places in the clusters of trees and underbrush, jagged rock formations, and dense shadows. The son of a bitch could be hiding there right now, watching him, gloating. But Magozzi didn't think so.

With a deep sigh, he took one last look at the water and headed back toward the barrier of squads that were lined up side by side in the parking lot. Blue and red lights still flashed, bathing the side of the *Nicollet* with a jerky, blood-and-bruise rainbow.

Gino had finally extricated himself from the melee on the boat and was ducking beneath fluttering ribbons of crime-scene tape, heading toward him. He was overdressed for the twenty-degree weather in a puffy down parka, fur-lined cap, and fat snowmobile mittens that were good to seventy below. Two crime-scene techs followed him, carrying a gurney that held a black zippered bag.

'You planning an Antarctic expedition later?' Magozzi asked.

Gino glowered at him. 'I'm sick of freezing my balls off. It's only October, for crying out loud. Whatever happened to Indian summer? I swear to God I'm going to move south. I hate this friggin' state. I hate winter. We're going to have trick-or-treaters out in snowmobile suits next week and every time you open the front door you're going to lose about a hundred dollars' worth of heat –'

Magozzi interrupted a rant that could go on until spring. 'So what have we got?'

Gino let out a tremendous sigh that filled the air around his face with billowy white clouds of frost. 'Same ol', same ol'. A nightmare from hell. What do you want first, gossip or facts?'

'Definitely gossip. The truth hurts too much.'

'Well, the mayor threw out his back bending over to kiss Hammond's ass – *apologizing*, if you can friggin' believe it, for causing such a ruckus. Stupid son of a bitch.'

'Which one?'

Gino smiled unpleasantly. 'Good question. At this point, I'd say they're interchangeable. Anyhow, the mayor quickly recovered from said back injury in time to save face in front of his biggest campaign contributor by openly chastising McLaren and Freedman for, quote, "letting this terrible thing happen."'

'You're not kidding, are you?'

'No, I'm not. Goddamn political asshole. Our guys were good, though. Just stood there and took it.'

'Jesus Christ. Remind me to write them up some

bonus time and hazard pay when we're doing hours on this thing.'

'I think a couple Purple Hearts would be more appropriate.'

Magozzi looked up and saw Red Chilton and two of his men disembarking from the boat. Even Red, normally unflappable, was looking a little worse for wear. Magozzi wouldn't have traded places with the man for all the gold in Fort Knox. 'How's Red doing? I didn't even see him when I was inside.'

'Ah, you know Red. Master of détente. Personally I think he's wasted in this field. He should be a diplomat.'

'Any sense of who's going to take the fall for this? I mean, when things shake out, people are going to wonder why thirty armed professionals on-site with a pre-warning couldn't stop this thing.'

'Well, that's the good news. Anant says the vic was probably dead for hours, long before anyone showed up. Magnusson never mentioned his private head when he was giving the tour. Dinky little thing with one of those plastic accordion doors – everybody assumed it was just a closet. Of course, ignorance is no excuse – Argo and our guys both did sweeps before any of the guests were on board. But Red's not passing the buck and neither are we. We'll all just keep our fingers crossed and hope this gets lost in the shuffle, if you know what I mean.'

Magozzi nodded. 'What else do you know?'

'The only thing I know for sure is that Hammond's lawyers are going to be up all night writing about fifty-two lawsuits. Wouldn't surprise me if Hammond tries to sue the dead guy's estate for emotional distress because he had the nerve to get killed. Of course, nothing holds water because Hammond was forewarned and he chose to ignore it.'

Magozzi smiled. 'So Hammond's going to be on the receiving end of some lawsuits.'

Gino winked. 'Let's just say he's going to find out who his real friends are. If he has any. Hell, *I* might sue him for emotional distress – I was helping Helen with her history homework when I got the call. What if she fails her test tomorrow? She'll be so damaged, her grades will start sliding, then she won't get into college – we're talking serious lost wages here. Anyhow, political intrigue and lawsuits aside, here's the scoop, straight from the Grimm Reaper and your Hindu buddy. Same old shit – my words, not theirs – .22 to the head. With one new wrinkle. Guy's got a fresh bite mark on his hand. Very recent. Like minutes premortem.'

'Terrific. Our boy's getting creative.'

'Yeah, that's what I thought, so I get all excited, thinking maybe we get some DNA, a bite mark we can match, like that, and then Anant tells me he thinks the vic bit himself.'

'What?'

'Yeah. Guy's got himself a serious overbite with some crooked canines. Match looks pretty good.'

'You want to tell me why the vic would bite himself?'

'Hey, it's late, I'm tired, and I don't want to go there. Rambachan will put it together. He always does.'

Magozzi looked over his partner's shoulder and saw the medical examiner's tall, lanky, unmistakable figure pacing the exterior deck of the ferry, his open coat flapping behind him, head bent in a search for clues

Magozzi could only guess at. When he caught his eye, he waved him over. Rambachan lifted one finger and went back to pacing, and Magozzi returned his attention to Gino. 'How are the interviews going?'

Gino snorted, scuffing at the frosty asphalt with his Sorels. 'Slow. They scattered like panicked deer when they saw the squads.' He looked irritably at the flashing turret lights. 'Can we shut these damn things off?' he bellowed to no one in particular. 'It took half an hour just to get a head count. Over three hundred guests. And every single one of them hates me.'

'That's a record for you, isn't it? Alienating three hundred people in one night?'

'You know what I had to do to those people? I mean they're all dressed to kill and ready to party and celebrating this really happy event, you know? And I have to go around with a friggin' Polaroid of a dead guy with a hole in his head just in case he might be their date or their father or whatever. Now you want to take a stab at the statistics? How many out of all those people do you think are going to puke when they have to look at a picture of a bloody corpse at a wedding reception?'

'Jesus, Gino . . .'

'Thirteen. Thirteen puked right on the spot. Goddamn boat smells like the drunk tank on Sunday morning. And the ones that didn't puke got hysterical. We should have been passing out Valium in little paper cups. "Here, take your pill and look at the dead guy." Man. I even felt sorry for the bride, and she was the one I really wanted to deck this afternoon. But she's just a kid, you know? Sure, a murder at your wedding reception sounds Agatha Christie when you're that age, but looking at the body is a whole different story. Here she is all decked out in white satin and lace with little pearl things in her hair and me, Mr Nice Guy, I make her look at a corpse on her wedding night. Christ, my stomach's a mess. I was scared shitless he belonged to one of them, you know?'

Magozzi nodded. 'But he didn't.'

'No. Nobody ever saw him before. So basically we've got nothing. No defensive wounds, no shell, no trace far as we can tell without labs. Just a guy in a suit with no wallet, just like in the game.'

'Which means more hurry up and wait for a print match or a Missing Persons before we can ID the victim.'

'Or maybe the ground search will turn up his wallet in a Dumpster, who knows?'

Magozzi shoved his hands in his pockets, searching for gloves that were on his front closet shelf. 'We need time of death to place the Monkeewrench people.'

'Between two and four is what we've got at this point. And I called the geek squad while you were on your way over, right after you called and told me they popped up from nowhere ten years ago. Now tell me that isn't weird.'

'It's weird.'

'Anyway, they all answered except MacBride, and get this: they all left work early, they all went home alone and stayed there. Not an alibi in the bunch that holds water, unless MacBride comes up with one when we track her down.'

'What did you tell them?'

'Zip is what I told them. Just asked where they were

between two and four, and told them we wanted them at the house for formal statements. Ten A.M. tomorrow. Didn't mention this little circus, but if any of them have a TV, that's a moot point.' Gino tipped his head at him. 'And you know what, buddy? Unless we rubber-hose them all and one of them breaks down and confesses, we're screwed. So far this guy is hitting once a day, and the next murder in the game is at you-know-where.'

Magozzi closed his eyes at the reminder. The fourth murder in the game was set at the Mall of America, and the logistics of covering a place that big were a cop's nightmare, not to mention the shit that would come down if Minnesota's number-one tourist attraction became a homicide crime scene. 'I don't know. My gut still tells me no. It isn't one of the Monkeewrench crew.'

Gino took off a mitten bigger than a small dog and started digging through the many pockets of his parka. 'Why? Just because they called us? It wouldn't be the first time the criminal reported the crime. Psychos get off on that shit, you know. Or maybe it's one of them trying to bring down the rest. They all know the game, and now you tell me they've got this no-past thing going. You ask me, there's just too much strange stuff going on with that bunch.'

Magozzi followed the pocket treasure hunt with his eyes. 'Sounds like you want it to be one of them.'

'Hell, yes, I do. It's either one of them or some anonymous player on that registration list, and last time I checked in with Louise, they'd only cleared about a hundred out of five hundred and some. She said it's practically impossible; every time they hit a red flag that tells them to look a little closer – a bogus address, billing addresses that don't match up with residential addresses, like that – their hands are tied. *Our* hands are tied. None of the Internet providers are giving up any subscriber information without a subpoena, and right now the only probable cause we've got is a hunch that our guy might be on that list. He could kill half the city before we get the legal thumbs-up to do that kind of privacy violation.'

'Almost makes me pine for the days of J. Edgar.'

'Damn right,' Gino said dispiritedly.

Magozzi wiggled his toes inside his shoes, figured he could feel about half of them. 'Monkeewrench could probably do it without subpocnas.'

Gino abandoned his pocket search and gaped at him. 'Arc you crazy?'

'If they've got the know-how to erase themselves, they've got the know-how to get us what we need without subpoenas and never leave a trace. We're out of time, Gino. We need information.'

'Great. So we'll bust the guy with inadmissible evidence and he'll walk anyhow.'

'If we get a real lead from their research, we won't need the inadmissible evidence to bust him. We'll find something else to nail him with.'

Gino grunted. 'Maybe. But asking civilians? And possible doers no less, to help eliminate suspects in a multiple homicide? We might as well call a psychic.'

Magozzi shook his head. 'I don't see that we've got any choice. As it stands now, every potential lead is a legal dead end. The only possible way to find the source is to trace those dead ends back to where they came from. Monkeewrench can do that and we can't. Even if we made Tommy break his sworn oath and several laws, he's just one guy. The only guy in the department with a prayer of tracking who the anonymous players really are. It all takes too much time –'

'And we haven't got time, I know, I know.' Gino stared at him for a long moment, then went back to digging in his pockets. 'If one of the partners is the killer, he or she sure as hell isn't going to help us out and trace themselves. We'd never know if we could trust their information or not. You think of that?'

Magozzi nodded grimly. 'I thought of that. I'm still going to ask them. What do we have to lose?'

'If they throw in a red herring to steer us away from one of them, we're losing time.'

'No more time than we are now, butting our heads up against brick walls . . . what the hell are you looking for, anyhow?'

'This!' With a triumphant grin, Gino pulled a plastic bag out of the last pocket he searched and dangled it in front of Magozzi. 'Salvation. Nirvana. Consolation for all the bad things in life.' He opened the bag and filled the air between them with the aroma of homemade chocolate chip cookies.

Magozzi accepted one and bit into it. 'I love Angela,' he said around a mouthful.

'I'll tell her.' Gino chewed happily. 'Hope it doesn't creep her out.' He glanced over at a few more couples disembarking the ferry. 'I suppose I should get back in there. Make sure McLaren isn't pocketing the phone numbers of all the bridesmaids.'

'Maybe we'll get lucky,' Magozzi said. 'Maybe one of

the guests spotted a tattooed beefer on a Harley or a two-hundred-pound sexpot.'

Gino snorted. 'This is Minnesota. Half the women here go two bills.'

'Yeah, but they're not that sexy.'

'More's the pity. What's her name? Annie what?'

'Belinsky. And with what you've got at home, you shouldn't be noticing.'

Gino smiled a little. 'I'd have to be dead.' He tugged up the collar of his parka. 'Damn, it's cold out here. Here comes the doc.'

Rambachan was cautiously disembarking the ferry, his eyes glued to the substantial, three-foot gangplank as if it were a rope bridge over the Grand Canyon. Magozzi watched him dodge the press and head toward them, his normally cheerful face drawn and weary, his gait a little unsteady.

'Good evening, Detectives.' Rambachan bobbed his head politely. Magozzi could have sworn his complexion was slightly gray.

'Dr Rambachan. I take it you're not too fond of boats.'

He gave them a sickly smile showing fewer teeth than usual. 'Excellent detective work. Yes, you are correct. I have a pathological fear of watercraft and become quite nauseous while on board.'

Magozzi marveled that a man who spent his days with putrefying corpses could actually get seasick on a docked boat. 'Sorry to keep ruining your evenings, Doc.'

'No rest for the wicked.' Rambachan tried for a rakish smile, obviously delighted that he'd had occasion to use an idiom. 'And not to worry. I have already telephoned my good wife to tell her I would be very late. These murders are becoming somebody's bad habit and I would like to complete this autopsy tonight. Perhaps it will shed new light on your investigation.'

Magozzi wanted to kiss him. 'We owe you, Doc. Thank you.'

'This is my job, Detective. I will call you immediately when I have something to report.' He turned to Gino and bowed his head slightly. 'I was honored to work with you tonight, Detective Rolseth. You were very gentle with the guests while performing a very unpleasant duty.'

Gino, unused to compliments from any quarter, blushed and blustered, 'Yeah, well, I could have done without it. Sucked rocks, is what it did.'

Rambachan brightened and looked at Magozzi. 'Sucked rocks? Would this be in the book?'

Magozzi suppressed a smile and shook his head. 'Probably not.'

'Then you will explain at another time?'

'With pleasure.'

'Excellent. Then good evening to you both.'

Gino waited until the Indian was out of earshot, then turned to Magozzi with a broad smile. 'What is with you two? You've got some little bonding thing going. I can barely understand the guy and you two chat it up like a couple of English lords over tea.'

Magozzi shrugged. 'I don't know. He's just so . . . polite. And so naïve. It's a nice combo. He thinks *How to Talk Minnesotan* is a linguistics book.'

Gino laughed out loud. 'I hope you told him.'

'Not yet . . .' Magozzi's cell phone chirped and he fumbled it out of his coat pocket. 'Damnit. Hang on, Gino . . . Magozzi!' he barked into the receiver.

He was quiet for a long time, and Gino swore he saw the beginnings of a smile.

'No kidding. You got an address for me?' He dug a piece of paper out of his pocket and scrawled down numbers and a street name. 'Funny place for a multimillionaire to live. Great work, Tommy. Now go home and get some rest. I'm going to need you early tomorrow.' He snapped the phone closed with a flourish.

'Good news?' Gino asked.

'Grace MacBride, or whoever she is, has six guns registered in her name. One of them's a .22.'

Gino nodded knowingly. 'She did it.'

'I'm going to head over there, see if I can catch her home, peg her from two to four, maybe take a look at the gun, and then ask her for some help with the registration list.'

'Nice touch. Could you help us find a killer, unless, of course, you're the killer, and if that's the case, could I take a look at your gun?'

Magozzi shrugged. 'You got any other ideas?'

'Yeah, I got an idea. Getting as far away from this case as I can. Jimmy and I were talking about that day-trading thing. Figured we could do it from Montana.'

22

Magozzi sped through side streets, turret light flashing, then picked up 94 East to St Paul. The freeway was nearly deserted at this hour – too late for the worker bees to be out, too early for the clubbers to head home – so he pushed the unmarked up toward ninety in the far left lane, wishing he had one of MPH's new Grand Ams instead of the doggy two-year-old Ford sedan.

Then again, why was he in such a hurry? He knew damn well Grace MacBride was no killer, and even if she were, she certainly wouldn't be wandering around her house drenched in blood carrying a smoking gun and looking guilty. The .22 registered in her name was the thinnest of coincidences – that particular gun was as common as potholes in this city – but it was an excuse to drop in on her, and he decided not to examine his reasons for wanting to do that too closely.

'Alibi. The registration list.' He said it aloud, as if giving voice to the feeble rationalization would make it more believable. His excessive speed was easier to justify. The broken car heater had mysteriously kicked in with a vengeance at eighty-five mph, and it was the first time he'd been warm since leaving City Hall.

He braked at the Cretin-Vandalia exit and turned off the turret light. By the time he drove the few blocks to Groveland Avenue, the temperature in the car had already dropped ten degrees and the plastic steering wheel started to feel like a circle of ice.

Even deep in the residential district, there were a few people out in spite of the cold. A group of preteens who should have been home in bed on a school night; a couple walking a long-haired dog so close to the ground it looked legless; a die-hard jogger who harbored the delusion that running past dark alleys and shadowy doorways was a healthy pastime. All of them wore gloves, even the kids, which made all of them smarter than he was.

He put one hand between his knees to warm his fingers and steered with the other, dreaming of his gloves at home on the closet shelf.

Grace MacBride's house was as modest as any in this quiet, working-class neighborhood, which seemed a little strange in view of her net worth. What was a multimillionaire doing living in a tiny two-story stucco with a detached garage? Another contradiction to add to the collection.

He parked on the opposite side of the street and studied the house for a moment while he exhaled frost into the cold car. Opaque shades covered all the windows; the only source of light was a high-intensity flood that illuminated a tiny front yard bereft of landscaping. No frivolous flower beds, no shrubbery, no decorative, welcoming touches – just a plain cement walk that led to a heavy, windowless door.

He shut off the car and climbed out, tugging his collar up around his ears. The thin microfiber trench that had seemed like a good fashion decision in August was laughably ineffectual now. But like every good

Minnesotan, except Gino, he'd wait until a near-death brush with hypothermia before he dragged out the down parka, as if wearing lighter clothing would somehow encourage the weather to adjust itself appropriately.

He crossed the deserted street and followed the arrow-straight walk up to a three-step cement stoop. He paused on the top step and studied the door.

The last time he'd seen a steel-clad door was on a homicide call at a suburban meth lab last spring. A pricey line of defense for drug dealers, mobsters, and the ultraparanoid. For an abused woman hiding out from a crazed ex-husband or boyfriend, it made good sense, as long as you had money, and it wasn't the first time that particular scenario had danced through his brain.

He'd seen the fear in her eyes the first time he'd met her, and in that instant he'd thought, *Abuse victim.* That idea had crumbled to dust within minutes. The victim mentality part was the problem. She didn't have a shred of it. Afraid, yes; incapacitated, no. She might put a steel door on her house and pack a Sig Sauer, but those were the actions of someone taking charge, preparing to meet danger, rather than hiding from it. Besides, the abused-woman scenario would only explain MacBride changing her identity – not all five of them.

He shook his head to clear it of thoughts going nowhere, noticed a gray plastic intercom box mounted on the door frame, and ironically, a rubber mat that said 'Welcome.' He wondered if that was Grace MacBride's idea of humor.

As he stepped onto the mat, he distinctly heard an

electronic whirring sound just above his head. He pinpointed the source quickly – a security camera, well camouflaged in the fascia of the eave, turning and focusing its ever-vigilant eye on him.

He knelt down and teased up a corner of the mat, exposing a pressure pad integrated into the concrete of the top step, obviously wired to the camera, and probably from there to an alarm somewhere in the house.

The pathology of paranoia kept rearing its ugly head, and on some level, it was incredibly disturbing. What justified this kind of security? If not an abusive ex, what then? Corporate espionage? He didn't think so. As he'd learned from Espinoza just tonight, you never had to leave the comfort of your own home to lie, cheat, or steal in a world that was inextricably linked together by the World Wide Web.

He stabbed the intercom button and waited, his breath coming in frosty puffs. For more than a minute, there was dead silence, then three metallic thunks – three dead bolts being released.

The steel door swung open and Grace MacBride stood before him, her pale skin flushed and moist. She was wearing baggy gray sweatpants, an oversized T-shirt, and a ponytail. She would have looked almost vulnerable if it hadn't been for the ankle holster and the derringer it held.

'It's eleven o'clock, Detective Magozzi.' Her voice was flat, noncommittal. She didn't seem particularly surprised that he'd shown up on her doorstep.

'I apologize for the hour, Ms MacBride. Am I interrupting anything?'

'My workout.'

He gestured toward the ankle holster. 'You carry when you work out?'

'I carry all the time, Detective, I told you that already. What do you want?'

A born hostess, Magozzi thought sarcastically. 'I want to look at your .22.'

'Do you have a warrant?' Her voice remained impassive, her gaze steady. Chalk one up for MacBride – she was either innocent or sociopathic.

Magozzi sighed, suddenly feeling exhausted. 'No, I don't have a warrant, but I can get one. I'll just stand here on this pressure pad and keep ringing your intruder alert or whatever the hell it is until Gino brings one over.'

'Am I a suspect?'

'Everyone's a suspect. Any reason you don't want me to see the gun?'

'Because this isn't a police state, Detective Magozzi.'

Goddamnit, she was snotty. No way she could have ever had a relationship with an abuser. With an attitude like hers, whoever it was would have killed her the first night.

'Ms MacBride, there are people dying out there and you're wasting time.'

The color of exertion on her cheeks turned the darker pink of fury. He'd hit a nerve. '*You're* wasting time, investigating the people who reported the crime instead of looking for the killer!'

He refused to rise to the bait. He just stood there in the cold, hoping she couldn't see him shiver beneath the thin coat, waiting for her to slam the door in his face. She surprised him.

'Oh, the hell with it. Come in and shut the damn door. And stay right there. Don't move a muscle.'

He stepped inside quickly, closed the door, and looked around. 'No retina scan?'

She glared at him. 'What are you talking about?'

Magozzi shrugged. 'You've got a pretty serious security system here.'

'I'm a pretty serious person,' she snapped, turning and stalking down the long, dim hallway. When she disappeared behind a swinging oak door, he took a few steps in, looking for some indication that the place was actually inhabited, but the foyer and hall were as empty and anonymous as the outside of the house.

Stairway to the left, two closed doors – living room and what? Den? – to the right. In between there was nothing but a well-polished maple floor and eggshell walls. If Grace MacBride had a personality, which he was beginning to doubt, there were no insights here.

He heard angry footsteps and the swinging door burst open again. Grace glowered at him from the doorway. 'I want this to be legit. If you want to see the gun, then you can look at it in the cabinet.'

'Fine. Better yet.'

She watched in what Magozzi could only classify as deep disapproval as he walked toward her. If the look was designed to make him feel like a blundering interloper, it missed its mark. It just set him on edge.

'Even you have to know this is ridiculous, Detective.'

He let the 'even you' part slide. *Detective 101. Do not respond to the verbal abuse of civilians.* 'Why is that?'

'You think I'd use a gun registered in my name to kill

people? You think I wouldn't have cleaned it if I'd used it to kill that poor girl yesterday?'

No mention of the riverboat killing, Magozzi noted. Either she didn't know about it, or was pretending not to. 'Of course you would have cleaned it. I would expect nothing less from you, Ms MacBride. But detective work is largely a tedious process of information gathering and report writing. My objective here is to note your ownership of the same caliber gun the killer used, and further note that I examined said gun with your permission and saw no evidence of recent firing.'

'You're covering your ass.'

'Absolutely. The first time I don't will be the time a killer leaves a gun dirty and covered with blood and wrapped in a sign that says "I Am the Murder Weapon."'

She swung the door open and gestured him into a stark, utilitarian kitchen with sparkling white tile and a stainless sink that looked like it had been spit-shined. Expensive pots and pans hung from a rack above a black granite countertop that was lined with the sort of appliances only a serious cook would have.

A covered pot simmered on low flame, filling the air with the savory aromas of garlic and wine. For some reason, he couldn't imagine Grace MacBride doing anything remotely domestic, but she obviously had a softer side, a side she went to great lengths to hide.

He didn't bother wondering why she was cooking at eleven o'clock at night, assuming almost everything she did would be a bit out of the norm. 'You have a dog?' he asked.

Grace frowned at him. 'Ye-es. Oh. The water bowl. Crack detective work.'

Magozzi ignored the comment. 'Where is he?'

'He's hiding. He's afraid of strangers.'

'Hmm. Is that something he picked up from you?'

She gave him an irritated look, then led him through an arched doorway into the living room, oddly placed at the rear of the house instead of the front. It was the polar opposite of the rest of the house – surprisingly warm, with overstuffed wing chairs and a big leather sofa that held an assortment of colorful down-filled pillows. A glass coffee table was stacked with computer magazines and ponderous-looking textbooks on computer programming languages. A willow basket of miniature pumpkins sat in the corner next to an urn filled with dried flowers and gourds. Another glimmer of her softer side.

He paid particular attention to the paintings, all originals, that covered the walls – an eclectic collection of stark black-and-white abstracts that had to be by the same artist as the painting in Mitch Cross's office, and two soft watercolor landscapes.

She knelt down in front of a fine mahogany cabinet that sat in the far corner of the room and slipped in a key. The interior was lined with thick red velvet and held the very formidable MacBride arsenal. She pulled out a Ruger .22 and handed it to him by the barrel.

He examined the gun, pulled back the slide, checked the load. Empty. Nothing in the chamber. And it was spotless with a light sheen of oil, as spit-shined as the kitchen sink.

'I don't suppose you'd want to turn this over to me . . .'

She exhaled sharply.

'I'll take that as a no.' He handed it back to her, then gestured toward the rest of her weapons. 'Nice collection. A lot of firepower.'

She was silent.

'Just what is it that you're so afraid of?'

'Taxes, cancer, the usual.'

'Guns aren't very effective against either of those things. Neither are steel doors.'

Still silent.

'Neither is erasing your past.'

Her eyes flickered a little.

'You want to tell me about that?'

'About what?'

'About what planet you and your friends lived on until you showed up here ten years ago.'

She looked off to the side, mouth clamped shut. Biting back temper, he decided.

'And just how much time have you wasted traveling that particular path?'

He shrugged. 'Not much. It was a real short path. I've got a computer wizard at the office tearing his hair out trying to get past your firewalls. Actually, he's now your biggest fan. Thinks you all should hire out to Witness Protection.' He watched for the slightest reaction, but she didn't even twitch. 'You know, if you were in the program, telling me would save us all a lot of trouble.'

She ignored him, put the Ruger away, locked the gun cabinet, then stood up and folded her arms across her chest. 'Is that all? Because if it is, I'd like to get back to my workout.'

Magozzi turned his attention to one of the watercolors, a city scene busy with uniformly happy people, remarkably detailed for the medium. A young artist, he thought, mixing the styles of the masters while searching for his own. The sociable subject matter seemed strangely out of place in a house designed as a fortress, owned by a woman who had clearly been born without smile muscles. He wondered what had made her buy it. 'Our people have been working the registration list you gave us.'

'And?'

'And it's slow.'

'Of course it's slow. And stupid.'

'Excuse me?'

'That list isn't going to do you a bit of good, and you know it. Even the dumbest killer wouldn't leave a name and address and telephone number so your uniforms could come knocking, and this one is not dumb . . .'

He opened his mouth to reply, but he wasn't fast enough.

'. . . and don't give me that song and dance about following procedure. Following the almighty procedure is what always bogs cops down. It wastes time and resources and energy that you damn well better be spending laying a trap for this guy, because he is rolling, and if he hits again, the victim is on your head, because you had a chance to stop him if you hadn't been so damn intent about crossing names off a list and checking out my .22 . . .'

'We *did* lay a trap for this guy,' Magozzi snapped

bitterly, suddenly furious that this strange, secretive, paranoid woman with no past was lecturing him on how to do his job; furious that this case was spiraling out of control with bodies stacking up like cordwood; furious at her lack of respect and her refusal to co-operate; and especially furious that he felt like he was missing something obvious about the whole damn case. 'Tammy Hammond's wedding reception was on the *Nicollet* tonight. Not only did we have ten guys on site, but Argo Security had another twenty and the damn place was safer than the White House. And guess what? We were still too late.' She just stared at him for a moment while his angry words registered, and then he saw all the righteous indignation drain from her eyes, leaving blue mirrors of devastation. *Christ, that had to be real*, he thought. *No way you couldn't fake a look like that.*

'Oh my God,' she whispered, and he heard her real voice, and saw her real face, and for just an instant felt a brand-new kind of guilt, as if he'd let her down personally.

In the next instant the look of devastation was gone, replaced by a fury that exceeded his own and a hatred directed squarely at him. 'You idiots.' Her voice was low, quiet, and she let the words hang there for a minute, making sure he knew she meant them. 'You were *too late?* We told you this was going to happen, we told you where, and now someone else died because you were *too late?*'

He felt his defenses kick in, knew they were wrong, but couldn't stop them. 'We were still scrambling around for permission to even be on that boat when this guy was murdered. Maybe you should have called us a little earlier to tell us one of your psycho players was using your game as a template for a killing spree. We weren't too late. You were.'

Christ, he sounded like a grade-school kid, batting away blame, hoping it would land on someone else. That made him angrier yet.

'Where were you between two and four?'

Her eyes seemed to harden and chill, blue water freezing. 'At work. Alone. No witnesses, no alibi. Everybody else left at noon. You want to arrest me, Detective? Make yourself feel better about blowing it?'

This was all wrong. Cops and witnesses – if that's all she was – weren't supposed to be adversaries, but this woman had been down on cops long before he met her. He was just the current target.

He moved his shoulders inside his coat, trying to loosen the muscles that felt like coiled springs. 'What I want is some cooperation. We need to pare down that registration list, get real names and addresses for all the bogus ones, and we don't have time to –'

'Do it legally?'

Magozzi didn't say anything

'Let's see if I've got this straight. You storm in here in the middle of the night violating all kinds of my civil rights, basically accusing me of murder, and now you're asking me to help you out?'

Magozzi wisely kept his mouth shut.

'You're a real piece of work, Detective.'

'Thank you.'

'Get the hell out of my house.'

His cell phone chirped as he was passing through the

kitchen. He tugged it out of his pocket, flipped it open, and snarled his name.

'Something wrong, sweetheart?' Gino said into his ear.

'Yeah, the market's down, India and Pakistan have nuclear weapons, and the heater in the car still isn't working.'

'Are you at MacBride's?'

'Yes.'

'Well, unless the phone's been ringing off the hook she's got the ringer off. Tell her about the interviews tomorrow. We got her friends coming in anyway, might as well do them all at once. Learn anything interesting over there?'

'My own shortcomings.'

Gino laughed. 'See you tomorrow, bud.'

Magozzi started to put the phone back in his pocket, then feeling a slight pang of guilt, wiped it surreptitiously on his coat and then laid it on the counter instead. He turned and looked at MacBride, standing under the archway into the living room, arms crossed over her chest in classic angry defense posture. 'Your friends are all coming down to give formal statements tomorrow morning at ten. They couldn't reach you.'

Her head moved almost imperceptibly. 'I have the ringer off.'

'That's what they thought. Can you make it?'

'Oh, sure, why not? Let's waste some more time together, shall we? Give this guy a shot at some more innocent victims before you decide to shut him down. What are you doing about the Mall of America?'

'I don't discuss ongoing police investigations with civilians.'

'Especially suspects.'

Magozzi looked at her for a long moment, then turned and strode down the hallway toward the front door. He jerked it open and gasped.

A black kid was standing on the stoop, his nowhere shoulders hunched inside a really good leather jacket. 'I'd like to see the lady of the house,' he said to Magozzi, weight shifting from one foot to the other, ready to run.

He never heard Grace moving up behind him, but he felt her.

'Jackson. What're you doing here?'

The kid's face relaxed a little. 'You okay?'

Grace nodded. 'Sure I'm okay.'

'Oh. Well, good. It's just that I saw that piece-of-shit car pull up and this guy get out, and . . .' Suspicious eyes climbed up Magozzi's chest to his face. 'He's carrying, you know.'

'It's all right. He's allowed. He's a cop.'

'Oh. Well, I was just checking, you know? Something about him didn't look right.'

'You've got a good eye, Jackson. Thanks for the thought.'

The kid took one more look at Magozzi, apparently decided he wasn't a threat, then hopped off the stoop and disappeared down the walk.

'What was that about? You hire local kids to watch the place?'

Grace eyed him steadily. 'No, he's my accomplice in all the murders.'

He heard the dead bolts slam home one by one while he was still on the walk, but he crossed the street, got into his car, started it up, then sat long enough to make it seem legitimate. Then he got out of the car, went back up to the door, and pressed the intercom button again.

She made him wait longer this time, intentionally, he was sure. At last the door swung open and she glared at him. 'Just because I didn't slam the door in your face the first time doesn't mean I won't do it now.'

'You can't.'

'Oh really? And why is that?'

'Because.' He pointed at the mat he stood on. 'It says "Welcome" right there.'

The sides of her mouth twitched a little in what might have been the beginnings of a smile. She controlled it admirably, he thought. 'What do you want, Detective?'

'I think I left my phone in the kitchen.'

'Oh, for God's sake.' She thumped away down the hall, dark ponytail bobbing, then reappeared almost instantly, his cell phone held at arm's length as if it were diseased.

'Sorry about that. Thanks.'

The door slammed hard behind him but he didn't care. He carried the phone by the antenna and, once inside the car, slipped it into a plastic evidence bag he took from a stack in the glove compartment.

Charlie was waiting for Grace on the other side of the swinging oak door, his tail stub twitching in a doggy question. 'It's okay, Charlie,' she reassured him. 'The big bad detective is gone.'

Charlie seemed satisfied with that and wandered back to his afghan nest on the sofa to resume the evening nap Magozzi had so rudely interrupted.

Grace stirred the pot of beef borguignonne that was simmering on the stove, put down the spoon, and clasped her hands to keep them from trembling. They felt cold.

She walked through the entire downstairs, turning on every light as she went, trying to chase away the darkness that was closing in on her again. The kid was going to be a problem. She shouldn't have helped him out in the park. Now he was trying to return the favor, keeping an eye out for her, hanging around, watching, and she couldn't have that. It was too damn dangerous.

A chiming sound stopped her when she passed the office door, the computer's alert for incoming e-mail. Probably one of her partners, or all of them, she thought, wondering if she'd gotten a call from the cops, too.

She went into the office, jiggled her mouse to restore the monitor, and pulled up her mailbox. One new message. She clicked on it and brought up the memo line. It read: FROM THE KILLER. Sent from one of those megaservers that offered free e-mail to anybody who wanted it.

She stared at the screen for a long, long time, her finger poised to click on the 'read new mail' button.

She wasn't sure if a minute or an hour had passed before she finally clicked open the message. Very slowly, familiar red pixels started to materialize on the screen with eerie slowness. It was the second screen of SKUD; the one that was supposed to say: 'Want to Play a Game?'

Only this message was a little different. This message had never been programmed into SKUD.

YOU'RE NOT PLAYING.

Grace started to shiver, and then to shake so badly she could barely fumble her way through Harley's phone number.

23

At five o'clock Wednesday morning, the phone next to Michael Halloran's bed started ringing and wouldn't stop. He stuck one hand out of the covers and felt goose bumps rise on his arm as his hand wandered blindly over the nightstand, searching for the phone, knocking over the clock and a water glass in the process. That brought his head out from beneath the down comforter. The cold in the bedroom made his hair hurt.

'Hello?' he croaked into the receiver, forgetting he was always supposed to answer with his title; forgetting his title for that matter. Sheriff of something.

'Mikey, is that you?'

Only one person in the world called him Mikey. 'Father Newberry,' he groaned.

'It's five o'clock, Mikey. Time to get up if you want to make six-o'clock Mass.'

Receiver still to his ear, he closed his eyes and fell immediately back to sleep.

'MIKEY!'

He snapped awake again. 'You call everybody in town to wake 'em up for Mass?' he squeaked.

'Just you.'

'I don't go to Mass anymore, Father, remember? Jeez, you're a sadistic old fart. What are you calling me for?'

'God can cure a hangover, you know.'

Halloran groaned again, vowing to move to a big city where everyone in town didn't know what he was doing every single goddamned minute. 'What makes you think I've got a hangover?'

'Because that heretic Lutheran's car was parked in your driveway all night . . .'

'How do you know that?'

'. . . which means the two of you probably stayed up all night drinking Scotch, and now your head's so heavy you can hardly lift it off the pillow.'

'Well, that shows what you know. I don't even know where my pillow is.' He looked around him on the bed for the AWOL pillow, eyes narrowed to slits, but he couldn't see anything. 'Besides, I'm blind.'

'It's dark. Turn on the light, sit up and listen.'

'That's too many instructions.'

'You didn't let Bonar drive home last night, did you?'

Halloran searched the fuzz in his mind for memories of the night before. They'd eaten the last of Ralph, he'd called the doctor in Atlanta, then they'd really started drinking . . .

Mike finally found the switch on the lamp, nearly screamed when he turned it on. Now he really was blind. 'Nope. We had a slumber party.'

'Cute. Listen, Mikey, how long are you going to keep this silly surveillance on the church? You've had a deputy parked in the lot since Monday.'

'It's just a precaution.'

'Well, it's bad for business.'

Mike tried to swallow, but it felt like he had a hair ball lodged in his throat. He dearly hoped he hadn't found a cat somewhere last night and licked it. 'That's why you called me at five o'clock in the morning? To tell me I'm cutting into your profits?'

'No, I called you to come to Mass, I told you.'

'I'm not coming to Mass. Goodbye.'

'I found something.'

Halloran brought the receiver back to his ear. 'What'd you say?'

'It was in one of the hymnal racks, two pews back from where the Kleinfeldts were sitting. Stuck in one of the hymnals, actually, in that gap between the cover and the binding that happens when the glue gets old and dried and pulls away, you know what I mean? Never would have found it if I hadn't dropped the book, so you probably shouldn't fire the men who were searching so hard . . .'

Halloran was fully awake now. '*What?* What did you find, Father?'

'Oh. Didn't I mention that? Well, it's a shell casing, if I'm not mistaken, and since it's been years since we've had target practice in the church, I was thinking it might be related to the murders.'

'You didn't touch it, did you?'

'I most certainly did not,' Father Newberry huffed, proud to be as informed in police procedure as any American with a television set. 'It's lying on the floor, right where it dropped, but of course the faithful will be arriving within the hour and I suppose they'll kick it all over the place . . .'

Halloran hit the ground running – well, figuratively, at least. In actuality he was shuffling across the bedroom floor with exaggerated care, trying not to jostle his head. 'Don't let anyone near it, Father. I'll be there as fast as I can.'

The old bastard was smiling so hard Mike could hear it in his voice. 'Good. You'll be here in time for Mass, then.'

Bonar was just stepping out of the bathroom as Mike was shuffling down the hall toward it. He was dressed, shaved, and looked disgustingly alert. 'Shower's all yours, buddy, and the coffee's on. Man, you look like hell. You shouldn't drink so much.'

Halloran peered blearily through puffy eyes. 'Who are you?'

Bonar chuckled. 'A vision of loveliness compared to you, my friend. Who called at this ungodly hour anyway?'

'An ungodly priest,' Halloran muttered, and then brightened, just a little. 'He found a shell casing in the church. Hasn't touched it. And since you're already up and dressed . . .'

'On my way. I'll see you at the office later.'

Halloran was smiling as he stepped into the shower. He wasn't going to make Mass after all.

24

Grace stood in her living room, smiling down at the three shadowy, snoring lumps on the floor. The fur-covered lump sensed his mistress's presence and looked up at her from the makeshift bed he'd made out of Harley's leg. Harley, apparently, could banish the demons on the floor simply by lying on it, making Charlie feel totally safe. Grace knew exactly how he felt.

Calling Harley last night had been a knee-jerk reaction, a perfectly rational antidote to the devastating fear Grace had felt. She could have called any one of them; his phone number just happened to be the first one to pop into her head. And then Harley had called Roadrunner because he was the best hacker of all of them. And then he'd called Annie because 'she'd castrate me if I didn't and I've grown fond of my testicles.' And they'd all come running without question, converging as a single unit to do battle against an unknown enemy. Circling the wagons, she thought.

'Charlie,' Grace whispered, patting her side in invitation. Charlie scrambled up and followed close on her heels as she crept quietly into the kitchen. She knelt down and stroked his head, then groped in the dark pantry for his bag of kibble and the special Jamaican Blue coffee she always kept on hand for Roadrunner. 'Good boy,' she said. 'It's okay, I'm not jealous.'

Charlie's tail swished back and forth in reply.

Grace found the kibble but was unsuccessful in her blind search for the coffee, so she hit a wall switch and turned on the soft, recessed overhead lights, hoping it wouldn't wake Harley and Roadrunner. With the gloom of early morning dispelled, she found the coffee immediately and noticed the row of empty Bordeaux bottles lined up on the counter. The throbbing of a headache she'd almost forgotten about renewed itself so she added two aspirin to her morning vitamins.

As she filled up the coffee decanter with bottled water from the fridge, the larger of the two lumps stirred and she heard Harley's sleep-gravelly voice rasp, 'I hope you're making coffee.'

'Lots of it, and extra-strong,' Grace whispered.

Harley groaned and rolled over, pulling the blanket up over his head.

Overhead, Grace heard the wooden floor in the upstairs spare bedroom creaking. A few minutes later, Annie emerged from the stairwell, fully made up and dressed to the nines in a burnt-orange wool suit with a scandalously short skirt. Hooked on the fingers of one hand was a pair of stiletto heels of the same pumpkin shade; trailing from the other, a dramatic black chiffon wrap trimmed with marabou feathers and sparkling black spangles. If Halloween could choose its own spokesmodel, Annie Belinsky would be it.

Grace gave her an approving thumbs-up. 'Very festive.'

They exchanged a giggle and a hug while Charlie crowded in between them to give Annie's hand a wash. Annie knelt down and ruffled the dog's fur. 'Hey, Charlie. You snuck out on me in the middle of the night, you cad. You know what that does to a girl's self-esteem?'

Charlie tongued her neck in a happy apology, then went back to the important business of eating.

'Your dog's a slut, you know that, Grace? Hey, those two bums still asleep?' she asked, peering into the living room.

Grace nodded and put a finger to her lips, then cringed as Annie smiled mischievously and sang out, 'Rise and shine you slobs!'

There was a brief pause, then Harley shouted back. 'Annie, you are a dead woman!'

Instead of running for cover and cowering in a corner at the sound of Harley's shout, Charlie lifted his head, barking playfully. It never ceased to amaze Grace that a dog with a pathological fear of almost everything was so perfectly comfortable with these people that even their shouts didn't scare him.

Roadrunner popped up, startled and looking a little shell-shocked. 'What? What?!'

'Nightmare, Roadrunner,' Harley rasped. 'Go back to sleep.'

Annie bustled around Grace and flipped the kitchen wall switch on high, blasting the adjacent living room with several hundred watts of light.

Harley lurched up to sitting position, emerging from under the blanket like a whale surfacing for air. 'You are a loathsome creature,' he mumbled, scrubbing at his wildly tangled ponytail. His mood lifted when he noticed her outfit and he gave her a very intentional once-over. 'What are you supposed to be? The Great Big Pumpkin?'

Annie scrunched herself up in Quasimodo style and clawed the air with her nails. 'Ha-ha. I'm the ghost of your worst Halloween nightmare past.'

'No, you're much sexier than she was.'

'Oh, for God's sake. Get up, it's already six A.M. *Breakfast* time. That mean anything to you, smart-ass?'

Harley cocked his head and gave Annie an adoring smile. 'It means I take back anything bad I've ever said about you.'

Charlie was now bounding into the living room like an overgrown puppy to start a gleeful campaign of face-licking. Harley fell on his back and submitted to the dog's ministrations. 'Help! Help! I'm being attacked by a mop!'

'You'll hurt his feelings,' Grace said, watching with a smile as the elated dog moved on to his next victim.

Roadrunner hugged Charlie and gave his back a vigorous scratching. 'You want to go for a jog, buddy?'

Charlie dropped to his haunches, his tongue lolling out of his mouth.

'Huh? What do you say?'

He barked his answer and loped toward the door.

Roadrunner yawned and stood up, looking almost fresh except for the large cowlick that stuck up from the back of his head. 'Is it okay if I take him out for a run?'

'I don't see why not.'

Harley looked around at them with a sour expression. 'What's the matter with you people? Why is everyone so goddamned perky?'

'Maybe because we didn't drink two bottles of wine apiece last night,' Annie said snidely.

'For your information, Miss Holier-Than-Thou, that is not wine, it's Bordeaux. And at two hundred bucks a bottle, I had to finish what your uncivilized palate could not. You don't open a bottle of '89 Lynch-Bages, have a glass, then chuck it.' He fumbled in his back pocket and pulled out his wallet on a chain. 'Roadrunner, stop at Mell-O Glaze on your way back and get me a box of those apple beignets.'

Roadrunner held up his hand. 'My treat.'

Harley's brows shot up. 'You're buying? What is this, the end of the world?'

'The end of the world comes when you stop being an asshole. See you guys in half an hour.'

Grace was unloading food from the refrigerator. 'Harley, go upstairs and lie down in the guest room. We'll call you for breakfast.'

Harley stood up and stretched. 'Nah, that's okay. Just give me a carton of orange juice and ten aspirin and I'll be fine.'

Grace held up a pitcher of orange juice. 'Come and get it.'

Harley strode into the kitchen, took the pitcher from her, and set it down on the counter. Then he took her by the shoulders and turned her to face him. 'I want you to know that I'm not afraid of cholesterol.'

Grace chuckled. 'Good thing, because I just went grocery shopping. Ham, bacon, eggs, sausage, potatoes, cheese . . .'

'I died and woke up in heaven.' He swooned, making a beeline for the coffeemaker.

Annie was now at the cutting board with sleeves rolled up and knife in hand, poised over an enormous ham. 'This reminds me of college,' she said happily, sawing off the first slab. 'Remember when we used to have crash-overs, then pull out whatever was left over in the fridge and cook it up in the morning?'

Grace went to work cracking eggs into a ceramic bowl. 'God, we made some disgusting stuff, didn't we?'

Harley grabbed three mugs from the cupboard and hovered by the coffeemaker, waiting impatiently for it to finish its cycle. 'What deranged individual made that lo mein omelet with goat cheese? Remember that? Jesus, that was disgusting.'

'It was Mitch,' Grace said. 'He was the only aspiring epicure in the bunch.'

'*Misguided* epicure,' Harley corrected her. 'Although I've got to admit, he's come a long way. Frankly, I think his skills are wasted on Diane. She's always eating unshelled birdseed and macrobiotic tree trimmings and crap like that.' Harley poured coffee and added a hefty dose of cream and sugar to his. 'Speaking of the ol' boy, he's probably already at the office having a nervous breakdown alone. I'd better give him a call and fill him in.'

'Invite him over for lo mein omelets,' Grace said.

Harley went into the office to call Mitch while Annie started her baking powder biscuits and Grace set the table. When Harley emerged five minutes later, he was shaking his head.

'What?' Annie and Grace asked simultaneously.

'Bad news, kids. The Monkeewrench connection to the murders blew wide open, along with all of Mitch's gaskets. We're all over the news.'

Grace sighed. 'It was bound to happen.'

'Just a matter of time,' Annie said, slapping dough back and forth between her hands. 'Anybody who played the game and saw the newspaper yesterday would have put two and two together, just like we did.'

Harley poured himself more coffee. 'Yeah, I know, but Mitch isn't taking it so well. Five clients already called him this morning to pull their accounts. Right now he's crunching numbers and he says it's not looking too good.'

'Did you tell him about the e-mail?' Annie asked.

'Well, I was going to, I meant to, but the poor guy was already totally undone, and if I told him about it I'd have to explain we've been here all night, that we didn't just pop over for an impromptu breakfast, and then he'd feel left out because nobody called him . . . you know. Figured it'd be better if we told him about it in person. Anyhow, he won't be joining us for breakfast.' Harley peered over Annie's shoulder and watched as she cut out little circles of dough. 'But on the plus side, that means more biscuits for me.'

Annie swatted him with a flour-covered hand.

A half hour later, they were all squeezed around the tiny kitchen table, finishing off an enormous spread of ham, bacon, potatoes, vegetable omelets, and Annie's legendary baking powder biscuits.

Roadrunner groaned and pushed his clean plate away. 'This beats trail mix any day, I can tell you that.'

Harley was aghast. 'That's all you can say? Better than trail mix? Jesus, Roadrunner, this is *paradise*.' He gave Annie and Grace an apologetic shrug on Roadrunner's behalf. 'Pearls before swine, you know.'

Roadrunner looked at his watch. 'I hate to be the

party crasher, but we're supposed to be at the cop shop giving interviews in a few hours. We should talk about the e-mail. Does anyone think it's the real thing or do we brush it off as a prank?'

'You tell us,' Grace said. 'You were up all night tracing it.'

Roadrunner shrugged. 'I never did get past that first firewall. Whoever did it is pretty good. I'll keep working on it.'

Harley reached for the coffee carafe and started refilling mugs. 'Probably some twisted little cyberfreak getting his anonymous fifteen minutes. According to Mitch, the press has this thing covered from hell to breakfast, especially with the Hammond wedding. So he sees his big chance to carve out his own little column for posterity. He plays psycho, gets his rocks off, and it's all good, clean fun to him. The next best thing to being there. Plus it gives him something for the scrapbooks, something to show the grandkids.'

Annie scowled. 'Nice. "Hey look, kids, your granpappy was a real sick asshole, what do you think of that?"'

'Lots of wackos out there,' Harley said. 'What I want to know is why he only sent it to Grace. Why not the main Monkeewrench e-mail? Or to one of us?'

Grace said, 'Think about it. If you were a nutcase and wanted to scare somebody, which e-mail address would you pick? Not Harley Davidson, probably not Roadrunner, and definitely not BallBuster.'

Annie looked up at the ceiling innocently.

'No, you'd send it to me. GraceM. That sounds safe.'

'Okay, so I'd be a bad psycho,' Harley confessed. 'So maybe the e-mail is from the killer, maybe it's from some harmless, wacked-out gamer. We'll play it safe and pretend it *is* from the killer. That brings up another topic.'

'What?' Annie asked, slapping Harley's hand as he reached for another biscuit. 'That's mine, pal.'

Harley relinquished the last biscuit to the baker. 'Well, doesn't anyone think this whole thing is a pretty amazing coincidence? I mean, what are the odds that this would happen to the same five people twice in a lifetime?'

Roadrunner frowned and started twisting his napkin. 'Makes me want to go out and buy a lottery ticket.'

'That's what I'm saying.'

'This is totally different,' Annie said sternly. 'Just some asshole playing the game.'

'That's what I figured, too,' Harley said. 'We all did. But after this e-mail, it got a little more personal and I got to thinking.' He hesitated and looked at Grace. 'What if it's *him?*'

Grace was absolutely stone-faced; she'd gotten very good at that over the years, but it didn't fool anyone at the table.

Roadrunner looked at her, saw what was inside, and shook his head vigorously. 'No way. There's no way he could find us, not in a million years. We all made sure of that. This is just a simple case of a homicidal maniac glomming onto a provocative concept and taking it to the extreme. He's a game player and this is the ultimate game.'

'I hope so, buddy,' Harley said, and for a moment

they were all so quiet that the chime of incoming e-mail from Grace's office sounded like an explosion.

'Oh, God.' Grace closed her eyes.

Roadrunner got up without a word, went to the office, then came back several shades paler. 'There's a new e-mail,' he said in a shaky voice. 'I don't know if it's from the killer, but I think from the details he gave, it won't be hard to figure it out.'

25

When the alarm went off at seven A.M. Wednesday morning, Magozzi figured he'd had about two hours of sleep, if you wanted to call it that. Mostly he'd tossed around in a quasi dream state, thrashing his sheets into a tangled ball at his feet, and he wouldn't have rested that well if it hadn't been for the double Scotch he'd downed before bed.

But even with the combined anesthesia of single malt and exhaustion, his brain had stayed in overdrive, tormenting him with a deluge of recapitulated data, ideas, and macabre images of the dead that stuttered to life in horrific black-and-white dreamscapes. Grace MacBride kept making guest appearances in his mental theater. He never really saw her face, just sensed her presence on the fringe of his subconscious where she floated like an angry ghost.

He'd gone back to the paddle wheeler last night, after he'd left her house. When he and Gino had wrapped things up there, they'd headed south to the Mall of America, cruised the empty parking ramps for an hour, then went back to the office to work the rosters.

The way he figured it, they probably didn't have a single friend left in the whole department. They'd called over a hundred men well after midnight, putting things together, and then they'd called the chief, who'd certainly called the mayor and the governor and God knew how many others. There might have been a senior citizen somewhere in the suburbs whose phone *hadn't* rung last night, but Magozzi didn't think so.

He showered and dressed in a stuporous fog, then headed downstairs, where the thermometer outside the kitchen window read fifteen degrees. He looked at it twice just to make sure, then hung his suitcoat over a kitchen chair, tucked his tie between the buttons of his shirt, and started making the first big breakfast he'd had in months. At this temperature, he rationalized, granola would be suicide. What he needed was calories.

He put bacon in one skillet, a lethal mix of eggs and cream in another, and popped in two slices of toast.

Late nights and cold mornings always made him miss Heather. Well, not Heather, specifically – what he really missed was the idea of marriage. Someone to come home to, another warm body in the house making warm body noises, a sympathetic ear, the companionable silence of understanding.

'So get a dog,' she'd said on the night she'd slapped the summons in his hand, right after telling him about the absolutely amazing number of men she'd met naked during the past year.

He'd spent bitter months cursing himself for a fool, grieving for a marriage he'd never had, suffering mightily under that egregious insult to his heritage and his machismo – what self-respecting hot-blooded Italian could live with himself after being dumped by a supposedly cold-blooded Swede?

He'd tried to assign blame to Heather, but mostly accepted it all, and gradually became a caricature of himself: an angry, brooding Italian.

Family and friends worried, and in their individual distinctively unhelpful ways, tried to help. His mother told him it was what he got for not marrying a nice Italian girl; Gino said he'd always had doubts about the woman, she was a lawyer, for chrissakes; but surprisingly, it was Anant Rambachan who showed him how to let it go.

Six months ago they'd been crouched over the body of a young girl who had found more to love about heroin than life, when, apropos of nothing, Anant suddenly sat back on his heels and said, 'It was, I believe, a very risky venture, Detective; marrying a woman whose name is grass.'

It had taken Magozzi a minute to catch up, to realize he was talking about Heather, and mentally he cringed. The whole damn city knew he'd been cuckolded.

'She laid down.' The Indian medical examiner smiled white in his dark skin, long-fingered hands spread in a gesture as matter of fact as if Magozzi had ended a meal instead of a marriage. 'It is simply the nature of grass to lie down, is it not?'

Anant was a big believer in the nature of things, and probably placed an inordinate value on symbols, at least from a Judeo-Christian perspective, but something in what he said, or maybe the way he said it, just cut through all the crap.

Magozzi had taken a breath that felt like his first in a year, and from that moment on, everything had been different. The rest of the cops thought he'd gotten laid; his mother was certain he'd started going to Mass again. He'd considered telling her a Hindu had shown him the light, but he wasn't sure her heart could take it.

He watched the morning news shows try to scare the shit out of the city while he ate his breakfast. The murders weren't just big news; they were the only news.

How much intrepid reporters had managed to discover scared him. They knew about the game, they'd put all three murders together, and worst of all, they knew the profiles of the next two victims. Murder four, a female shopper at the Mall of America; murder five, an art teacher.

'Our sources tell us there are twenty murders in the Monkeewrench game,' one of the morning newscasters intoned. He was young, new, and looked like a Ken doll. Magozzi didn't know him. 'Which begs the question, are there seventeen more victims somewhere in this city, innocently going about their daily lives, unaware that they have been marked for death by a psychopathic killer?'

'Jesus Christ.' Magozzi hit the mute button and dove for the phone. It blurped an aborted ring just as he picked up the receiver.

'I've been ringing your cell for the last hour,' Gino said without preamble.

'We dropped it at the lab last night, remember?'

'Oh. Yeah. I forgot. Christ, I'm operating on about three brain cells here. You catch the news?'

'Just now. Channel Ten has the game up to victim five.'

'They all do. Papers, too. Looks like none of the players calling the tip lines got past the fifth murder.'

Magozzi stretched to reach a piece of bacon off his plate. 'You want to go to work or do you want to go shopping?'

‘Shopping?’

‘Megamall’s going to be empty.’

‘Very funny. What are you chewing?’

‘Animal fat. Bacon.’

Gino was silent for a moment. ‘Well, that clinches it. It’s the end of the world.’

It was nearly eight o’clock when Magozzi cruised past City Hall and almost decided to turn around and go right back home.

Satellite vans lined both sides of the street, and only half of them were local. He saw Duluth, Milwaukee, even Chicago, and a slew of low-end rental cars that meant freelancers and wire stringers were here in force.

A few reporters were doing stand-ups in front of the building, and the sidewalk was a mess of cables. They’d make the network news tonight for sure, and then the city council members would shit bricks at what the story would do to the Minneapolis convention trade.

He circled the block and parked in the ramp, where clerks and secretaries would have a hard time finding an empty space this day, because all the cowardly detectives had chosen to slink in a back door. Gino’s Volvo wagon was there; so was Langer’s brand-new Dodge Ram pickup; even Tommy Espinoza’s beloved ’41 Chevy was perilously crowded into door-ding territory.

Gino was waiting for him inside the door, still wearing his overcoat, sipping coffee from a mug that said *World’s Best Grandmother*. He’d missed a full square inch of whiskers on his left cheek with the razor, and little swollen pockets of purplish flesh rode high under his eyes.

'Jeez, it took you long enough. Come on.' He grabbed Magozzi by the elbow and started propelling him down the hall, past the elevator.

'We've got to get upstairs. Meeting starts in ten minutes.'

'I know, I know, we're just going to make a short stop first.'

'Where?' Magozzi asked.

'Secretarial pool.'

'We've got a secretarial pool?'

Gino pushed him through a doorway into a large office filled with computer stations. 'Don't call it that. They get really pissed, and you don't want to piss these girls off or they won't give you any coffee. And don't call them "girls," either.'

'There's nobody in here.'

'They're in the coffee room.'

'Can I call it the coffee room?'

Gino gave an exasperated snort. 'I hate it when you don't get enough sleep. You get punchy and weird.'

'I get weird, you get wired. How much coffee have you had anyway?'

'Not enough.' He led him toward a doorway on the back wall and poked his head in. 'Here he is, ladies, just like I promised. Detective Leo Magozzi, the primary on these murders.' He jerked Magozzi into the tiny room where half a dozen women of various shapes and ages smiled at him.

'Good morning, Detective Magozzi,' they chimed like a parochial grade-school class greeting a visiting priest.

'Good morning, ladies.' He forced a pleasant smile, wondering what the hell he was doing in there, trying to remember if you were allowed to call adult females 'ladies' anymore. The room was small, hot, and smelled like Starbucks, only better.

A tiny, fiftyish woman pushed a warm mug into his hand. 'Here you are, Detective Magozzi.' She smiled up at him. 'And you come right back whenever you want a refill. Detective Rolseth told us you boys have been up all night trying to solve these terrible murders, and we want you to know how much we appreciate all your hard work.'

'Uh, thank you.' Magozzi smiled uncertainly. Nobody'd ever thanked him for doing his job before, and it was a little embarrassing. Because he didn't know what else he was supposed to do, he took a sip from the mug. 'Oh my God.'

Gino was rocking back and forth on his heels, grinning. 'Is that incredible or what? They make it in that thing.' He jabbed a stubby finger toward an old-fashioned glass pot perking on the hot plate. 'I'm telling you, it's a lost art. Walked in this morning, followed my nose, and discovered treasure. Never would have known these ladies were down here if I hadn't been dodging that circus out front. Thank you very kindly, ladies.'

There was a round of 'thank *you*'s from the table of women as they left.

'Was that a kick or what?' Gino asked as they weaved around empty computer stations on their way out. Every desk held photos, green plants, knickknacks; pieces of home that workers with real lives couldn't leave behind. 'They think we're hot stuff. Not a bad start to a day that's going to go down the toilet in about three seconds.'

'What's a primary?' Magozzi asked him.

'They all watch that Brit cop show on PBS – you know, the female dick who bosses around all the guys who actually have real dicks? Over there they call the lead detective the primary.'

'We don't have "lead" detectives or primaries or whatever.'

'Hey, I was just trying to get you a cup of coffee. Me, I can get by on charm. Figured you needed a title.'

Chief Malcherson was waiting for them in the upstairs hallway, and if you wanted to know how bad things were, all you had to do was look at the man. Every strand of his thick white hair lay in its proper place, his pale blue shirt was rigor-mortis starched, his long face freshly shaven and composed. But his suitcoat was unbuttoned. This was a genuinely catastrophic event.

'Morning, Chief,' Magozzi and Gino said together.

'You two saw the papers, the TV?'

Both detectives nodded.

'The press ate me alive when I came in. Chewed me up, spit me out, then stomped on what was left.'

'And you look it, sir,' Magozzi said, eliciting a very slight smile from the chief, one of the few they would see for a long time.

'You actually ran the gauntlet at the front door?' Gino asked, amazed.

'Some of us have to come in the front door, Rolseth. Otherwise people might think that we don't have a handle on this case; that we don't have a suspect; that we don't have a clue who is doing these murders or how to protect our citizens; and that we're afraid to face the press.' He looked from one detective to the other. 'They want to know if we're going to close the Megamall, if we're going to close the schools, if we're going to put armed guards around every teacher in the city, and most of all, they want the victim profiles on the other murders in the game because they "have a responsibility to warn the public."'

He released a heavy sigh and shoved both hands in his trouser pockets, which was truly alarming. The suit was a wool blend work of art, and Magozzi would have bet a year's salary that those pockets had never felt the chief's hands before.

'Monkeewrench took that game off the net yesterday morning, right after they read about the cemetery murder,' Gino reminded him. 'Nobody – except the people working this case and the Monkeewrench geeks – has seen any of the murder scenarios past number seven. So that business about seventeen more vics marked for death is a load of sensationalistic crap.'

Malcherson said sarcastically, 'And I'm sure the public will be as relieved as we were to learn only four more of them will die, not seventeen.' He sighed and glanced down the hallway toward the task force room. 'We've got some decisions to make, and we've got to make them fast.'

'Like what?'

'Like do we shut down the Mall of America?'

'Jesus,' Gino muttered. 'Even if it wasn't a stupid idea, we don't have the authority to do that, do we?'

'According to the attorney general, we do. Imminent danger to the public, something like that. And incidentally, Rolseth, before you repeat your sentiments beyond this hallway, you should know that a lot of the people I've been talking to don't think it's "stupid" to close the mall to save a life. Including some of the people on the task force.'

Gino rolled his eyes. 'Damnit, it's not that simple. They're not thinking it through . . .'

Malcherson held up his hand to stop him. 'I know that, and you know that, but we're not going to convince anyone else by opening with the unequivocal statement that their idea is stupid.'

Gino sighed and nodded.

'What's the mall's position?' Magozzi asked.

There was no humor in Malcherson's smile. 'No one is going to touch this one. Not the mall management, not the mayor of Bloomington, or the governor, for that matter. It's our decision.'

Gino gave a disgusted snort. 'No one wants to take the heat for shutting it down, and no one wants to be left holding the bag if we don't shut it down and someone gets hit out there.'

'Exactly.'

'So we get the backlash. It's a no-win situation, and once again the cops get to be the bad guys. Well, this just sucks.'

Malcherson glanced at his watch. 'We've got exactly one hour to decide. We keep it open, I've got commitments from the Highway Patrol and almost every sheriff's department in the state to help out with extra officers.'

'For how long?' Magozzi asked.

'As long as they can.'

'Not long then.'

'Probably not.' He blew out a long exhale and looked down at the floor. 'Plus I've got two suits in my office.'

'Shit,' Gino said.

'Right now it's an offer. Manpower if we need it, which we might, so we'd better think carefully before we decline; and profiling help.'

'Profiling?' Magozzi said. 'That's a crock. There is no profiling this guy. He's not a sexual predator, not sticking to a victim type, hell, they'd be hard-pressed to prove serial with no forensics beyond the gun caliber. The FBI's got nothing to offer here. They just want in.'

'If it's Internet-related, it's Federal, and they *are* in. Technically, of course, we have no hard evidence of the Internet connection, just conjecture; so for the moment they're standing down. But politically, having them on board might not be such a bad idea. No harm in spreading the blame around.'

Magozzi bit down on the impulse to say that this case was about catching a killer, not about spreading blame, but in his position, the chief had to juggle both of those balls. 'Can we hold off? See what shakes out in the meeting?'

Malcherson nodded. 'That's what I told them.'

Gino's cell phone chirped from deep in his overcoat pocket. 'Yeah, Rolseth here.' He listened, brows elevated slightly. 'Got it.' He folded up the phone and tucked it back in his pocket. 'The Monkeewrench partners just walked in the front door. All five of them together.'

Magozzi frowned. ‘You told them to come in at ten, right?’

‘That’s right. Eager beavers.’

Magozzi shrugged. ‘Let ’em wait.’

26

With most of the department in the task force meeting, Gloria had the homicide room to herself, unless you counted Roger Delaney, which she didn't. He was a short, cocky son of a bitch with slicked-back hair, bad teeth, and a penchant for butt-slapping that had nearly gotten him killed the one and only time he'd laid a hand on her fine black ass. He was two-fingering a keyboard in a back corner while Gloria manned the front desk and the phones.

She'd already had over a dozen calls about the Monkeewrench murders. Would-be witnesses who saw the killer in a dream, or knew for a fact their brother-in-law or boss or pizza delivery boy had done it. She marked them all dutifully in a log, as if they had merit, because sometimes psychos kooky enough to kill were kooky enough to call the cops and talk about it.

Between phone calls it was so quiet she could hear the hesitant clicks of Roger's keyboard and the sporadic trickle of water passing through a coffeemaker that hadn't been cleaned in months.

Normally the homicide room was buzzing with activity, detectives busy with cold cases in the lulls between new ones, working narco or sex crimes or helping out the gang detail when people on the street had the good sense to stop killing each other for a time, and the silence made her irritable. So did the desk sergeant keeping all the media people corralled downstairs on a day when she'd dressed for television, wrapping her big beautiful black body in a combination kaftan/sari of browns and oranges that looked like Africa even if she'd bought it at Kmart. She'd wrapped her wild black hair in a matching scarf, bought ten new nails with half-moons twinkling gold in mahogany enamel, and knew the TV people would be all over her because the fools always jumped all over what they thought was ethnic, even though they didn't have a clue. But they had to see her first.

She was drumming her long nails on the desktop, trying to think of an excuse to sashay down to the press room, when she heard voices in the hall and perked up a little. At this point she was so desperate for a diversion she didn't care if it was a scruffy walk-in with a hot tip on the JFK assassination.

The first one through the door was white and slender and strung so tight she might have asked for a urine sample if the woman hadn't looked at her straight on, then nodded with respect. 'Good morning. I'm Grace MacBride. We're here to see Detectives Magozzi and Rolseth.'

'I'm sorry, the detectives are in a meeting right now . . .' The words died in her throat as the rest of them filed in. Her sharp brown eyes brushed over a guy in one-piece bright yellow Lycra so tall and skinny you could use him as a pole for vaulting; a ponytailed, bearded linebacker of a man in black leather; a pale guy in a to-die-for suit who looked like he was CEO of something; and then a wonderfully, beautifully fat woman with flashing eyes who sashayed better than

Gloria on her best days, head to toe in Gloria's favorite color, orange. My oh my. A white woman with fashion flair.

'We're the owners of Monkeewrench.' Grace MacBride recaptured Gloria's attention. 'We were asked to come in this morning.'

Gloria gave the circus troupe a hasty, skeptical once-over, wondering what on earth would bring such a diverse group together. 'That's right. I've got you down, but not until ten. You're almost two hours early. You can have a seat over there –'

'No. There's no time.' MacBride's response was so fast and sharp it put Gloria off for a minute.

'Excuse me?'

'We need to see them right now. Please call them.'

Oh, now, this was intolerable. The words had been civil enough, but they'd been delivered like an order, and Gloria didn't take orders very well, especially not from some skinny white broad with an attitude. She stood up and leaned stiff-armed on her desk, using her great size as intimidation.

'Listen, honey, if you think I am going to walk into a meeting of armed men and women and tell them sorry, they have to break it up now because Ms Grace MacBride wants to see them, you've got another think coming. You may rule the little world in that Monkeewrench office of yours, but in this one, you operate at the pleasure of the detectives, not the other way around, so you might as well take a seat, because you're going to have a very long wait.'

Grace MacBride just smiled at her.

*

There was a big tag board on wheels positioned in the center front of the task force room today, holding morgue photos of the three victims, crime-scene photos, and blowups of the staged photos from the game. The desk was angled off to the side.

Everyone was seated when Magozzi, Gino, and the chief walked in, and they were all looking at the pictures.

It was a funny thing, Magozzi thought. Most people looked at morgue photos and jerked their eyes away just as fast as they could. Homicide cops – good homicide cops – spent a lot of time staring at the pictures of dead victims, absorbing details surviving family members never saw, unwittingly forming some kind of bond with people they'd never known in life, making a kind of unspoken promise.

In one way it was a little morbid, he supposed, and in another, it was almost tender. Anyone who said you had to shut off your emotions to be a homicide cop had it exactly backward.

'Okay, listen up, everyone.' Magozzi piled a thick stack of stapled handouts on the table in the front of the task force room and took a seat on the edge of the desk. 'Fresh off the copier. We may have caught a break today, thanks to Dr Rambachan, who stayed up all night working on the paddle wheeler vic. Speaking of which, I'd like to thank everyone for the extra hours they've been putting in. I'll give you a quick briefing, but if you'd like some light reading later, the actual autopsy report is included in your handout.'

There were a few chuckles and a couple sleepy groans as the task force that still wasn't officially a task force lined up like zombies to retrieve the new material. Most of them had pulled a double yesterday, and Magozzi wondered if the son of a bitch who was responsible was suffering similarly or if his tweaked-out brain chemicals were keeping him wired.

He took the last swallow from the mug of great coffee the women downstairs had given him and continued. 'Victim number three is Wilbur Daniels.'

'His name was Wilbur?' Johnny McLaren asked. He and Patrol Sergeant Freedman were sitting together this morning, bonded by what they surely considered their personal failure on the paddleboat last night. They both looked exhausted and defeated.

Magozzi looked from one to the other, then threw them a bone. 'You did good work on the boat last night.'

'Right,' Freedman rumbled in a sarcastic basso-profundo. 'The operation was a success but the patient died.'

'He was dead a long time before you got there,' Magozzi reminded him, deciding that if they needed any more head-patting than that, they were going to have to go to the department shrink. Right now he just didn't have the time. 'Wilbur Daniels, forty-two years old, ID'd through military prints from a stint in the army back in the eighties. Never been married and we're still trying to find next of kin. He is . . . was . . . employed as a marketing rep for Devon Office Supplies on Washington for six years and we have his boss on ice downstairs waiting to be interviewed. You up for it, Louise?'

'You bet.'

'Note that Dr Rambachan found semen in his underwear and has determined that Wilbur Daniels ejaculated very near the time of his death. He also bit his own hand, presumably out of passion, so there was obviously a sexual element involved. Whether or not it has anything to do with the killer, we don't know yet.'

'So maybe he was just wanking in the bathroom and got a little surprise in the form of a bullet to the head,' Louise offered.

'Possible. Or maybe the killer brought him there under the auspices of a little afternoon delight.'

'So if our doer's a man, that makes Daniels a fag,' Louise stated frankly.

'Not very PC, Louise,' Gino said.

She tossed her head indignantly. 'Hey, it's okay for me to say "fag."' She turned her attention back to Magozzi. 'So if he was gay, what are you thinking? Maybe a series of hate crimes?'

'Not at this point,' Magozzi said. 'We don't have any info on the girl on the angel yet, but there's absolutely no indication that the jogger was a homosexual. But that Wilbur Daniels might have been is a possibility to keep in mind when we retrace his steps before he set foot on that paddle wheeler. And that takes us to page three of the autopsy report. Stomach contents.'

'Oh, God, I haven't even had breakfast yet,' Detective Peterson groaned. He was a recent transfer from St Paul, whip-thin with a pallor to his skin that made Magozzi think meat hadn't passed his lips in several years.

'Okay, there was beer and eight mostly undigested mini corn dogs in the vic's stomach. The very sort of mini corn dogs they serve at Steamboat Parker's Grill down by the river and nowhere else in the general vicinity. He was there less than an hour before he was shot on the boat. McLaren, you get down there with his photo as soon as they open. Maybe somebody remembers him, or better yet, maybe he was with someone, and if so, then chances are pretty good that's our killer and we can have a sketch worked up for the media.'

Aaron Langer, fresh from outside in a black topcoat and leather gloves, sporting violet circles under his eyes, strode into the conference room waving a sheet of paper. 'Sorry I'm late. We just got an ID on the girl in the cemetery. Maybe something we can work with.'

'Terrific. Tell us what you've got.'

Langer peeled off his gloves, assumed his lectern demeanor, and addressed the room. 'Missing Persons got a call from the Mounties last night. A Toronto couple had reported their eighteen-year-old daughter missing after she took a Greyhound to Denver via Minneapolis. The bus stopped at the downtown terminal two nights ago, with a layover.'

'The night of the cemetery murder,' Magozzi said.

'Right. Her name was Alena Vershovsky. She and her parents emigrated from Kiev five years ago. Her parents are also both computer programmers, which might mean nothing – half the Russian immigrants are computer programmers. But something to bear in mind. Anyhow, a family friend in Denver met her bus yesterday, but she wasn't on it. We just confirmed a match on the dental records. I've got two guys on their way down to the terminal now, and we can all pray somebody can give us a visual on this piece of shit.'

There was a long silence. Nobody had ever heard Langer curse before.

'Any chance she was a homosexual?'

'Doesn't seem likely. Apparently she had a pretty active dating life. But who knows? Anybody can swing both ways. Why?'

'It's a possibility with the guy on the paddle wheeler. We were hoping for a common thread.'

Langer shrugged. 'Nothing pops so far.'

'Okay, let's leave it alone for now. So we'll have people canvassing the bus terminal and Steamboat Parker's, looking for someone who was in both places, and we've got a team still working the registration list of game-players . . .'

'We're never going to get anything out of that list,' Louise Washington complained. 'I worked an extra shift on that thing last night and only cleared five players.'

Magozzi nodded grimly. 'I know it's slow, but we've got to keep working it. Freedman? How are they doing on the door-to-doors?'

'During the day? Slow as crippled snails. Most of the people who signed on to the game with legitimate addresses apparently have legitimate jobs, because nobody's home. We're going to be knocking on a lot of doors after dark. Plus you took a lot of my people for the mall.'

'I know. Couldn't be helped.'

'Is our presence on the street compromised?' Chief Malcherson asked Freedman.

'It's thin, sir.'

'How thin?'

'I wouldn't want it to get any thinner.'

Magozzi nodded. 'Okay. We're getting some highway patrol and county people to help out. You put them where you need to fill the holes. Gino, you want to lay out the mall?'

'Yeah.' Gino pushed away from the wall by the door and managed to stand semi-upright. 'Murder number four in the game, folks, staged at the Mall of America.'

Everyone started flipping through their files, looking for the fourth murder scenario.

'In the parking ramps, right?' Louise Washington asked.

'Right. And since this dirtbag's been doing one every twenty-four, we gotta figure it goes down today. In the ramps, in a car, no specific make or model. We were a day late and a dollar short on the riverboat, and we don't want to make that mistake again, so Magozzi and I scoped the place last night, put together some shift rosters, and had people in place by four A.M. We've got two officers on every ramp level, and mall management called in all their security, which gives us another set of eyes on each deck. They also doubled up monitors on the closed-circuit cameras.'

'So it's covered,' Sergeant Freedman said.

Gino snorted softly. 'Not even close. They've got acres of ramp out there on four to five different levels and space for thousands of cars. We could pull everyone on the force and there's still no way in hell we've got enough people to monitor a space that big as closely as we should.'

'You see the newscasts this morning?' Louise asked. 'Everyone in the city knows the next target is a shopper at that mall. No one's going to go there today.'

'From your lips to God's ear,' Gino said. 'But I don't think it's going to happen. You know the deal. Nobody thinks they're going to be the victim. It's always someone else. They'll listen to the news and they'll take precautions – careful to look in the backseat before they get in the car, maybe go with a friend instead of alone – but the news is also covering our presence out there, remember, which is going to make a lot of people feel safer than they should, and they will go. They get over a hundred thousand people a day out there, and even if half of them decide to stay home, that still leaves fifty thousand for the killer to pick from.'

There was silence in the room for a moment, then Sergeant Freedman repeated his sentiments from yesterday, when he was talking about the paddle wheeler. 'Shut it down.'

'For Christ's sake, yes,' Johnny McLaren agreed quickly. 'It's a no-brainer, isn't it? Shut the place down, no shoppers, no shoppers get killed. What's the downside?'

Gino shook his head. 'I'll tell you the downside. What are you going to do? Shut it down indefinitely? Which first of all is illegal, and second of all you're going to throw the whole state economy into a tailspin, and third of all, what's to keep the guy from just waiting till we open it up again?'

'So just shut it down until we catch this guy,' Freedman suggested.

Magozzi said quietly, 'As of right now, the only shot

we've got at catching this guy is staking out the places we can that we know he's going to hit. We close the mall, we lose the chance.'

'And what if we miss him?' McLaren was insistent. 'You said yourselves there's no way we can cover the ramps completely. So what if he slips past us? What if someone else dies because we didn't close the goddamned mall?!'

'What if we shut it down for just a couple of days?' Langer asked. 'We could divert all the manpower to the door-to-doors on the registration list, catch him that way, or maybe we'll get lucky at Steamboat Parker's or the terminal. Maybe someone saw him –'

'And maybe not,' Magozzi said. 'And maybe he's not on that registration list. Maybe he got into that game through a back door even the Monkeewrench people can't find. Then what?'

Chief Malcherson stood up so suddenly he almost knocked over his chair. 'Is that possible?'

Magozzi shrugged. 'Anything's possible. The geeks at Monkeewrench say no, there's no way anybody could hack into their site, but that's what the people at the CIA said before that thirteen-year-old hacker downloaded their eyes-only files, remember?'

All the color seemed to drain from Malcherson's ruddy face. 'You said no player got past murder seven,' he almost whispered.

'If he came in a back door, he's got them all.'

'Dear God.' Malcherson sank back down into his chair.

'At least this hit's in a specific location,' Gino interjected. 'From now on, it just gets worse. The next one's a teacher in a classroom. You know how many teachers there are in the Cities alone? So what do we do? Stake out all the schools, a cop in each one? We don't have enough cops in the whole goddamned country to cover that kind of ground. And let me tell you that if you shut down the Mall of America to save a shopper, you damn well better shut down every school in the state to save a teacher, not to mention sparing little Johnny Whoever the trauma of seeing his teacher's brain get splattered all over the blackboard . . .'

'Gino . . .' Magozzi tried to interrupt, but Gino was rolling, losing it, his voice climbing the pitch and volume ladder, his fists clenched, his face flushed.

'. . . so what you've got is some *fucking* psycho paralyzing thc whole city, because after the teacher you've got the ER tech, and what are you gonna do then? Stop the ambulances? You realize what would happen if *they* all stayed home . . . ?'

A sharp rap on the door behind him made Gino jump, and Magozzi figured if he didn't have a heart attack right then, he probably never would. He saw Gloria's dark face peering through the glass to make sure it was clear before she opened the door and stepped inside. Gino looked like he was going to kill her.

'Those Monkeewrench people are downstairs,' she said, 'and they are making a serious fuss.'

Gino snapped at her. 'Then sit on 'em Gloria. We're busy in here.'

'Okay, but I think you should know the queen bee –'

'MacBride?'

'Yeah, her. The little black-haired whippet. Anyway, she's standing right outside the press room. Said she'd give you five minutes before she walks in there and starts talking.'

'About what?' Gino demanded.

Gloria lifted one big shoulder, shifting the yards and yards of orange and brown material that covered her body in a way that was somehow indecent. 'About how the Keystone cops – and I'm quoting here, you understand; that's not me talkin', that's her – are sittin' on their asses upstairs ignoring people downstairs who have been contacted by the killer.'

Magozzi caught his breath. So did everyone else. '*What?*'

'That's what she said, and that's all she said. Won't talk to me. Just you two.'

'Get them up here,' Gino growled.

'You got it. Leo? Gino? I need a personal word in the hall.' She swished out the door in a swirl of material.

'Smoke 'em if you got 'em,' Magozzi said, hopping off the desk, catching Chief Malcherson's alarmed expression, as if someone would actually have the nerve to light up in a government building.

He and Gino followed Gloria out to the hall, closing the door behind them.

'You want to tell me whose prints were on this, Leo?' She dug in the voluminous folds of her dress and handed over Magozzi's cell phone.

'No.'

'Well, whatever rock you turned over sure woke up the dragon. We got a hit on the prints, but the FBI's got a cover on it. No name, no nothin'. Nancy over in

Latents tried to shine up to 'em, and all they'd give her was that they were flagged, and that they were on an open file. But here's the interesting part. You know those suits waiting in the chief's office? About three milliseconds after I got the call, they were slithering all over my desk real casual-like, saying, Gee, you know those prints Detective Magozzi ran through AFIS last night? Well, somehow we lost the name on the ten-card, can you give it to us again?' She paused for an eloquent snort of disgust. 'Like I was going to fall for that one, even if I knew anything. Which I don't,' she added pointedly. Gloria didn't like to be out of the loop.

Magozzi looked at Gino. 'What do you think?'

'Curiouser and curiouser.'

'Okay, Gloria. I'll tell you what you do. Tell them we need to see that file, to have it faxed over here, and we'll be down to take a look at it when we're finished up here.'

'They're not going to do that. They've got a cover on that file, I told you.'

'I know. Tell 'em anyway.'

'And when they refuse?'

'Fuck 'em,' Gino said.

Gloria scowled at him. 'You fuck 'em. I've got standards.' She turned and clopped away down the hall.

Langer and Peterson were getting ready to leave when Gino and Magozzi reentered the room.

'We're on mall relief in an hour,' Langer explained.

'Sit tight for a minute,' Magozzi said. 'I want everybody's take on these Monkeewrench people.'

'Good,' Langer took a seat happily. 'I want to see

the cop-hater who carries all the time. MacBride, right?'

'Right.'

'Oh, this should be good.' Louise walked up to the coffeemaker and grabbed a cup. 'Shoot-out in the task force room.'

'I've got a uniform at the door. No one gets past one of my men with a weapon.' Freedman glowered at her as she passed his chair.

She smiled and patted his huge head. 'I know that, honey. Just kidding.'

'Did everyone see that?' Freedman looked around at the others. 'She called me honey and she patted my head. That's sexual harassment.'

'In your dreams, baby.'

'Now she called me baby. I don't have to take this . . .'

Magozzi looked on from the front of the room, feeling a little like a grade-school teacher watching a class of miscreants spin out of control, and that was all right. In this job, jumping from murder to mischief in the space of a second was par for the course. Maybe essential.

Gino stepped over to stand beside him, smiling as he watched Louise shaking a donut over Freedman's head, dusting him with white powder. 'Keystone cops,' he said.

'Yep.'

'You gonna let MacBride and her crew walk in and see this?'

Magozzi shrugged. 'You do the time, might as well do the crime.'

'Magozzi?' Chief Malcherson was standing at the

board of victim photos. 'Just out of curiosity, who was the killer in the game?'

Magozzi got busy adjusting his tie. 'The chief of police, sir.'

27

When the Monkeewrench entourage filed into the room, the ambient temperature seemed to drop about ten degrees. Magozzi wasn't sure if the human iceberg leading the pack was responsible or if it was the collective hostility of a roomful of defensive cops. If it was the latter, MacBride seemed utterly oblivious to the chilly reception.

She was wearing the same canvas duster and high English riding boots she'd worn at the Monkeewrench loft the day before. Everything black, right down to the jeans and T-shirt beneath. He'd already decided that for this woman it wasn't a fashion statement, more like a uniform that served a function he hadn't completely figured out yet. He put the jeans and T-shirt off to comfort, and the duster to hide the gun, but the boots were a mystery. They were that thick, rigid leather that never yields, made for riding, not walking, and you had to think they were hot and uncomfortable as hell.

The duster flapped open as she walked, exposing the empty leather holster, and most of the eyes in the room went to that. Nothing made cops more nervous than armed civilians.

Her hair swung as she turned to face the room, as dark and loose as her eyes were cool and steady, and while the cop in Magozzi bristled at the arrogance of her demeanor, the artist in him was struck again by that kind of pure physical beauty that makes you take a quick mental step backward, simply because you don't see it very often.

None of which mitigated her irritating bitchiness one iota.

He gave her a curt nod, which she returned in kind, along with a searing glance that seemed to be a challenge of some sort. Just what she was challenging, he had no idea. His competency? His suit? His existence on the planet? Maybe all of the above. But he had no interest in petty brinksmanship right now; he only cared about what she had to say.

Magozzi watched the faces of his detectives shift from angry to curious as the bizarre assemblage gathered in a cluster close to the door. Grace MacBride in her fox-hunter/gunslinger garb; Roadrunner towering in bright yellow Lycra, looking disturbingly like a pencil; the husky, leather-clad Harley Davidson with his ponytail and beard; fat Annie Belinsky in an impossibly orange getup, exuding sensuality no *Playboy* centerfold had ever come close to; and Mitch Cross, whose conservative appearance looked positively eccentric next to the others. Magozzi still couldn't quite figure him into the picture. He stood off to one side, looking confused, displaced, and on the verge of meltdown.

Cross and Chief Malcherson had a lot in common, he realized – right down to the expensive suits and the high blood pressure. Maybe the two of them could get together later for beers and Xanax.

Gino stared at the group with the dull disbelief of a World War II vet suddenly transported to Woodstock, then moved back along the wall, distancing himself.

Magozzi didn't waste any time with polite preambles or introductions. 'Ms MacBride, you have our curiosity and attention.'

Grace didn't waste time with niceties, either. She took a step forward and delivered her information abruptly, with all the emotion of one of her computers spitting out data. 'I received an e-mail last night with a memo line that read, "From the Killer."'

There were a few soft snickers from the detectives. MacBride waited them out. 'The message itself was much more creative, a clever modification of the game's opening graphics screen.' She looked at Magozzi. 'Has everyone seen what the opening graphics page is supposed to look like?'

Magozzi nodded. 'Part of their handouts. "Want to play a game?," right?'

'Right.' She returned her attention to the room. 'The sender manipulated those graphics so instead it said, "You're not playing."'

Magozzi felt a little chill creep up his spine. Patrol Sergeant Freedman dispelled it almost immediately with an impatient bass rumble.

'You're probably going to get a million of those, now that the media's got the Monkeewrench connection. Somebody's just yanking your chain.'

Grace nodded at the big black cop. 'That's what we thought last night. But another message came this morning.' She took a deep breath and exhaled silently. Magozzi supposed that was the Grace MacBride version of an attack of nerves. 'This one said, "Wilbur bit his hand. No accounting for taste. Are you ready to play yet?"'

No one in the room moved. No one even blinked.

Grace looked from face to face. 'Well? Was that his name? The victim on the paddle wheeler?'

Gino pushed away from the wall. 'Yeah, that was his name. And it wasn't released to the press. Neither was the bite mark. Which is real interesting. Looks like you people have information only the shooter would know.'

Grace nodded woodenly. 'Then there's no doubt. The e-mails are from the killer.'

'Or one of you is the killer,' Gino was quick to suggest. 'Sending yourselves e-mails, coming to play with the stupid cops . . . one scenario's as good as the other.'

A soft, disgruntled murmuring rose from the Monkeewrench crew. Grace shot them a quick glance and they went silent.

'You have copies of the e-mails?' Magozzi asked.

She shook her head. 'They were programmed to erase after they were opened.'

'How convenient,' said Gino. 'No way to trace them. No way to prove you *didn't* send them to yourself.'

Grace gave him a long, steady look, but there was an angry quaver in her voice. 'You're a typical cop, Detective Rolseth, with a typical cop's tunnel vision.'

Gino emitted a long-suffering sigh and looked at the ceiling.

'You've already decided that one of us is guilty, and you just can't get past that. But you'd better. Because if you're wrong, and you'd better believe that you are, while you're wasting your resources investigating us, someone out there is just going to keep killing.'

Gino started to open his mouth, but Chief Malcherson raised one finger to keep him silent. 'I'm Chief Malcherson, Ms MacBride, and I can assure you that this is a broad investigation. We're not focusing on any particular suspects at this point.'

This time the snickers came from the Monkeewrench crew, who knew better.

'Let's just go with this for a minute,' said Magozzi. 'So the killer's contacting you, egging you on. He wants you to play the game. What the hell does that mean?'

Grace shrugged. 'We don't know. We're guessing he wants us to try to find him. Hiding is no fun unless someone is looking for you. So that's what we've been doing. The e-mails themselves may have disappeared, but not the log. We spent all night tracing the first one. And bear in mind that although we did trace it to a specific location, we believe this location is false. The sender has a relatively high level of computer proficiency and we all agree that he literally drew us a cyber map that routed us there, when in all likelihood, it was actually sent from somewhere very nearby.'

Tommy Espinoza stood and introduced himself then, and asked a series of technical questions that might as well have been in Greek, as far as Magozzi was concerned. MacBride and her clan were duly impressed with Tommy's knowledge and after five minutes of Q & A, they were deep in the midst of techno-geek bonding.

It was Gino who finally interrupted, making no attempt to keep the irritation out of his voice. 'Look, I'm just tickled pink you're all hitting it off, but can you postpone your little lovefest until you tell the rest of us where the hell that e-mail supposedly came from?'

Magozzi nodded. 'Tommy, after we wrap up here, you can take them to an interview room and get a full briefing on the computer angle.'

Tommy gave Magozzi a chagrined smile. 'Sorry, Leo, Gino.'

'It came from a private Catholic school in upstate New York,' Grace said.

'Saint Peter's School of the Holy Cross, Cardiff, New York,' Roadrunner put in.

The room was silent.

'We were hoping that the location would have some significance to you and the investigation, because it certainly has no significance to any of us.' Grace reached deep into the pocket of her duster, pulled out a folded slip of white notebook paper, and passed it to Magozzi. 'Here's the school's phone number. You won't find him there, but it might be a clue, intentional or otherwise.'

Magozzi unfolded the paper and stared at the precise, draftsman-quality script that could only belong to Grace MacBride. 'We'll check it out.'

'You know,' Louise offered, 'the first vic was a seminary student. Maybe he went there.'

'Maybe,' Magozzi said. 'Or maybe we can match a name with someone from the registration list.' It was such a long shot he almost laughed out loud, but he figured that would be bad for morale. Or whatever was left of it. Things were just never that easy.

'If he continues to make contact,' Grace went on, 'the chances of tracing him back to his real location improve. The mistake most hackers make is the arrogant belief that nobody plays the game better, that there isn't a chance they'll get caught. So they keep hacking into the same sites longer than they should, tempting fate, leaving little cyber footprints, and eventually someone finds them and follows them. It doesn't matter how good you are. There's always, always somebody better.' She looked at Roadrunner, who nodded, and then at Tommy, who smiled at her.

It was the same with serial killers, Magozzi thought. They often started to feel invincible when they literally got away with murder. They got arrogant, maybe a little bored, so they upped the stakes, left more clues. A lot of serial homicides were solved for that very reason.

Grace sighed. 'You will have our full cooperation on this, of course.' The offer was genuine, but the tone in which she said it made it clear that her cooperation was a reluctant consortium with the enemy. 'We'll interface with Detective Espinoza on the technical aspects, and until we receive a new message, we'll continue to attempt to trace back to the current message's true origin.'

'And you'll keep us informed of any new messages you receive,' Gino said. It was a command, not a question.

'Absolutely.'

'You get an e-mail at four A.M., I want a call by four-oh-one. Can we route your e-mail to Tommy so he has instantaneous access to any message you might receive?'

Grace nodded at Tommy. 'We'll work something out. We'll set up an on-line link. I'll give you my password.'

'Wait a minute,' Magozzi interrupted. '*Your* password? Are you saying these e-mails were sent to you, personally?'

Grace MacBride hesitated only a fraction of a second. 'Yes.'

'Not the company.'

'Generally, to the company. Specifically directed to my mailbox.'

Louise Washington sucked air in through her teeth. 'Whoa. You have any enemies, Ms MacBride?'

'Outside of this room? No, I don't think so.'

Her crew smiled at that, even Mitch Cross. So did a few of the detectives.

Chief Malcherson gave her one of his political nice smiles. 'You have no enemies in this room, Ms MacBride. No enemies in this department. If our questioning seems a bit curt, it's only because we're under a great deal of pressure with this case. I'm sure you understand.'

'I understand perfectly. Yesterday the police were told that a murder was going to take place on a paddleboat. It wasn't a very large area to cover, and in spite of that, you were unable to either trap the killer or save the life of an innocent man. I imagine that kind of abysmal failure brings a great deal of pressure to bear on your department.'

Now she had enemies in the room, Magozzi thought. For a moment everyone was silent; every pair of eyes riveted hatefully on Grace MacBride. Gino, predictably, was the one to fire an answering shot.

'Yeah, well, while you're passing out black marks, you just might want to lay a couple on yourselves. If we're still pretending that one of you isn't the killer, then there's somebody else out there following this piece-of-crap game you psychos dreamed up like a goddamned blueprint, and I don't care how you try to justify it so you can sleep at night, the fact is that we've cleaned up three bodies in two days that would not have been there if it weren't for you people.'

'Not "you people," Detective Rolseth,' Grace replied quietly. 'Me. The game was my idea.'

If there was remorse in there, Magozzi didn't hear it. But there was something almost plaintive in what she said next.

'Did you close the Mall of America?' Her eyes darted from face to face, but no one answered. She looked at Chief Malcherson. 'You have to close it. You have to.'

A lot of the detectives shifted in their seats, maybe a little uncomfortable to find themselves on the same side as the professed cop-hater.

'That wasn't a viable option,' the chief said, and it was clear that he was uncomfortable, too.

'You did it before,' Grace pressed him. 'When you thought that escaped prisoner went into the mall, you evacuated everyone, shut it down in a matter of minutes.'

Chief Malcherson sighed. 'We didn't *think* he went into the mall. The police in pursuit *saw* him enter the ramps. He posed an obvious and immediate threat. This is a very different situation.'

Langer stood up abruptly. 'Speaking of the mall . . .'

Magozzi blessed him silently and jerked a thumb toward the door. 'Right. You and Peterson, go. McLaren, you've got Steamboat Parker's. Louise, when you finish with Daniels's boss, check in with the team canvassing the bus station. The rest of you are on the registration list. Check in with Freedman; he'll be making the street assignments.'

'Detective?' Roadrunner took one gangly step forward and fluttered a sheaf of papers. 'We cleaned up the registration list a little. Thought it might help.'

Magozzi looked at Grace, who returned his gaze coldly. Perfect, he thought. I sneak around stealing her fingerprints, and she gives me the help I ask for. 'This is Roadrunner, everyone. What do you mean, you cleaned it up?'

'Well . . . you know . . .' His bony shoulders twitched in a nervous shrug. 'We just made sure there was a legitimate address for everyone who signed on.'

'*Everyone?*' Gino asked. 'All five hundred eighty-some?'

'Well . . . yeah . . .' And now all Roadrunner's body parts started moving at once. His eyes shifted from side to side, the corners of his mouth tightened in a guilty smile, his head bobbed, and his shoulders kept going up and down. Pinocchio manned by a mad puppeteer. 'We had a lot of orders from people who signed on. And I mean a lot. Almost four hundred. We cross-checked the mailing addresses against their credit card records, and cross-checked those addresses against . . . um . . . other sources . . .'

Magozzi suppressed a smile, wondering how many government databases had been violated last night, not caring at all. 'What about all the bogus names and addresses? Claude Balls, that type of thing?'

'We found them all,' Grace MacBride said impatiently. 'There were no complicated trails, nothing to indicate that anyone on that list was making a serious effort to hide their identity. Some of them were probably kids having a little fun; a lot were probably ordinary people trying to preserve their privacy and stay off mailing lists; but not one of the names on that list demonstrated anything close to the kind of computer skills we ran up against tracing those e-mails. We don't think the killer is on that list, but if you insist on checking them out, you now have a name and a legitimate address for every single one of them.'

Magozzi took the papers from Roadrunner and stared down at them. 'Good. That'll help. But if he isn't on here . . .'

'Then he got into the site through a back door.' She finished his thought. 'And that means he has the whole game.'

Chief Malcherson just closed his eyes.

Ten minutes later, Magozzi was at his desk on hold with St Peter's, suffering through a grating, tinny version of an organ fugue.

Gino walked up with two large white deli bags that smelled like heaven. He plopped a jumbo roast beef sandwich and a large coffee down in front of him. 'You look pissed, Leo.'

'Some nun put me on hold. It's a little early for lunch, isn't it?'

Gino glanced at his watch. 'Hell, no. It's nine-thirty already.' He settled in at his own desk with a triple-decker turkey club.

Magozzi put the phone on speaker and the music

leaked out in all its low-fidelity glory. Gino stared at the phone in disbelief. 'God, that should be illegal.'

'Everybody sells out to Muzak eventually. Even Bach. Any word from the mall?'

'All's quiet on the western front,' Gino mumbled through a mouthful.

The organ music stopped abruptly and a frail, elderly female voice answered. 'Hello?'

Magozzi snatched the receiver and introduced himself to the Mother Superior of St Peter's.

After five minutes, Magozzi was fully satisfied that St Peter's was a dead end. Yes, the school had computers, no, the students didn't have unsupervised access to them, yes some students had their own computers, but when he mentioned that he was investigating a multiple homicide case in Minneapolis, she just laughed.

'You won't find your suspect here, Detective. We stopped taking older children years ago – our oldest class is the fifth grade.'

And of course all the St Peter's employees, past and present, were either nuns or priests, none of whom were a good fit for the profile of a traveling homicidal maniac. But she was cooperative, patient, and sweet as could be, although Magozzi harbored a deeply ingrained mistrust of sweet old Mother Superiors from his own childhood experiences. He just knew there was a big wooden ruler lurking in the black folds of her habit.

By the end of the conversation, he'd apparently charmed her enough to take pity on him. With a heartfelt 'God bless you,' she passed him on to Sister Mary Margaret in records.

When he finally finished with Sister Mary Margaret,

Gino had already lain waste to most of his sandwich and half a piece of chocolate pie. 'So what's the news from New York?'

'Not much. Probably dead in the water, although their record keeper is a computer fanatic and has every single scrap of data from the past thirty years computerized and stored on-line.'

'Suspect?'

'Highly unlikely. She's a sixty-year-old nun in a wheelchair.'

'So what's this "sexy voice" bullshit I overheard? I know you've been single for a while, but even you wouldn't stoop to seducing an elderly, disabled nun.'

Magozzi smiled. 'She sounded like Lauren Bacall and I told her so. Then she gave me the password so we can access all their data.'

'Great. So what do we do now, print out a list of every student who was ever enrolled and see if we get a match from the registration list, or what?'

'I guess. For all the good it will do. How's Tommy doing with the Monkeewrench bunch?'

'They're all jammed into that fast-food wastebasket he calls an office, busier than a bunch of psycho bees. Poked my head in a couple times, got sick of hearing him say, "Gee, man, that's so cool." Friggin' fawning turncoat, is what he is. You still want to interview 'em?'

'Oh yeah.' Magozzi unwrapped his sandwich and smeared horseradish from a little plastic packet on the obscenely large pile of meat. So much for the diet. He'd taken one bite when Chief Malcherson appeared at his elbow.

'The FBI has left the building,' he said.

Gino nearly spit out a mouthful of turkey club. Chief Malcherson never joked – ever – and this one wasn't bad.

'Hey, Chief, you're a funny guy.'

'What do you mean? What was funny about that?'

Gino and Magozzi exchanged a glance and went poker-faced. 'Nothing, sir. So the suits are gone. Hope they didn't go away mad.'

Malcherson moved around the desk to look directly at Magozzi. 'Whose fingerprints did you submit to AFIS last night?'

'I'd rather not say just yet.'

Malcherson's white brows shot halfway up his forehead. 'Excuse me?'

Magozzi took a breath. 'Chief, I'm not trying to keep you out of the loop, but if I tell you, you're going to have to tell them, and I'm not so sure that's a good idea just yet. I'm going to have to ask you to trust me on this for a while.'

Malcherson stared at him for a long time, but his brows went back to their normal resting place. 'They said they wouldn't even talk about letting us look at the file, whose ever it is, until we give them a name to go with the prints.'

Magozzi shrugged. 'They won't give us the file no matter what we do.'

'Probably not. Can you work around that?'

'We're trying. I'll let you know as soon as I have something.'

After Malcherson left, Gino leaned across his desk and said quietly, 'I'm not real comfortable crossing swords with the Feds for these people, buddy.'

'You want to bail?'

'Not on your life. I said I wasn't comfortable; I didn't say I wasn't having fun. I'd like to know what we're protecting MacBride from, though.'

'We're going to find that out right now.'

28

The streets of Calumet were frosty and still as Halloran drove to work over two hours after Bonar had left for the church, bag in hand for Father Newberry's shell casing.

There had been record-breaking cold temperatures the night before, and the town's love affair with Halloween was certainly going to suffer for it. Decorative cornstalks huddled around front yard lampposts, their dried leaves ragged from the wind, and on almost every porch a carved pumpkin sagged in on itself, as if it had sucked in too deep a breath.

The streets outside the office were strangely empty without all the media trucks, vanished like thieves in the night now that the town had gone a whole twenty-four hours without a grisly death.

Goddamned vultures, he thought, cursing the press first, then the cold as he got out of his car, and then his own foolishness as his head pounded with every step he took toward his office. He vowed never, ever to drink that much again, which he did every time he drank that much.

Settled at his desk at last, a third cup of coffee sloshing in his queasy stomach, he cosigned a waiting stack of payroll checks, then had dispatch call Sharon Mueller in off the road. He spent the next hour alone with his hangover and the Internet, waiting for her.

She breezed in smelling like fresh air and soap, which somehow seemed at odds with the rattle of cuffs on her belt and the big gun tucked under her arm. She slipped her hat from her head, setting off a round of static in her short hair. A lot of the strands stood straight up, looking excited.

'Close the door.'

'I like the sound of that.' She sat down across from his desk and looked at him expectantly. 'Business or personal?'

'Business, of course.'

'Because if it's personal, I should close the blinds.'

Halloran blinked at her, slowly. Blinking hurt this morning. 'We had kind of a development on the Kleinfeldt thing last night.'

'I know. I ran into Bonar outside. He filled me in. What do you need? Deep background on hermaphrodites from someone with a penny-ante U of W psych degree?'

Halloran sighed, wondering why it was that women remembered every stupid thing you ever said, word for word. 'I think I apologized for that crack.'

'Did you? I can't remember.'

He couldn't figure her out. She was ripping on him; he knew that; but she was smiling, too, and that didn't make any more sense than smelling like soap when she looked like a warrior. He tipped his head as if the altered view would offer more insight, but his headache slid to that side of his skull and punished him for such idiocy. 'You want to work this or not?'

'I want to work it.'

'All right. The Kleinfeldts – the Bradfords back then

– lived in Atlanta for four years. After the birth of their child –'

'You sound just like Bonar. Everybody else under twenty you call a kid. This one you call "the child," as if he, she, or it were Christ or something. What's the deal?'

'We're at sea without the correct pronoun?'

'Don't be flip. This is serious.'

Halloran stared at her, waiting for his brain to catch up to hers, not at all surprised when it didn't. Kid, child . . . what did it matter? 'I'm trying to give you an assignment here, and you're questioning my semantics. Is it possible for you to keep quiet for thirty seconds so I can tell you what I want done?'

Sharon just looked at him.

'Well, is it?'

She continued to look at him, saying nothing, and he finally got it. She was keeping quiet. God, she was irritating.

'Okay. Back to Atlanta. So sometime after the birth of their kid/child/banana . . .'

One side of her mouth twitched a little.

'. . . the Kleinfeldts move to New York City and stay there for twelve years. Kid had to go to school, right?' He pushed a thick stack of freshly printed pages over to her side of the desk. 'That's a list of all the accredited schools in the city, public and private. Find the right one.'

He sat back and waited for the outburst that was sure to come. He had no clue how many schools there were – hundreds, for sure – he just knew that it had taken his printer the better part of half an hour to print them all out. 'It's a lot of phone calls. Hire some temps to help you out, but if anyone gets a hit, I want you talking to the administration, not them.'

She was flipping through the stack of papers, looking strangely calm for someone who was supposed to explode at any moment. 'I won't need any temps,' she said absently, scanning the last few pages as she got up from her chair and walked toward the door. 'But you don't have the right list here.'

'What do you mean I don't have the right list? That's *all* the schools.'

She flapped a hand dismissively. 'Never mind. I'll take care of it.'

Bonar walked in as she walked out. Mike thought maybe he'd put in a revolving door.

'I wish she wouldn't have cut her hair,' Bonar said.

'Why?'

He sank into the chair Sharon had just vacated. 'I don't know. She's scarier with short hair. Did you give her the schools?'

Halloran nodded. 'Fifty-some pages of them. She turned down the temps. Thinks she can do it on her own.'

'That's crazy.'

'I know. I give her an hour before she comes back begging for help.'

Bonar smiled a little, then grew serious. 'No prints on the shell casing.'

'I figured.'

'And you broke the padre's heart. I would have stayed for Mass myself, just to make him feel better, but he kept calling me a heretic.'

'He's just trying to win you over.'

'A subtle effort, at best.' He shifted his belly with his forearm, as if it were a large animal he carried around, then licked his finger and started paging through his notebook. 'The boys tidied up a few things yesterday. There were no charters in or out of any airfield within a hundred miles on Sunday; no guests that rang any bells at any of the local motels. Couples, mostly; a few hunters, but we cleared all of them. I figure whoever it was drove in, did the deed, then drove right out, and we don't have a chance in hell of finding out where they came from or where they were going. I went through every traffic citation in the county for the whole weekend, ours and HP, just on the off chance somebody stopped a speeder who was wild-eyed and covered with blood, but no joy. I separated the single-driver, no-passenger tickets in case we get something to check them against later, but I have to tell you, I feel like we're just spinning our wheels here.'

'Excuse me?' Sharon rapped lightly on the door frame, then came in.

'Change your mind about the temps?'

She was dragging a chair from the corner over next to Bonar's. 'The temps . . . ? Oh, no, of course not.' She settled into the chair and pulled a little notebook from her breast pocket. 'I found the kid's school.'

Halloran glanced at his watch, then looked up at her in disbelief. 'There were hundreds of schools on that list, and you found the right one in fifteen minutes?'

'No, I found the right school in about five minutes. The rest of the time I was on the phone with them.' Bonar and Halloran were both gaping at her. She shrugged, a little embarrassed. 'I got lucky.'

‘Lucky?’ Bonar’s thick brows were halfway up his forehead. ‘You call that lucky? Well, holy mackerel, woman, rub my head so I can go buy a lottery ticket.’

Sharon giggled softly, and Halloran realized it was the first time he’d heard her make such a benign sound. It was pretty appealing. ‘I told you you gave me the wrong list, Mike, so I made my own . . . You didn’t want that thing back, did you? It weighed a ton. I threw it in the trash.’

Halloran shook his head slowly, trying not to look dumb.

‘Anyway, from what Bonar told me about these parents from hell, I figured they wouldn’t want the kid anywhere near them, and to me, that said boarding school. Catholic, natch, since they’re such religious freaks, and as far from New York City as they could get without going out of the state so they can still get the resident tuition and tax break. There weren’t that many, believe it or not.’

She paused for a breath and flipped open her own little notebook. ‘And that’s when I got lucky. Yeah, it was a short list, but it was the second one I called.’ She plopped the notebook down on Halloran’s desk and spun it as if he could actually read her writing.

‘Is this shorthand?’

She scowled and leaned over to look at the book. ‘No, it’s not shorthand. That’s perfectly legible handwriting, see?’ She stabbed a finger at the scribbling. ‘Saint Peter’s School of the Holy Cross in Cardiff. That’s a little town in the Finger Lakes region. The Mother Superior’s been there since the sixties, and the minute I mentioned the Bradfords, she knew exactly who I was talking about. Remembers the kid because there wasn't a single parental visit in the twelve years the kid lived there.' She stopped and looked at them both, then spoke more softly. 'Not one.'

'Christ,' Bonar muttered, and then everyone was silent for a moment.

'Go on,' Halloran said at last. 'Did you get a pronoun for us?'

Sharon nodded absently, looking out the window. 'He. A little boy, name of Brian. Five years old when they dropped him off.'

Halloran waited for her to shift back to no-nonsense mode, knowing it wouldn't take long. You couldn't get bogged down in sympathy when you worked with abused kids, she'd told him once. It paralyzed you, made you totally ineffective. Two seconds later she looked back at him, brown eyes sharp and focused once again, and he thought maybe he liked her better the other way.

'Did the school know he was a hermaphrodite?' he asked.

'Not from the Bradfords, but they found out soon enough, at his first physical. "The Aberration," is what the Mother Superior called it, delicate-tongued old bitch . . . sorry. I keep forgetting you're Catholic.'

'Lapsed.'

'Whatever. Anyway, since he was presented as a boy when he was dumped there, they treated him as a boy, and as far as she knew, a few nuns and the doctor were the only ones who ever knew.'

'What, this school had individual showers? Private rooms?' Bonar asked.

Sharon smiled ruefully. 'Hermaphrodites don't generally drop their pants in the company of their peers, particularly if the condition is obvious, as it apparently was in this case.' She took back her notebook and flipped a few pages. 'His parents never showed up again, never called. Paid the whole tuition the day they dropped him off. As for the kid, he was a loner, naturally, but very bright. He got his high-school diploma when he was sixteen, and then he disappeared, too. They got a transcript request a couple years later, otherwise they never saw or heard from him again.'

Halloran blew out a sigh and leaned back. 'Where'd they send the transcript?'

Sharon smiled a little. 'Georgia State in Atlanta. Interesting, isn't it? Right back to where he was born, but the Mother Superior said something else that interests me more.' She stopped, intentionally, Halloran thought, smiling like a kid with a secret.

'You want me to beg?'

'Desperately.'

Bonar laughed. 'Come on, what have you got?'

Sharon took a breath and swallowed the canary. 'The Mother Superior said that in all the years she's been at the school they have never once gotten a call from a law enforcement agency before, and wasn't it peculiar that this morning she had two.'

Halloran frowned at her. 'You and who else?'

'Minneapolis PD.'

'Did she say what they wanted?'

'Something to do with computers and an e-mail address, but that's all she'd tell me. Damn nuns think there's a confidentiality agreement every time they open their mouths. She said we'd have to ask Minneapolis if we wanted to know more.' She tore a sheet off her notebook and passed it to Halloran. 'Here's the name and number of the guy who called. Maybe it's nothing, but it seemed like a hell of a coincidence. Gave me a bad feeling.'

'Detective . . . what's the name? I can't read this.'

'Magozzi. Detective Leo Magozzi.'

'What's the "H" stand for?'

Sharon smiled at him. 'Homicide.'

29

Magozzi decided to interview the Monkeewrench partners in the task force room. The psychologists would have told him he was making a big mistake. It was too large a space, too open. Claustrophobic surroundings were a real plus when you were trying to get information from the reluctant. After a few hours in one of the tiny interview rooms downstairs, most people would tell you anything, just to get out.

But Magozzi didn't have a few hours to wear down this group. If he was going to wage psychological warfare, it had to be high-impact. Before they came in he arranged chairs in a straight line in the front – no kindergarten semicircle to make anyone feel too secure, and no desks or tables to hide behind. Leave them open, vulnerable, and put nothing between them and the big board where eight-by-ten glossies of the dead looked down at them.

He took his usual place with one hip cocked on the front desk, friendly teacher facing the class. But he'd placed the chairs very close to the desk, less than three feet away. He'd be in their space, and from what he knew of these people, that would make them uncomfortable enough.

Gino brought them in, closed the door, then leaned against it, arms folded across his chest.

'Please have a seat.' Magozzi gestured at the arrow-straight row of chairs, and watched in bemused silence as they instinctively negated his foolish attempts at psychology. Without a moment's hesitation or a single exchanged word, they all moved their chairs a few feet back from the desk and into the forbidden semicircle, Grace MacBride in the center, the others fanned protectively around her. He wondered if they realized how obvious it was.

At least they looked at the pictures; every one of them. The twenty-year-old seminary student who'd found jogging a deadly pastime, his youthful features as serene and composed as they had probably been in life; Wilbur Daniels, whose broad, flabby face looked deceptively innocent on an autopsy table; and most disturbing of all, the seventeen-year-old Russian girl who looked heartbreakingly childlike with all the makeup washed away. Rambachan had done that with great and tender care, before her mother came to see her.

Grace MacBride looked quietly at each photograph for a prolonged moment, as if she were forcing herself to do it, as if she owed it to them. The rest of them swept the board with their eyes very fast, not a masochist in the group. Except maybe for Roadrunner.

The crime-scene photos were up there, too; terrifying duplicates of the crime-scene photos in the game and Roadrunner couldn't take his eyes off the girl on the stone angel, no doubt remembering the night he had positioned himself in that very place, setting the stage for the girl's murder. 'Jesus God,' he mumbled, and finally looked away.

Annie Belinsky turned a hateful glare on Magozzi. 'Cheap shot, Detective.'

He didn't even bother to pretend ignorance. 'You didn't notice them when you were in here earlier?'

'Sure we noticed them.' She pursed her pumpkin orange lips angrily. 'But they weren't staring right at us.'

'Would you like me to turn the board around so you don't have to look at them?'

Harley Davidson shifted his bulk with a squeak of leather. 'What I want is for you to say whatever the hell you're going to say so we can get out of here and get back to work trying to trace this guy.'

Magozzi raised his brows. 'Good. We're all on the same page.' He looked at each of them in turn, and he did it slowly, letting the silence hang there, letting them read into it whatever they liked. The room was deathly still. 'I'm going to lay this out to you the way we see it, and then you're going to have to decide whether or not to answer our questions. And then you're going to have to live with that decision.'

'What, no thumbscrews?' Mitch Cross asked bitterly.

'We don't use thumbscrews anymore, asshole,' Gino snarled from the door, confirming that he and Mitch Cross would probably never be bowling partners. 'Too slow.'

Magozzi shot him a warning look, then turned back to the others. 'The thing is, you people are too tangled up in this case, and the longer it goes on, the more alarm bells go off. At first we thought it might be simple. That maybe there is some nut out there who just played your game and thought it would be fun to act it out for real. Then we found out that none of you is who you pretend to be, that there's something back there you're all hiding. We don't know if you're criminals on the lam, victims on the run, or both at the same time. Maybe there are warrants out all over the country for who you really are. Maybe you ticked off the mob, we don't know.

'And today you tell us you're supposedly getting messages from the killer. Now you people might not think there's a connection between what's happening now and whatever the hell happened to send you underground over ten years ago, but to objective observers, all of you, and especially Grace MacBride, are in this so deep you'd have to be blind not to see it.'

Roadrunner looked nervously at his friends. Annie Belinsky, sitting next to him, squeezed his arm with a plump hand in either reassurance or warning. He took a breath that sounded too big for such a stick of a man.

'What we do know,' Magozzi continued, 'is that Grace MacBride lives in a fortress with more firepower than a small army, and now I find out she's a sealed file in an open FBI investigation.'

The whole group caught their breath at once, like a single organism. 'How the hell did you find that out?' Harley demanded.

Grace was staring at him, her blue eyes flat and cold, hiding the mental acrobatics that were probably going on inside her head. After a moment her lips tightened. 'Damnit. The cell phone. You ran my prints.'

Magozzi nodded. 'The Feds had them flagged, and so far they refuse to tell us why. Now whether you were a suspect or a victim in their case, I have no clue, but the whole thing is starting to smell. You just moved sky-high on the suspect list, and the longer you hold back information that might help, the higher you go.'

Mitch shot up from his chair with a suddenness that surprised even his friends. Gino was three steps toward him from the door so fast no one had seen him move, his reaction time honed by years with volatile perps whose sudden movements never meant anything good. 'We can't tell you anything!' he shouted, and Magozzi took note of his word choice. *Can't*, not *won't*.

Gino stopped where he was, still watchful. 'Why not?'

Mitch had delicate nostrils for a man, and they flared visibly when he breathed too hard. 'Because Grace's life might depend on it, that's why!' He blinked in sudden confusion, perhaps startled by the sound of his own raised voice.

'Sit down, Mitch,' Grace MacBride said quietly. 'Please.'

They all turned to look at her, surprised she had spoken at all. Mitch hesitated, then eased back down into his chair. He looked like a whipped dog.

'Grace, don't,' Annie said gently. 'It isn't necessary. This is a totally different thing. What happened then has nothing to do with what's happening now.'

'And maybe you're just hoping it doesn't,' Magozzi suggested quietly.

'No, damnit.' Harley Davidson was looking straight at him, shaking his head so hard his ponytail swung from side to side. 'It's not worth the chance.'

'I agree,' Roadrunner mumbled at the floor, and Magozzi guessed that was about as defiant as this obviously timid man ever got.

Grace MacBride took a deep breath, then opened her mouth to speak.

'Grace!' Annie hissed before she had a chance. 'They're cops, for Christ's sake! You're going to trust cops?'

'So much for the Friendly Policeman myth,' Gino said sarcastically, and Annie turned on him.

'Cops – cops just like you – nearly got her killed!'

Magozzi and Gino exchanged a quick glance, but said nothing. There was a little crack in the wall now, and they both knew all they could do was wait.

'They've got my prints,' Grace MacBride said. 'It's just a matter of time now anyway.' She was sitting straight in her chair, her hands resting quietly in her lap, one elbow held slightly to the side to accommodate the empty shoulder holster. 'Ten years ago we were all seniors at Georgia State in Atlanta.'

'Goddamnit.' Harley closed his eyes and shook his head sadly. The rest of the Monkeewrench crew seemed to sag in their chairs as something slipped away from them they couldn't get back.

'Five people were murdered on campus that fall,' Grace continued, her voice a brutal monotone, her eyes fixed on Magozzi's face.

'Jesus Christ,' Gino murmured involuntarily. 'I remember that. You were there?'

'Oh, yes.'

Magozzi nodded carefully, reminding himself to breathe. He hadn't known for certain what had sent these people underground, but this kind of nightmare was the last thing he had expected. He remembered the murders, and the firestorm of publicity. 'This is the case that's in the sealed FBI file?'

'That's right.'

'That doesn't make sense. Why would they seal that file? It was all over the news for weeks . . .'

'Not all of it,' Annie said dryly. 'There were certain things that never became public information. The Atlanta police didn't even have all of it, and the FBI wants to keep it that way.'

Magozzi let that one ride. Sure, it was possible the FBI would seal a file to cover some perceived wrongdoing, but it was also possible they'd do it to protect evidence or witnesses. 'Okay.' He glanced at Grace. She was pale, obviously tense, looking straight ahead. 'I take it you were suspects, or at least acquainted with the victims.'

Grace spoke with all the emotion of someone reading a grocery list. 'Kathy Martin, Daniella Farcell, my roommates. Professor Marian Amburson, my counselor and art instructor. Johnny Bricker. I dated Johnny for a while, we stayed close even after we broke it off.' She kept looking at him, but she didn't say anymore.

'That's four,' Magozzi nudged her gently, and she moved her head in the tiniest nod.

'After the fourth murder, because I was so close to all the victims, the Atlanta police and the FBI decided I was what they called an oblique target. That whoever was doing it was trying to punish me by eliminating the people I cared about, the people I depended on. So they gave me a new friend and set a trap. Libbie Herold, FBI, second year out of the academy. She was very good. Very professional. On her fourth day as my new roommate, he killed her, too.'

Magozzi held her gaze because she seemed to be demanding that. Everyone else was looking down at their laps or the floor or their hands, places you look when you want to distance yourself from what's going on around you. After what seemed like a decent interval, if such a thing were possible at all, he asked her, 'What about this group? Were you all friends at that point?'

She nodded, lips curved slightly in a knowing smile that held no humor. 'More than friends. We were family. And we still are. And yes, the FBI looked at all of us . . .'

'With a magnifying glass,' Harley put in. His face was flushed and his tone was sharp, bitter. 'And don't think we don't know what you're thinking. The cops and the Feds took us down the same road. Either Grace was killing her own friends, or more likely, since none of us ever bought it, one of us was doing it. Broke their hearts when they couldn't pin it on us, or at least it would have if any of those scumbags had had hearts.'

For the first time Magozzi saw the part of Harley Davidson he wouldn't want to meet in a dark alley. He wasn't just bitter; he was seething with a rage that hadn't tempered a bit in all these years. He'd seen the same thing in Grace MacBride; a touch of it in all of them, and it made him nervous. They didn't just mistrust authority; they hated it. He wondered if any or all of them were mad enough to kill. Harley certainly looked like he was. His head was lowered, his hands clenched into fists on his thighs.

The big man took a couple of deep breaths, blowing them out slowly, reining it in. 'Anyway, the FBI wanted to try another plant, but Grace decided she didn't want to play their reindeer games anymore, didn't want to wait around to see if the killer would get to the rest of us. So we disappeared.' He jerked his head toward Roadrunner. 'This guy's the genius who did it. Wiped us all right out. Far as we know, the Feebs were still groping around blind till you sent in Grace's prints, and for that, Detective, it is my sincerest wish that your balls rot slowly and painfully and then fall off.'

Magozzi smiled a little. 'The prints piqued the FBI's interest, all right, and now I see why. They never made an arrest, did they? And Ms MacBride was their only connection –'

'They were using her as bait.' Mitch Cross was furious, too, but his anger was colder than Davidson's, and somehow more disturbing.

'And now, thanks to you,' Harley said, 'they know where we are, they know Grace's new identity, and all the killer has to do is access their records –'

'We never put a name on the prints,' Magozzi interrupted, leaving Harley with his mouth open on his last word. 'The only people who know they belong to Ms MacBride are in this room, and we've got no problem with it staying that way.'

Harley closed his mouth, but they all still eyed Magozzi with suspicion.

'Okay, just a minute.' Gino walked over to the front desk and sat behind it, frowning down at the scarred wooden surface. 'Are you telling me you all just walked away from everything? Three-plus years of college, friends, families . . .'

'We don't have families.' Roadrunner frowned at him as if he were supposed to know that. 'That's how we all hooked up in the first place. Everybody on campus went home for holidays, and there we were, darn near the only people eating in the cafeteria. One day we all moved to the same table. Called ourselves the Orphan Club.' He smiled at the memory, which to Magozzi's amazement was apparently a pleasant one.

Mitch Cross was looking superior again, now that the secrets were all out and there was nothing left to bluster about. 'So now you know everything. Are you satisfied, Magozzi?' He used his last name like a weapon, leaving off the title.

'Not quite. If Ms MacBride was never the direct target in Atlanta, if the rest of you, as the people closest to her, were probably a lot higher on that killer's hit list – why is she the one who carries a gun and lives in a vault?'

The five exchanged sheepish glances.

'Uh, actually.' Roadrunner scratched his left earlobe. 'We all have pretty decent security systems, and . . .'

'We all carry.' Mitch shrugged. 'As I'm sure your desk sergeant will tell you if he ever gets his mouth closed again.'

Harley chuckled. 'He was pretty surprised when we all checked weapons on the way in.'

'You *all* carry guns?'

'All the time,' Harley said matter-of-factly, 'just like Grace. Hers is just a little bigger, that's all, a little more obvious.'

'Jesus Christ.' Gino shuddered a little, thinking back to when they'd first walked into the Monkeewrench office, never imagining that they'd been entering an armed camp. 'You've all got permits?'

Mitch snorted softly. 'You think we're idiots? You think we'd tell you we carried if we didn't have permits?'

'I'll tell you what I think,' Magozzi said quietly, looking at each one of them. 'Apparently all of you live under tight security and carry guns because every single one of you has been looking over your shoulder for the past ten years, thinking this killer was going to track you down. And now that it looks like that might have happened, every one of you is saying, oh no, it's totally unrelated, it can't possibly be the same guy. You said cops have tunnel vision? Well, I'm here to tell you we don't hold a candle to you people in that department.'

Roadrunner was frowning hard, biting his lower lip. 'But it *could* be some psycho just playing the game. It's not impossible. You know how many serial killers are operating in this country at any given moment?'

'As it happens, I do. Upwards of two hundred. And yes, it's possible. Anything's possible. But it would be a hell of a coincidence, so we're going to be looking at this, and we're going to need to know a lot more about what happened in Atlanta.'

Annie Belinsky's eyes shot up to his in a panic. A movement in her lap caught his eye, and he glanced down and saw her wagging a finger back and forth almost imperceptibly, warning him to back off. That wouldn't have stopped him, but the naked plea in her eyes did.

He hesitated, his eyes still locked on Belinsky's. 'We'll get in touch with you later.'

Her long lashes fluttered closed briefly, then she got up from her chair. 'So we're finished here.'

'For now,' Magozzi replied. 'I want numbers, cells, if you've got them, for all of you before you leave. Write 'em down, give 'em to Gloria. And I want to know where you're going to be, today, tonight, tomorrow.'

He and Gino watched silently as the five filed out of the room, then Gino got up and closed the door and turned to face his partner. 'You've got about five seconds to explain to me why you let those people out of here, and then another five to call downstairs and have them stopped before they leave the building.'

'That's what you think we should do?'

'Damn straight that's what I think we should do. And I'll tell you why. Because A, I don't care if the Feds couldn't pin anything on them in Georgia, one of them was the killer then, and he's the killer now, because that's the only thing that makes sense. And B, said killer is going to pick up his gun and go dust somebody at the mall unless we lock him up.'

'We can't hold them, and they're all smart enough to know that.'

'We could lose them in transport for about a day and a half, at least until we can turn the screws on the FBI and get some straight answers. And then I want to talk to the locals who gave carry permits to a bunch of nutcases like that. Shit, they barely let *us* carry.'

'We're going to get a little more information first.'

'Oh yeah? From where?'

'From Annie Belinsky. She'll be back in a minute.'

Gino opened his mouth just as the door opened behind him. He turned and stared as Annie Belinsky breezed in on a cloud of orange.

'You tryin' to catch flies with that thing, sugar?' She put a long orange nail under Gino's chin and closed his mouth, then sauntered over to Magozzi and looked straight at him. 'Thank you,' she said.

'You're welcome. But it was a conditional reprieve.'

'I know the rules.'

'Uh, excuse me for living.' Gino was scowling. 'How the hell did you know she was coming back? And what the hell are you talking about? You two got some psychic thing going here or what?'

Annie snagged her purse from where she'd tucked it under her chair and held it aloft with one finger. 'This is how he knew I was coming back, and as for some psychic connection, well' – she smiled at Magozzi and her drawl deepened – 'your friend here's got some dynamite eyes, haven't you ever noticed that?'

'Oh, sure,' Gino said. 'Every day I sit across from him and wish I had peepers that special.'

'Well, you should. He talks with them just as clear as snowmelt runnin' into a creek, and that's how we made our agreement. He lived up to his part, now I'm here to give him my tit for his tat.'

Gino blinked several times, rapidly, then decided not to touch that one.

Annie sighed sharply, all business now, and the drawl faded a bit as the tempo of her speech increased. 'I've got about five minutes before one of them figures I've been spirited away to the drunk tank or something and comes runnin' to save me, so tell me what you want to know about Atlanta.'

'I want to know what you didn't want me to ask Ms MacBride.'

'Well.' She took a breath, let it out slowly. 'That would be just about everything. For starters, the Atlanta murders were totally different than what's going down here, which is one of the reasons we aren't thinking it's the same killer. I don't have to tell you how rare it is for a serial killer to change the way he kills; in particular, the weapon he uses.'

'It could happen.'

'Yes, of course it could,' she said impatiently, 'but rarely, like I said. Especially when there's some sort of ritual involved, which seemed to be the case in Atlanta. That animal used an X-Acto knife.'

'I don't remember reading about that,' Gino said.

'It was one of the things the cops held back. He cut their Achilles tendons first, so they couldn't get away . . .'

Oh Jesus, Magozzi thought, feeling sick. *That's why she always wears the boots.*

'. . . and then he slashed the femoral arteries. They bled out. It took a while.'

'Christ.' Gino looked a full shade paler than he had a minute ago.

'Grace found Kathy and Daniella – those were her roommates – when she came back to her room after a night out. She was a smart girl. She didn't go in. Just opened the door, turned on the light, then ran like hell. But there was a lot of blood, and she had to have seen that.'

'Shit,' Gino grumbled. 'That would have put me right in a rubber room.'

Annie looked at him. 'She had a tough childhood. It made her strong. And the Valium didn't hurt either. The school brought in a psychiatrist, and he put her on what he called a maintenance dose.'

'Why the hell didn't she just pack up and leave?' Magozzi asked. 'I would have.'

'And go where? Back to a string of foster homes that had been their own nightmares? We were all the family any of us had, and we stayed together.' She looked off to the side briefly, frowning. 'A better question is why the rest of us were so goddamned stupid we didn't drag her out of there right then, before the other murders. We've been kicking ourselves for that ever since, but none of us knew what was coming.' She took another deep breath and dug in her purse for a cigarette and lighter. 'I'm going to smoke in a government building, fellas. You want to stop me, you're going to have to wrestle me to the ground.'

'Tempting,' Gino said, handing her a cup to use as an ashtray.

'Thanks.' She took a long drag and made the task force room smell the way it had in the old days. 'Marian Amburson and Johnny Bricker were killed a few days later, and the FBI came down on us like a swarm of locusts. While the rest of us were locked up in interview rooms for damn near two days, they had Grace to themselves. That's when they set up the trap with Libbie Herold.'

'The FBI agent.'

'Right. What they did was put them both in a little house off in the corner of the campus, away from the high traffic of the dorms. Easier to stake out, they said, easier to protect. Grace was scared to death. She was a kid, you know? And they were asking her to play bait for a killer. She didn't want to do it. All she wanted was to get the hell out of there, and I think if we'd been able to get to her, we would have all taken off right then and there.'

'What do you mean, if you'd been able to get to her?' Gino asked.

Annie pursed her lips and frowned hard, looked out the window. 'Even after they let the rest of us go, they wouldn't let us see her. They said she was in "protective custody" and no one could see her; no one could talk to her. We didn't even know where she was.' She smiled bitterly at the memory. 'What they were really doing, of course, was isolating her, taking away her support structure so the only ones she had left to depend on were them.'

Jesus, Magozzi thought.

'And then they started hammering on how if anyone else got killed it would be on Grace's head unless she helped them nail the killer, and pretty soon they had her believing it. So they've got Grace locked away in this house with a very well-armed agent, and there's nothing to worry about, they said, because Libbie always wore a wire and help was always just outside the door.' She paused, closed her eyes, and took a deep breath. 'But somebody fucked up, big time. Maybe Libbie's wire didn't work, maybe the guys staking out the house looked away at the wrong time – who knows what really happened? One morning Libbie didn't check in when she was supposed to, and when the agents went in after them, they found Libbie's body in the bedroom, lying in a lake of blood, her legs nearly sawed off. They found Grace in the closet, all scrunched up against a back corner. She scratched those agents up pretty good when they tried to get her out, but she didn't say a word. Didn't scream, didn't cry, nothing. She was in the psych ward at Atlanta General for a week. Then we took her away.'

Gino was leaning against the wall by the door, looking down at the floor. Magozzi was watching Annie look around aimlessly, as if she'd misplaced the thread of her thought and hoped to see it somewhere in the room.

Finally she took a last drag off her cigarette and dropped it in the coffee at the bottom of the cup. 'Anyway, that's what happened in Atlanta.' She slid her eyes sideways to look at Magozzi. 'We don't ever talk about this; not in front of Grace.'

Magozzi nodded, watched her slip her purse strap over her shoulder and head for the door. Gino stepped aside and opened it for her.

She turned back at the last minute. 'Your computer guy, Tommy What's-his-name.'

'Espinoza.'

Annie nodded. 'He's good. He was making all the right moves trying to hack into that sealed FBI file.'

'What makes you think he's trying to do that?'

Annie shrugged prettily. 'He left us in the room for a minute. And don't blame the boy. He locked up his computer first, and it was a very sophisticated lock. Would have stopped all but about three people in the world.'

Magozzi smiled ruefully. 'And Roadrunner's one of them.'

'Yes, he is. Anyway, on the off chance he ever breaks through, there's probably a thing or two in that file that might give you pause. Might as well hear it from me first.'

'What's that?'

'Another thing the FBI used to get Grace to co-operate. They were going to reopen a dismissed case on one of her friends, make a little trouble if they could.'

'And that case was . . . ?'

Annie touched the sides of her mouth with a finger to keep her lipstick in line. 'I stabbed a man to death the year before I entered the U.' She looked at Gino, whose mouth had dropped open again, and gave him a smile that would have blown a less substantial man away. 'Flies, sugar,' she reminded him with a tap under his chin, and then she sashayed out the door.

Grace was waiting for her by the elevator. She was leaning against the wall on one shoulder, looking like a model-turned-cowboy in the long black duster, wearing one of those tiny, knowing smiles that always gave Annie the creeps.

'You spilled your guts, didn't you, Annie?'

'Actually, I spilled your guts, darlin'. And a little bit of mine.'

Grace pushed away from the wall and looked down at the floor, dark hair curtaining the sides of her face. 'If I'd thought they needed to know everything, I would have told them. I can talk about it now. I'm not going to fall to pieces.'

'They did need to know everything, if only to keep them on track and off our backs, and there's no reason on God's green earth that you should ever have to talk about it. Not to them, not to anyone.' Annie's mouth was set in a stubborn line. 'Damnit. I was getting to like Minneapolis. If that Tommy character gets into that file, our cover's blown and we're going to have to leave, start all over again.'

Grace pushed the elevator button, her eyes on the little lights over the door. 'We did what we could. It's a waiting game now.'

30

For a full five minutes after Annie Belinsky had left the room, Magozzi and Gino just sat in the chairs that faced the board of victim photos, saying nothing, digesting what she had told them about Atlanta.

'What are you thinking?' Magozzi finally asked.

Gino grunted. 'That I should go out and shoot an FBI agent, just to make myself feel better.'

'There were cops there, too. You can't lay it all on the FBI.'

'Yeah, I know. That's even worse.' He turned his head and looked at Magozzi. 'It doesn't take MacBride off the suspect list, you know. If anything, it makes her a better pick. It'd be a real kick for a killer, wouldn't it? Off a bunch of people and have everyone feeling sorry for you, thinking you're a victim? And there's another thing that bothers me. If she's not the killer and she really went through all that shit, you'd think she'd be loony tunes for the rest of her life.'

'Apparently she was, for a while.'

'A week. You could fake it for that long standing on your head.'

Magozzi sighed. 'She didn't do it, Gino.'

'You sure you're not doing your thinking a little south of the border?'

Magozzi leaned back in the chair and rubbed at his eyes. 'I'm not sure I'm thinking at all. Let's work it out.'

There was a big old blackboard in the back of the task force room that hadn't been used in years. Everything was neater now. They used tagboards with digital photos and computer comparison charts and probability charts and graphics that would have made Disney weep. But for Gino Rolseth and Leo Magozzi, there was something about writing stuff down with your own hand that helped the thinking process.

They went to the board now and started diagramming it all out, breathing in the dusty smell of chalk, rubbing their fingers together where all the moisture had been sucked out of their skin.

'Okay,' Gino said, stepping back and taking a look. 'It's just as goddamned clear as a bell, isn't it? About ten years ago you've got a series of killings at Georgia State, and the Monkeewrench people are in it up to their eyeballs. Now we've got a series of killings in Minneapolis and guess who's here? You know what the odds are that any human being on the planet will be directly affected by a serial killer in his lifetime? And these people hit the jackpot twice. One of them did it. No doubt about it.'

Magozzi looked at the board for a long time. 'Still doesn't make sense that one of them would want to ruin their own company.'

'Excuse me.' Gino rolled his eyes. 'But you gotta assume whoever dresses up a girl, hangs her on a cemetery statue, then shoots her in the head isn't exactly taking the elevator all the way to the top floor. Besides, every one of them's got enough money stashed to last a lifetime. So they lose the company. So what? Ain't like they're gonna be homeless.'

Magozzi looked at the list of Georgia killings, then the list of Minneapolis killings, lines connecting all of them to the five people who had just been in this room. 'What's the motive?'

'Hell, I don't know. One of them doesn't like the direction the company's going – this game was a big jump from the little birdie cartoons they were programming for the kindergarten crowd, you know . . .'

'Mitch Cross doesn't seem to like the game much. He wouldn't even go to the photo shoot in the cemetery, remember?'

'There you go.'

'Okay,' Magozzi said. 'So the game offends Cross's sensibilities and he thinks it's a bad business decision. But he's outvoted, so he snaps and decides to destroy the company he helped build by killing a bunch of people he never met. Kind of an overreaction, don't you think?'

'He didn't just "snap." The guy's a maniac. An out-of-control killer. He already offed five people back in Georgia, remember?'

'What was his motive then?'

Gino pursed his lips and stared at the board, looking for the answer. 'Don't know.'

'And if he's that out of control how come there's a ten-year interval between killings?'

Gino pulled at his tie, jaw jutting. 'Don't know that, either.'

'Let's plug somebody else in. How about Belinsky? She just blithely informed us that she stabbed a man to death before her freshman year in college, for Christ's sake.'

'Don't try to break my heart here, Leo. You're just going after her because I went after MacBride.' He took a step back from the board and scrubbed at the patch of whiskers he'd missed. 'Truth is, I don't really like either one of them, sexist pig that I am. I've had it in my head right from the start that it's a man. What about the other two? Mutt and Jeff?'

'Nothing jumped out in what Tommy dug up on them from the last ten years. Aside from the fact that Roadrunner sees a shrink twice a week and Harley has a subscription to *Soldier of Fortune*.'

'*Soldier of Fortune*, huh? That's scary.'

'He gets *Architectural Digest*, too. That's scarier yet.' Magozzi went to the front desk and brought back the file on the Monkeewrench partners Tommy Espinoza had left on his desk the night before. 'I gave it a quick read-through, but nothing popped for me either. The short and sweet is that Harley Davidson turns out to be quite the bon vivant. Second lowest net worth, after Belinsky. Expensive taste, patron of the arts, wine connoisseur . . .'

'You've gotta be kidding.'

'See for yourself. Spends money like a drunken sailor. Has about five million in classic motorcycles stashed in the garage of his little ten-thousand-square-foot house and his dining-out expenses would pay our salaries.'

'That's obscene.' Gino sat down and started pawing through the printout on Harley. 'Holy shit. *A hundred and fifteen thousand dollars* on Bordeaux futures last month? What the hell is a Bordeaux future?'

'Like corn futures, hog futures, only wine. Reads like

a Robin Leach script for "Lifestyles of the Rich and Famous," doesn't it?'

Gino looked up. 'This is bizarre. But not necessarily incriminating. I was hoping for a correspondence course in serial killing, something like that.'

Magozzi smiled. 'He's got a Victoria's Secret charge account that runs him a few grand a year.'

'*What?*'

'Yep.'

'Is he wearing it or giving it away?'

'That, Tommy couldn't tell us. But put that together with dinners out and his romantic weekend getaways to Saint Bart's and I'm guessing he likes the ladies.'

Gino looked thoroughly depressed. 'Shit. And I wanted to hate this guy. How can you hate a guy like that? What about the Human Pencil?'

Magozzi pulled up a chair next to Gino. 'Can't tell much from the kind of records Tommy was able to access, except the shrink thing. He's got a nice fat investment portfolio he leaves pretty much alone, a house on Nicollet Island, and nothing really interesting in the money trail. Aside from bicycle and computer stuff, and some pretty generous charitable donations, he doesn't seem to spend any.'

'What kind of charities?'

Magozzi shrugged. 'Homeless shelters, domestic-abuse centers, youth-at-risk programs, stuff like that.'

'The kind of places he probably spent a lot of time in as a kid.'

'Probably.'

Gino sighed and closed the folder. 'He's kind of a sad sack, isn't he?'

'A sad sack with a carry permit and four registered guns.'

'Not exactly a standout in that group. Still, he's a misfit weirdo loner who most likely had a bad childhood, keeps to himself, and likes his guns. Is that classic, or what?'

Magozzi sighed and ran a hand through his hair. 'Actually, it sounds like half the cops on the force.' He stood up and went back to the blackboard. 'The truth is we could plug in any one of the five and make them fit some psycho-in-training profile. These are strange people, Gino.'

'Tell me about it.'

'But there's nothing solid that says any of them are doing the killing.' Magozzi bounced his chalk in his hands a few times, then drew an X with a circle around it beneath the list of Monkeewrench names.

'That's a kiss inside a hug, right?' Gino asked.

'That's our other option, Mr X. Some creep fixated on Grace, did the killings in Georgia, lost track of them, or maybe went to the big house for a while on another rap. He gets out, finds them, and starts killing again.' He cocked his head and looked at Gino. 'It's a possibility. We've got to consider it.'

'Along with the possibility that the two series of murders aren't related at all. That this is just some new psycho playing their stupid-ass game.' He blew out a disgusted sigh. 'So basically we're nowhere, right where we've been all along.'

Magozzi nodded. 'I'd say that just about sums it up.' He tossed the chalk in the tray and brushed the white dust from his fingers. 'And I'll tell you something else.

We've got to find a way to put round-the-clock tails on these people.'

'What are we going to use, the Girl Scouts? Half the law enforcement in the state is out at the mall. We're so short on the street I was thinking of robbing a bank myself.'

'We've got to do it. Monkeewrench is in this too deep. If it's not one of them, it's someone with a serious beef against one or all of them. And you can bet your pension that if he's starting to make contact, he's feeling a need to get closer. That's straight out of *Profiling for Dummies.* And e-mails aren't going to keep him satisfied for long.'

Gino swiped a hand over the top of his thinning hair. 'So you think he's going to try to make personal contact soon.'

'I think it's a pretty safe bet.'

Detective Aaron Langer stopped by one of the huge concrete pillars that supported the parking deck above and watched two women and four kids pile out of an old Suburban. He followed them with his eyes until they made it to the walkway that led to Macy's, wondering what the hell was wrong with people these days. You tell them there's probably going to be a shooting at the Mall of America and what do they do? They bring their kids. Jesus.

He started walking back toward Nordstrom, head swiveling right and left, trying to watch everything. It was just after one o'clock and the parking decks were almost full. When he'd dressed for work this morning he'd imagined patrolling an enormous empty slab of concrete, so he'd worn the warm Perry Ellis overcoat his wife had gotten him for his birthday. Now the black wool was filthy from brushing up against cars that weren't supposed to be there, that shouldn't have been there if their owners had had half a brain. The upside was that the killer probably wouldn't be able to find a parking space.

They had two uniforms and four mall security types on each level of the massive parking decks, twenty unmarkeds cruising the ramps nonstop, and ten detectives on foot coordinating the patrols. He was responsible for levels P-4 through P-7 in the West ramps, an assignment that had particularly pleased his wife since he'd be close to Macy's, and that had simply blown him away. Here he was putting himself in the line of fire, and all she could think of was that he could go in on a break and pick up a pair of the nylons she liked while they were still on sale. He'd told her he probably wouldn't have time, what with dodging a psychopathic killer and all, and she'd just rolled her eyes and told him not to be silly, that there was no way a murderer would show up at the one place everyone was expecting him.

And that, he assumed, was undoubtedly the same logic all these other shoppers were employing today. And they were probably right.

He was scanning the rows to his right and nearly ran into a guy from Channel 10 with a handheld. Another reason for the killer to stay home. The media was damn near as strong a presence on the parking decks as law enforcement. So far he'd had six requests for on-camera interviews, interrupting his surveillance, irritating the hell out of him.

'Hey! Watch where you're going, buddy!' the cameraman complained.

Langer tapped the leather badge clipped to his breast pocket.

'Oh, sorry, Detective.' The camera whirred to life. 'Could you answer a few questions, Detective?'

'Sorry, I'm working.'

The cameraman trotted after him, infuriatingly persistent. 'How long do the police plan to keep up this kind of intensive patrolling, Detective? Are there other areas of the city being left without protection while so much of the force is diverted to the Mall of America?'

Langer stopped and looked down at the shoes that were too thin-soled for walking on cold concrete, then he looked straight up into the camera and smiled. This guy wanted an interview? He'd give him a friggin' interview. 'What are you doing here, buddy? Making a snuff film? Trying to catch a murder on tape so you can show it to the kiddies on the five-o'clock news?'

The camera shut off abruptly, and the cameraman eased the unit off his shoulder and looked at Langer with a wounded expression. 'Hey, I'm just doing my job here. Covering the story.'

'Really. You know maybe I could buy that if you'd just come down here to film all the hullabaloo and then left, but the fact is you've all been here as long as I have.' He glanced at his watch. 'That's three hours so far, so don't give me that business about covering a story when what you're really doing is waiting for it to happen, which in this case means you're waiting to film one of your viewers getting her head blown off. Now I don't know what that makes you, but I do know it ought to make you ashamed.'

Langer walked away, disgusted with the media, disgusted with the kind of society that had created the media, and mostly disgusted with himself for letting it get to him.

'Langer?'

He keyed his shoulder radio and turned his mouth to talk into it. 'Right here.'

'We've got your deck covered if you want to break for lunch.'

'Where are you?'

'Turn around.'

He did, and saw one of the unmarkeds pulling up beside him, Detective Peterson grinning behind the wheel. He'd been assigned as one of the floaters who covered sectors for the rest of them when they took a break. 'How're they hanging, guy?'

'They aren't hanging. They're shriveled up and tucked up and hiding from this damn cold.' He stamped his feet to get the blood moving and looked around. There was more foot traffic now, probably morning shoppers heading back to their cars to miss the afternoon rush hour. 'It's getting busy,' he said. 'Maybe I'll wait awhile till it slows down.'

'It ain't gonna slow down. From here on in it's just busy, busy, busy. Now you got the lunch crowd leaving, and when that's done the after-school crowd gets here, then the after-work crowd . . .' Peterson pulled into a handicapped spot and got out of the car. 'Besides, I think I can handle it. I'm a detective, just like you. Wanna see my badge?'

'All right, all right.' Langer smiled a little. 'But you parked in a handicapped spot.'

'Up yours, Langer.' Peterson's eyes were busy, scanning the area with an acuity that made Langer feel better about heading inside where it was warm. 'And haven't you noticed? There are no handicapped people here today. That's the one and only contingent that had enough brains to stay home.'

At that moment a wheelchair emerged from the walkway to Nordstrom, making him a liar.

Peterson glared at the sad little mini-procession as if they'd intentionally timed their appearance to make him look bad. 'Okay, I take it back. That makes nobody in this state who had the brains to stay away from here today. There's about fifty million kids down in Camp Snoopy, can you believe that? You know what it reminds me of? Public hangings. Witch burnings. That place in Rome where everybody went to see gladiators kill each other . . .'

'The Coliseum,' Langer said distantly, staring at the occupant of the wheelchair, trapped in a time warp he visited occasionally to torture himself. The woman was carefully bundled up against the cold, bowed over by age, and even from a distance he could see the trademark empty gaze of Alzheimer's. He shivered inside his coat, looking at that old woman and seeing his mother before the disease had finally relented and let her die last year.

'Yeah, the Coliseum,' Peterson was saying. 'I didn't think anybody was going to show up here today, and now the mall people say they've broken every attendance record in the book. Either all these people are just flat-out stupid, or they've got some kind of a bloodlust thing going, like they came here just because they heard something horrible was going to happen. Almost creeps me out more than the killings.'

'Minnesota nice,' Langer mumbled, finally tearing his eyes away from the woman in the chair, hating himself for staring.

He'd been on the other end of that morbid, curious stare times beyond counting, whenever he'd wheeled his mother out of the nursing home, patting himself on the back for being such a good son, such a dutiful son, taking his mother to the park or the mall or the McDonald's on the corner, just as if she were still a real person. He would push the chair and look at the back of her head, which looked pretty much the same as it always had, and pretend that she was still in there.

But the people who looked at the front knew better, and their stares said the awful emperor-has-no-clothes truth – excuse me, sir, but did you know your mother is drooling? urinating? having a bowel movement right here in the middle of McDonald's? Those noisy, talkative, cruel stares had awakened the coward that had always been in him, and that coward found a million reasons not to visit his mother today, or this week, or this month, until eventually, she curled up like a pea in a pod and died on the night shift when the only nurse was busy.

'Langer? You okay?'

Oh, Jesus. Stop looking at her.

'Yeah. Fine.' He turned to Peterson and startled the man with his pathetic attempt at a smile. 'Just tired. And cold.'

'Well, get inside, man. Get something hot to eat.'

'Right. Thanks.'

If he'd been half a man, half a decent person, he would have gone over to help with the familiar struggle of loading into a car the uncoordinated, unresponsive collection of mindless body parts that Alzheimer's makes of a perfectly good human being. Lord knew he'd done it enough times to have it down. But the coward still prevailed, and now that he'd finally managed to look away, he found it almost impossible to look back. Just a quick glance as he passed even with the wheelchair, several rows to his right. Just a quick jerk of the eyes to see that all had been accomplished without him.

He trotted across the deck to the mall entrance, and once inside, he covered the considerable distance from Nordstrom to Macy's very quickly, a man chased by ghosts. By the time he'd passed the shoe department, his mind had quieted enough to prod him gently with what he had really seen in that quick glance back in the parking ramp, in that quick jerk of the eyes. He froze in mid-stride, never feeling the angry shopper who ran into his back, or hearing the muttered expletive.

'Jesus Christ.' He said it very quietly, no offense, and then he turned and started running back the way he had come, head turned sideways to shout instructions into the radio for Peterson, sick with the knowledge that the person who had been pushing the wheelchair loaded the old woman into one car, *and then got into the one next to it and drove away.*

He tried to tell himself it was only a coincidence; just another caretaker beaten down by frustration, finally shrugging off a burden that had become too heavy to carry. But he didn't believe it.

Langer was running hard, having a hard time dodging all the shoppers, partly because there were so goddamned many of them, partly because his eyes were watering, making it hard to see.

Or maybe he was crying, because sometimes people with Alzheimer's looked like they were dead, and sometimes people who were dead looked like they had Alzheimer's.

31

They'd lost daylight savings time last Saturday night, and by 5:30 Halloran's office was gloomy with that oppressive kind of half-light that settles when the sunlight weakens, like an old light bulb fading away before it blows out completely.

He sighed and snapped on the green-shaded desk lamp, postponing the need for the sterile glare of the overhead fluorescents. He'd never noticed the buzzing until Sharon had mentioned it. Ever since, it had been driving him crazy, especially at times like these, when the day tour had left and the building was quiet.

He perked up at the sound of Bonar's voice in the outer office, and raised his brows when his friend's considerable bulk filled the doorway. He'd apparently showered in the locker room downstairs, and had exchanged his uniform for slacks with an honest-to-God crease, a turtleneck sweater, and a sport coat. Halloran could smell Old Spice all the way across the room.

'You look very handsome.'

'I already have a date.'

'You taking Marjorie to dinner?'

'That was the original plan. Out to dinner, and then back to her place where I suspect I would have been forced to lay waste to the woman.' He tossed his overcoat on the couch in disgust.

'Did I hear past tense?'

'Actually, I think it might have been future perfect. Did Minneapolis call you back yet?'

Halloran tossed his pen on the desk. 'No, the arrogant asshole from Minneapolis did not call me back.'

Bonar clucked his tongue in a scold. 'You have to talk nicely to the big policemen in the big city or they won't share.'

'Damnit, I've left three messages for this man. You can't tell me he hasn't had five minutes sometime in the past six hours to make a courtesy call to another department.'

'I wouldn't bet on that.' Bonar glanced at the dark screen of the television in the corner. 'You didn't watch the news, did you?'

'Hell, no. I've been having too much fun writing a report for the commissioners, who want very badly for us to arrest someone for the Kleinfeldts' murders, preferably someone from very far away who has no connection with our county at all. A Colombian drug lord passing through on his way back to Bogotá would be ideal.'

Bonar's smile was grim. 'Well, they had the TV on down in dispatch. I caught a piece of it on my way up here. Magozzi was the name of that detective, right?'

'Right.'

'Well, he happens to be the lucky lead on those murders in Minneapolis, and another went down this afternoon. At the Mall of America, no less. The whole city's going nuts.'

Halloran frowned. 'You mean the computer game thing?'

Bonar nodded. 'And before you make the quantum

leap and pretend you thought of it first, I've already been there. His call to the school had something to do with computers, and since chances are pretty slim he's working anything but this case right now, that means the school is somehow connected to the computer game murders.'

Halloran straightened in his chair. 'Jesus.'

Bonar shoved his hands in his pants pockets and started pacing. 'So the Minneapolis murders are connected to a Catholic school in upstate New York, and our murders are connected to that same school, or at least they are if the kid did it, which makes you want to believe our murders are connected to their murders, right?'

'Wrong. I don't want to believe that at all.'

'Me neither. And maybe they aren't, because he's looking for a current e-mail address, and we're looking for a kid who lived there years ago before they even had computers. All the way up here I've been trying to figure out how a computer game killer in Minneapolis jibes with a family killing in Calumet, and there's nothing there except a coincidence that makes your head hurt.' He sighed and eased down on the couch, elbows braced on his knees, hands dangling between his legs. 'I'm getting Sharon's bad feeling about this.'

Halloran put his elbows on the desk and stared straight ahead, thinking hard. After a few minutes, he decided it was a futile exercise. He needed more information, and he wasn't even sure that would help.

'I've got to call Marjorie and cancel,' Bonar said, standing abruptly.

'And do what?'

Bonar looked blank. 'I don't know. Wait for Magozzi to call, I guess. This thing's driving me nuts.'

'Go,' Halloran said. 'Take your cell, and if I get through to him, I'll call you.'

32

Charlie was totally confused. His ordered doggy world was upside down. Yes, he was sitting in the Adirondack chair next to his mistress, normally his favorite place in the world, but it was the wrong time of day, she wasn't in her sitting-in-the-chair clothes, and there was no water running out of the long snake under the tree.

He was brave for as long as he could stand it, then he clambered off his chair, climbed up onto her lap, and started licking her face, whining, demanding an explanation.

Grace put her arms around him and pressed her head against his, giving comfort, and taking it. 'Oh, Charlie, I killed another one,' she whispered, closing her eyes.

Your fault, Grace. All your fault.

The news about the Megamall murder had flashed over the Internet less than an hour ago. She'd been alone in the loft then, still working on tracing the e-mails long after everyone else had left.

For a long time, she simply sat there, numb, reading the bulletin over and over.

Harley, Annie, and Roadrunner had called moments later, all worried about her, and Mitch had called from his car soon after that. He was running between client meetings, trying to put out the fires that were consuming the company, and he'd heard the news over the radio. Grace reassured them all that she was fine, even as she staggered under the burden of this new blame, added to the old one she'd been carrying for ten years.

Your fault then, and your fault now. Your game, your idea, your fault.

She'd left the loft immediately, wanting more than anything else to be alone in the house that fear had built, with the dog that fear had created, because it was only there she felt properly punished.

A scrambling sound on the north wall of the fence pricked Charlie's ears and sent Grace's hand immediately to her shoulder holster. She almost smiled to see the gun in her hand, pointed toward the sound, because she hadn't realized that she still wanted to live that badly, and part of her wondered why.

Two small black hands appeared at the top of the fence, followed by a small black face. Dark eyes widened at the sight of the gun. 'Jeez, Grace, don't shoot me.'

She relaxed and put the Sig back in the holster. 'What are you doing here, Jackson?'

He swung one leg over the fence and slid down into the backyard, then strolled over as if scaling an eight-foot fence to pay a visit was a normal course of events. 'I saw you drive in. You never come home this early. Figured something was up.' He stopped in front of her, tipped his head, and frowned. 'You don't look so good.'

'I don't feel so good.'

Now that was funny. To her partners, who had known and loved her for years, she lied like crazy, telling them she was fine. To this annoying kid she'd met only twice, her traitorous mouth had decided to tell the truth.

Jackson dropped to a cross-legged position on the drying grass, holding out a hand for Charlie to lick. 'What happened?'

'There was another murder today.'

'Yeah, at the mall. Bad juju. The Monkeewrench Killer strikes again. Victim number four in the game.'

Grace looked away from him, over at the magnolia, troubled by the way he'd said it; that murder could be such a casual thing to a nine-year-old. 'Well, I'm Monkeewrench.' Confession to a kid-priest. 'I designed that game.'

A slow smile spread over the dark young face. 'No shit? Man, that is so cool. I love that game.'

She turned to look at him with sad astonishment. 'Jackson. Four people have died because I created that game.'

He gave her the raspberry. For God's sake she was confessing a mortal sin and the kid was giving her the raspberry.

'That is such bullshit. They died 'cause some wacko shot 'em. C'mere, Charlie.' He patted his leg and Charlie left Grace's lap with no apology at all to roll on the grass with a boy who granted absolution with the word 'bullshit.'

She watched them play for a time, losing herself in the immediacy of life that comes naturally to boys and dogs and few others; and then she took Jackson in the house and sat him at the table, and while she was making something for them all to eat, she asked him about his life. And he asked about hers.

It was dark when she and Charlie walked him home,

all of them breathing frosty plumes into air that had grown hard with cold after sunset.

'I want to give you something.' Jackson dug under his T-shirt, pulled out a chain, and peeled it over his head. He held up the silver cross, glinting in the light from the streetlamps. 'You know what this is?'

'Sure. It's a crucifix. Where'd you get it?'

'My mom gave it to me so I wouldn't be afraid when she died.'

Grace closed her eyes briefly and dropped to her heels so she could look him in the eye. 'Your mom's dead?'

'Yeah. Last year. Cancer.' He slipped the chain over her head and then smiled at her, white teeth in a black night. 'There. Now you'll be safe.'

33

Pandemonium, Magozzi thought, dodging hustling bodies to get to his desk in the homicide room. There just wasn't another word for it.

All the shifts were in, crowding at desks, vying for phones and computers, a hive of disconnected creatures stumbling over one another, shouting to be heard. Delivery people were lined up at Gloria's desk balancing pizza boxes and bags of Thai and Chinese and God knew what else, while a furious Gloria yelled for people to come pay for their damn food and get it off her desk.

A general din from beyond the room added to the confusion. The press had jammed the hallway, filming everything, hollering questions at the hapless uniform posted at the door, who probably should have been made to check his gun, just so he didn't shoot anybody. And they weren't going to leave anytime soon.

Magozzi glanced at the muted TV in the corner and watched it like a silent movie. They were linked to the satellite feed now, live on every station in the city.

Chief Malcherson was locked in his office, the phone glued to his ear, probably talking to the mayor or the council members or maybe even the governor, trying to explain what had gone wrong at the Mall of America, who was to blame, and what the hell they were going to do next. Magozzi couldn't begin to imagine what he was telling them. There were no pat answers, and for the very first time since he'd first walked into the Monkeewrench office, he was beginning to think there was no solution. This psycho was just going to keep killing people one by one, and there wasn't a goddamned thing they could do about it.

And for the second time in twenty-four hours, none of the Monkeewrench people could come up with a solid alibi. At the time of the mall murder, supposedly Annie, Harley, and Roadrunner were in their respective homes alone, Grace was at the loft, and Mitch was in his car between client calls. No witnesses for any of them. It was starting to smell, even to Magozzi – for people that usually stuck together twelve hours out of every twenty-four, it seemed pretty damn coincidental that every time they weren't together, somebody got killed.

'Hey, Leo.' Patrol Sergeant Eaton Freedman looked up miserably from a desk that looked like doll furniture with him sitting at it. 'Bad scene today.' He'd been coordinating the door-to-doors on the registration list all day, and was the only member of the task force who hadn't made it out to the mall. 'I hear Langer took it hard.'

'He was pretty wrecked. We sent him home. Peterson isn't much better off. Walking wounded.' They both glanced over at a desk in a far corner where Detective Peterson sat with his head in his hands.

Freedman shook his big head. 'I don't get it. Woman was long dead by the time they saw her, right?'

'Oh yeah. We've got a scene in one of the dressing rooms in the Nordstrom store. Looks like he did her there, then just wheeled her out. They aren't shouldering the blame for that one, but if there's a next one, they figure it's on their heads.'

Freedman nodded sympathetically. By this time everyone in the department knew that Langer and Peterson had seen the shooter, had been within range, and not only did he get away, neither detective could describe him. 'It's not their fault. It's this damn cold,' he said angrily. 'You could walk into your own mother on the street and not recognize her.'

And the sketchy description both Peterson and Langer had given on the scene seemed to prove the point. One of those long, puffy down coats with a furred hood, a heavy stocking cap, a scarf wrapped around the lower face – typical garb for Minnesota when the mercury fell and the winds rose, not at all suspicious – and the person beneath all that could have been anyone from Marilyn Monroe to a German shepherd. Frigid weather made for a hell of a disguise.

'But it wasn't that!' Langer had shouted at him back at the mall, refusing the salvation of any excuse. 'You don't understand! I never even *looked* at the person pushing it! I'm a trained observer! I'm supposed to see everything! And all I saw was the woman in the wheelchair!' He'd been shaking by that time, with cold, surely, and some personal demon Magozzi didn't have a handle on yet.

Peterson had said pretty much the same thing, but where Langer had jumped into a hair shirt like it was the only garment on the planet, Peterson had just been kicking himself in the ass.

'Hey, Leo.'

He turned at a gentle nudge on his shoulder and

got a whiff of Gloria's perfume. Something faint and flowery and expensive, and the best thing he'd smelled all day. God, he loved having women around.

'Rambo called,' she told him, pushing a pile of pink message slips into his hand. 'You got a slug from the mall vic, a good one, lots of rifling. He's still working on her, but he thought you'd want to know that right away. And that sheriff from Wisconsin has been calling all day. The man is driving me nuts.'

'What's he want?'

'I don't know. He won't leave a message, and he won't tell me jackshit.'

'I'll take care of it.' Magozzi sighed and turned back to Freedman, glanced down at the sheaf of papers he was working on, row after row of print almost solid with yellow highlighter. 'That the registration list?'

Freedman gave a glum nod. 'Even with the right names and addresses, it's going to take days, maybe weeks to knock on this many doors, and that was before half my teams got diverted to the mall. Besides, I keep hearing what that MacBride woman said, about him not being on the list at all, and I gotta wonder if we aren't just spinning our wheels with this thing.'

'You and me both.' Magozzi pushed at the scowl line between his brows. It felt deep and permanent. 'You still got people out there?'

'Twenty teams of two, working round the clock. We never sleep.'

'Keep at it.' Magozzi gave him a pat on a shoulder that felt like rock, then dragged himself over to his desk. He eased down into his chair like an old man and just sat there for a moment, letting his brain idle.

Gino was already settled in at the desk facing his, yelling into the phone, a finger stuck in his other ear to block out the noise around him. 'I don't know when I'll get home, so what I want to know is this: What are you wearing right this minute?' he hollered, making Magozzi smile.

That was the thing about Gino. No matter what was going down, when he checked in with Angela, it was all about them, and only about them. Magozzi envied him so much it hurt.

34

Sheriff Halloran finally got through to Detective Leo Magozzi at 8 P.M., and the only reason he connected at all was because he'd threatened to lay an obstruction of justice charge on some overly protective secretary who was ten times scarier than Sharon.

'That is such a load of bullshit,' she'd told him.

'I know, but I'm desperate.'

For some reason that made her laugh, and now he had the man himself on the phone. He sounded genuinely contrite, and genuinely exhausted. 'Sorry, Sheriff . . . Halloran, is it?'

'Right. From Kingsford County, Wisconsin.'

'Well, I'm sorry I couldn't get back to you, Sheriff. Things have really been hitting the fan here today.'

'Mall of America. I heard it on the news, and I'll try to be quick . . .'

'Wait a minute. Kingsford County. Oh, man, son of a bitch I am sorry. You're the one who lost a man this week, aren't you?'

'Deputy Daniel Peltier,' Halloran said, and then for some reason he added, 'Danny.'

'I want you to know all of us here were really sorry to hear about that. Hell of a thing, losing a man that way.'

'Hell of a thing to lose a man any way.'

'I hear you. And listen, I can't believe you didn't get

a call from the chief, but I know we're sending a car for the service . . .'

'I did hear from your chief, and we appreciate it. That's not why I'm calling, Detective Magozzi.'

'Oh?'

'The thing is, I got your name from the Mother Superior at Saint Peter's School in New York.'

The detective was silent for so long Halloran could hear snatches of a half dozen urgent conversations in the background.

'Detective Magozzi? You still there?'

'Yeah. Sorry. You caught me a little off guard. I've just been trying to think what to make of that. May I ask why you had a conversation with the people at Saint Peter's today?'

Halloran released a long, slow breath, the way he did just before he eased back on the trigger at the firing range. 'We had a double homicide here the day Deputy Peltier was killed.'

'Yeah, the old couple in the church. I read about it. Just a sec.' He covered the mouthpiece and raised his voice. 'Could you people hold it down, please?' As far as Halloran could tell, the background noise didn't diminish much. 'Sorry, Sheriff. You were saying?'

'I'll make it real short, Detective. Our only lead on a suspect in that double homicide led us straight to that school, and when we called there this morning and found out you had called them, too . . .'

Someone on the Minneapolis end was hollering about a pizza, and Magozzi didn't even bother to cover the mouthpiece this time, he just yelled, 'GOD-DAMNIT, SHUT THE FUCK UP!'

And then there was total silence on both ends.

'Excuse the language, Sheriff.'

Halloran smiled. 'No problem. Sounds like every movie about city cops I ever saw.'

'Yeah, well, they weren't filmed in this area code. I've got a chief who loves to lecture on the deterioration of the English language as a moral indicator of the decline of civilization. So you think your killer had ties to that school.'

'Maybe. It's a long story.'

'Tell you what. I'm caught out in the main room here, and this place is a zoo tonight. Let me get to someplace quiet and call you back.'

'This is pretty much a shot in the dark, Detective. We've got nothing solid that would suggest what we're dealing with is in any way connected to your murders. The coincidence bothered us, though.'

'I'd like to hear what you've got.'

'I'll wait for your call.'

'So what was that about?' Gino asked, biting the end off of a huge piece of pepperoni pizza, catching a hanging string of mozzarella with his tongue.

'I don't know. Could be just a weird coincidence. Come on.' Magozzi pushed himself up from his chair and started weaving through the desks toward an interview room.

Gino followed, tomato sauce plopping to the floor behind him in a bloody trail. 'Cops don't believe in coincidence. I heard it on "Law and Order."'

'Well then, it must be true. Remember that old couple killed in a church in Wisconsin earlier this week?'

'Sure I remember. Deputy walked into their house

later and got blown away by a rigged shotgun. Survivalists or something. Don't you want a piece of this? It ain't Angela's, but it ain't bad.'

'No thanks. That was the sheriff over there. Says they traced a suspect to Saint Peter's School in New York.'

Gino stopped walking. '*Our* Saint Peter's?'

Gino kept checking in at the small interview room where Magozzi was talking to Halloran and by the time he'd hung up, Gino looked like he was ready to climb the walls. 'Well?'

Magozzi propped his feet up on a chair and stared at the scuffed suede toes of his black Hush Puppies. 'Weird stuff, Gino.'

'How weird?'

'Weird enough so that Sheriff Halloran is driving over here sometime tonight.'

'So who's the suspect he traced to Saint Peter's School?'

'The old couple's kid. Apparently they dumped him there when he was five, never came back. That was twenty-six years ago.'

Gino closed the door on the noise from the homicide room and just stood there for a minute, trying to get his head around parents who could abandon a child. It wasn't like he hadn't seen it a hundred times before; he just never could get used to it.

Magozzi was looking at him. 'The kid was a hermaphrodite, Gino.'

'Wha-at?'

Magozzi nodded. 'Boy and girl, all at once. Halloran talked to the doc who delivered him – or her – and he said the parents were religious freaks, figured the kid was God's punishment or some crap like that. They refused the surgery that would have made the kid one or the other. God knows what the first five years of his life were like. Eventually they dropped him at Saint Peter's, paid twelve years' tuition in advance, and just split.'

'You keep saying "him."'

'He was dressed as a boy when he arrived, so the school treated him as a boy. And named him.'

Gino frowned. 'What do you mean, they named him?'

Magozzi grabbed a yellow legal pad from the table and started thumbing through his notes, his expression grim. 'The kid didn't have a first name when he got there. The Mother Superior told one of Halloran's people she didn't think anyone had ever talked to him in his life up to that point – the kid could barely speak. Anyhow, they called him Brian. Brian Bradford.'

Gino looked at the back wall of the spartan room with its single narrow window. 'You know what the miracle is here? That Sheriff Halloran is even bothering to look for whoever killed these dirtbags. I take it he ran the name.'

'And got nothing. No hits on any Brian Bradford with his DOB.'

Gino sighed and rubbed the back of his neck. 'All right. So Halloran's shooter grows up at this obscure Catholic boarding school in New York, and our shooter lays an e-mail path to that very same school. One-in-a-million odds. One coincidence too many. Let's find him and have him picked up.'

'It's not that easy.'

'Well, shit, I must be psychic. I knew you were going to say that.'

'He disappeared when he was sixteen.'

'Aw, Jeez.' Gino jerked a chair out from the table and sat down. 'You notice that everybody involved with this damn case keeps dropping off the face of the earth? I'm starting to look down at my legs every now and then just to make sure I'm still here.'

Magozzi flipped a page on the tablet. 'Looks like the Kleinfeldts – that's the old couple – had been running from somebody for a long time. They'd been in New York the longest – twelve years – but before that, the sheriff traced them back through God knows how many name changes and locations across the country. They really started hopping around about the same time their kid picked up his diploma and walked away from Saint Peter's. City to city, state to state, changing their names every time.'

'Hiding.'

'Right. They'd stay in one place for a while, then something happened. B and E in their apartment in Chicago, all their clothes cut up, feces all over the walls, furniture slashed, every dish broken, the next day they were gone. They turn up in Denver with brand-new names, stay there a few months until some U-Haul the locals couldn't trace rams them from behind, tries to push them off a cliff. They disappear again. Then in California, somebody blows up their million-dollar house. Fortunately for the happy couple, they're living in the guest house by the pool. The local who caught it believed they knew somebody was coming, and he didn't even know the history.'

'Man.' Gino shook his head.

'Next time we see them they're the Kleinfeldts in Wisconsin, and by this time they must have learned to cover their tracks pretty well, because it's ten years before their little shadow turns up, and this time they think they're ready.'

'The rigged shotgun that caught the deputy.'

'Yeah. But the shooter got them in the church instead, the one place they couldn't set booby traps. Twenty-two to the head, both of them. One of the slugs was useless, flattened inside the man's skull so there was damn near nothing left; but the one they pulled out of the missus lodged in brain tissue. It's got some rifling. Halloran's driving it over tonight. Doesn't trust it anywhere but inside his own pocket.'

Gino was playing with a piece of pizza crust, balancing it on end on the table, turning it to balance on the other end. 'Does Halloran have anything solid? Anything that makes him absolutely sure it's their kid?'

'A couple of things, I don't know if you'd call them solid, exactly. The Kleinfeldts were murdered on their kid's birthday, if you want to start stacking up coincidences. Plus he's got some psych wiz in the department who says there are road signs all over the place that make it real personal. The feces on the wall in the Chicago apartment, for instance. Apparently that's a classic sociopathic kid-against-parents thing. And there's something they held back from the media.'

Magozzi looked down at a mass of dark scribbling on the tablet, where his note-taking had deteriorated into meaningless slashes. 'After he shot them in the church, he opened their clothes, carved big crosses in their chests – damn near flayed them, the ME said – and then he dressed them again.'

Gino licked his lips, swallowed. 'Well, that sure sounds personal.'

'It gets worse. The slug he's bringing didn't kill the old woman, not right away. Mrs Kleinfeldt was alive when he carved her up.'

Gino tipped his chair back on two legs and closed his eyes, and all his years showed on his face. 'Anything besides the Catholic school connection to tie our shooter to his?'

Magozzi nodded. 'Now this you're going to like.'

'Well, good, because I haven't liked any of it so far.'

'After the kid graduated Saint Peter's and took off, the school got a transcript request from Georgia State in Atlanta.'

Gino's chair came down with a bang. 'Holy shit.'

'That's where he was born, Gino. Atlanta. Looks like Brian Bradford was going home.'

'Holy shit.'

'You already said that.'

'Goddamn.'

'Ah, an original thought.'

'Just a minute, just a minute.' Gino was excited now. He jumped up and started circling the scarred wooden table, frowning hard while his thoughts went a mile a minute. 'He's five, twenty-six years ago – that puts him on campus about the same time as the murders . . .'

'And the same time as the Monkeewrench people.'

'None of whom have alibis for any of the murders.' Gino looked at him. 'Goddamnit, Leo, we've got to find a way to lock these people up.'

'You figure out a way to do it, you let me know. In the meantime, we've got to at least cover them.'

'And we've got to get their real names. Maybe one of them's Bradford.'

Magozzi reached for the phone. 'I'll check with Tommy, see if he cracked into that FBI file yet . . .'

'Don't bother. I checked in with him while you were on the phone. He's still tearing his hair out over that one. Said something about being one click away from entry when he ran smack-dab into some new firewall he can't penetrate.'

Magozzi frowned. 'That's funny. He told me he could hack through FBI security in his sleep.'

'Yeah, well, he doesn't think so anymore. You know what we oughta do? Round them all up again, make them drop their drawers, and check their equipment, see if anybody has too much.'

'I think that might be illegal.'

'Maybe we could get them to volunteer.'

Magozzi laughed. 'Right, go ahead. Call Annie Belinsky and ask her to lift her skirt, I dare you.'

Gino snorted. 'Not her. There is no way on God's earth you could be that much of a woman, and part man at the same time. Besides, she wouldn't hurt a fly.'

'Except that one guy she says she knifed to death.'

'Who I am absolutely sure deserved it,' Gino said. He sat down again and leaned his elbows on the table and stared at his hands. 'You know, this just keeps getting worse. Now we don't even know if we're looking for a woman or a man.'

Magozzi tossed his pen on the desk and pushed the phone toward Gino.

'Who am I calling?'

'Atlanta PD. See if they've got a Brian Bradford in their book on the campus murders. And if they don't, have them check admissions at the Atlanta campus. If Bradford went there, he used the transcript from Saint Peter's. Even if he changed his name afterwards, we ought to be able to dig up some kind of a trail.'

Gino stabbed at the numbers with a sausage-like finger. 'It's almost ten o'clock there. The university's been closed for hours.'

'They're the cops. Tell them to track down somebody who can open the office and check it out.'

'Okay, but I'm using your name.'

Chief Malcherson waved Magozzi and Gino into his office, then gestured for them to close the door and sit down. Magozzi wondered if the whole meeting was going to be conducted in sign language, and then decided that if he'd spent as many hours in front of the press and on the phone as the chief had today, he probably wouldn't feel like talking either.

It took them ten full minutes to bring him up to speed. He listened without interrupting as he rolled down his cuffs, buttoned his collar, and adjusted his tie, getting ready to run the media gauntlet as he left the building. He tried straightening his white hair with his hands, but it was hopeless. Too much mousse, Magozzi thought.

'So Atlanta PD is going to pull their files on the campus murders, but the Brian Bradford name didn't ring any bells with the detective Gino talked to, and he worked the case,' Magozzi finished. 'But the Monkeewrench connection is definitely tightening up with this Wisconsin thing. They're either suspects or targets, but either way, we need to cover all five of them, full-time.'

'I agree.' The chief got up and slipped his topcoat from a wooden hanger on the tree in the corner. 'But you're going to have to pull people from the roster you already have. We've been running through officers like water, and the well just went dry.'

'Come on, Chief,' Gino complained. 'Everybody we've got is already at the end of their second double in two days. What about getting some more highway patrol or loaners from all those sheriffs' departments who were so hot to trot yesterday?'

'Not a chance. All the locals are keeping their people close to home, including the district HPs, trying to cover the schools.'

'Even out-state?' Magozzi asked. 'That's ridiculous. This guy hasn't hit outside the city limits once.'

Malcherson shook his head. 'Doesn't matter. They've got constituencies to answer to, just like we do, and their people want their officers on their turf, not ours.'

'Christ.' Gino flung himself against the back of his chair, disgusted. 'That's stupid. If he hits at all, chances are he's going to hit in a Minneapolis school, and how the fuck are we supposed to cover them?'

It was a measure of Malcherson's weariness that he didn't climb all over Gino for his language. He just rebuked him with a glance, shrugged into his topcoat, and started to button it. 'I just got off the phone with the governor. He's closing all the metro and suburban schools tomorrow. It'll be on the ten-o'clock news.'

Gino shook his head. 'I knew it. Here we go. We

now have a psychopath running the whole damn city, just like I said, and it's all downhill from here. Tomorrow we close the schools, next day we shut down the ambulances . . .'

'What did you expect him to do?' Malcherson almost raised his voice. 'We're losing a person a day, and there aren't many people in this state who think the Minneapolis Police Department can do a damn thing about it, including the governor!' He looked once at each of them, then dropped his eyes and released the breath that had been turning his face red. 'Sorry. Not your fault. Not anybody's fault. I've just been on the phone too long.'

'They've been beating on you pretty hard, eh?' Gino asked, and Malcherson barked a soft, humorless laugh.

'That new council member – Wellburg, or whatever his name is – had the temerity to call and ask me why I wasn't doing anything about the murders, and by that time I'd been through the wringer so many times I told him because I just didn't want to. I imagine that will be on the ten-o'clock news, too.'

He sighed and looked off into a corner, no doubt wondering if he'd have a job after the regular city council meeting tomorrow. 'Listen, all I can tell you is to work with what you've got. Take some of the uniforms off the registration list – sounds like that's not going anywhere anyway – hell, lock all the Monkeewrench people in a room and you two can take turns standing guard at the door.' He paused for a deep breath. 'Or else let the FBI in. Give them a name for those prints and they'll be tickled to death to run surveillance on anyone you want.'

Magozzi shifted uncomfortably in his chair. 'I don't want to do that, sir.'

Malcherson blinked, surprised. Magozzi never called him 'sir.' 'If you get a match on that slug from Wisconsin, they're going to be in this up to their eyebrows tomorrow anyway. It'll be their case then.'

'I know.'

'You'll have to turn over all your files. Every scrap of paper.'

Magozzi nodded carefully, and Malcherson's eyes narrowed.

'You didn't write it down, did you? You're not ever going to tell them whose prints they were. Or me, for that matter. Wait. Don't answer that. I'd have to suspend you.' He sighed again, straightened his lapels, and grabbed a briefcase from his desk. 'Gentlemen, I'm going home. I'm going to walk the dog and have a drink with my wife, or maybe the other way around, depending on which one is talking to me. Gino, give my best to Angela.'

'She'll be pleased you thought of her, Chief.'

Malcherson stopped at the door, a little smile on his face. 'You know, she probably will be. She's that kind of person. God knows what you did to deserve her, Rolseth, but I assume it was in a former life.' He closed the door quietly behind him.

After he left Gino turned and eyed Magozzi. 'Are you ever going to tell the chief they're MacBride's prints?'

Magozzi shrugged.

'You got any idea what kind of shitstorm is going to come down on you if she turns out to be the shooter?'

'MacBride isn't the shooter, Gino.'

Gino slid down in the chair until his butt was on the edge, leaned his head back, and closed his eyes. 'Wish I was as positive about her as you are. So what do we do now, Kemosabi?'

'What the chief said, I guess. We'll have Freedman pull some uniforms out of his hat to put on them, starting with third watch.'

Gino lifted his wrist and opened his eyes a slit to peer at his watch. 'Third doesn't start for a few hours.'

'Yeah. I thought we'd cover them till then.'

'Excuse me, but we're two and they're five.'

'They're all going to be in the same place. They left their schedule with Gloria, remember? I checked it earlier.'

'You gotta call Angela. She's gonna scream like a banshee.'

Magozzi smiled. 'Angela never raised her voice in her life.'

'Yeah, you're right. But she'll whimper. I hate that.' Gino pushed himself out of his chair and stretched. 'So where are we headed?'

Magozzi grinned at him.

'Oh, shit. It's bad, isn't it?'

35

Halloran had just hung up with Detective Magozzi and was rising from his chair when Sharon Mueller walked into his office. He froze there for a minute, half in and half out of the chair, then sank back down slowly, speechless.

Apparently his reaction pleased her, because she smiled at him. 'Gee, thanks, Halloran.'

'You're wearing a dress,' he told her, just in case she hadn't noticed.

He'd never seen her in anything but her uniform. Straight brown pants, brown shirt and tie, clunky regulation shoes, and of course the ten pounds of hardware they all wore on their belts. Not to mention the gun. Which she wasn't wearing. Probably thought it would clash with the clingy little red thing that rode low on the top and high on the bottom.

She hiked the skirt a little to show about four hundred feet of leg and he nearly passed out. 'And high heels,' she pointed out, which was a good thing since he hadn't gotten down that far yet and probably never would.

He looked up at her face to be polite, and was startled to see a little makeup, which she never wore and didn't need. A smoky color on her eyelids and a sleek shine on her lips that made them look like they were made of colored water. It just wasn't fair, gilding the lily like that.

'I've never seen you out of uniform before,' he said.

'This is a uniform. It's my date uniform. We're going out.'

'Okay,' he said without thinking, and then remembered. 'Only I can't.'

Her dark eyes narrowed a little. 'Why not?'

'I have to catch bad guys.'

She blew out a noisy sigh and her shoulders slumped a little, which made her breasts move under the red fabric, and he had to look down at his hands. They were just lying there on the desk, fingers slightly curled, lazy sons of bitches doing nothing, looking stupid, no help at all.

'I know you're not gay, Halloran . . .'

'Oh dear. The secret's out.'

'. . . so what's the deal? Two years and you've never hit on me. Not once.'

He cleared his throat. 'I'm not allowed to sexually harass officers under me. It says so right in the police manual.'

'That's not funny.'

'I wasn't trying to be funny. It really does say so in the police manual.'

She tightened her lips and he waited for all the colored water to run out, surprised when it didn't. 'Fine. Then I'll harass you. Let's get out of here so I can get started.'

He felt his mouth move into one of those Harrison Ford shit-eating-grin looks. Here he was in a nearly empty building with a woman in a red dress he'd wanted since she'd stood in front of him two years ago, shoving her application in his face, and *she* was seducing *him*.

Women probably did that to Harrison Ford all the time. No wonder he looked like that.

'You're not going to catch any bad guys here tonight anyway.'

The shit-eating grin slipped away. She'd waved his little sheriff's star in front of him without even realizing what she was doing. 'Well, that's the thing,' he sighed, getting up and gathering papers and folders and photos that were spread all over his desk, stuffing them into the box that had become the Kleinfeldt file. 'I'm going to Minneapolis tonight.'

She was silent for a beat, and he felt the change in her like a sudden drop in barometric pressure. Woman to deputy, all business, just like that. 'What happened?'

He hefted the box under one arm and grabbed his coat from the back of his chair. 'I've got to go to the evidence room and then get going. It's a long drive.' He flipped off the lights, closed and locked the door to his office, then headed downstairs. She was hot on his heels.

'It's the same guy, isn't it?' she needled him, trotting in her little high heels to keep up. 'The Monkeewrench Killer is our guy.'

'The Monkeewrench Killer? Where'd you hear that?'

'That's the media moniker. And he's our guy, right?'

'Maybe. They got a .22 slug from the Mall of America shooting this afternoon, enough rifling to run a comparison with the one we pulled out of Mrs Kleinfeldt.'

She kept firing questions at him, oblivious to Cleaton looking up from where he was ogling Melissa in the dispatch booth, his jaw dropping when he got a look at Sharon in a red dress. Why had Minneapolis PD called the Catholic boarding school? What were they looking for? Was the killer doing any creative carving on his victims over there? Were they getting any forensics help from the scenes, and, bizarrely, what did Detective Magozzi sound like?

He told her everything they had, which wasn't much, including the fact that Magozzi sounded like a nice enough guy who was just about at the end of his rope.

'It makes perfect sense,' she said as they went down the tiled steps to the basement.

'What do you mean?'

She was excited, walking fast, talking fast, ahead of him now in the narrow hall, heading for the wire mesh door at the end. 'The Kleinfeldts were his first; the people he really wanted to kill. That one was personal. Hence the crosses in the chests.'

Halloran raised his brows at 'hence.' He couldn't remember anyone ever saying that word aloud before.

'That MO didn't transfer to his next victims, because he doesn't care about them, doesn't even think of them as people. It isn't personal anymore. It's just business.'

'Business? What kind of business?' He unlocked the mesh gate and pushed it open.

'Monkey business.' She wrinkled her nose when he didn't laugh at her joke. 'I don't know what kind of business, but he's got a goal in mind, something very specific he wants to accomplish.'

'The feeling in Minneapolis is he's just doing this for fun. Playing the game, beating everybody.' He set the box on a table and fumbled on the wall for the light switch. Fluorescents flickered to white life overhead and revealed rows of metal shelves holding boxes of evidence from cases that went back into the last century. Kingsford County never threw anything away.

Sharon walked straight to the nearest shelf, pulled out a small box, and checked the label on the plastic bag inside. 'But why play the game at all? If shooting people in the head was enough to give him his jollies, he could just off anybody, anywhere. Don't you see?' She walked over and tucked the bag in Halloran's breast pocket, closed the flap, and pressed her hand against it. 'He's gone to a lot of trouble to follow this game very precisely, and he's taking some big risks. Like at the mall today. He had to know that place was crawling with cops, just waiting for him. Not exactly a killer's ideal venue. And still he did it. Why?'

Her hand was still pressed flat against his breast pocket, and he wondered if she could feel his heartbeat, much too fast and hard for a man standing still. 'Maybe he wants to make the cops look bad.'

'Maybe. Then you've got to ask, what's he got against cops? What's the history? Because there is a reason for this, no matter how twisted it seems to the rest of us, and when you figure out the reason, you're just a step away.'

'You learn all this in those psych classes?'

She smiled up at him. 'Among other things. Are you ready to go?'

'Uh-huh.' But he didn't move, because if he did, she'd take her hand away from his pocket and he figured his heart might get cold.

'I've got to make a quick stop at my place, change into a uniform.'

'You're not going.'

'Of course I am. It's the middle of the night, it's a six-, seven-hour drive. You'll fall asleep and run into a tree.'

He thought about that for a minute. 'I'll take Bonar.'

She jerked her hand away from his chest, took a step back, and glared at him, eyes outflashing the lights overhead. 'Oh, now that's great, Halloran. Thanks a lot. I've worked this case just as hard as Bonar has, so what's the problem? What is it? Afraid showing up with a female deputy will make you look bad to the big macho city dicks?'

'Oh, for Christ's sake.' Halloran had her by the upper arms and up against the wall before she took her next breath, his face so close to hers his vision blurred, his body flat and pressing hard until he felt every single thing she had under the little red dress. 'What I'm afraid of' – he talked with his mouth right against hers and swore he tasted colored water – 'is that I'll never get to Minneapolis if I take you along.'

He kissed her for a long time – years, or maybe three seconds – and then her mouth moved and opened under his and he had to throw his hands against the wall on either side of her just to stay upright.

He figured he had two choices: take her right there against the wall in the Kingsford County evidence room, or drive all the way across the state in the middle of the night to chase a killer and keep his job.

He'd just decided that there wasn't a man alive who needed any job that bad when she pushed him away. Her eyes were wide and she was breathing through her mouth. 'Damnit, Mike, I nearly fainted.'

Here came the Harrison Ford shit-eating grin again.

He would have given a million bucks to be back in high school right then, just so he could go to the locker room tomorrow morning and tell the guys, hey, I kissed a girl last night and she nearly fainted.

'You'd better go.'

He moved into her again. 'I'm not in that much of a hurry.'

She ducked under his arms and quick-stepped away from him to the doorway, her skirt swirling, showing knee and thigh and the lacey top of a nylon. 'Neither am I,' she said, looking right at him. 'That's why you'd better go.'

He was so dumbfounded that she could just walk away from him like that, click those little heels all the way down the hall and then trot up the stairs, that it never occurred to him to think that she had given in too easily about riding along to Minneapolis.

An hour later, Halloran and Bonar were on Highway 29 heading west, a thermos of Marjorie's coffee between them, two full cups steaming in the holders. Bonar was driving the first leg with the apparent intention of getting it over with as soon as possible. He had the cruise set at eighty and the roof lights flashing.

'Never thought you'd be in this much of a hurry to get to the big city.'

'I'm not. I hate cities. Smog, crime, parking meters, cities suck. But I am going to make it to Eat 'n Run Truck Stop in Five Corners before it closes. Best damn roast beef and gravy in the state.'

'I thought you and Marjorie went to Hidden Haven for dinner.'

'That was hours ago.'

'You can't eat roast beef and gravy in a car.'

'I can eat roast beef and gravy on a stick, but the truth is, I was thinking of you. Sharon said you didn't eat dinner.'

'When did you talk to Sharon?'

'Between jumping out of Marjorie's bed and running to my place to change into a uniform.'

'She called you? Why?'

'To tell me to stop and get you something to eat. You should probably marry that girl.'

'I'm too young to get married.'

'You're damn near too old to reproduce.'

'We haven't even had a date yet.'

'Do that first.' Bonar swerved to avoid the remains of raccoon on the road. 'I heard the "yet," by the way.'

Halloran slid down in the seat and closed his eyes.

'I went by Danny's folks' tonight to pay my respects.'

Halloran opened his eyes.

'They said you were over there this morning. Drove them to the funeral home, helped them make all the arrangements.'

'I had some time.'

'Bullshit you did. You're a nice guy, Mike. Suck it up.'

Halloran closed his eyes again. Yeah. That's what he was, all right. A nice guy. Helped the grieving parents of a kid he'd gotten killed get ready to put him in the ground. What a prince.

'They said the funeral's Monday.'

Halloran nodded. 'Danny's sister is in France somewhere. She couldn't get back until Sunday.'

'I don't think I've ever been to a Monday funeral.'

'I wish to God we didn't have to go to this one.'

36

Diane hurried away from a cluster of admirers when Grace, Harley, Roadrunner, and Annie entered the art gallery, gliding toward them on a cloud of white silk.

She embraced them all, then took both of Grace's hands in hers and stepped back, smiling. 'You dressed up.'

'Only for you.' Grace smiled back.

'Huh?' Harley frowned at Grace's trademark black jeans, T-shirt, and duster. 'What are you talking about? That's what she wears every day.'

'Harley, you are such a cretin,' Diane scolded him.

'I keep telling him that,' Annie said.

'She's wearing the Moschino T-shirt,' Diane pointed out. 'And if that isn't dressing up I don't know what is.'

Harley leaned over and peered at Grace's T-shirt. 'Looks like Fruit Of The Loom to me.'

Diane shook her head in bemused exasperation, then looked from one to the other. 'You didn't have to come tonight. I know how bad things have been.'

'Sugar, are you out of your mind? Have we ever missed one of your openings?' Annie asked. 'Besides, this is just what we needed.'

Roadrunner nodded. 'Yeah. Especially after the thing at the mall today.'

Diane took his hand and squeezed it. 'Just let that

all go for a couple hours. And I have something that I think will help.' She raised her hand and a uniformed waiter came over with a tray of champagne.

'I love this woman,' Harley said, taking a glass from the tray and draining it, then grabbing another. 'Where's that sack-of-shit husband of yours?'

Diane waved a hand vaguely toward the crowd at the buffet table. 'You know Mitch. Doing what he does best. When I left he was selling the most expensive piece here to some poor man who bought his last painting in a gas station parking lot.' She sighed and glanced fondly over at Mitch. 'It's distracting him, anyway. He needed that.'

She turned back to them with a regretful smile. 'I have to go mingle now, but please stay as long as you'd like. Eat, drink, be merry, and leave when you have to. It means the world that you all came tonight.'

She held Grace back when the others made an immediate beeline for the buffet table. 'How are you holding up? This has to be worse for you than anyone else.'

Grace reached out and gave her a hug. 'I get by with a little help from my friends,' she quoted the Beatles. 'Just like always.'

Gino and Magozzi parked in a pay-box lot and walked the last block in the cold, looking like a couple of B-movie mobsters in their flapping trench coats.

The Acton-Schlesinger Gallery was housed on the top floor of yet another renovated warehouse very much like the Monkeewrench building, and only a few blocks away. A brass plaque at the entrance of the building informed visitors that this had once housed a clothing manufacturer that specialized in men's under-garments.

Gino was sullen and defensive as he and Magozzi entered the vacuous downstairs foyer, no doubt anticipating the pretentious snobbery and general nostril-gazing he was certain he would be subjected to from the crowd upstairs.

'With that kind of attitude, you *are* going to get snubbed,' Magozzi admonished him.

'You just wait and see, Leo. I've been to stuff like this before with Angela and if you aren't pale as a ghost, emaciated, and dressed head to toe in black, they won't give you the time of day.'

'You're going to see what you want to see,' Magozzi sighed. 'Me, I'm just looking forward to seeing what kind of woman married a neurotic mess like Cross.'

The gallery space was vast and spartan, with gleaming blond floors and vaulted bare-beamed ceilings that glowed with soft track lighting. Abstract art hung from steel partitions that were arranged in labyrinthine fashion throughout the space. Elegant patrons with elevated chins and ennui-filled eyes milled through the maze like well-dressed rats, sipping pink champagne from crystal stemware.

An attractive young woman dressed in the requisite black uniform greeted them with a tray of champagne flutes. Her face had a fresh innocence to it despite the generous application of white powder, and the smile was demure, although the effect was mostly lost behind blood-red lipstick. To her credit, she didn't bat an eye at their rumpled suits that were beginning to look slept in. 'Welcome, gentlemen. May I offer you some champagne?'

Magozzi and Gino looked at each other. The prospect of an alcoholic beverage had them both salivating.

'Billecart-Salmon,' she enticed.

'I guess that's supposed to be good, huh?' Gino asked her.

'Better than good.'

He looked back at Magozzi. 'We on duty?' he whispered.

Magozzi bit his lower lip. 'Not in an official capacity, I don't think.'

Gino beamed at the young woman and took two flutes. 'You are an angel from heaven. Bless you, my child.'

Her demure smile broadened to a grin. She seemed grateful to have found two patrons who wouldn't have apoplexy if she broke character. 'Anytime. I'll keep my eye out for empties.'

'You know, this place ain't so bad after all,' Gino said, smacking his lips and surveying the surroundings. 'Best-tasting champagne I ever had, even if it is pink.'

Magozzi savored the glowing warmth of carbonated alcohol hitting his bloodstream fast. The feeling was vaguely familiar to him – he'd experienced it once or twice about a thousand years ago – it was called relaxation. He took another sip. 'I suppose we should make the rounds.'

Gino drained his glass. 'I like it here on the periphery. Let's just stay here and get bombed, let Halloran take over when he gets into town.'

They indulged their wishful thinking for another

minute, then entered the fray, pausing briefly at the first wall of Diane Cross's paintings, all distinctively styled black-and-whites like the abstract in Mitch Cross's office, and the ones hanging in MacBride's living room.

Magozzi nodded to himself, understanding that marriage and friendship would explain the display of such works, much as a parent hangs the crayoned renderings of a beloved child on the refrigerator, but not understanding at all an entire exhibit of such careless starkness in a gallery as prestigious as this.

He apologized mentally to Vermeer and van Gogh, masters of light and color, for a world that now paid homage to chic over genius.

The Monkeewrench crew wasn't hard to spot in the sea of sleek fashionistas. Grace MacBride and Harley Davidson, engaged in a private conversation at the moment, most closely resembled the gallery's majority of denizens. Both of them could have passed for either patrons or artists, she in her black duster, he encased in enough black leather to dress a rodeo.

Annie stood a few feet away, coquettishly deflecting the attentions of a handsome young man in a vintage tuxedo. Somehow she'd found the time and change of wardrobe to magically transform herself into a semi-formal butterfly adorned in diaphanous, hand-painted chiffon. Magozzi remembered what Espinoza had said about her clothing budget, and he believed it.

Roadrunner, obviously suffering from sensory overload, hovered alone against a far wall in his perennial Lycra – formal black for this occasion – shifting uncomfortably from foot to foot. He offered them a weak wave, then went back to his pacing.

Gino shook his head in genuine sympathy. 'Poor guy looks like an antelope in a pack of lions.'

'Where's Mitch?'

Gino didn't hear him. 'Annie is the only one who looks like she's having fun,' he sighed.

'I think she always has fun. So Mitch – he's the only missing person.'

Gino tore his eyes away from Annie and cocked a thumb toward a linen-covered buffet table groaning under the weight of sushi and floral arrangements. 'There he is.'

Magozzi saw him then, next to a tall blond woman in a white silk gown. There was no question she was the artist – adoring fans clustered around her, vying for audience, and she graciously attended them all while managing to cosset her husband like a cherished pet.

So that was Diane Cross. The artist, the star, and obviously a doting wife. Not a ten-star stunner, maybe, but attractive in that wholesome, athletic sort of way so many Midwesterners aspired to.

The girl who'd greeted them appeared miraculously with a fresh bottle. 'Don't look so surprised,' she laughed, refilling their glasses. 'I told you I'd keep an eye out for empties.'

'Well, cheers to you,' Gino said. 'Do you think you could fill up my friend over there, too? The tall skinny guy?'

'Sure.' She drifted away toward Roadrunner and Gino gave Magozzi a wink.

'I'm going to make my way over there, see if Super Geek had any more luck tracing those e-mails.'

Roadrunner almost looked grateful when Gino

approached him, then his face twisted in confusion, remembering that he was supposed to be taking sides. 'Detective,' he said warily.

'You look like you're about as happy to be here as I am.'

Roadrunner twirled his glass between his fingers nervously. 'Yeah.'

'Any new progress on the e-mails?'

'No.' His eyes narrowed suspiciously. 'Are you playing good cop now?'

Gino laughed. 'No, I'm always the bad cop. But I'm off-duty, sort of. From now on, you've all got your own personal police protection, courtesy of MPD. We're just filling in till the swing shift gets assigned.'

Roadrunner looked alarmed. 'You mean . . . you're *tailing* us?'

Gino shrugged good-naturedly. 'Surveillance, protection – either way you look at it, everybody's safer.'

Roadrunner frowned at him for a minute, then sighed. 'Okay. I guess that makes sense, from a cop's point of view.'

'Only view I got, buddy. So you get dragged to this kind of stuff often?'

'Pretty much. Courtesy to Mitch and Diane, you know?'

'What do you think of the art?'

He shrugged in halfhearted apology. 'Hey, I don't know shit about art. Coming to the shows always makes me feel like an idiot.'

'Well, if any of these people came to your office to see your work, you'd make them feel like idiots, so then it'd be even.'

‘Yeah, I guess so.’

Harley appeared from out of nowhere, which was hard to believe, given his mass. He placed himself between Roadrunner and Gino like a protective father defending his son against the neighborhood bully. ‘You checking up on us, Detective?’

‘Basically. I was just telling Roadrunner here, we got a car on each of you from now on.’

Harley looked Gino hard in the eye. ‘So you’re covering Grace?’

‘You bet.’

‘Well, I sure as hell hope you’re better at covering her than you were covering the goddamned Megamall.’

Gino glared at him. ‘You’re pretty fucking mouthy for a guy who doesn’t have an alibi for any of these murders.’

‘And you’re pretty fucking self-righteous for a guy who knew the last two murders were going down and didn’t stop them.’

Gino looked down into his glass, blowing out a silent whistle, counting to ten. ‘Okay, buddy,’ he finally said, ‘I’m a little buzzed right now, and I’m guessing you are too, which is why you forgot this whole shitload of a case is messing up your doorstep as much as ours.’

Harley glared at him for a minute, then slowly his shoulders slumped and he deflated like a spent balloon. ‘I didn’t forget, Detective,’ he said quietly. ‘Christ, we’re never going to forget. That’s the problem. Grace still blames herself for Georgia and now she’s taking the hits for these, too. We’re worried about her and it makes us crazy. Jesus, what a fucking mess.’

Gino eyed him speculatively. It hadn’t been an

apology exactly, but it was close enough. 'Fucking mess. I'll drink to that.' He lifted his flute and acknowledged Harley with a slight nod before draining his glass. 'You know what? These damn glasses are too small.'

Harley nodded. 'Sit tight. I know where they keep the bottles.'

Ten minutes and almost a bottle later, Gino was starting to think that Harley wasn't such a bad guy after all – in fact, they seemed to have a lot in common. They both hated abstract art, liked pink champagne, and loved to eat. Roadrunner seemed pretty decent, too, especially for a techno-wienie.

They were all standing shoulder to shoulder in front of a painting of bold, distorted strokes that stretched upward like chunks of pulled taffy, trying to make sense of it.

'So what do you think this is supposed to be?' Gino asked.

'Hell if I know,' Harley said. 'Black-and-white shit. I think they're supposed to be people.'

'They're clothespins,' Roadrunner said with great certainty.

'Nah,' Gino disagreed amiably. 'Gotta be people. See the legs? And those fat globs of paint on the bottom are feet. Besides, why would anybody do abstracts of clothespins? They're already abstract, aren't they?'

Harley finished off the rest of the champagne straight from the bottle. 'Good point, Detective.'

'You have to wonder if they're supposed to be anything,' Roadrunner said, slurring his words slightly. 'What if all this contemporary art stuff was just a scam?

What if they just pour a bunch of paint on a canvas and hope it turns into something some pseudo-intellectual art critic says is profound?'

'That's exactly what I think,' Harley started to say, but then a stunning blond in a tight black dress sidled up next to him and touched his arm. 'Is this your work?'

Harley concentrated hard to keep his jaw from falling open. 'Uh . . . no.'

'Oh.' She looked around uncomfortably, searching for a polite way to extricate herself from her obvious mistake.

'It is a . . . moving piece, though, isn't it?' Harley added quickly.

Roadrunner and Gino pretended to ignore the exchange, but they were both smiling smugly.

'Oh, yes! I think it's incredible!' the blond gushed with renewed interest. 'Whoever did these is quite talented. So what's your interpretation of this one?'

Harley leaned back on the rundown heels of his motorcycle boots. 'Well, I think it's a poignant representation of the contemporary dichotomy between homogeneity and global diversity.'

Next to him, Roadrunner bent forward and coughed into his hand, stifling a laugh. Gino looked away.

The blond's eyes brightened in admiration. 'I can see that. You know, with the contrast between the black . . . and the white.'

'Exactly. A bold statement. Black. And then, white. I think there are some racial undertones, too.'

'I still think they're clothespins,' Roadrunner said quietly.

The blond frowned over at him, crinkles of irritation creasing her forehead. 'What did you say?'

'I said they're clothespins. Black and white clothespins,' Roadrunner repeated.

She nodded. 'I see your point. The clothespins represent rural artifacts in a complicated world . . .'

'And I think they're people with teeny-weeny heads and big fat shapeless feet.' Gino upped the stakes.

'Okay. I could see that, too. The suggestion of motor function overriding mental function as a general condition of mankind; the rigidity of the torsos and the emptiness of the background hinting at a paralysis of spirit that has rendered life meaningless . . .'

'A combined representation of paganism and Judeo-Christianity enveloped in hopelessness.' Harley gave a sage nod.

The blond looked as if she'd just had an epiphany. 'Perhaps it's trying to talk to us about being spiritually bereft.'

Gino's eyes were watering from the effort of holding back his laughter. He looked into his empty glass. 'My major concern at the moment is the fact that I'm alcoholically bereft. If you'll excuse me?' He turned and sought out the girl with the tray; Roadrunner examined his options and decided to take up his old station by the far wall.

Across the gallery, Magozzi had waited to approach Grace until she was alone – a window of opportunity that had proven to be rare as hen's teeth. He shouldn't have been surprised – aloof, dark-haired beauties were universally alluring to men, whether your passion was art or punk rock or reading back issues of *Field &*

Stream during half time. And if you were clueless to the fact that this particular beauty had a very nasty temper and a loaded Sig lodged under her armpit, she probably seemed like fair game.

She watched him approach, her expression absolutely neutral. They stood there and stared at each other for a moment, then Magozzi said, 'There are some things I need to ask you.'

'I was alone at the office. No witnesses. No alibi.'

'I know. It wasn't that.'

'What, then?'

Magozzi looked around, hesitating, stalling. 'It's not that easy. I shouldn't be talking to you at all.'

'Because I'm a suspect?'

'Something like that.'

She didn't say anything; she just stood there waiting, not helping him at all.

'Can I give you a lift home?' he finally asked. 'We could talk on the way.' When she didn't answer right away, he added, 'It's important.'

She thought about it for a minute. 'I've got my car. You can ride along if you want.'

'Give me a few minutes. I'll meet you downstairs.'

Magozzi made a quick circuit of the gallery and finally found Gino just coming out of the restroom. 'Hey, buddy.' Gino slapped him on the back. 'You taken a leak yet? They got phones in there, right on a little table with curvy legs . . .'

'I'm going to ride home with MacBride.'

Gino blinked once, then tried to lower his brows in a scowl, but champagne spoiled the effort, leaving one brow up so he merely looked whimsical. 'You're gonna date a suspect?'

'It's not a date.'

Gino tried to absorb that, tucked his lower lip inward. 'You gonna look under her skirt?'

Magozzi covered his eyes with his hand and shook his head. 'Look, Gino, you don't know where I am, you don't know what I'm doing, okay?'

'Damn right I don't know what you're doing. Do you?'

'Hell, no. Can you catch a cab?'

Gino tipped back on his heels and came perilously close to falling over before he righted himself. 'Well, buddy, as it happens, I just talked to Angela. She found a last-minute sitter, and she's meeting me next door for a drink in fifteen minutes. First real date since the Accident.'

'No shit?'

'No shit.'

'You're a lucky man, Gino.'

'Yes I am.'

37

Magozzi was playing with the passenger-seat controls in Grace's Range Rover. By the time he found the seat heater and the lumbar control, he was seriously considering a career as a gigolo.

They were two blocks away from the gallery when Grace said, 'You put a tail on me.'

Magozzi glanced in the side mirror and saw the squad half a block back. 'Kind of conspicuous, isn't it?'

'Just me?'

'All of you.' He counted to twenty and was almost disappointed when she didn't jump all over him. 'Don't tell me you're okay with that.'

Grace sighed and draped her wrists over the top of the steering wheel. 'Magozzi, I'm tired. And you know what? I'm past caring about a lot of things. Now, did you really have something you wanted to talk to me about, or did you just want a ride in my car?'

'I want to know your real names.'

She took the ramp onto I-94, then shot into the far left lane and accelerated. It was a full minute before she spoke again. 'I take it Tommy hasn't hacked into the FBI file yet.'

'You know damn well he hasn't. You made sure of that.'

Grace didn't say anything.

'He ran into the firewall you put on it. And don't

bother to deny it. You did it this morning, probably when you realized he was good enough to crack through FBI security, so you beefed it up a little. You're speeding.'

'You don't get it, do you?' Grace said quietly. 'If anyone ever connects who we are now with who we were in Atlanta, we'd have to disappear again, start all over.'

'Because you're afraid the Atlanta killer would find you.'

'Exactly.'

'He already has.'

Grace sighed heavily. 'Maybe. Maybe it's the same guy, but what if it isn't? What if this really is just some new crazy playing the game, and because we buy into the theory that it's the same guy, we get careless and he finds us again? Can you guarantee it's the same man? That we've got absolutely nothing to lose by blowing our cover?'

Magozzi thought about that. 'No. I can't guarantee it. Not tonight, anyway. But I might be able to tomorrow.'

'Then tomorrow I'll tell you our real names.' She turned her head and looked at him. 'Why is it so important to you to know who we were, Magozzi? There's no magic back there, just ordinary names.'

'I'll get to that.'

'When?'

'To tell you the truth, I'm kind of going out on a limb here. Giving you information about an ongoing homicide investigation isn't exactly procedure.'

Grace looked at him briefly, then back at the road. 'Something broke, didn't it?'

'Maybe.' He rubbed at the ache that was just starting

in his temples. Exhaustion and champagne were a bad combination. 'If there's a chance you might know anything about it, I've got to ask you. If my instincts are right, it could break the case. If they're wrong . . . shit, I don't even want to go there.'

'You're not making a lot of sense.'

'I know. I hope to make more sense later. I guess at the very least I'd like to be looking you in the eye if I go out on that limb.'

'You expect me to invite you into my house?'

'We could stop somewhere else. A coffee shop, bar, whatever.'

Grace shook her head and kept heading toward home.

While Grace put the Range Rover in the garage, Magozzi went out to where the squad was just pulling up to the curb. When the uniform rolled down the window, he recognized Andy Garfield, one of the older patrols who had the savvy to go inside, but absolutely no interest in leaving the streets.

'She was doing eighty-three in a fifty-five, Magozzi. How fast do you think she goes when she doesn't have a cop in the right seat?'

'God knows. How the hell are you, Garfield?'

'Better.'

'I heard Sheila came out all right.'

'Yeah. We were scared shitless for a week, but it was just a cyst.'

'Gino told me. We raised a glass.' He glanced over his shoulder when he heard Grace's boots on the front walk. 'I'm going to be inside for a while. Heads up out here, okay?'

'You got it.'

Up at the door Grace was just inserting her key card when Magozzi came up behind her. 'Garfield's on you tonight. He's a good man.'

'Is that supposed to make me feel better?'

'I don't know. It makes me feel better.'

When she cracked the fortress door a wire-haired mutt was right there, doing a little tap dance, his tongue lolling. His doggy expression shifted comically from great joy to utter shock when he realized Grace wasn't alone, but surprisingly, he didn't run away. He merely kept a wary eye on Magozzi, who was careful to keep his movements slow and predictable.

'So this is the dog that's afraid of strangers? He doesn't seem too afraid now.'

Grace bent over and ruffled his fur. 'Hey, Charlie.' She looked back at Magozzi. 'I guess he remembers you. Or at least the smell of you. Probably figures if you were invited back, you're pretty harmless. Of course, he doesn't realize that you weren't invited either time. That might change his mind.'

'What happened to his tail?'

'I don't know. He was a stray.'

Magozzi knelt down and extended his hand slowly. 'Hey, Charlie. It's okay.'

Charlie scrutinized the offered hand from a distance, then stretched his nose forward tentatively. The stub of his tail wiggled back and forth a couple times.

'He's wagging his stump at me.'

Grace rolled her eyes. 'You sound excited.'

'My standards have dropped a lot in the past week.'

Grace hung her duster in a closet, looked at Magozzi

for a moment, then finally held out a hand for his coat. He stared at her hand for a moment, confused by the unexpected gesture of civility, then scrambled out of his topcoat in record time. 'You're amazingly hospitable when you're tired.'

She just sighed, hung up his coat, and then headed down the hallway toward the kitchen. Charlie scampered behind her, and Magozzi followed, with considerably more dignity, he thought.

'Sit down if you want,' Grace said.

Magozzi pulled up a chair at the kitchen table, then watched, absolutely amazed, as Charlie climbed up into the chair opposite him and sat there like a person.

Grace chose to remain standing, leaning against the counter instead of sitting. Magozzi decided she was big on taking the high ground, moral and otherwise.

'Okay, Magozzi. I'm looking you in the eye. Talk.'

He took a deep breath and let it out slowly and climbed out all the way to the edge of that shaky old limb. 'Let me rattle off some names and you tell me if they mean anything to you.'

'Oh boy. Word association.'

'Does the name Calumet mean anything to you?'

'Baking powder,' she said without batting an eye. 'Did I pass?'

'No, you failed. How about Kleinfeldt?'

'Nothing. So what's Calumet?'

'A small town in Wisconsin.'

'Wisconsin is a state, isn't it?'

Magozzi smiled. 'You're actually funny. Does anyone else know that?'

'Just you.'

'How about Brian Bradford?'

She didn't hesitate. 'Nope.'

'You sure?'

Grace studied him for a minute. 'That's the big one, isn't it?'

Magozzi nodded.

'I've never known a Brian Bradford. I've never known a Bradford, for that matter.'

'No chance that one of your friends might have gone by that name back in Atlanta?'

She pulled out a chair, sat down, and looked him straight in the eye. 'No. No chance at all. And you're going to have to take my word for that, Magozzi.'

Magozzi let out a long, weary breath. He hadn't realized how much hope he'd pinned on MacBride knowing the name until just now, when the hope had suddenly disappeared.

'This Brian Bradford – is he the killer?' Grace asked quietly.

'We think so. He grew up at Saint Peter's . . .'

Grace's eyes widened at that.

'. . . and we think he might have been at the university in Atlanta the same time you were.'

'Jesus.' She closed her eyes and her hand moved reflexively toward her holster, then dropped back to her lap. 'It's the same killer.'

'More and more, it's starting to look that way. We're working some things, trying to confirm his presence in Atlanta. Saint Peter's got a transcript request from the university; we've got people down there checking admissions.'

The sound of chimes from another room was gentle,

musical, but Grace jumped in her seat and caught her breath.

'What's wrong?'

'e-mail,' she whispered, staring past him down the hall.

'From him?'

'I don't know.' She sounded small, helpless.

'Chcck it out while I'm here.'

She looked at him with the expression of someone about to go to the gallows, then led him down the hall into the tiny office and settled in the chair. He watched over her shoulder while she clicked on the monitor and pulled up her mailbox screen. There was one e-mail, with the same memo line as before: 'From thc Killcr.'

She looked over her shoulder at him. 'I hate this, Magozzi.'

She took a deep breath and clicked the 'read' button. There were no red pixels this time, no modified opening screen, just a simple text message:

I'm disappointed in you, Grace. You can't even play your own game. And to think I'm right in your backyard.

Magozzi had his gun drawn and was out the back door before Grace had even finished reading the message.

The backyard was empty. Grace had flipped on a bank of floods by the time he'd made it down the three steps onto the grass, but all he saw was a single tree, a couple of chairs, and a solid wood fence attached to the house, too high for easy scaling. He called dispatch on his cell, got patched through to Garfield, and rattled off instructions while he checked the fence inch by inch, looking for scrapes on the wood, footprints, anything.

When he came back into the house he found Grace sitting stiffly in a recliner in the living room, Charlie in her lap, her Sig in her right hand, finger on the trigger, ready. Magozzi thought it was the saddest thing he had ever seen.

'Jesus, Grace,' he said, startled to hear her first name slip out. If she heard it, she didn't let on, or perhaps she just didn't care.

'Nothing, right?' she asked calmly.

'We've got Saint Paul sweeping the neighborhood, cars and foot patrols, but if he was here tonight, he's probably long gone. I'm going to check the rest of the house.'

'I already did that.'

'Christ.'

'It's my house, Magozzi.'

'I'm going to check it anyway.'

She shrugged apathetically.

She was sitting in the same place when he got back.

'Are you just going to sit there all night with a gun in your hand?'

'It wouldn't be the first time.'

Magozzi dragged his fingers through his hair, looked around the room, then settled into a corner of the couch.

Grace eyed him curiously. 'What are you doing?'

He didn't even look at her. 'I'm not leaving.'

'That's not necessary.'

'I'm still not leaving.'

38

It was still dark when Halloran and Bonar headed down the steep hill at Hudson and over the bridge that crossed the St Croix River into Minnesota. Halloran was driving now, and considering that he'd only managed about an hour of sleep, he was feeling pretty good, pumped, like he was heading toward the end of things.

Bonar was sleeping like a baby in the passenger seat, and Halloran flashed back to the last time they'd driven across state to the Twin Cities with two cases of beer in the trunk and a couple of Springsteen concert tickets locked in the glove compartment. They'd been kids then, Bonar had been about a hundred pounds lighter, and the world had seemed such a benign place.

He caught himself wondering what Danny Peltier had been doing then – skinning his knees on a skateboard, probably – and then spent the next ten minutes trying to push the image out of his mind.

Minneapolis did it for him, when he took the downtown exit off 94. 'Hey, Bonar.' He nudged a plump shoulder and Bonar's eyes opened immediately, clear and focused as a kid's. There was none of that groggy transition state where every adult's IQ seems to hover somewhere between zero and fifty before the first cup of coffee; Bonar always passed from sleep to wakefulness in a single heartbeat, alert and ready for anything.

'How about that.' He grinned as he leaned forward

and peered up through the windshield. 'They left the lights on for us.'

The skyline had changed a lot since they'd been here last. A dozen new buildings soared straight up from the roots of downtown, pillars of white and golden light vying with the old IDS tower for sky space.

Halloran had always thought of Minneapolis as a young city, a female city; pretty and modest and proper, trying hard not to be too intrusive. Now it looked as if the youngster had grown up, and he wondered if it would feel the same.

'It's gotten a lot bigger since we were here.'

Bonar reached for the thermos on the floor between his feet. 'Yep. Cancer of the landscape, that's what cities are, and the nature of cancer is that it just keeps growing. You want some coffee?'

'Oh, come on, look at the lights. It's pretty. And yes to the coffee.'

Bonar reached for the plastic Conoco cup in the holder and peered inside. 'Did you put a butt out in here?'

'No I did not.'

'Well, there's something in here.' He opened his window and tossed the dregs of old coffee outside. 'I don't want to know what it was.'

They passed a bank thermometer that read twenty degrees, but from the cold air blowing into the car, Halloran thought that was pretty optimistic. He'd heard once that all the thermometers in Minnesota were calibrated ten degrees high, just to keep the population from moving en masse. 'Close the window, would you? It's freezing.'

Bonar stuck his nose out the window like a dog and inhaled deeply before he closed it. 'Snow today. You can smell it.' He passed over the filled Conoco cup and poured an inch or two in his own mug. Not that he needed the caffeine. He actually drank the stuff for the taste, which was a mistake in this case. He shuddered after the first sip. 'God, this is terrible.'

'It was a gas station, not a Starbuck's, what do you expect?'

'I would expect that a man with a gun could get better coffee than this, even at a gas station. Where are we? What street is this?'

'Hennepin.'

'You know where you're going?'

'Sure. City Hall.'

'You know how to find it?'

'I figured I'd just drive around until I found it.'

Bonar dug in his shirt pocket, pulled out a many-folded piece of paper, and smoothed it open on his broad thighs.

'What's that?'

'A map of downtown Minneapolis, driving directions to City Hall. Turn right at the next light.'

'Where'd you get it?'

'Off Marjorie's computer.'

Halloran turned on the map light and glanced over at the paper. It looked like a real map. 'No kidding.'

'No kidding. You type in where you are, where you want to go, and bingo. It prints up a map and driving directions. Pretty cool, huh?'

'I don't know. Kind of takes all the fun out of it.'

They parked at the end of a line of patrol cars in the

middle lane of a side street wider than any road in Calumet, and walked around the city-block-sized stone building and went in the front door. A bleary-eyed uniform directed them down a hall to the Homicide office.

There were a lot of people around for this hour, Halloran thought, and all of them looked tired. Everyone they passed nodded politely, but they all eyed their brown uniforms with the quick, intense take of a cop, focusing particularly on their sidearms.

Just as they entered the Homicide division, Bonar leaned over and whispered, 'Nobody stopped us. You dress like a cop, you could walk in here and take the whole building.'

'Who'd want it?' Halloran asked, looking around at the tiny, characterless reception room with a sliding glass window set in one wall. Through the glass he caught a glimpse of the larger room beyond, the gray government-issue desks, the unlovely walls and cubicles of an office space designed for business and nothing else.

A very large black woman, just shrugging out of a heavy winter coat, appeared on the other side of the glass and looked them up and down for a long moment before sliding open the window. 'Halloran, right?' she said, and Halloran recognized her voice from the phone.

'Sheriff Mike Halloran, Deputy Bonar Carlson, Kingsford County, Wisconsin.' They both put their badges on the counter and opened them up so she could see the pictures. 'And you've got to be Gloria. You and I had quite a few conversations yesterday, if I'm not mistaken.' He smiled at her.

'Uh-huh. Haven't had that many calls from the same man in one day since Terrance Beluda was afraid he'd knocked me up. Bonar. What kind of a name is that?'

'Norwegian,' Bonar said, still a little wide-eyed from her remark about being knocked up.

'Huh. I thought I'd heard them all. And you people think black folks have weird names. Come on in, fellas. Find yourselves an empty seat while I give Leo a call.'

She buzzed them through the interior door as she picked up a phone, and a dozen pairs of eyes lifted from what they were doing and gave them the once-over. Halloran felt like a grade-school transfer standing in front of his new classmates. 'Morning.' He nodded to the one closest to them, a wasted-looking man with a prominent Adam's apple, a scruffy beard, and a black woolen cap with a moth hole right in front.

'Now why are you talking to that dirtbag?' Gloria chided as she came up behind him.

'Dirtbag? I figured he was undercover.' Halloran turned to give her a sheepish smile, then quelled the impulse to reach for his sunglasses. Her dress was carmine red with bright orange pumpkin appliqués. It was a miracle, he decided, because somehow she made it work.

'My, my, you boys are from the country, aren't you? Looks like old Gloria's going to have to take you under her wing.'

Bonar rocked back on his heels, smiling. 'Praise Jesus.'

Brown eyes flashed at him, then softened almost immediately. Halloran saw it and shook his head. Didn't matter what Bonar ever said to a woman, and half the time he had his foot so far in his mouth he nearly choked to death. It was something about his face – a gentleness, innocence, something – that made women forgive him damn near anything.

'Leo's on his way. You've got your slug, right?'

Halloran patted his pocket and felt his heart have a flashback to when Sharon's hand had done the same thing.

'Well, I can have someone take you to the lab now, or if you want, you can just cool your heels till he arrives.'

'How about if you just bring us up to date on this case while we wait for Detective Magozzi?' Bonar asked.

She arched a well-plucked brow. 'You're talking to a secretary, not a cop.'

Bonar grinned at her and Halloran gave her ten seconds before she started spilling her guts.

'Well . . .'

So he was wrong. Five seconds.

'You want to know what I'm supposed to know, or what I really know?'

Bonar's grin broadened. 'What you really know. But mostly I want to know how you get your hair in all those tiny braids. I've always wanted to know that. They're really small, like Cinderella's mice did it or something.'

Gloria rolled her eyes toward Halloran. 'Has this man ever even seen a black woman before?'

'I don't think so.'

39

Magozzi didn't think it mattered if you were a pauper or a millionaire. There were a few solid, basic human pleasures that followed you from childhood to old age, and one of them was waking up to the smell of good coffee that someone else had made.

He opened his eyes and looked at the ceiling of Grace MacBride's living room. The slats on one of the blackout blinds hadn't closed all the way, and slices of weak sunlight painted the ceiling. For some reason that filled him with optimism.

A new blanket covered him, a down comforter that hadn't been there when he'd fallen asleep last night. He lifted the edge and peered beneath it to see the navy blue wool he remembered, and then sat up and looked through the archway to the empty kitchen. She'd covered him while he slept. She'd gotten up, made coffee, and at some point she'd put another blanket over him so he wouldn't get cold. The knowledge of that made his chest hurt.

He found them in the backyard, Charlie sitting in one Adirondack chair, Grace in the other. She was bundled in a white terry robe, her dark hair wet and curling over the collar, steam rising from a coffee mug in her left hand. Her right was tucked in her robe pocket, and even from a distance, he could see the lumpy outline of her gun beneath the fabric. A hose ran at the base of the magnolia tree, and the trickle of water put music in the stillness of morning. But, damn, it was cold.

'It's freezing out here,' he said as he walked down the back steps, careful not to slosh the fresh coffee in his mug. He could see his breath, and frosty grass crackled under his shoes.

Charlie turned his head and smiled at him. He could see his breath, too.

'Put on your coat,' Grace told him without turning around.

'Already did.' Magozzi crouched next to Charlie's chair and scratched the wiry coat behind the dog's ears. Charlie sighed audibly and leaned his head into Magozzi's hand. 'This is terrific coffee.' He looked over at Grace and found her smiling at him. It was a smile he hadn't seen before, and it made him feel like he'd done something right. He couldn't remember the last time a woman's expression had made him feel that way, and decided he'd better identify his good deed so he could repeat it in the future. 'What?'

'You didn't kick Charlie out of his chair.'

'Oh. Well. It's his chair.'

Grace smiled again.

'And I would have kicked him out, but I was afraid he'd rip my arm off.' He looked down at where the vicious beast was furiously licking his hand, and for a second he slipped into the Americana picture of a man and a woman and a dog and a house as if it were real, and as if he belonged there. 'You shouldn't be out here alone,' he said suddenly, and Grace's smile vanished.

'This is my backyard. *My* place.' She glared at him for

a moment, erasing that one small thing he'd done right. He might as well have kicked the dog off the chair. Except he really liked the dog. Finally she sighed and looked back at the magnolia. 'Besides, I had to water the tree.'

Magozzi sipped his coffee and absorbed the lesson. Don't ever suggest to Grace MacBride that she should alter her routine to avoid being slaughtered in her backyard. He concentrated on suppressing the protective instinct that had followed man out of the caves. It was a stupid instinct anyway, he thought, because it had failed to make the evolutionary adjustment that would accommodate women who carried big guns in their robe pockets. He stared at the water puddling around the trunk of the magnolia, and decided it was a safe conversational topic. 'It's kind of late in the year for that, isn't it?'

Grace shook her head and dark curls stiff with cold moved against the white robe. She shouldn't be out here in the cold with wet hair, either, but Magozzi wasn't about to tell her that. 'Never too late to water your trees. Not until the ground freezes, anyway. Do you live in a house?'

'Just like a normal person.'

'I'm not the target. I never was.'

God, she was hopping around the conversation like the Easter bunny. Magozzi was having trouble keeping up. Apparently that was painfully obvious.

'That's why I'm not afraid to be out here alone,' she explained. 'He doesn't want to kill me. He just wants me to – stop.'

'Stop what?'

She gave a desultory shrug. 'I've been trying to figure that out for years. The profiler the FBI brought in in Georgia theorized that the killer's intent was "psychological emasculation," whatever the hell that is. That he felt I had some kind of power over his life he was trying to eliminate, and that apparently killing me wouldn't do it.'

'Interesting.'

'You think so? I always thought it was gobbledygook. Nobody has any power when they're dead.'

'Martyrs do.'

'Oh.' Her lips circled the word and stayed there for a second. 'That's true.'

'Dead lovers.'

'Dead lovers?'

Magozzi nodded. 'Sure. You take a couple – any couple – right at the beginning when everything's hot and new, you know? And then say the guy dies, in a car wreck, a war, whatever, before he has a chance to get old or potbellied or inconsiderate, and what have you got? Dead lover. Most powerful people in the world. Can't compete with them.'

Grace turned to look at him, frowning and smiling at the same time. 'Personal experience?'

'Nope. As far as my ex was concerned, I couldn't compete with the live ones.'

She reached over to stroke Charlie's neck. 'I talked to the others this morning, told them what happened last night.'

Magozzi winced, and she caught it.

'Relax, Magozzi. I didn't ask them about Brian Bradford, mostly because if I didn't know him, they wouldn't either. Anyway, they're afraid for me. They want us all to disappear again.'

'Is that what you want?'

She thought about it for a while, then made a broad gesture that took in the fence, the security, ten years of fearful vigilance Magozzi couldn't even imagine. 'I want all this to be over. I want it to end.'

They both jumped when his cell phone burped in his pocket.

He stood up and flipped it open. 'Magozzi.'

'Good morning, Detective.'

Magozzi took a beat, confused. Only cops called his cell, and he couldn't remember any of them ever saying 'good morning.'

'This is Lieutenant Parker, Atlanta Police Department.' The drawl came through on 'lieutenant,' which explained everything.

'Yeah, Lieutenant. You find anything for us?'

'Nothing that's going to make your day, I'm afraid. According to Mrs Francher – she's the admissions director, and she's been working with me on this all night – a Brian Bradford was admitted to the university, but she can't find any record that he ever actually registered.'

'Oh.' Magozzi packed a lot of disappointment into that single syllable. 'Well, thanks for –'

'Whoa. Slow down a minute, Detective. It seems this was a little peculiar. When an admitted student doesn't register, that leaves the school with an empty slot they fill up with someone else. Otherwise you've got a bed going to waste in the freshman dorms, an empty chair in the classrooms . . .'

'Okay. Right.'

'But that didn't happen in this case.'

Magozzi frowned. 'I don't get it.'

'Neither did Mrs Francher. So she checked the numbers – freshman admissions against freshman registrations – and they matched. Right on the money.'

Magozzi closed his eyes and focused, waiting for his brain to kick in. Get rid of the woman, the dog, the morning coffee, the fleeting illusion of normalcy; go back to the cop. 'So he was there. Just not as Brian Bradford.'

Lieutenant Parker said, 'That's what we were thinking. Apparently if he changed his name legally between admission and registration, the name Brian Bradford would never show up in the school records, but the numbers would still match.'

'He'd have to prove it, though, right? Show the documents before you'd let him register? Otherwise Joe Blow off the street could just come in and use Brian Bradford's transcript and SAT scores . . .'

'True enough. But that doesn't mean the documents were legitimate, and Mrs Francher isn't a hundred percent sure the university was double-checking such things back then. I checked the state records for you, just in case. No Brian Bradford ever applied for a name change in Georgia.'

'Okay, okay, wait a minute . . .' Magozzi frowned, thinking hard, then his brow cleared. 'So what that leaves us is a name on that list of registered students that doesn't belong. One name that isn't on the admissions list. That's our guy.'

Lieutenant Parker sighed through the phone. 'And

that's a problem. The freshman class that year was over five thousand, and nothing was computerized. What we're looking at is hard copies. Two lists, five thousand-plus names each, and they aren't even alphabetized. The names were entered when the clerks got around to it. The lists are going to have to be checked against each other by hand, name by name. Even after you eliminate the names that are obviously female . . .'

'Can't do that. It could be either.'

There was a short silence. 'You know, Detective, sometimes I just can't understand why people think southerners are so eccentric. Hell, we're down here pulling alligators off golf courses while you boys up north get all the really interesting cases.'

Magozzi smiled. 'He was born in Atlanta, if that makes you feel any better.'

'Well, it does. The South's reputation is intact. Are you going to call me when this is all over, Detective, give me the whole story so I have something to talk about on the eighteenth green?'

'I'll give you my word on that, if you fax me those lists this morning.'

'There might be some privacy issues. I'll have to check with legal.'

Magozzi took a breath, tried to keep his voice steady. 'He's killed six people in under a week, Lieutenant.'

A soft whistle came over the wire. 'I'll light some fires, Detective. Give me your fax number.'

Magozzi gave him the number, then flipped the phone closed and looked over at Grace. She was sitting very still, watching him.

'That's why the name didn't ring a bell,' she said softly. 'He could have been anybody.'

Magozzi looked down into his mug, sadly empty now.

'Those lists from the university – we could probably help you with those. We've got some comparative analysis software . . .'

He was shaking his head, but he met her eyes. 'I've got to go. I don't want you to be alone today.'

'We'll be at the loft. All of us.'

'Okay.' He turned and started to leave, then turned and looked back at her. 'Thanks for the extra blanket.'

She almost smiled, then tipped her head a little sideways, like a child assessing an adult, and for the life of him, he couldn't read her eyes. 'Did you ever think it was me, Magozzi?'

'Not for one second.'

40

Gloria looked Magozzi up and down when he got into the office. He rubbed his cheek and heard the rasp of twenty-four-hour whiskers.

'This is my macho look.'

'Hmph. You sleep in those clothes, Leo?'

'As a matter of fact I did.'

'Some macho. First sleepover with a woman since your divorce and you kept your clothes on.'

Magozzi looked at her, exasperated. 'Is there anything about my life you don't know?'

'Yes. I don't know why you had your first sleepover with a woman since your divorce and kept your clothes on.'

'It was not a sleepover. It was surveillance, protection, interrogation . . . Oh, the hell with it. Where'd you put Kingsford County?'

'They're in the task force room with Gino, who, I might add, managed to shower, shave, change clothes, and still get here before you did. You've got funny curly hairs on your jacket.'

Magozzi peered down and brushed off his lapels. 'She has a dog.'

'Looks like you had more luck with the dog than the woman.'

'Very funny. Listen, no one uses the fax today, okay? And I mean no one. I'm looking for a big one from

Atlanta, and I don't want them getting a busy signal when they try to start sending.'

'How big?'

'I don't know. Big. Find me when it starts to come through.' Magozzi left the Homicide office and took the stairs up to the task force room.

He caught a glimpse of his reflection in the glass top of the door, thought he looked like a mobster, then shifted his focus into the room. Gino, Sheriff Halloran, and his deputy were all standing in front of the big board that held photos of the victims and crime scenes. They had their hands in their pockets and their expressions were sober.

The sheriff was a surprise. Tall and dark and sharp-eyed; not even close to the fair-haired, paunchy good old country boy Magozzi had pictured, although from the size of his shoulders he did look like he threw hundred-pound hay bales around in his spare time. The deputy was shorter, closer to the stereotype with a Santa Claus belly that must be making Gino feel positively svelte.

When he opened the door Gino looked over and said, 'There he is. What did I tell you? Tall, dark, mean-looking guy.' He gestured at Magozzi. 'Short, blond, lovable guy.' He stuck his thumb in his chest. 'Just like you two. I'm telling you, it's like we're a couple sets of twins that got mixed up. Like that movie with Lily Tomlin and, who was it?' He scratched his head.

'Bette Midler,' the deputy offered.

'Yeah, her. Magozzi, meet Mike Halloran and Bonar Carlson. Jeez, guys, I'm sorry. He usually looks a little better than this.'

Bonar Carlson grabbed his hand. 'I think you look very pretty.'

'Thank you.'

Sheriff Halloran jerked his head toward his deputy. 'I didn't want to bring him, but it was either him or a good-looking woman.'

'No choice, then.' Magozzi shook his hand.

'None at all. I hear you spent the night with one of your suspects.'

'I guess there are probably a couple people in Outer Mongolia that haven't heard about that yet.'

Gino said, 'Anything's possible. She got another e-mail, huh?'

'Yeah. Tommy's on it, or at least he was last night.'

'He's still here, hunched over his machines like a mad troll. I don't think he's been home since this thing started. His eyes are starting to move in different directions.'

'Well, Sheriff, did Gino bring you up to date?'

'Actually . . .'

'Didn't have to,' Gino broke in. 'Gloria told them everything before I got here, including your shorts size. We sent the slug over to the lab. David's on his way in. He'll run it first thing.' He frowned at the board where he'd tacked up morgue and scene photos of the Mall of America victim. 'There's our girl from yesterday. Marian Siskel, forty-two years old, and you're not going to believe this. She was mall security, monitored the closed-circuit cameras, just finished her shift and apparently decided to try on a few things at the Nordstrom sale before she headed home. Crime Scene got a ton of trace from the dressing room where she got hit.

Said it's gonna take them ten years to sort through it.'

Magozzi looked over the new photos, comparing the actual crime-scene shot of the dead woman in the car with the staged photo from the game. The similarities were uncanny. His eyes moved to the next game photo – a woman in an artist's smock slumped on the floor beneath a classroom chalkboard. Halloran followed his gaze.

'That's the next one?' he asked.

Magozzi nodded. 'Only it won't happen. Not today, at least. Governor closed all the schools.'

'And the crime scenes aren't giving you anything?'

'Nothing we can use. We're not going to catch him that way.'

The sheriff moved his big shoulders inside his jacket, as if he were trying to dislodge a weight, Magozzi thought. 'We've got a funeral for our deputy Monday,' he said solemnly, and Magozzi understood immediately that the deputy's death was the weight he was carrying, and that it was probably way too heavy. 'I'd really like to tell Danny's folks this thing got put to bed.'

'We'll work it hard,' Magozzi said.

Deputy Bonar Carlson was looking at the right side of the board, at all the crime scenes to come. 'This is real bad.'

'It's a lot better than it was before you called,' Magozzi said. 'If the slug you took out of the Kleinfeldt woman matches the one we got from our victim yesterday, chances are pretty good that Brian Bradford is our man – or woman – and I think things could start to come together real fast.' He told them about the call from Atlanta.

‘Five thousand names?’ Gino looked at him in disbelief.

‘Plus,’ Magozzi corrected.

‘Great,’ Gino said dispiritedly. ‘More lists. The troops are going to love that.’

‘The registration list was always a long shot. Not these. He’s on this one,’ Magozzi said. ‘He’s got to be.’

‘There’s a lot riding on those slugs matching up,’ Halloran said.

‘Just about everything,’ Magozzi agreed.

‘I almost forgot.’ Gino hefted two copy paper boxes from the desk. ‘Tommy finally cracked into the FBI file. All seven hundred pages.’

‘My goodness,’ Magozzi said. ‘Are there Cliffs Notes?’

‘Not exactly. But I took a peek. There’s a ten-page index of witnesses they interviewed. Looks like half of Atlanta, but at least it’s alphabetized.’

‘God bless the anal-retentive FBI,’ Magozzi said. ‘I don’t suppose there was a Brian Bradford on the list.’

‘Of course not.’

On their way out of the building Magozzi saw another brown shirt walking toward them down the hall. He figured it was one of the new Hennepin County deputies he hadn’t met yet, certain that he wouldn’t have forgotten any officer that filled out a uniform in quite that way.

‘Good grief,’ Deputy Carlson said, and he and Sheriff Halloran stopped dead and stared at the approaching woman. She had short dark hair and sharp brown eyes that were fixed on the sheriff, and not much else.

'Morning, Sheriff, Bonar,' she said when she was close enough for Magozzi to see the Kingsford County insignia on her heavy jacket. 'Did the slugs match?'

Halloran blinked at her as if she were an apparition, opened his mouth to say something that was probably unprofessional, then changed his mind. 'Detective Magozzi, Detective Rolseth, this is Deputy Sharon Mueller. She was the one who found the link to Saint Peter's.'

She gave them a brief nod. 'What about the slugs?'

Deputy Carlson sighed. 'God, Sharon, were you raised by wolves? Say hello to the nice detectives. Shake their hands. Pretend you're civilized.'

She gave Bonar an exasperated look, then quickly shook Magozzi's hand, then Gino's. 'Okay. Now will somebody tell me about the slugs?'

'They just went down to the lab,' Magozzi said. 'They'll call when they've got something. We were just going to grab some breakfast.'

'Good deal. I'm starving. What's in the boxes?'

Gino shifted the copy paper boxes to his right hip. 'Open FBI file on a case the Monkeewrench partners were involved in years ago. Light reading over breakfast.'

'God, I hate reading FBI files,' Sharon muttered and promptly started walking toward the exit, forcing the four men to hurry to keep up.

Gino was grinning, always content to walk behind a good-looking woman, Magozzi and Bonar trailed behind, and at the end of the line Halloran was shaking his head, wondering when the hell Sharon had read FBI files and what the hell she was doing there.

They were almost at the door when two men in suits hurried to intercept them. The taller one led the charge, long legs eating up the hall floor. Give him a big round shield, the man could be a Viking, Magozzi thought. He glanced at the younger, grim-faced man trotting to keep up, but careful to remain a deferential step behind. Silent, obedient attack dog. There, and not there.

'Uh-oh,' Gino said under his breath. 'They sent the big gun today.'

'Magozzi! Rolseth!'

Magozzi stopped reluctantly and waited, recognizing the taller man as Paul Shafer, special agent in charge of the Minneapolis FBI office. 'Hey, Paul. I didn't know you ever actually left the office. What's up?'

Shafer was FBI first, Norwegian second, and human being third. 'This.' He waved a thin, official-looking folder. 'You get the file, we get the name to go with those prints you ran.'

Magozzi tensed for a minute, then forced his shoulders to slump. 'Aw, shit.' He looked at the folder and sighed heavily. 'Damnit, Paul, you sure you don't want to give me that file in the spirit of agency cooperation or something?'

Shafer looked stern. 'We get the name, you get the file. That's the deal.'

'Well, that's the problem. We don't exactly have a name.'

'Excuse me?'

Magozzi looked embarrassed. 'Yeah, I know how it sounds, but you've got to understand, we were running prints like crazy the night of the riverboat killing. There were hundreds of people there, you know? And the uniforms were tearing their hair trying to get prints before people left, and . . . Well, the guys were rushed and frazzled and some of them were green, and the thing is, when we went back to check the ones we ran, we found a couple of cards that didn't have names on them. Like the one you're interested in.'

'What?'

Gino nodded grimly. 'You think you're pissed? We don't even know which cop took the prints, which means we can't nail his ass. Man, I hope this wasn't a ten most wanted or something.'

Shafer's hard blue eyes were shooting fire. He looked from Magozzi to Gino, little creaky wheels slipping on the gears inside his head as he tried to decide if he was being had. 'This is bullshit, Magozzi.' He wasn't buying it retail, but Magozzi figured he liked the idea of MPD screwing up so much that maybe a part of him wanted to believe it.

'I could make up a name,' Magozzi offered. 'Would you give me the file then?'

Shafer's eyes narrowed suspiciously. 'If you don't know who the prints belong to, the file wouldn't interest you at all.'

Magozzi nodded. 'Yeah. You're right. I got caught up in the contest.'

Shafer glared at him for a moment, then shifted his suspicion to Halloran and his crew, who were all standing to one side with identical poker faces. 'Something going on with Wisconsin I should know about?'

Magozzi and Gino exchanged a quick, nervous glance. If Shafer found out they were looking at an interstate connection on the Monkeewrench case, the FBI would take over in a heartbeat, and all the subterfuge about the prints would be for nothing. Damnit, Halloran didn't know any better, they should have thought to warn him to keep his mouth shut about what he was doing there, but who expected an ambush?

Shit, shit, shit, Magozzi thought, holding his breath, waiting for Halloran to start yammering about the Kleinfeldts, the slug in the lab, the St Peter's connection. He nearly jumped out of his skin when the sheriff took a quick step toward Shafer and held out his hand.

'Sheriff Halloran, sir, and Deputies Carlson and Mueller, Kingsford County, Wisconsin.' He grabbed Shafer's hand and nearly shook it off, wearing the best shit-kicker grin Magozzi had ever seen outside of a movie theater. 'Real pleasure to meet you, sir. We don't see many Federal officers in our neck of the woods. Just on TV. This is a real treat.'

'Uh . . .'

'The detectives here were going to give us a hand with a prickly little case we've got going back home, but I can see now we couldn't have picked a worse time. Bonar, Sharon, shake hands with the man.'

Goddamnit, Magozzi thought, suppressing a smile. I'm going to kiss this guy later. He looked sideways at Gino, and had to look away quickly before they both burst out laughing.

Sharon shook Shafer's hand with her eyes cast down demurely, then Bonar stepped up to the plate with a look of awe seldom seen outside Graceland.

'Deputy Bonar Carlson, sir. A genuine pleasure, sir.'

Shafer tried for a smile, but it came off weak. FBI

agents were not trained to deal with groupies. 'Well, thank you, I'm sure the pleasure is all . . . Wait a minute.' His head swiveled to Sharon. 'Did you say Sharon Mueller? *The* Sharon Mueller? *The Profiles of Abuse?*'

Everyone did a little mental double take and looked at Sharon, who was cringing a little, wearing a pained smile. 'That's right.'

'Well, by God.' Paul Shafer beamed at her. 'Then the pleasure really is all mine. They're using your paper at Quantico, you know. Attended a seminar on it myself last summer. You turned some old ideas right on their heads.'

'Yes, well . . .'

'Magozzi.' Shafer turned to him. 'Take some advice. After you give these people the help they need on their case, let this woman take a look at the Monkeewrench files before she leaves. She's one of the best we've got in profiling outside the Bureau, and God knows you could use all the input you can get.'

'I'll do that.' Magozzi smiled pleasantly. 'We've got no problems at all sharing files with other agencies.'

Shafer's eyes tightened slightly at the barb, then he and the attack dog turned and went out the door.

'Pricks,' Gino muttered the minute the door closed behind them. 'Did you see that little pissant folder they were going to pass off as the file?'

Magozzi was looking at Sharon, confused. 'You're FBI?'

'No . . . Well, I consult sometimes.' Her eyes darted sideways to Halloran, whose mouth was open.

'So whose name is really on those prints that got those boys so excited?' Bonar asked.

Magozzi and Gino looked at each other. 'One of the Monkeewrench people,' Magozzi finally said.

Bonar tipped his head, waited for a minute, then said, 'Okay.'

41

They sat at a big circular booth in the back of the diner, drinking coffee while Magozzi and Gino tag-teamed, laying out the whole investigation right from the beginning, more for Sharon's sake than Halloran's or Bonar's, who had already gotten an earful from Gloria.

It was peculiar, Magozzi thought, that he felt like he'd been living this case forever, but it took only five minutes to lay out just about everything they knew.

Everyone went silent when a fiftyish waitress in a red wig and a green uniform came over and laid enough cholesterol on the table to kill a platoon. Sausage, bacon, eggs, pancakes drooling butter – and that was just on Bonar's plate. Magozzi looked down at his dry English muffin and black coffee and contemplated suicide.

'"Gee, Mr FBI Man, we don't get many Federal officers up in our neck of the woods,"' Gino was sing-songing around a mouthful of waffle. 'Christ, Halloran, I thought I'd die.'

'Well, we don't, as a rule.' Halloran shrugged amiably, then his face darkened and he looked at Sharon, sitting on his left. 'Of course, that was before I knew I had one of them working for me.'

'Oh, for God's sake, Halloran.' Sharon chased a ball of scrambled egg around her plate, finally stabbed it viciously. 'I told you, I don't work for them. They asked,

I turned them down. Every now and then they want a consult, and the pay is good, and God knows what I get from the county isn't, so I run a profile. No big deal.'

Gino sat back in the booth. 'The FBI recruited you?'

'They recruit everybody.' She shrugged, then she looked straight at Halloran, chewed on her toast for a minute, and said, 'Three times what I make at Kingsford, one month paid vacation the first year, six weeks the next, and a house.'

'A *house?*' Gino's eyes widened. 'Jeez, they must want you bad. Why didn't you take it?'

She sighed and laid down her fork, then leaned across the table toward Gino and said confidentially, 'Because I like my job, and I'm in love with my boss.'

Bonar nearly choked on his coffee. Magozzi grinned and looked at Halloran. He was looking straight ahead, his face beet-red.

'Unrequited?' Gino asked conversationally, ignoring the rest of them.

'I don't know. He hasn't decided yet.'

'Bummer.'

Halloran closed his eyes. 'Jesus, Sharon . . .'

Magozzi took pity on him. The man was obviously out of his league with women, and Magozzi knew how that felt. 'Okay, back to the bad guys. Did you pick up anything on the kid from the Kleinfeldts' house? Photos, baby books, anything?'

Bonar snorted. 'Not a scrap. They erased that kid like he'd died.'

'But he's smart,' Halloran said, digging into a pile of strawberry pancakes. 'IQ of 163, last time he was tested.'

‘Where’d you get that?’ Bonar asked.

‘I called back Saint Peter’s while I was waiting to hear from Leo yesterday; talked to one of the nuns who did double-duty as a counselor back then. I was really looking for something we could use for ID, like a birthmark, maybe, or some hobby or special interest he might have kept up that would give us something to look for . . .’

‘That was good,’ Gino said.

‘. . . but she couldn’t think of anything. Just that he aced every test they ever gave him, he was a good kid, and she liked him.’ He set down his cup and sighed. ‘And that he was sad. That’s what she said.’

Gino pushed away his empty plate. ‘Aw, shit, don’t tell me that. That’s just the kind of thing some sleaze-ball defense attorney is going to climb all over. More of this poor-me victim crap, guy couldn’t help killing all those people, see, because he was born with all these boobs and balls and dicks –’

‘Gino,’ Sharon interrupted gently. ‘He’s not a killer because he’s a hermaphrodite, and there isn’t a mental health professional in the country that would support that as a defense.’

‘Oh, yeah? Reassure me.’

‘From the limited studies we’ve got, it’s pretty clear that hermaphrodites tend to be passive, not aggressive, when life goes wrong for them, and almost always turn any hostility inward, against themselves. They’re just people, Gino, that’s all. But like all people, they’re subject to the same genetic glitches and environmental conditions that just might create a sociopath. Even so, I couldn’t find a single recorded case of a hermaphrodite convicted of homicide, and frankly, I can't think of another statistical group in the country that can make that claim. This person doesn't kill because he's a hermaphrodite; he's a killer who just happens to be one.'

Gino grunted, obviously unconvinced. 'Maybe so, but that still doesn't mean some dirtbag lawyer isn't going to try to capitalize on it.'

'Don't mind him,' Magozzi said. 'He's been this way ever since O.J.'

Sharon started to move dishes aside. 'You guys mind if I look at the file?'

'Go for it,' Magozzi said, handing over one of the heavy boxes.

She lifted the cover and started thumbing through pages very fast. 'None of your witnesses could pin it down as male or female?'

Gino shook his head. 'No witnesses at all with the jogger – he was the first one, hit after dark on a trail down by the river. Lots of trees, lots of cover, you would have had to be damn near on top of him to see anything. The second one was the girl on the statue in the cemetery . . .'

Sharon grimaced as she continued flipping through the pages, speed-reading. 'I read about it. Really spooky.'

'You should have been there. Would have curled the hair on your balls . . .' Gino hesitated. 'Shit, is that sexual harassment?'

Sharon looked up and batted her eyes at him.

'Anyway, cemetery closes up tight at sundown, and this was in pretty deep. Not a lot of mourners around in the middle of the night. We tracked the victim back to the bus depot, but no joy there. Nobody could even ID her, let alone place her with anybody.'

Magozzi said, 'There was a maybe with the guy on the riverboat. He was at a local restaurant less than an hour before he was killed. Waitress there put him with someone out on the street after he left, thought it might have been a woman, but hedged when we tried to pin her down. Clothes could have gone either way.'

Gino leaned back in the booth and sighed. 'So far the only people who saw the shooter for sure were at the mall yesterday – cops, no less – and even they couldn't nail it down. Whoever it was was all bundled up in one of those big puffy coats with a hood. No way to tell for sure.'

'Wow.' Sharon shook her head and sucked air through her teeth. 'You've got four murders and not a single witness. You know how rare that is?' She tapped the piece of paper she'd been reading. 'And from the looks of this, the same thing happened in Georgia.'

'And Wisconsin,' Halloran said grimly. 'If this is Brian Bradford, he's done eleven that we know about, clean as a whistle, and we don't even know if we're looking for a man or a woman or both.'

Sharon said, 'I'd guess woman.'

Magozzi raised his brows. 'Why?'

'Just a hunch. He'd want to be whatever his body told him to be, of course, and just because both sets of sex organs were fully developed doesn't mean the hormone production isn't prejudiced toward one or the other. More estrogen, he'll want to be a woman; more testosterone, the other way. But all things being equal, from a psychological standpoint, my guess is he'd want to be the opposite of what his parents chose, and they dropped him at the school dressed as a boy.'

'Huh.' Gino pondered that, then looked down his nose at Magozzi. 'There you go. Probably a woman, and that means probably Grace MacBride, just like I been telling you.'

Bonar's thick eyebrows twitched together over his nose and seemed to lock in place. Magozzi watched, fascinated, wondering if he'd ever get them apart again. 'You got a feeling about MacBride?' Bonar asked Gino, snagging a discarded piece of toast from Sharon's plate.

'I don't know. She's screwed up enough, if you ask me,' Gino said. 'She's got her house locked up like Bank of America, she carries all the time, and she hates cops.'

'Sounds like half the people in America so far,' Halloran noted.

'And that's not "screwed up," anyway,' Sharon put in. 'If she *weren't* trying to protect herself after what happened to her in Georgia, now *that* would be suspicious.'

Gino pursed his lips and thought about that. 'Damn, Leo, you are a stupid son of a bitch. That's the best argument for MacBride not being the killer I ever heard, and you never thought of it. But you know what? It kind of puts the kibosh on the rest of the geeks. They all thought they were targets of the Georgia killer, so they all carry, too, and apparently have security systems just about as tight as MacBride's.'

'But that doesn't really eliminate anybody, does it?' Bonar asked. 'If one of them was the killer, for instance, and the other four were scared, the killer better pretend to be scared, too.'

Gino groaned and dragged his hands down over his face. 'This just keeps going round and round.' His cell phone rang and he pulled it out of his pocket. He listened for a second, said, 'Thanks, David,' then flipped it closed and gave a thumbs-up. 'The slugs are a perfect match.'

Everyone took a breath.

'Goddamn,' Halloran murmured. 'It really is the kid. What do you think of that.'

'And . . .' Gino got up and started to fish out his wallet, '. . . we got about a zillion pages coming in on the fax from Georgia State.'

'What's coming from Georgia?' Sharon asked.

Magozzi was on his feet, tossing bills on the table. 'Two lists from Georgia State, about five, six thousand names each. Brian Bradford's on the admissions list, but not on the freshmen registration list, but the numbers still match up.'

Sharon thought about it for two seconds, then jumped up and started stuffing papers back into the box. 'He changed his name. Did you check court records?'

'Yeah, Atlanta did. No record of a Brian Bradford applying for a name change in Georgia. He might not have done it legally. Could have just altered the records at the U.'

She snapped the box cover closed and started digging in her pockets for change. 'Yeah, maybe. Nothing in New York, either?'

Gino and Magozzi looked at each other for a minute,

then Magozzi reached for his cell, punched in Tommy Espinoza's number, and looked over at Gino while it was ringing. 'We gotta hire more women.'

Bonar was grinning, patting Sharon on the head while she tried to slap his hand away.

42

Tommy called Magozzi while they were still in the car, heading back to City Hall. New York's name changes were recorded county by county, not statewide, and some of the counties weren't computerized that far back. It was going to take some time.

'Keep at it,' Magozzi told him.

'No luck?' Gino took the corner around City Hall too fast, and then had to do some fancy steering to avoid a Channel Ten camera crew crossing the street. Or maybe he was trying to hit them; Magozzi wasn't sure.

Magozzi told him what Tommy had said. 'In the meantime, we're going to have to do it the hard way. Comparing those two lists, name by name.'

Gino squealed into the parking ramp, checking his rearview mirror to make sure Halloran's car was still behind him. 'There, you see? Sharon's idea about checking New York didn't do us a bit of good, so we don't need to hire more women after all.'

'That's a relief. We get any more women with guns in this town I'm going to have to move to Florida.'

'*All* the women in Florida have guns.'

'Yeah, but most of them are older than I am. I figure I could outdraw them.'

'Are you kidding? Think about it. Those old retired

broads got nothing to do all day but sit around the senior center practicing their quick draws. You ask me, Florida's the scariest state in the union.'

Tommy Espinoza hadn't left his tiny, littered cubicle in twenty-four hours. He'd felt the exhaustion creep up on him from time to time and his eyes felt like they were bleeding, but the thrill of the hunt had kept his adrenaline pumping. It was a rare moment when your boss (who happened to be a law enforcement officer) commanded you (also a law enforcement officer) to do something illegal in the line of duty. And cracking into the FBI was definitely illegal.

That had been the first high. The second had been breaking through the extra firewall the Monkeewrench people had set in place to block his entry. It had been good. Hell, it had been amazing, but by God he'd beat it, and his cheeks still ached from smiling.

The whole process had taken longer than it should have because he'd been extra careful to cover his steps in consideration of the MPD. It was bad enough when Joe Blow hacked into a Federal organization, but the cops? He didn't even want to think about what kind of fallout would precipitate if they ever managed to trace his surreptitious journey into J. Edgar's hallowed ground back to City Hall.

Tracking a name change was going to be a cakewalk compared to the FBI file. Tedious, time-consuming, maybe, but still a cakewalk.

He was searching county by county, alphabetically, and he was already up to the Ds. He typed in Delaware, entered his search parameters for Brian Bradford, and sat back and waited.

Gloria was still collecting pages out of the fax machine when Magozzi, Gino, and the Kingsford County bunch all walked into the Homicide office. A nearby table already held a thick stack of paper.

'You better hope this thing doesn't up and die,' she told Magozzi without looking up. 'You've got about fifty, sixty pages over on the table. Heading says Admissions. Now there's a bunch more coming through called Registrations. You want to tell me what this mess is?'

'Salvation, maybe.' Magozzi watched the fax feed out a page crammed with single-spaced names. 'There's a Brian Bradford somewhere on the admissions list. By the time he registered he was calling himself something else. We've got to compare the two lists and find the name on the registration list that isn't on the admissions list.'

'Lord in heaven.' Gloria shook her head until her tiny braids trembled. 'You could grow old doing that. So you think this Brian Bradford's the shooter?'

'That's what we think.'

Sheriff Halloran picked up a page from the table and squinted at it. 'Man, that's small print. How many names to a page, you figure?'

Sharon squeezed in next to him to look. 'A hundred, at least.'

A phone started to ring on one of the desks, and kept ringing until Gino walked over and answered it. For the first time Magozzi took a good look around the room. Johnny McLaren had a phone pressed to his ear in his cubicle in the back; other than that, the place was deserted. 'Where the hell is everybody?'

Gloria shot him an exasperated look. 'Wouldn't hurt you to turn on your radio every now and then. There's a nasty domestic down on thirty-seventh – some guy holding a shotgun on his ex and three kids – plus about a million 911 calls. This city's popcorn on a hot plate today. Everybody's seeing strangers with guns everywhere.'

'Shit. I've got to have bodies to work this list.'

Gloria glanced over her shoulder at the Kingsford County people. 'What about those bodies? Can people from Wisconsin read?'

Bonar stepped forward, grinning. 'I'll read if I can sit next to Gloria.'

She folded orange lips over a smile and went back to work at the fax machine.

Gino came over to the table with a cell phone pressed to his ear. He looked down at the lists and grimaced. 'Christ, that's a lot of names. This is going to take forever.'

Magozzi asked, 'Who're you talking to?'

'Becker. He picked up the surveillance on MacBride from Garfield. Now she's at the Monkeewrench offices, and apparently so are the rest of them. All the tails are parked out front, looks like a goddamned police convention . . . Yeah, Becker, I'm still here.' He listened for a minute, rolling his eyes. 'Okay, okay, you stay put, and one other car. Send the rest back to the house . . . Christ, Becker, I don't care, just pick one.' He snapped the phone closed. 'Man, that was one rocket scientist. Who the hell is Becker anyway?'

'Don't know him.'

'He sounds like he's about twelve. He checked with the Monkeewrench people. They're all staying put except Cross; he's leaving before noon; so I left one car to cover him, and Becker at the warehouse.'

'Okay. We're going to need some help from outside with these lists. Think you could get someone to cut the coffee ladies loose to come up here and read?'

Gino brightened immediately. 'I bet they'd bring their own coffee.'

'I bet they would.'

Bonar made a face into the cup he'd filled from the grimy homicide pot. 'Sure hope they didn't make this stuff.'

'Oh, Bonar.' Gino gave him a benevolent smile. 'Come, my son. I'm going to lead you to heaven. Contrary to popular opinion, that happens to be downstairs . . .'

Sharon was thumbing through the stack of paper on the table. 'So you think you'll have enough help with the list?' she asked Magozzi.

'You have someplace you need to be?'

'Well, I was thinking . . . you're covering the Monkeewrench crew, right?'

'Yeah. Have been since last night.'

'Is this protective surveillance, or suspect surveillance?'

'Yes.'

'Any chance I could get in there and get a look at these people? Maybe talk to them a bit, scope them out . . .'

Magozzi raised a brow. 'You think you can spot a hermaphrodite?'

Sharon shook her head impatiently. 'Of course not. But I'm not bad at spotting psychopaths. Interviewed a couple hundred of them for that FBI paper.'

Magozzi glanced over her head at Sheriff Halloran, who was trying his best not to look alarmed. 'Your deputy, your call, Sheriff.'

Halloran's jaw tightened and his brows worked. He looked at Magozzi, not Sharon. 'I lost one deputy this week. I'm not too keen on putting another one in harm's way if I don't have to.'

'I'll be in and out,' Sharon said. 'And you've got other officers on site, right?'

Magozzi nodded. 'Right outside the building.'

'Which won't do you a damn bit of good if you're locked inside with a killer,' Halloran said.

She closed her eyes and sighed. 'First of all, I'm not exactly defenseless, and second of all, you heard Gino say they're all there. All five of them. Even if one of them *is* the shooter, he or she is not likely to start gunning down cops in front of the rest of them. Especially with more cops right outside.'

Halloran's expression was dark, but his eyes were steady. 'There's no reason for you to go there.'

'Really. I thought looking for the bad guy was why you brought us here.'

'I didn't bring you here,' Halloran reminded her.

Sharon looked up at him, eyes flashing, jaw jutting. 'Yeah, well, I certainly hope that wasn't because you were trying to protect me or something stupid like that, because I'm not going to do the citizens of Kingsford County a hell of a lot of good as a deputy if my commanding officer won't let me out on the street for fear I'll stub my toe.'

'We'll get him with the list!' Halloran snapped, his face reddening.

The rising voices had attracted McLaren's attention. He was leaning forward at his desk in the back, a half-smile on his face, phone pressed to his chest so the tedious business of some homicide call didn't interfere with his enjoyment of the fireworks in his own front yard. He waggled red brows at Maggozi.

Gloria seemed to be having a good time, too. She was rocking back on her platform heels, beaming at Sharon like a well-loved child, and even though she would never have said, 'You go, girl' out loud, because that was what people expected a black woman to say, the expression was written all over her face.

Magozzi, on the other hand, was decidedly uncomfortable. Cop-cop confrontations were not good; man-woman confrontations were flat-out terrifying, and this one was both. He decided to take charge of the situation and end this right now. 'Okay, listen, you two . . .'

Sharon spun her head and looked at him.

Or maybe he should just let them work this out for themselves.

'Listen, Mike.' Sharon turned her attention back to Halloran. 'Even if we get a name off those lists, that doesn't mean we've got the shooter. He could have changed his name a dozen times since then, and it could take days to trace from then to now, especially if it's one of the Monkeewrench owners. We are light-years behind those people when it comes to altering computer records. But if I could spend just a little time with them, ask the right questions, maybe I could see something in one of them, or jog loose a memory about somebody they knew in Georgia.'

Sheriff Halloran was trying to scowl at her, but Magozzi thought he just looked helpless. Poor guy. Apparently Sharon took pity on him, too, because her voice softened.

'It's what I do, Mike. And I'm good at it. You know I am.'

Halloran was remembering what he'd told Danny Peltier on the way out to the Kleinfeldts': that Sharon was the best interrogator he had. There seemed to be a strange sort of synchronicity at work here; things coming together in a way that was tying his stomach into knots.

Suddenly there was the startling sound of complete silence, and Magozzi realized the fax machine had stopped. 'Tell me it didn't die,' he begged Gloria.

She pulled out the stack of papers in the tray and looked at the number on the last one. 'Nope. This is the whole lollapalooza.' She added the papers to a stack on the table just as Gino and Bonar entered the office carrying coffee-making paraphernalia. A line of women trailed behind, looking around with eyes as wide as those of the grade-schoolers who tramped through on occasional field trips.

'Well, Mike?' Sharon asked quickly, wanting this settled before the confusion of new arrivals gave him an excuse to postpone his decision.

'I'll go with you.'

She shook her head firmly. 'It doesn't work that way. I'm not going to get any information out of anybody with you hovering. You're too intimidating.'

'*I'm* too intimidating?'

'I'll wear a vest. I'll take a shoulder unit and leave it on. You can listen to every word.'

Halloran looked down and saw Sharon the cop, in the shapeless brown uniform with the cuffs and the Mace and the big gun she could shoot faster and better than anyone on the force. But in his mind's eye he saw Sharon in the red dress, looking small and hopeful with colored water on her lips. 'I'm going with you,' he said, and when she opened her mouth to protest again, he added, 'But I'll wait outside.'

After Sharon and Halloran left for the Monkeewrench warehouse, Magozzi looked around at his new workforce and immediately regretted letting them go. Gino and Bonar had brought fifteen women up from data entry downstairs, and now they were clustered together in a whispering, tittering pack, uncertain and nervous in this strange environment.

Their demeanor changed when Gino started to explain what they needed done, and even before he finished the women were dragging chairs around the table near the fax, dividing the pages of the registration list, organizing themselves like an army of ants with a single purpose.

Gino, always smart enough to know when he'd become superfluous, stepped over to talk to Magozzi. 'This is going to work.'

'Looks like it.' Magozzi watched one of the women fussing over Bonar, putting him in a chair, handing him a sheaf of pages, setting a mug of steaming coffee at his right hand. Bonar took a sip, feigned an ecstatic swoon, and got a pat on his head for his trouble.

'I stopped and talked to Tommy. He's running a couple of searches through the FBI file, looking for the geeks' real names so maybe we could check them through the list first. He found MacBride right off the bat, since she was the focus. No way we can figure the rest of them. There's a ton of witness and friend interviews, but no physical characteristics, just names.'

Magozzi slid his eyes sideways to look at him, tried not to ask, but finally he couldn't stand it. 'All right, damnit, what's her real name?'

Gino handed him a small folded piece of paper.

Magozzi opened it, looked at it, and frowned. 'No way.'

'I kid you not. Jane Doe. Tommy checked it all the way back to her birth certificate. That's her real name, all right. Just about the saddest thing I ever heard.'

Magozzi took a deep breath, then shook his head and handed the paper back to Gino. 'Have them check it through first. I've got to call Monkeewrench and tell them Sharon's on her way.'

Gino nodded. 'Call dispatch while you're at it so they can give Becker a heads up, or he'll probably shoot her before she gets to the door.'

43

Roadrunner was at his desk in the loft, eating a Twinkie, of all things, and there was no clearer indication that he was having a bad day. Not only had he overslept for the first time in fifteen years, but when he had finally regained consciousness, it had been with a splitting headache and a stomach so sour he couldn't even contemplate coffee. He blamed the champagne and swore off the stuff for the rest of his life.

Even Annie, usually the last to arrive at the office, had beaten him in that morning. Now she was swishing over in a brown satin ensemble that was covered from top to bottom with tiers of velvet, leaf-shaped cutouts in autumn colors. She was carrying a mug of coffee and a white bakery bag. She set the coffee down in front of him. 'Here you go, Sleeping Beauty.' She eyed his yellow sponge breakfast suspiciously. 'I thought you said Hostess was the devil's workshop.'

Roadrunner looked guiltily at the Twinkie and set it down. 'They are, but I was hungry. The Food and Fuel is a little weak on the food part and I didn't have time for anything else.' He eyed her outfit. 'You look like a tree.'

'Honesty will never get you a date, pal.' She dug in the bag and slapped a cherry turnover down on his desk. 'If you're going to poison yourself with sugar and fat, at least do it without the preservatives. The

Russians used Twinkies to preserve Lenin, did you know that?'

Roadrunner gave her a crooked smile and took the turnover. 'Thanks, Annie. You look like a *pretty* tree.'

'Uh-uh. Too little, too late.'

'Where is everybody?'

'Harley walked down to Liquor World to get a little hair of the dog. Grace went with him.'

'How is she?'

Annie clicked her tongue against her teeth. 'Okay, I guess, considering. But she doesn't want to leave.'

Roadrunner looked alarmed. 'But we *have* to leave. We all agreed.'

'*We* all agreed. Grace agreed to meet, to talk about it, that's all. She's not going to go, Roadrunner. She's not going to run this time.'

'Oh, man, Annie, he was in her backyard. There isn't any doubt now, is there? This is the guy – he's back. And he's close. Jesus, she can't stay here.'

'Settle down. I talked to Mitch, he's on his way over. When we're all together, we'll find a way to talk her into it.'

The elevator rumbled up a few minutes later and Mitch emerged, looking wild-eyed and worse than anyone had ever seen him.

'Good Lord, Mitchell, what *is* the matter?' Annie asked.

He gaped at her. 'Are you kidding? You mean aside from the fact that there's a killer stalking Grace, the company is going bankrupt, and we have to disappear and start all over again?'

'Yeah. Aside from that.'

Mitch collapsed into a chair and dragged his hands down his face. 'Christ. I told Diane we were thinking about leaving and she just freaked. You know what this means, don't you? She'd have to stop painting. She's at the top of her career, she has stuff hanging all over the world, and now she's going to have to drop off the face of the earth and give it all up.'

They were all silent for a moment. It was Roadrunner who finally spoke. 'You know, Mitch . . . you don't have to go. You're married. You have obligations the rest of us don't. Your family's got to come first.'

Mitch looked aghast. 'This *is* my family. This has *always* been my family. If Grace goes, if the rest of you go, I go.' He pressed his palms into his eye sockets. 'Shit, this is such a fucking mess I can't believe it. I'm not even supposed to be here. I *promised* Diane I wouldn't come here today. I gave her my fucking word. And the minute she left for the gallery, I snuck out like some guilty, FUCKING KID.'

'Jesus, Mitch,' Roadrunner said. 'Take it easy. You're going to have a heart attack.'

'I should be so lucky. Anyway, I can't stick around for long. I've got to get back home before Diane does. Where the hell are Grace and Harley?'

The elevator started down, answering a call from below. 'That's them,' Annie said. 'And before they get up here, you should know that Grace said she doesn't want to go.'

They'd had a meeting like this once before, Grace remembered. Only that time the others had all been standing around her hospital bed in the psych ward at

Atlanta General. She'd been young, scared out of her mind, half in the bag from whatever tranquilizers they had dripping into her arm, and images of Libbie Herold bleeding to death on the other side of that closet door had still been playing on the inside of her head. In that state, she probably would have gone to the bunker with Hitler if he'd told her to.

But not this time. This time she was just too goddamned tired. She wanted it over, one way or the other.

'Damnit, Grace, it's different this time!' Harley was pacing around their circle of chairs, smacking a beefy fist into his palm, making the dragons on his arms twitch and ripple. 'He's totally focused on you. He was in your backyard, for chrissake! This time you *are* the target, can't you see that?'

'That's why I don't have to run this time, Harley. This time it's my risk, and only mine.'

'Grace.' Roadrunner leaned forward in his chair and grabbed her hands with long, bony fingers. 'We could just go for a little while, until they catch him, then we could come back. It wouldn't have to be forever.'

Grace squeezed his fingers and smiled. 'If I disappear, he disappears, just like last time. And then maybe I'll have another ten years of looking over my shoulder before he finds me again, and then it will start all over. The cops are getting close. Let's give it another day or two.'

'The cops are hopeless!' Roadrunner said. 'They were all over the Megamall and look what happened! And how about the paddleboat? You should have seen the men they had down there, and they didn't do a damn bit of good!'

Harley stopped pacing and looked at Roadrunner. 'Are you telling us you were down at the paddleboat landing when that guy was killed?'

Roadrunner gave him an irritable look. 'Obviously not, or I would have seen the killer. By the time I got there the cops and the security people were already there.'

'You stupid shit, are you crazy? Do you realize what they would have thought if they'd seen you there?'

'I just wanted to make sure they had it covered, that's all! I didn't want anyone else to die!' Roadrunner shouted, and for a minute it looked like he was going to burst into tears.

Grace patted his hand and smiled at him.

By the time Magozzi called to tell Grace Deputy Sharon Mueller was on her way, Mitch was in his office gathering paperwork to take home, Annie was across the street picking up takeout from an Italian deli, and the rest of them were hard at work on the only thing that remained for them to do – tracing the e-mails.

There was a hissing sound as Harley opened his second beer. 'We're going to get this son of a bitch,' he muttered at his monitor.

44

Halloran sat in the driver's seat of the cruiser, listening to the crackle of static from his shoulder unit, feeling like a coiled spring about to shoot through the windshield.

The minute the warehouse door had closed behind Sharon, the radios had stopped working, and he'd panicked. He'd jumped out of the car and run across the street to the MPD unit parked there, scaring the hell out of a blond kid behind the wheel who looked about ten years too young to be wearing a uniform.

'Oh yeah,' Becker said after Halloran's hurried explanation. 'We have a lot of trouble with reception in some of these old buildings. Some kind of metal they used to reinforce the concrete plays hell with the radios. Should clear up when she gets upstairs where there are some windows.'

So now he was waiting, counting seconds in his head like a kid trying to figure out how far away lightning was. She'd do a walk-through of the big downstairs garage before going upstairs; that was a given; but goddamnit how long would that take? She'd already been in there three minutes and forty-four seconds.

Sharon had locked the shoulder radio transmit key in the 'on' position before she left the car, and on her way to the intercom box next to the big warehouse door, she'd heard Halloran say, 'I can hear you breathing.'

Something like a mild electrical shock – startling, but most certainly not unpleasant – had run through her body when he'd said that. She smiled now, remembering the feeling.

She'd heard the radio start to clutter up the minute the door closed behind her, and figured she had about five minutes to check the garage and get upstairs before Halloran started shooting his way in.

For two long years she'd felt nothing coming off him except the indifferent waves of a man who worked hard to keep whatever he was really feeling under tight control. But in the last few days she'd poked a big hole in that indifference and let the caveman out. Never mind that she could outdraw, outshoot, and probably outfight the guy, for all the difference in their sizes. Halloran felt a primitive compulsion to protect her, and Sharon felt a primitive compulsion to let him. That, she figured, was the way it was supposed to be.

She didn't like the garage, although there was no reason she could find to feel that way. It was well lit, spotlessly clean, and completely devoid of shadowy nooks and crannies. She could see damn near every inch of it without taking a step, and there was no reason in the world to expect that anyone else was down there; but still, she felt uneasy.

She held her breath for as long as she could and listened to the tomb-like silence.

Nothing.

There were two cars parked near the back wall: a black Range Rover and a Mercedes, both silent, both dark. A mountain bike and a big Harley Hog leaned on their kickstands nearby.

She dropped to a crouch and peered beneath the cars, feeling a little silly for doing it. And when she stood up again, she did something even sillier. For the first time in her life outside of a target range, she unsnapped her holster, lifted out the big 9mm, and chambered a round. The unmistakable ratcheting echoed in the big empty space, and just the sound of it embarrassed her a little.

Better safe than sorry, she rationalized, sweeping her gaze along the back wall as she started to walk toward it. There was a freight elevator in the center that had rumbled down as she entered, with interior lights that showed it was empty behind the wooden grate.

In the back left corner was a man-sized door marked STAIRWAY. In the right corner was another door with a black-and-yellow high-voltage sign on the front.

Cars first, she told herself, *then the doors, and why the hell are my hands sweating?*

Grace was staring mindlessly at her computer screen, mesmerized into near stupor by the white blur of tracking information that was scrolling down her monitor.

The Wisconsin deputy Magozzi had sent over had just called from downstairs. Grace had talked to her for a few minutes, then used the remote to key her in and send the elevator down.

Mitch came out of his office, lugging his briefcase and laptop. His suitcoat was rolled up in a ball under his arm. He stopped at Grace's desk and put his hand on her shoulder. 'I'm going to take off. Are you okay?'

She covered his hand with hers and smiled at him.

'I'm going to be fine. You go home and take care of Diane.'

Mitch looked at her for a long moment, giving her everything with his eyes, like he always did. 'You know, Grace,' he said softly so he couldn't be overheard, 'if you change your mind about leaving, I'll be right beside you. Nothing could keep me from that. Nothing.'

It was always there between them, this remnant of a first love that men seemed to cling to for all of their lives. But usually Mitch wasn't this overt and it made Grace a little uncomfortable. 'I know that. Go home, Mitch.'

He looked at her for a moment longer, then turned for the elevator.

'I sent it down for that deputy Magozzi sent over,' Grace remembered. 'She should be up in a few minutes.'

Mitch shook his head. 'I'll take the stairs. See you guys.' He waved to Roadrunner and Harley, who were so focused on their monitors they just lifted their hands in farewell without looking up.

Down in the garage Sharon was hurrying now, rubber-soled shoes squeaking on the concrete as she walked past the open freight elevator.

She figured she'd eaten up three minutes checking the cars and the padlocked door with the high-voltage sign on it, and she was starting to worry about Halloran calling out the National Guard before she could check the stairway and get upstairs, where she hoped the radio would work again.

She still had her gun drawn, but by now her uneasiness was fading and her hands had stopped sweating. Any enclosed space would tell you if it was empty, if you just listened to your senses, and once she'd checked out the cars and banished the mental bugaboo of the only viable hiding places, all of her senses came through loud and clear, telling her she was absolutely alone down there.

She was ten feet from the stairwell door when it opened suddenly and one of the Monkeewrench geeks bopped out, then froze comically at the sight of her gun. 'Oh my God. Don't shoot!'

Sharon relaxed. 'Sorry.' She smiled a little sheepishly and looked down to holster her gun. 'I'm Deputy Sharon Mueller . . .' she started to say, and then she looked up and saw only eyes, and in that instant she knew she had just made the biggest mistake of her life.

Both her hands jerked automatically, one toward the useless radio on her shoulder, the other to her holster, and all the time she was thinking crazily, *See, Halloran? I told you I might be able to see something, I told you I was good at this . . .*

. . . and her hands were still moving, too fast to see, too slow to do any good, and then she heard a soft popping sound and felt a bite on her throat above the vest, *goddamnit, above the fucking useless vest*, and then there was a gush of something warm and wet running down her shirt and her right finger moved spasmodically against nothing but air, trying to pull a trigger that wasn't there again and again and again.

Magozzi hurried down the hall toward Tommy's office, took a step inside the door, and skidded on an empty

Chee-tos bag. 'Jesus Christ, Tommy, this place is like a minefield. What have you got?'

Tommy stabbed a finger at the monitor in front of him. 'I got a name. D. Emanuel. That's your boy.'

'That's Bradford?'

Tommy grinned and rubbed his Buddha belly. 'You bet your ass. First I checked the county Saint Peter's School is in, and then I was going alphabetically until I figured a high-school kid wouldn't travel too far, so I did the adjacent counties and got a hit on the second one. Livingston County. Brian Bradford changed his name to D. Emanuel the day after his eighteenth birthday.'

Magozzi grabbed the phone and punched the extension for Homicide. 'No first name?'

'Nope. Just D.' He gestured at another monitor. 'I'm running a New York and Georgia search on D. Emanuel now, see if anything pops.'

'Gino!' Magozzi barked into the phone. 'The kid changed his name to D. Emanuel. Check it on the lists.' He was just hanging up the phone when Tommy frowned at one of the monitors.

'Well, that's weird.'

'What?'

'I got a marriage certificate for D. Emanuel in Georgia. But this can't be right.' He leaned closer to the monitor as if that would make the information more clear. 'This D. Emanuel married James Mitchell . . . It's got to be a different one.'

Magozzi was tense, almost rigid. 'No it doesn't.'

'Same-sex marriages in Georgia? I don't think so.'

'Brian Bradford is a hermaphrodite.'

Tommy's jaw dropped. 'You're shitting me. Why didn't you tell me that before?'

'We didn't tell anyone.'

Tommy was looking at the screen, shaking his head. 'James Mitchell. I've seen that name.'

'It's about as common as dirt.'

'No, I mean recently. Give me a minute. Christ, it had to be in the FBI file. That's the only thing I've been working on.' He slid over to another keyboard and started typing frantically.

The phone rang and Magozzi snatched it off the hook.

'That's it, Leo. D. Emanuel was on the registration list, but not the admissions list. He's the guy. Is Tommy running it?'

'Yeah, we're working on it. I'll let you know.'

45

'Roadrunner, Harley?' Grace said quietly. 'I just got another message.'

Harley and Roadrunner tore over to her desk and hovered over either shoulder to look at her monitor.

'Open it, Grace,' Harley said.

Grace clicked the mouse and a single message line appeared on the screen:

I DIDN'T WANT TO HAVE TO DO THIS

'Jesus,' Roadrunner whispered. 'What's that supposed to mean?'

Suddenly the lights in the office snapped out and the monitor flickered. The e-mail disappeared and was replaced by a blue screen. A few seconds later, the monitor started drawing a power grid schematic.

'Power failure warning.' Roadrunner stated the obvious.

'Lot of good that does,' Harley said. 'We already know the power failed.'

'Says the main isn't receiving power,' Grace said. 'What exactly does that mean?'

'Means there's probably a big trunk line outage somewhere,' Harley said. 'Shit. It could be a while.'

He walked over to the windows and opened the louvered blinds, for all the good it did. The sun was behind a black wall of clouds that looked like they weren't going anywhere soon. 'Darkest goddamned day of the year and we lose power.'

'Why isn't the generator kicking in?' Grace asked. 'I thought we had it set up to take over automatically.'

Harley shrugged. 'Who knows? We've probably never had the thing running or serviced since we got it. It's like a car battery – use it or lose it. I'll go down and take a look. Roadrunner, how much battery time do we have on the computers?'

'Around two hours.'

'I'll report it to the power company and start making backups of our drives,' Grace said. 'You guys go see if you can't get the generator running.'

'Where the hell is the generator, anyhow?' Roadrunner asked.

'It's in the power room in the garage.'

Roadrunner looked confused.

Harley rolled his eyes. 'Didn't you ever notice the door with the big yellow high-voltage sign on it . . . never mind. You're hopeless. Come on, let's go.'

'But the elevator runs on electricity.'

Harley sighed impatiently. 'The stairs, Roadrunner.'

'Oh yeah.'

Roadrunner had reluctantly taken the lead down the dark stairwell, carefully mincing a slow side step to accommodate his size-fourteen feet. But the farther down they descended, the darker and more tomb-like the stairwell became and the more nervous he got.

'Damnit,' Harley barked suddenly, his voice reverberating in the concrete sarcophagus and nearly sending Roadrunner into the next world.

'WHAT?!' Roadrunner shrieked.

Harley paused to peel a big, sticky cobweb out of his beard. 'Spiders. Sorry, buddy, didn't mean to scare you. It's just hard to remember all your phobias.'

'You're telling me you're not creeped out by this?' he asked angrily.

'Oh, I'm plenty creeped out, don't you worry.'

'Well, I can't see a damn thing,' Roadrunner complained. He reached up and smacked one of the dark, wall-mounted light fixtures as if his ire could produce light. 'And what about these? Aren't they the glowy things that are supposed to stay on all the time?'

'Yes, but the glowy things operate on battery and if you don't change the batteries, they stop glowing eventually,' Harley said in a tone more suitable for a toddler.

'We need a flashlight. Why didn't we bring a flashlight?'

'Because we're stupid. And don't even think of asking me to run up and get one. Just keep moving. There's a deputy down here somewhere and cops always carry those big-ass five-trillion-candlepower flashlights.'

Roadrunner was suddenly seized by a volley of sneezes that could have qualified him for the Guinness record book.

'Jesus, you okay?' Harley asked when he'd finally finished.

Roadrunner sniffled, then moved forward again. 'Yeah. But somebody needs to clean this place out,' he said in a nasal voice. 'There's enough dust in here to plant a garden.'

Harley grunted as one of his lug-soled motorcycle

boots caught on a concrete riser. When he reached out to grab the railing for support he made contact with something furry. 'Fuck!' he squealed, snatching his hand back and holding it close to his chest. 'Don't touch anything. I think I just felt up a rodent.'

Roadrunner sneezed again. 'This place is hermetically sealed. If a rodent ever managed to get in here, it'd be dead by now.'

'Oh yeah? So what else is furry, the size of Rhode Island, and has a heartbeat?'

'Probably just a spore cluster.'

'What the fuck's a spore cluster?'

'I don't know. The stuff that's making me sneeze.'

'You just keep telling yourself that, Roadrunner.'

'We should have brought a flashlight.'

'Shut up. Where the fuck is the door?'

'You say "fuck" a lot when you're nervous.'

'Who's nervous?'

There was a hollow thunk as Roadrunner collided with the steel door. 'Ouch.'

'Good job. You found the door.'

Roadrunner pushed on the steel bar and the door swung open onto the garage, which was even darker than the stairwell had been.

'Deputy Mueller?' Harley called out. The only answer was his own echo. 'Deputy? Are you down here?' More silence.

'If she were here, she wouldn't be sitting quietly in the dark waiting to ambush us,' Roadrunner said.

'Good point. So she's not down here. Probably took off when the lights went out. We're going to have to do this without light.' He paused, imagining the layout of the garage in his mind. 'Okay, the generator room is directly across from us, on the other side of the garage,' Harley said. 'Grab onto my shirt and we'll grope our way down the wall.'

Roadrunner clamped onto Harley with a death grip and shuffled behind him blindly. 'Ick. The floor is sticky. Is your hog leaking oil again?'

'My hog has never leaked oil. Okay, we're here.' He dug in his jacket pocket, pulled out his key ring, and started feeling each one, searching for the small padlock key. 'What I'd like to know is why we have a padlock on the generator room. It's not like anyone is going to steal a two-thousand-pound chunk of metal.'

He finally found the right key, popped the padlock, and opened the door.

The power room was even blacker than the rest of the garage, if such a thing were possible. It took a moment for their eyes to find the hulking form of the generator in the corner. They clambered over to it, trying to decipher its parts with their hands.

'So what am I feeling for?' Roadrunner asked.

Harley scratched his beard. 'Check the cords, connections, and let me know if you find any buttons. I think this thing is supposed to have a reset switch on it somewhere.'

Roadrunner reached out blindly and found a dangling cable that seemed like it should be connected to something, but what did he know? He'd failed shop class in high school two years in a row before the frustrated teacher had finally given him a passing grade in exchange for help with what had then been a state-of-the-art Kay-Pro computer.

As he maneuvered around the generator to get a better grip on the cable, his head connected painfully with a very sharp metal object attached to the wall. 'Ooowww!' he squawked, stumbling back and holding his head.

'God, you're a klutz. You're going to end up killing yourself one day.'

'Hey, it's dark, okay?'

'What did you run into?'

Roadrunner reached out and felt the offending piece of metal. 'It's . . . a metal box. On the wall.'

'That's the breaker box. Hey, good idea. Maybe we just tripped something.'

'Yeah. That's what I was thinking. That's why I just gashed my head on it,' Roadrunner grumbled.

Harley squeezed next to Roadrunner and felt around for the box. 'Okay. I found it.' He pulled open the cover and started feeling around inside. 'I can't see shit, but one of the switches is facing a different direction.'

There was a click and suddenly the lights blazed on. 'YES!' Harley shouted victoriously.

'Thank God . . .'

And then the door to the room slammed shut on them with a deafening metallic thud.

'Oh shit!' Roadrunner panicked.

'Don't worry, buddy. Door doesn't lock automatically. Against code. Here, I'll show you.' He walked over and reached for the handle.

Outside the generator room, a pair of gloved hands slipped the padlock through the hasp and snapped it shut.

46

Magozzi was hunched over Tommy's shoulder, breathing down his neck. 'Why is this taking so long?'

'It's a seven-hundred-page file. I just started . . .'

One of Tommy's other computers chirped. He nudged Leo back and rolled his chair over to a computer on a side table. 'Monkeewrench just got another message.' He squinted at the monitor and read aloud: '"I didn't want to have to do this." Man, what do you suppose that means?'

'Who knows?' Magozzi started to say, but then a shrill alarm started to sound. 'What the hell is that?'

Tommy was rigid, unblinking, totally focused on the monitor as a line of numbers and letters flashed on and off beneath the message. 'Goddamnit,' he whispered, then turned to Leo, his eyes wide. 'Goddamnit, Leo, there are no firewalls. It's a direct line. This message came from the Monkeewrench computers.'

Magozzi froze for a second and heard a roaring in his ears. 'What are you saying?'

'The guy's *there*, Leo. *Right now.*'

Harley was using his shoulder as a battering ram. The door rattled in its metal frame, but it wasn't going to give anytime this century. 'God-*damn*-it!'

'I thought you said it didn't lock from the inside.'

Harley took another run at the door. 'It's not supposed to.'

'Harley, give it up. You're not going to break down a metal door.'

'Any better ideas?'

'You have your cell?'

'Roadrunner, we're in a concrete room inside another concrete room underground. A cell phone is not going to work.'

'I just saw a movie where this guy is in an underground bunker in Iraq during Desert Storm and *that* cell phone worked.'

'That's fucking Hollywood for you.' He grabbed the knob and started shaking it in pure frustration.

'Harley?' Roadrunner said in a small voice behind him.

'Yeah, what?'

'Am I bleeding? Like, a lot?'

Harley turned and saw Roadrunner touching his head where he'd run into the breaker box. 'You have a big, red goose egg that's starting to turn blue now, but no blood.' He followed Roadrunner's worried gaze down to the floor. The concrete was covered in bloody footprints.

Their footprints.

'Oh Jesus Christ, Harley. That wasn't oil out there,' Roadrunner whispered.

And suddenly everything clicked – the power that shouldn't have gone out, but did; the door that wasn't supposed to lock, but did – Harley let out an anguished roar and pulled out his .357 and leveled it at the doorknob.

'JESUS FUCKING CHRIST, WHAT THE FUCK ARE YOU DOING?!' Roadrunner screamed. 'You can't shoot a steel door in a concrete room, you're going to shred us to ribbons!'

'I know that!' Harley's hand was shaking; Roadrunner's eyes followed the muzzle of the gun as it wobbled back and forth. 'I know that,' he said again, this time in a whisper, and when he turned to look at Roadrunner, he was crying. 'He's here, Roadrunner. And Grace is up there alone.'

And then they heard the elevator, rising.

'Grace?'

'Magozzi, is that you?'

'Grace, do you trust me?' He was running through the office, dodging desks, pushing aside anyone who got in his way, cell phone pressed to his ear so hard it would hurt for days.

'No, I don't trust you.'

'Yes you do, Grace. You trust me with your life. You've got to. The killer's there! Get out! Get out of there right now! Right this second . . . Jesus Christ goddamnit it to hell!'

'What?' Gino was pumping, panting behind him.

'I lost her.'

'Goddamnit,' Gino echoed, and they were in the hall, down the stairs, racing for the front door because that was closest to the car, knocking over the anchor from Channel Ten, rocking a stationary camera, hitting the bar on the door so hard Magozzi thought for a minute it might go right through the glass.

He'd hit redial the second he'd gotten disconnected,

and the phone at Monkeewrench kept ringing, ringing in his ear.

Grace stood frozen at her desk, phone pressed to her ear, her eyes wide and fixed on the elevator across the loft. She could hear the grind of the gears as it rose; she could see the cables moving through the wooden grate.

'Magozzi?' she whispered frantically into the phone, and heard nothing in her ear but dead air.

Do you trust me, Grace?

Her hand was shaking so badly that the receiver rattled when she set it down on the desk.

The killer's there! Get out! Get out of there right now!

She heard her heart pounding against the wall of her chest, she heard the hum of the computers and the oblivious twitter of a bird outside the window.

And over it all, she heard the elevator, coming up.

Run! Hide, goddamnit! She dropped to a crouch behind her desk and in a flash she was back in that closet in Georgia ten years ago, doing what FBI Special Agent Libbie Herold told her to do. She'd heard her heart pounding then, too, and other sounds: the quick padding of Libbie's bare feet across the wooden floor, toes still wet from her shower; the creak of a floorboard in the hall, and then a *snick, snick*, coming from the bedroom doorway. Through dusty louvers she saw Libbie's bare legs wobble back into view, and then there was a flash of metal that opened her thighs in two bloody smiles that spilled a red lake on the floor. And through it all, Grace hadn't made a sound. She'd just cowered in her laughable hiding place, eyes wide with terror as she waited for her turn, doing nothing to help Libbie Herold, doing nothing to save herself. *Doing nothing.*

Run and hide. It was an instinct so ingrained, so powerful, that in an instant it had overridden the exhaustive training of the last ten years. The defense classes, the bodybuilding, the target practice, all of it useless as Grace cowered now as she had ten years ago, waiting, doing nothing.

Like any prey, she tried to make herself smaller, pressing her arms tight against her sides, hugging herself, and then suddenly she felt the gun and remembered who she was. Who she had created from that ruined girl in the closet.

She glanced over her shoulder at the window that led to the fire escape. She could still make it. Out the window, down the stairs, onto the safety of the street . . .

Not this time. She closed her eyes briefly and turned back to the elevator. It was almost all the way up. Too late to race past it to the stairwell, but time enough to pull the Sig from its holster and chamber a round; time enough to dart forward to the cover behind Annie's desk and steady the gun in both hands on the smooth wooden surface.

This is your entire world when you shoot, her first firearms instructor had lectured over and over again. *Your gun hand, your target, and the path between. Nothing else exists.*

She'd been in that world a hundred times, a thousand, firing fifteen rounds in a pattern so close the holes all overlapped. Ironically, the deafening noise of the target range had provided her only moments of real peace, when the world around her blurred and disappeared and there was only that narrow, sharply focused path demanding her attention.

She felt the peace settle on her now as she put pressure on the trigger and saw only her gun, and the grate of the elevator door.

She breathed in through her nose, out through her mouth, and waited with eerie calm to kill her first human being.

Magozzi was driving so fast the Ford fishtailed when he took the turn onto Hennepin through a red light. Pedestrians and bikers scattered in front of the wailing siren and the screech of tires. Gino was in the passenger seat, one hand braced on the dash, yelling the warehouse address into the radio, calling for ERT and backup, broadcasting a possible officer down.

Sharon Mueller wasn't responding to radio calls.

The top of the elevator rose slowly into Grace's line of sight, then the interior, and when it was level with the floor, it clunked to a stop.

Grace's heart stopped with it, and then broke into a million pieces. She heard it break in her ears, and felt the clatter of all its parts against the inside of her ribs.

There was no killer in the elevator. Only Mitch, slumped against the side wall, staring at his sprawled legs with blue, sightless eyes, wearing bloody Armani. The side of his head that faced her was utterly gone, inside out, as if someone had pulled off his ear like a pressure cap, letting his wonderful brain spill out.

No, no, no. Grace felt an anguished, outraged wail

threatening to rise from her throat, and knew that that sound, if she let it come, would be her surrender.

So she looked away from strong curled hands that had touched her with tenderness, dead eyes that had loved her once and forever, and let the hatred come instead, filling her up.

She moved silently, quickly, boots barely scuffing as she crept around the desk, past the elevator *don't look!* toward the stairwell, gun held at arm's length, leading the way.

The door opened fast, but Grace was faster, down on one knee, holding her breath, finger increasing the pressure on the trigger until she felt that tiny tug of resistance that came a hair's breadth before firing . . .

. . . and then Diane stepped clear of the door and froze, staring down at the muzzle of Grace's gun.

She was in heavy sweats and her running shoes, a canvas purse slung over her shoulder. Her blond hair was snagged up in a ponytail, and her face was flushed and twisted and terrified. 'I . . . I . . . I . . .'

Grace jumped to her feet, grabbed Diane's arm, and pulled her against the wall, all the while keeping her eyes and gun trained on the door as it eased closed. 'Goddamnit, Diane . . .' she hissed close to her ear, 'did you see anyone? Harley? Roadrunner? Annie?'

Diane made a tiny, keening noise in her throat, and Grace felt her start to collapse next to her. She jerked her eyes away from the door for a second, saw Diane staring at Mitch's body in the elevator, her mouth open and her breath coming very fast.

'Look what you did, Grace,' she whimpered. 'Look what you did.'

Grace flinched as if she'd been slapped, looked down at her gun, then realized what Diane must be thinking. 'For God's sake, Diane, I didn't do that!' she whispered frantically, jerking Diane to her other side, standing between her and the awful thing in the elevator. 'Listen to me, we don't have time, there's a deputy downstairs, did you see her?'

Diane was moving her head, trying to see past Grace to the elevator. Her eyes were wild, open too far, a circle of white showing around the blue.

Grace shook her arm. 'Don't look at that, Diane. Look at me.'

Empty blue eyes slid slowly to Grace's. They seemed pathetic, resigned, as ruined as Mitch's head. 'What?' she asked dully.

'Did you see anyone downstairs?'

Diane's head went up and down. 'Woman cop.' Her throat moved in a convulsive swallow. 'She's dead . . . messy . . .'

'Oh, God.' Grace closed her eyes briefly. 'What about the others? Harley, Annie . . .'

Diane shook her head mindlessly.

Jesus, Grace thought, she isn't even blinking. I know where she's going. I've been in that place, I remember. She pinched the skin of Diane's arm hard enough to make her gasp in surprise and jerk backward.

'You hurt me.' It began as an anguished whisper and crescendoed to an awful wail. 'You hurt me you HURT ME YOU HURT ME . . .'

Grace slammed her free hand over Diane's mouth, pushing her back against the wall, hissing into her face. 'I'm sorry. I had to do that. Now listen to me. I have to go downstairs. I have to find Harley and Roadrunner' – *and please God let Annie not be here; let her be safe outside, standing in line at the restaurant, impatient and pissed and sassy and alive* . . . 'Do you understand, Diane? I have to go, and I can't leave you up here alone. You have to come with me, behind me, all right? I won't let anything happen to you, I promise.'

Because this time she had a gun, by God, and this time she was ready. No one else was going to pay with their life for the dubious privilege of being part of hers.

'We can't go, Grace.'

'We *have* to go. Just for a little while.' Grace was thinking fast, talking fast, feeling precious seconds tick away, cursing the imagination that saw Harley and Roadrunner and Annie somewhere downstairs, bleeding to death while goddamned stupid selfish Diane . . . She stopped and took a breath, redirected that good, strong anger away from Diane, back toward the killer.

'Come on, Diane. It's time to leave,' she said reasonably. 'You told me that once, remember? And you were right. Remember?'

Diane blinked at her. 'The hospital.'

'Right. I was in the hospital, and you told me that sometimes we just have to walk away from things. That everything would be better if I just went away. And that's what we did, remember . . .'

'But . . .' Diane looked at her helplessly. 'I didn't mean it that way. We weren't all supposed to go.'

Grace felt a tiny hitch in the world. 'What?'

'You were supposed to go. Not me, not Mitch, just you, but then everybody went, everybody had to follow Grace and I had to go, too, and now see what you've done?' She was crying hard now. She dug in her purse for a tissue and pulled out a silenced .45 and stuck it in Grace's chest.

47

Magozzi bit the inside of his cheek as he took the turn onto Washington on two wheels, tasted blood while he waited an eternity for four tires to find the pavement again, then jammed his foot against the floorboards.

They slid sideways to a stop in front of the warehouse in time to see Halloran spread-legged in front of the little green door, emptying his clip at the lock with booming explosions that sent shrapnel flying all over the place. Thc trunk was popped on an MPD unit parked across the street, and a young patrolman was sprinting toward Halloran with a twelve-gauge and a tire iron.

Magozzi and Gino were out of the car before it stopped rocking after the hard stop, doors left hanging open, coattails flapping as they ran for the door. Magozzi grabbed the shotgun barrel and jerked it down before Halloran started shooting. 'No! It's steel! Wait for the ram!'

Halloran darted wild eyes toward him, then grabbed the tire iron and started hammering it into the crack where steel door met steel frame.

Magozzi froze for an instant, paralyzed by hopelessness, hearing a chorus of sirens coming in from all different directions. 'Fire escape,' he said suddenly, and started to run for the side of the building before the words were out of his mouth. 'Take the front!' he yelled at Gino over his shoulder, just as the toothy grill of a fire department emergency vehicle nosed around the corner.

One minute for the ram, he thought. *Maybe two. It's going to be okay. It's going to be okay . . .*

His cell phone rang when he was on the fire escape and Tommy yelled into his ear. 'Leo! I found it! It's Mitch Cross! James Mitchell is Mitch Cross and D. Emanuel is his wife!'

Magozzi pounded up the metal stairs and threw his cell phone over the railing.

All the air had left Grace's lungs in a rush, as if the sudden pressure of the .45 against her chest had pushed it out.

She hadn't been ready after all. Her own gun was pointed off to the right, still trained on the stairwell door, and through the shock and the fear she was thinking, *She could fire two rounds into my heart before I could swing the Sig around . . .*

Diane was looking at her with the empty, soulless eyes Sharon Mueller had seen in those last seconds before the bullet found her throat, eyes that Grace had never seen before. The waterworks had stopped the second she'd pulled out the .45. 'I brought the big gun today, too,' she said quietly. 'I like the .22 better, but I needed to be sure. You have to be really close with the .22. Really precise.'

It took a long moment for it all to sink in. Oh, sure, quiet, proper Diane who was squeamish about guns and who never so much as raised her voice had just shoved a .45 into her chest, but until the moment she mentioned the .22, the thought that she was the Monkeewrench killer had never entered Grace's mind.

'Oh no.' Disbelief spilled involuntarily from lips that felt thick and useless, from a mind that was threatening to stop altogether. 'You? You killed all those people? My God, Diane, why?'

'Well, self-preservation, I suppose.'

'But . . . you didn't even know those people. They were just . . . profiles. In a *game*, for God's sake. *It was just a game.*'

Diane actually smiled at her, and it was so frightening Grace's knees almost buckled. 'That's exactly it. I knew you'd understand. I was actually killing the game, not real people.' Her eyes narrowed slightly. 'Mitch tried to talk you out of that game, but you just wouldn't listen, would you? Do you have any idea what you put that man through?'

'You murdered people because Mitch *didn't like the game?*'

'Oh, Grace, don't be ridiculous. It was much more than that. The game was going to destroy us. It was the *end of everything!*' She paused a moment, head slightly tipped, listening.

Grace heard it, too. A siren. Distant. On its way here, or somewhere else? Diane didn't seem a bit troubled by it, which terrified her.

'Anyway,' Diane continued calmly, 'I had to stop it before players started to get to level fifteen. Cops play games like that, you know. What if some of them in Atlanta saw that little crime scene you dreamed up and started asking questions?'

Grace's thoughts were spinning, colliding, trying to

make sense of insanity. 'What are you talking about?'

'Murder fifteen, Grace. You laid it all out for them. A half a dozen agencies and hundreds of cops couldn't figure out who killed the people in Atlanta, and you told them with one stinking little clue in your stinking little game. Thanks a lot, Grace, for almost ruining my life. Obviously, I had to stop the game before anyone saw it. And I did. Killed a few people and you pulled it right off the web, just like I knew you would. But then those stupid cops sent your prints to the FBI, and that brought up the Atlanta murders anyway, and everything just started to fall apart.'

More sirens. A lot more, and they were close. Diane didn't bat an eye.

Maybe she doesn't hear them. Get her to listen. What was in murder fifteen? What clue was she talking about? No. Don't think about that. It isn't important now. Just try to distract her so you can move the Sig slowly, slowly, a fraction of an inch at a time . . .

'The police are coming, Diane. Listen to the sirens.'

'Oh, don't worry about them. It's all part of the plan. Would you like to know the plan? It's really quite ingenious. My original intention today was to kill just you, of course. I didn't want to kill everyone, because then there'd be no Monkeewrench and Mitch would be unhappy, but . . . you know how it is. People just kept getting in the way.' She frowned, irritated. 'Like that woman cop downstairs. Now that ruined everything. What the hell was she doing here anyway? Did you know she was from Wisconsin? I saw it on the patch on her shirt.' She tapped her forefinger against her lips, puzzling over something, then her face cleared abruptly. 'Anyway, by the time the cops manage to break into the building – and I should give you a nod of thanks here, Grace, for this very excellent security system – I'll be hysterical. I think I can do that pretty well. I've been practicing. And then all I have to do is tell them you just snapped and started killing people and I had to shoot you in self-defense. You know the FBI is just going to love that. They always wanted to believe you were the killer in Georgia anyway, and now they can, and they'll get to close that pesky file. So everybody's happy.'

Her eyes darted to the elevator, then back, and her face darkened. 'Well, not completely happy. It really pisses me off, Grace, that you made me kill Mitch.'

Your fault, Grace. All your fault.

'He loved you,' Grace mumbled, and suddenly the Sig was so heavy, and her arm was so tired. Had she moved it another fraction of an inch toward Diane? She wasn't sure. 'How could you kill him?'

Diane's eyes narrowed and Grace searched them for rage, hatred, some kind of human emotion, but all she saw was annoyance. 'Well, that was not my fault. He was not supposed to be here. He promised. HE PROMISED. He walked in on me right after I shot that woman cop, and then of course I had to explain the plan, and *naturally* he didn't want me to kill his precious Grace.'

And then in a conversational tone so ordinary it made the hairs rise on Grace's arms: 'We had the worst fight of our marriage, Grace. The absolute worst. He was going to kill me, his very own wife, just to keep me from killing you, do you believe that?'

Yes, Grace believed that. Mitch would have done anything for her. Anything. She tried to imagine what it must have been like for him, finding out his wife of ten years was a murderer. But he'd lived with her, damnit. How can you live with someone for that long and not just know? 'I don't understand how you kept it from him all these years.'

Diane was puzzled. 'What are you talking about?'

'Georgia.'

And now she was amused. Enormously amused. 'Oh, Grace! You think I killed the people in Georgia? Oh, God, that's funny. Why on earth would I have done that? Mitch killed them.'

Grace stared at her, stupefied. Her ears recorded gunfire from somewhere outside; a lot of shots, close together, but her mind refused to accept the information for processing. 'That's crazy. Mitch would never . . .' she started to say, and Diane laughed a little, mirthlessly.

'It wasn't the brightest thing he'd ever done, but he wasn't thinking that clearly in those days. I suppose he had some twisted idea that if he just eliminated all the people around you, you'd run right into his arms. It didn't work, of course, so he had to satisfy himself to be . . . what? Your best friend?'

Grace nodded, numb.

'I happened to be following him the day he killed that Johnny person you used to date – oh, for heaven's sake, the irony just struck me. Ten years ago I walked in on him after he'd killed someone; this morning he walked in on me after I'd killed someone. Huh. Full circle.'

Her eyes seemed to lose their focus as her mind drifted a little before coming back with a snap. 'Anyway, I'd already chosen Mitch as the man I was going to marry, so it worked out perfectly. I got the husband I wanted, he got a wife who couldn't testify against him.' She wrinkled her nose in distaste. 'And everything would have been fine if the FBI hadn't locked you up in that house with Libbie Herold. I'm telling you, Grace, that just sent him right over the edge, not being able to get to you. Personally, I think he may have been just a little bit psychotic then, hell-bent on "rescuing" you, and I couldn't talk him out of it. And that's when he lost the necklace.'

'Necklace?'

Irritated, Diane pushed the .45 harder into Grace's chest. 'Grace, try to keep up! *The* necklace. Your little Speedo joke.'

And then Grace saw it. In the game, clutched in the hand of murder victim fifteen, and in real life, around Mitch's neck all those years ago in college. Always under his shirt or sweater so no one else would see it.

'The idiot lost it when he was killing that woman FBI agent, which wasn't a problem until you put the damn necklace in that damn game and then put it on the goddamned Internet. And when the Atlanta cops see that they're going to remember it's just like the one they have in the evidence locker. Then guess what happens? They'll come up here and start asking questions, how you came up with that idea, and you'll tell them, gee, I gave Mitch a necklace just like that back when we were in college in *Atlanta,* and that would be it, end of story, because Libbie Herold cut him. His blood was all over the scene. And now with all the DNA testing . . .'

Grace was barely listening. Mind, body, spirit – they were all numb. The rage she'd been counting on, the hatred that had filled her up and made her strong, had drained away in a flood of hopelessness.

It had all been for nothing. Silly, really, when she thought about it. All that security to protect herself from a killer who'd been beside her every step of the way. All that sharp-eyed paranoia, suspicion of every strange face, when she'd been too blind, too *stupid* to see the truth behind one of the faces she thought she knew best.

The Sig was growing heavier, and the muscles in her outstretched arm were starting to cramp. Why was she holding it there anyway? She would never have a chance to use it.

Suddenly there were terrible noises from downstairs. Something big crashing, metal against metal, again and again.

Diane's eyes flickered. 'Oh dear. The cavalry is getting serious. I guess we'd better finish up here. What the hell are you doing?'

Grace blinked, a little confused.

'With your neck, damnit! What are you doing with your neck?'

She felt it then, between her fingers. Even as her gun hand had sagged toward the floor, her other one had crept to the chain she'd tucked inside her T-shirt, pulling out the cross that Jackson had given her. It hadn't been a conscious gesture. You didn't live through a life like Grace's and retain a belief in talismans, religious or otherwise. But when she touched the cross she saw the young boy's solemn brown eyes looking up at her, imploring her to wear it. He believed. Maybe that was why she had reached for it; to connect with the fragment of trust that life hadn't beaten out of him yet.

Grace, do you trust me?. . . as if she owed him that, because he had trusted her first.

What a precious thing trust was; a fragile thing. That was what Jackson had really given her. Jackson and Harley and Annie and Roadrunner and Charlie, and even Magozzi, who shouldn't have trusted her at all, but did . . .

'It's nothing. Just a cross. See?'

Diane took a quick step backward, and for the first time in what seemed like hours, Grace took a breath without the .45 pressed against her chest.

Diane was staring at the cross, transfixed, as it swung back and forth in Grace's hand, catching the light from the loft windows, sparkling. 'I had one of those,' she whispered, touching her own throat, feeling a phantom. 'Mother Superior gave it to me, but . . . I think I threw it away.'

She was lost in a memory Grace couldn't begin to imagine, distracted for just a split second by whatever she was seeing behind those staring eyes. And in that second Grace felt the heat of an adrenaline surge that started to raise her gun hand, saw the stairwell door open slowly, slowly; saw a woman in a brown uniform soaked in blood crawling on her belly, a gun shaking in both hands, then the muzzle sagging, clattering to the wooden floor as she lost her tenuous grip . . .

In the next second Diane's eyes blinked, jerked to the woman on the floor, and faster than Grace could follow, Diane angled the .45 toward the door at the same time the Sig was rising, and then the loft seemed to explode in a volley of deafening gunfire.

Diane was flung sideways and went down very fast, her head hitting the floor hard with a sound that would feed nightmares forever. There was blood, a lot of blood, flowing from so many wounds in Diane's head and body that Grace couldn't make sense of it at all.

She looked down at the Sig Sauer in her hand, confused. She'd fired once? Twice? Certainly no more than that, there hadn't been time, and besides, the gun had been rising, barely above floor level, and she could see where the bullets had ripped and shattered the polished maple.

He rose slowly from his crouch behind Annie's desk so he wouldn't startle her, gun pointed down, but still clenched tightly in both hands.

'Magozzi,' Grace whispered, and then again, 'Magozzi.'

It was only his name. He'd heard it all his life, but hearing it right now from Grace MacBride made his heart hurt. 'And Halloran,' he said, looking toward the stairwell door.

Grace followed his eyes and saw a big man in a brown uniform bent over the bleeding woman, pressing his hand against the wound in her throat, crying like a child.

Grace heard a lot of yelling from the stairwell, up through the elevator. What seemed like a thousand voices calling unintelligible words, and her heart picked out three voices from all the rest, booming out her name.

'Thank you, thank you,' she whispered mindlessly, even as she was dropping her gun, running to help the injured woman, oblivious to the tears streaming down her face. She was thinking of Annie and Harley and Roadrunner, alive, by God, alive; of Jackson and Magozzi, the man called Halloran and the woman bleeding beneath his hand – all the people who had saved her at last.

Gino and Magozzi stood on the curb outside the warehouse, watching the ambulance speed away toward Hennepin County General. There were three police escorts, lights and sirens going full blast: two MPD units in front, and Bonar behind in the Wisconsin cruiser. Halloran had insisted on riding with Sharon. The med techs had been foolish enough to tell him they were sorry, but he couldn't ride in the ambulance, and Halloran hadn't said a thing. He'd just pulled out his gun and pointed it at them, and the techs had changed their minds in a hurry.

'Techs said it doesn't look good,' Gino said.

'I heard.'

'How many cops do you know would have dragged themselves up all those stairs with a wound like that?'

'I'd like to think most of them would.'

Gino shook his head. 'I don't know. It was really something.'

Magozzi nodded. 'They were both something. Halloran jumped through that door and damn near emptied his clip before I could get off a second round.'

Gino sighed. 'I might have to rethink my position on Wisconsin cops. What was the deal with MacBride anyway? Why was she chasing the gurney like that?'

Magozzi closed his eyes, remembering Grace running alongside the gurney as they wheeled it through the garage, jerking the crucifix off her neck, frantically wrapping the chain around Sharon's wrist.

Is she Catholic? one of the techs had asked her.

I don't know. Don't let them take that off her.

'She was doing what she could, Gino.'

'Huh.' Gino turned and looked at Grace, Harley, Roadrunner, and Annie, huddled in a circle by the door with the shell-shocked expression of war victims. 'Wonder if she's gonna go loopy after this.'

Magozzi looked over his shoulder at Grace. She was almost buried under the arms of her friends, but she raised her eyes to his almost immediately, as if he'd spoken her name. 'I don't think so,' he said.

48

It was a hot day for late October, close to eighty degrees, and the sky was cloudless, a deep, hurtful blue.

It was the pomp and circumstance, Halloran thought, that made cop funerals so goddamned sad. Milwaukee had sent the bagpipes, and they were wailing now for all the men and women in uniform who couldn't, because it wouldn't be seemly.

God, there were hundreds of them. So many figures in brown and blue, sparkles of polished brass winking in the sunlight, decorating the autumn-dried, gentle slopes where tombstones sprouted.

He'd seen plates from a dozen states besides Wisconsin in the somber motorcade that had crawled the two miles from St Luke's Catholic Church to the Calumet Cemetery.

He searched the faces closest to the grave and saw his own people standing at rigid attention. A lot of them were crying, unashamed. The bagpipes hadn't done it for them.

Halloran's own eyes were dry, as if the tears he had shed in that warehouse in Minneapolis were all that his body contained.

It was almost over now. The flag had been folded and presented, the salute had been fired, startling a flock of blackbirds up from the adjacent field, and now the bugle was crying, sending the familiar notes of Taps into the awful stillness of this perfect autumn day. He heard Bonar beside him, softly clearing his throat.

It took over half an hour for all the mourners to leave. Halloran and Bonar were sitting on a concrete bench under a big cottonwood. A few leaves clung stubbornly to the crown, gold against blue.

'It wasn't your fault, Mike,' Bonar said after a long silence. 'You get to be sad, but not guilty. It wasn't your fault.'

'Don't, Bonar.'

'Okay.'

Father Newberry seemed to float down the slope toward them, his black vestments sweeping the dried grass. He was wearing one of those beatific smiles priests always wear when they put someone into the ground, as if they were seeing them off on a grand journey instead of into the nothingness Halloran believed in. Sadistic bastards.

'Mikey,' the sadistic bastard said gently.

'Hello, Father.' Halloran showed the priest his eyes for a moment, then looked down at the ground, found an ant at his feet, climbing a blade of grass.

'Mikey,' Father Newberry said again, even more gently, but Halloran wouldn't look up. He would not be comforted. He refused.

Bonar gave Father Newberry a helpless shrug, and the priest nodded his understanding.

'Mikey, I thought you'd want to know. The keys you left at the station the day Danny was killed . . .'

Halloran winced.

'. . . they didn't fit the Kleinfeldts' front door.'

Halloran remained still for a moment, taking it in, then he raised his head slowly. 'What do you mean?'

The priest's smile was faint, elusive. 'Well, I think I told you they left everything to the church, so yesterday I picked up the keys from your office and went out there to see to some things' – his fingers fumbled at his chest, then closed around the ornate crucifix hanging there – 'and it was the strangest thing. None of them fit, Mikey. I tried them again and again, but none of them fit the front door. I called your office. A couple of your deputies are going to go back out there with me tomorrow, but it won't make any difference. The key simply isn't there.'

'I don't understand.'

Father Newberry sighed. 'The Kleinfeldts were frightened people. Perhaps they never carried a key to the house with them. Probably they kept it hidden on the property, although I did look in the obvious places and couldn't find it. I suppose it will turn up eventually. But the point is that even if you had remembered the keys, Mikey, you wouldn't have been able to open the front door. Danny would still have gone around to the back. Do you understand?'

Halloran stared at the priest for a long time, then dropped his eyes and found the ant again, stupid ant, still wasting the moments of his brief life climbing up and down the same damned blade of grass.

Goddamnit, he'd made so many mistakes. The list of 'what ifs' seemed endless, and damning. What if he'd refused to let Sharon go to the warehouse? What if he'd let her go, but refused to stay outside? What if he'd gone to the back door instead of Danny? What if he'd broken one of those goddamned windows and they'd both just gone in the front?

But at least with Danny, the biggest 'what if' was crossed off the list. *What if I'd just remembered the keys? Well, Halloran, it wouldn't have changed a goddamned thing.* There was a little salvation in that knowledge. Halloran grabbed it and held on tight, and when he could finally trust his voice, he said, 'Thank you, Father. Thank you for telling me that.'

The old priest breathed out a sigh of relief.

Bonar stood up and arched his back, big belly thrusting forward like the prow of a ship. 'I'll walk you up to your car, Father.'

'Thank you, Bonar.' And when they were up the slope a bit, out of Halloran's hearing, he whispered, 'Will you tell me what happened in Minneapolis? I've only been getting bits and pieces.'

'If you promise not to proselytize.'

Bonar talked nonstop as they climbed, then dipped down into a little hollow, then up the last hill to where Father Newberry's car was parked near the entrance. He told him everything, refusing to insult the man with a whitewashed version, and then he opened the car door and watched as the priest settled solemnly in his seat, put his hands on the wheel, then sighed heavily.

'So much sadness,' Father Newberry said. 'So much more than I imagined.' He touched the crucifix again, then looked up at Bonar. 'Are you going back to Minneapolis with Mikey?'

'Later this afternoon.'

'Will you tell Deputy Mueller I've been praying for her?'

'She was talking pretty good yesterday. Doc says it'll take some time, but she's going to be fine.'

'Of course she is. As I said, I've been praying for her.'

Bonar smiled. 'I'll tell her she owes it all to a Catholic priest. That'll frost her nuggets.' He sighed and looked down the hill, where Halloran was just getting up from the concrete bench. 'It was a nice Mass, Father. Really nice. You saw Danny out in style.'

'Thank you, Bonar.' Father Newberry reached for the handle to close the door, but Bonar held it open.

'Father?'

'Yes, Bonar?'

'Well, I was just wondering . . . when we check things into evidence we're pretty precise. Like take a ring of keys, for example. We don't just write down "a key ring," we record how many keys, whether they're house keys, padlock keys, car keys, like that.'

'Really.'

'Yes, really. So what I was thinking was that when the deputies go back out there with you tomorrow, they'll be checking the log against the keys on that ring, you know, to make sure one didn't get lost or something.'

'Oh.' The priest was staring straight ahead through the windshield. His face was absolutely expressionless. 'That's very interesting, Bonar. Thank you very much for telling me. I never realized police procedure was so . . .'

'Precise.'

'Yes.'

Bonar straightened and closed the car door, then bent at the waist to smile through the open window.

'Keys are tough things to keep track of. I bet I got a million keys in my junk drawer at home. Don't know what half of 'em are for.'

Father Newberry turned his head and looked Bonar right in the eye. 'I have a drawer just like that at the rectory.'

'I thought you might.'

Bonar stood in the road and watched the car pull away, veering a little from side to side, as if the driver were a bit unsteady under the burden he'd chosen to carry. He was thinking that in all his life the old priest had probably never committed so great a sin, or so great a good.

'Hey, Bonar.' Halloran came up beside him.

'Hey. How're you doing?'

Halloran took a breath and looked back down the hill toward Danny Peltier's grave. 'Better. A lot better.'

49

On Monday afternoon, the day of Danny Peltier's funeral, Magozzi and Gino went to the hospital to visit Sharon.

Except for the dark circles under her eyes, her skin was almost the same color as the white bandage covering her throat, and she had that certain stillness of survivors who have not yet quite rejoined the living. But when she opened her eyes, Magozzi thought she looked terrific.

'I was wondering when you guys would show up.' She smiled.

'Shows what you know,' Gino grumbled. 'We were here on and off the whole time you were in ICU. So were all the Monkeewrench people.'

'Really? How come none of you came back when I was awake?'

Magozzi smiled. 'Are you kidding? Halloran guarded this door like a junkyard dog. We had to wait for him to leave the state before we could sneak in for a statement. Are you up for this?'

'Sure. Throat's still a little sore, but at least I stopped spitting blood, which really grossed me out.'

Gino dragged a chair up to the bed. 'Doc says you'll be out of here in a week.'

'Yeah, I was lucky. If it had been anything bigger

than a .22, I'd be talking to you from the other side right now.'

'Damn right you were lucky,' Gino said. 'The .22 was probably the first thing Diane grabbed when she reached into her bag. What I can't figure is why she didn't plug you again and finish you off.'

Sharon rolled her head toward Magozzi. 'Is he always this diplomatic?'

'Pretty much.'

'Well, I think she was going to, but Mitch walked in. He probably saved my life.'

'You saw that?' Magozzi asked.

'Yeah, I was in and out. She was over the edge by that time. She told him flat-out she came there to kill Grace. He pulled a gun on her, did you know that? He was going to kill his own wife so she didn't kill Grace. So she shot him, boom. Blew him away right next to me. And then I lost it for a while.'

Gino nodded. 'Well, while you were in dreamland, she dragged Mitch's body into the elevator, then cut the power and unplugged the generator so it wouldn't kick on. That brought Harley and Roadrunner down in the dark – that's why they didn't see you – and then she locked them in the generator room and went upstairs to finish off Grace.'

'That's when I came to again, when the stairwell door closed. I heard voices and I knew she was up there with MacBride. So I went upstairs.'

Gino rolled his eyes. 'You crawled up a flight of stairs in the dark, bleeding like a stuck pig. You're a pistol, lady.'

'Yeah, right. I didn't even get off a shot.'

Magozzi walked over to the bed and took her hands. 'You were amazing. You saved Grace's life.' He thumbed the silver crucifix wrapped around her wrist like a bracelet.

'Don't know where that came from and I can't unclasp the damn thing.'

'Just leave it for a couple days.' Magozzi smiled, noticing how tired she looked now that he was closer. 'You want to rest now?'

'Hell, no, I don't want to rest, I want to know what's happening.'

Gino smiled. God, he loved cops. Shoot 'em up, nearly kill 'em, put 'em in a coma for a day or two and they still wake up cops, and the first thing they want to know is what went down. 'The bad guys are dead,' he said.

'Come on, Gino . . .'

'It's wrapping up in a hurry. The hair your ME pulled put Diane Cross at the church in Calumet and the blood work came back on the Kleinfeldts. She was their kid all right. She'd been tracking them ever since she left Saint Peter's.'

'And she finally found them.'

'Found them, did them, and signed them with her new last name,' Magozzi said. 'We figure that's what the crosses she carved in their chests were all about.'

'I'm going to get my Ph.D. with this,' Sharon said. 'She had the surgery, right?'

'Yeah,' Gino said. 'Week after his eighteenth birthday, Brian Bradford went under the knife, got a few extra parts removed, and changed his name to D.

Emanuel, which incidentally happens to be the Mother Superior's name before she was promoted. Sister Emanuel. Then Brian, now the dishy Diane, enrolls at Georgia State – honors computer science major, by the way, which explains the high-test firewalls on the e-mails she sent to Grace. Anyway, she sets her sights on Mitch Cross, who was James Mitchell at that point – Christ, I hate this case. Everybody's got a million names and one of 'em's got two sexes.'

Sharon closed her eyes and leaned back farther into her pillow. 'But she wasn't the slasher in Georgia. That was Mitch.'

'Right. Turns out Diane's been saving that boy's ass for ten years. Alibied him right off the suspect list for the Atlanta killings, then saved him again by stopping the SKUD game when the necklace clue threatened to blow the whole thing wide open.'

Sharon's eyes fluttered open. 'That's the part I don't get. You'd think the cops would have asked Grace about that necklace back in Atlanta.'

'Well, there were tons, and I mean tons of trace at the crime scene – it was student housing and the last five hundred residents had left something or other behind. By the time they sorted through it all and got around to questioning their material witnesses, the material witnesses had disappeared without a trace. All five of them have been wanted by the FBI for questioning the whole time.'

'That's why the FBI had apoplexy when you ran MacBride's prints.'

'Exactly.'

Sharon yawned and closed her eyes again. 'I'm telling

you, the penis is the root of all evil. This whole thing started because ten years ago Mitch had some sick fixation on MacBride and started bumping off the competition.'

Gino smiled. 'Yeah, but the really interesting thing is, it probably wasn't the first time.'

Sharon's eyes opened. 'What do you mean?'

Magozzi said, 'Once we had his real name, all the records popped. His parents died in a suspicious house fire when he was thirteen. Juvie was looking at him, but couldn't prove anything. Then he was pulled in for stalking some high-school girl, and a month later her boyfriend and brother turned up dead. Stabbed to death.'

'Jesus,' Sharon murmured.

'Yeah,' Gino said. 'Again, no proof, but it looks like MacBride wasn't his first obsession.'

Sharon pushed herself up on her elbows, wincing, and looked at Magozzi. 'Have you told MacBride this yet?'

'She knows Mitch killed the people in Georgia, I was there when Diane told her. But not the rest.'

'You've got to tell her.'

'We will, eventually. We were taking it easy on them for a –'

'No. You've got to tell her now. Don't you get it? She's been carrying the blame for Georgia for ten years. She thinks this guy *only* killed because of her, that she created some kind of a monster. She needs to know there's a history there, that Mitch was damaged goods long before she met him.'

She sagged back on the pillow and closed her eyes, exhausted. 'Go tell her, Magozzi.'

It was dusk when Magozzi pulled up to the curb in front of Grace's house. Jackson was in the front yard, rolling in the grass with Charlie. He jumped to his feet when Magozzi came up the walk, and Charlie butted his leg, whining a greeting. He dropped to a crouch and scratched behind the dog's ears, looking up at Jackson.

'How is she?'

Jackson moved his thin shoulders in a worried shrug. 'I don't know. She doesn't say much. The rest of them left a little while ago, but they'll be back. She's better when they're around.' He rolled troubled eyes up to Magozzi. 'She's still scared. I don't get that. It's over, right?'

Magozzi nodded, pushed to his feet. 'It's going to take a while. You keeping an eye on her?'

'You bet your white ass I am.'

It took a long time for Grace to answer the door. He listened to the metallic thunks of all the dead bolts sliding back, and then she opened the door a crack and looked out.

Her dark hair was loose and tousled, weeping around her shoulders, and it hurt him to look into her eyes. She was wearing the white bathrobe, which was all wrong for this time of day. The outline of the Sig bulged in her pocket. He wondered if she'd ever be able to put it away.

'Can I come in?' he asked, and he was about to say that there were things he needed to tell her, things that might help, that maybe *he* could help if she'd just give him half a chance –

She just stood there looking at him, and he couldn't read her eyes, but he had a fearful flashback to the night she'd slammed the door behind him, because he was a cop, because they always fought, because he was inextricably linked to a nightmare she couldn't put behind her.

Let her go, he told himself.

Yeah, right.

'I'm not leaving, Grace.'

Her eyebrows shifted up a notch.

'I'm not. I won't do it. I'm not leaving until you talk to me, and if you won't let me in, I'll just sit out here on your front step until I'm a hundred years old. You'll get ticketed for littering.'

She tipped her head sideways a little, no more than an inch, but something in her eyes changed, as if maybe there was a small, small smile somewhere inside her head that might, in time, make it outside to her mouth.

'Come on in, Magozzi.'

She took his hand and led him inside, leaving the door wide open behind them.

An exclusive extract from

Live Bait

The new thriller by

P. J. Tracy

Published June 2004

I

It was just after sunrise and still raining when Lily found her husband's body. He was lying faceup on the asphalt apron in front of the greenhouse, eyes and mouth open, collecting rainwater.

Even dead, he looked quite handsome in this position, gravity pulling back the loose, wrinkled skin of his face, smoothing away eighty-four years of pain and smiles and worries.

Lily stood over him for a moment, wincing when the raindrops plopped noisily onto his eyes.

I hate eyedrops.

Morey, hold still. Stop blinking.

Stop blinking, she says, while she pours chemicals into my eyes.

Hush. It's not chemicals. Natural tears, see? It says so right on the bottle.

You expect a blind man to read?

A little grain of sand in your eye and suddenly you're blind. Big, tough guy.

And they're not natural tears. What do they do? Go to funerals and hold little bottles under crying people? No, they mix chemicals together and call it natural tears. It's false advertising, is what it is. These are unnatural tears. A little bottle of lies.

Shut up, old man.

This is the thing, Lily. Nothing should pretend to be what it's not. Everything should have a big label that says what it is so there's no confusion. Like the fertilizer we used on the bedding plants that year that killed all our ladybugs, what was it called?

Plant So Green.

Right. So it should have been called Plant So Green Ladybug So Dead. Forget the tiny print on the back you can't read. Real truth in labeling, that's what we need. This is a good rule. God should follow such a rule.

Morey!

What can I say? He made a big mistake there. Would it have been such a problem for Him to make things look like what they are? I mean, He's God, right? This is something He could do. Think about it. You've got a guy at the door with this great smile and nice face and you let him in and he kills your whole family. This is God's mistake. Evil should look evil. Then you don't let it in.

You, of all people, should know it's not that simple.

It's exactly that simple.

Lily took a breath, then sat on her heels – a young posture for such an old woman, but her knees were still good, still strong and flexible. She couldn't get Morey's eyes to close all the way, and with them open only a slit, he looked sinister. It was the first thing that had frightened Lily in a very long time. She wouldn't look at them as she pushed back the darkened silver hair the rain had plastered to his skull.

One of her fingers slipped into a hole on the side of his head and she froze. 'Oh, no,' she whispered, then rose quickly, wiping her fingers on her overalls.

'I told you so, Morey,' she scolded her husband one last time. 'I told you so.'

2

April in Minnesota was always unpredictable, but once every decade or so, it got downright sadistic, fluctuating wildly between tantalizing promises of spring and the last, angry death throes of a stubborn winter that had no intention of going quietly.

It had been just such a year. Last week, a freak snowstorm had blustered in on what *had* been the warmest April on record, scaring the hell out of the budding trees and launching statewide discussions of a mass migration to Florida.

But spring had eventually prevailed, and right now she was busy playing kiss-and-make-up, and doing a damn fine job of it. The mercury was pushing seventy-five, the snow-stunned flora had rallied with a shameless explosion of neon green, and best of all, the mother lode of mosquito larvae was still percolating in the lakes and swamps. Giddy, sun-starved Minnesotans were out in force, cherishing the temporary delusion that the state was actually habitable.

Detective Leo Magozzi was stretched out on a decrepit chaise on his front porch, Sunday paper in one hand, a mug of coffee in the other. He hadn't forgotten about last week's snowstorm and he was pragmatic enough to know that it wasn't too late for another, but there was no point in letting cynicism ruin a perfectly beautiful day. Besides, it was a rare thing when he could practice the sloth he'd always aspired to – homicide detectives' vacations were always contingent on murderers' vacations, and murderers seemed to be the hardest-working citizens in the country. But for some inexplicable reason, Minneapolis was enjoying the longest murder-free spell in years. As his partner, Gino Rolseth, had put it so eloquently: Homicide was dead. For the past few months they'd had nothing to do but work cold cases, and if they ever solved all of them, they'd be back on the beat, frisking transvestites and wishing they'd been dentists instead of cops.

Magozzi sipped his coffee and watched as the neighborhood masochists engaged in all manner of personal torture, huffing and puffing and sweating as they raced furiously against a climatic clock that would have them locked indoors again in a few months' time. They jogged, they Rollerbladed, they ran with their dogs, and celebrated every degree that rose on the thermometer by shedding another article of clothing.

It was one of the things Magozzi loved most about Minnesotans. Fat, thin, muscled, or flabby, there were no self-conscious people in this state when the weather got warm, and by the time you got a nice day like this one, most of them were half naked. Of course this was not always a good thing, certainly not in the case of Jim, his extremely hirsute next-door neighbor. You could never be really sure if Jim were wearing a shirt or not. He was out there now, possibly shirtless, possibly not, hard at work preparing the flower beds that would put him in pole position for next month's Beautiful Gardens of the Twin Cities Tour. If Jim was trying to shame Magozzi into being a better homeowner, it wasn't going to work.

He looked out at his own sorry excuse for a yard – a couple of mud puddles from last night's rain, some brave dandelions, and a few blue spruce in various stages of demise. Occasionally he had a fleeting memory of what the place had looked like before the divorce. Flowers everywhere, Kentucky bluegrass standing at attention, and Heather out there each day with sharp instruments and a stern expression, frightening plants into submission. She'd been good at frightening things into submission – it had certainly worked on him, and he'd been armed.

He was on his second cup of coffee and almost to the sports section when a Volvo station wagon pulled into the driveway. Gino Rolseth hopped out, lugging an enormous cooler and a bag of Kingsford. His belly tested the generous limits of a Tommy Bahama shirt, and beefy legs poked out from a terrible pair of plaid Bermuda shorts.

'Hey, Leo!' He lumbered up onto the porch and dropped the cooler. 'I come bearing gifts of animal flesh and fermented grain.'

Magozzi lifted a dark brow. 'At eight o'clock in the morning? Tell me this means Angela finally kicked your sorry ass out, so I can call her and propose.'

'You should be so lucky. This is charity. Angela's folks took her and the kids to some craft thing at Maplewood Mall, so I had a free Sunday, thought I'd liven up your so-called life.'

Magozzi got up and looked into the cooler. 'What's a craft thing?'

'You know, those places with all the booths where people knit houses out of old grocery bags and stuff like that.'

Magozzi rummaged in the cooler and pulled out a package of sickly-looking, plump, gray-white sausages. 'What are these things that look like your legs?'

'Those are uncooked brats, imported all the way from Milwaukee, you food pygmy. Where's your grill?'

Magozzi gestured toward a rusty old Weber in the corner of the porch.

Gino nudged it with his foot and it collapsed. 'We're going to need duct tape.'

Magozzi hefted a suspicious-looking, dark orange brick of cheese. 'Twelve-year cheddar? Is that legal?'

Gino grinned. 'That stuff'll make you weep with joy, I promise. Got it at a great little cheese house in Door County. Somebody forgot about a wheel in the cellar and found it twelve years later, covered in about a foot of mold. Nirvana, my friend. Pure nirvana. It's amazing what a cow and some bacteria can do.'

Magozzi sniffed it and cringed. 'Oh yeah. Every time I see a cow I think, Hey, wouldn't it be great to get some bacteria and really do something with this thing. Why do you have a file folder in the cooler?'

'It's a cold case.'

'Very funny.'

Gino lifted the grill and another leg fell off in a shower of rust. 'This one's from ninety-four. Thought we could take a look at it later. You know, just to keep our hand in, in case anyone ever kills somebody in this town again. You remember hearing anything about the Valensky case?'

Magozzi sat down on the chaise and opened the folder. 'Sort of. The plumber, right?'

'That's the one. Shot seven times, three of them in places I don't even want to think about.'

'Plumbers charge too much.'

'Tell me about it. But other than that, this guy was damn near a candidate for sainthood. Some Polack who actually made it out of the war alive, emigrated to the good old US of A, started a business, married, had three kids, deacon at his church, scout leader, the whole American dream, then bled to death on his own bathroom floor after someone used him for target practice.'

'Suspects?'

'Hell no. According to the reports in there, everybody loved him. Case dried up in about two seconds.'

Magozzi grunted and tossed the folder on the floor. 'Most guys with a free Sunday would probably find something else to do, like sit on a bench at Lake Calhoun and count bikinis.'

'Yeah, well, I'm a crime fighter, I have a higher purpose.' Gino ran a hand through his hedge of closely cropped blond hair, reconsidering. 'Besides, it's probably too early for bikinis.'

They got the call before Magozzi had finished duct-taping the legs back on his grill. Gino had gone inside to unload the cooler, and when he came back out to the porch he was beaming.

'Hey, want to go see a body?'

Magozzi sat back on his heels and frowned. 'You found a body in my kitchen?'

'Nah, Phone rang while I was in there, so I picked up. Dispatch got an honest-to-God homicide call. Uptown Nursery. The owner's wife found him this morning by one of the greenhouses and figured it was a heart attack, because the guy is pushing eighty-five and what else would drop a man that age? So she called the funeral director. He finds a bullet hole in the guy's head and calls nine-one-one.'

Magozzi looked wistfully at the grill and sighed. 'So what happened to the on-duty guys who are supposed to be taking this?'

'Tinker and Peterson. Just what I wanted to know. They just took a call at the train yard over in Northeast. Found some poor bastard tied to the tracks.'

Magozzi winced.

'Nah, don't worry. Train never hit him.'

'So he's okay?'

'Nope, he's dead.'

Magozzi looked at him expectantly.

'Don't look at me. That's all I got.' He jumped when his shirt pocket spit out an irritating, tinny version of Beethoven's Fifth.

'What *is* that?'

Gino pulled his cell phone out of his pocket and stabbed viciously at buttons half the size of his chubby fingers. 'Goddamnit. Helen keeps programming in all these weird rings 'cause she knows I got no clue how to change it.'

Magozzi grinned. 'That's funny.'

Beethoven spoke again.

'Fourteen-year-olds are only funny when they belong to somebody else . . . shit I'm gonna invent one of these things with big fat buttons and make a jillion dollars. Hello, this is Rolseth.'

Magozzi stood and brushed the rust off his hands, listened to Gino grunt into the phone for a few seconds, then went inside to lock up. By the time he got back out to the porch, Gino had retrieved his gun from the car and was hooking it to the belt that almost held up his Bermuda shorts. He looked like an armed and dangerous tourist.

'I don't suppose you've got a pair of pants that would fit me.'

Magozzi just smiled at him.

'Aw, shut up. That was Langer on the phone. He and McLaren just got called in for a suspected homicide – "suspected" meaning someone did a little interior design with a few gallons of blood, but there's no body. And guess what?'

'He wants us to take it?'

'Nah, Dispatch told him we were on the nursery thing, that's why he called. The bloody house is just a few blocks over.'

Magozzi frowned. 'That's a pretty decent neighborhood.'

'Right. Not exactly a killing field, and all of a sudden we've got two possibles in one day. And there's another thing. The guy who lives in that house is – or was – also in his eighties, just like our guy.'

Magozzi thought about that for a minute. 'He's thinking cluster? What, that some psycho's running around killing old people?'

Gino shrugged. 'He was just giving us a heads-up. Thought we should keep in touch in case something clicks.'

Magozzi sighed, looked longingly at the Weber. 'So we're back in business.'

'Big-time.' Gino paused for a moment. 'You ever think there's something wrong with a job where you only have something to do if someone gets murdered?'

'Every day, buddy.'

3

Marty Pullman was sitting on the closed toilet lid in his downstairs bathroom, staring down the muzzle of a 357 Magnum. The round black hole looked very large, which worried him. Worse yet, the toilet faced the big mirror on the sliding doors that enclosed the bathtub, and he wasn't too keen on watching his own snuff film. He thought about it for a minute, then got into the bathtub and slid the doors closed behind him.

He smiled a little as he aimed the shower nozzle toward the back of the tub and turned the spray on full blast. He may have made a mess of his life, but he sure as hell wasn't going to make a mess of his death.

Finally satisfied, he sat down in the tub and put the muzzle in his mouth. Water poured over his head, his clothes, his shoes.

He hesitated for just a few seconds, wondering again what, if anything, he'd done last night. Not that it would matter now, he thought, slipping his thumb through the trigger guard.

'Mr Pullman?'

Marty froze, his thumb quivering on the trigger. Goddamn it, he was hallucinating. He had to be. No one ever came to this house, and certainly no one would just let himself in – except maybe a Jehovah's Witness, which made him glad he had the gun.

'Mr Pullman?' The male voice was louder now,

closer, and he sounded young. 'Are you in there, sir?' A forceful knock rattled the bathroom door in its frame.

The gun tasted terrible as he pulled it from his mouth, and he spat into the water swirling toward the drain. 'Who is it?' he shouted, trying his best to sound scary and aggressive.

'Sorry to disturb you, Mr Pullman, but Mrs Gilbert told me to break the door down if I had to.'

'Who the hell are you and how do you know Lily?' Marty shouted.

'Jeff Montgomery, sir? I work at the nursery?'

The kid spoke only in questions. God, that was irritating. Marty looked down at the gun and sighed. He was never going to get this done. 'Stay right where you are. I'll be out in a minute.'

He scrambled out of the tub, stripped out of his drenched clothes, then stuffed gun, clothes, and shoes into the hamper. He wrapped a towel around his waist, then opened the bathroom door.

A tall, good-looking kid – eighteen or nineteen at most – was standing awkwardly in the hallway, hands stuffed into his jeans pockets.

'Okay. Here I am. Now tell me why Lily wanted you to break my door down.'

Jeff Montgomery had big blue eyes that grew comically wide when he noticed the thick scar that slashed a diagonal across Marty's bare chest. He looked away quickly.

'Uh . . . I didn't actually break down your door? It was open? And Mrs Gilbert has been trying to call you forever, but no one answered your phone? And jeez, Mr Pullman, I'm really sorry, but Mr Gilbert passed away.'

Marty didn't move for a minute; didn't even blink; then he rubbed the heel of his hand hard against his forehead, as if it would help him absorb the information. 'What?' he whispered. 'Morey's dead?'

The kid pressed his lips together and scowled down at the floor, trying not to cry, and Marty's opinion of him shot up a few degrees, even if he did end every sentence with a question mark. Anyone who liked Morey enough to cry for him couldn't be all bad.

'He was shot, Mr Pullman. Someone shot Mr Gilbert.'

Marty didn't say anything, but he felt the blood drain from his face as if someone had just pulled a plug. He sagged sideways against the bathroom door frame, glad it was there to hold him up.

Jesus Christ, he hated this world.

4

'Come on, Leo. Stop at Target or someplace so I can buy a pair of pants,' Gino grumbled from the passenger seat.

Magozzi shook his head. 'Can't. Crime scene's getting older by the minute.'

Gino plucked unhappily at the legs of his shorts. 'This is totally unprofessional.' He blew out a noisy sigh and looked out the window.

He'd always liked this part of Minneapolis. They were on Calhoun Parkway now, circling Lake Calhoun only a little slower than the bikers who decorated the asphalt trail in their brightly colored costumes. There were even a few windsurfers out today, dancing across the water with their triangle sails.

'Damn, I hate this part.'

'At least we don't have to tell her,' Magozzi said. 'That's something.'

'Yeah, I suppose. But we still have to ask her questions, like did she shoot her husband in the head.'

'That's why we get the big bucks.'

There was a squad on the street and another one blocking the driveway of the Uptown Nursery when Magozzi and Gino arrived. A couple of uniforms were standing around with rolls of yellow crime-scene tape, looking lost. Magozzi showed his badge when one of them approached the window. 'You got a grid staked out? You want us to park on the street?'

The uniform took off his hat and wiped his shiny forehead with a sleeve. It was already hot in the sun, especially on asphalt. 'Hell, I don't know, Detective. We got no clue where to string the tape.'

'Gee, how about around the body?' Gino suggested.

The cop bristled a little. 'Yeah, well the wife moved the body.'

'*What?*'

'That's right. She found him outside and moved him into the greenhouse. Said she didn't want to leave him out in the rain.'

Magozzi groaned. 'Oh, man.'

'Lock her up,' Gino muttered. 'Tampering with evidence, destroying a crime scene. Lock her up and throw away the key. She probably killed him anyway.'

'She's about a million years old, Detective.'

'Yeah, well that's the thing about guns. Old people, kids, anybody can use 'em. They're equal-opportunity murder weapons.' He got out of the car and slammed the door and started walking slowly toward the big greenhouse in front, eyes down in case the rain had missed a bloody footprint or something.

The uniform watched him go, shaking his head. 'That is not a happy man.'

'Normally he is,' Magozzi replied. 'He's just pissed because I wouldn't let him stop and change into some long pants before we came here.'

'You gotta give him points, then. Those are some bad legs.'

'Who belongs to the other squad?'

'Viegs and Berman. They're walking the block, hitting the neighbors. Couple of bike patrols are babysitting the body inside, but I wouldn't be surprised if the old lady has them watering plants or something.'

'Yeah?'

The uniform wiped his brow with his sleeve again. 'She's a piece of work, that one.'

'You got a feeling about her?'

'Yeah. I got a feeling her husband's getting the first rest he's had in years.'

Magozzi caught up to Gino in the middle of the lot, staring at the hearse angled in front of the greenhouse.

'We got no crime scene,' Gino grumbled. 'Rain trashed it first, then the funeral director drove his tank all over it, and . . . oh, man. Are you seeing what I'm seeing?'

Behind and almost hidden by the hearse was a white '66 Chevy Malibu convertible, red leather interior, positively cherry. Gino had lusted after it from the first time he'd seen it.

'Huh,' Magozzi grunted. 'What do you think?'

Gino clucked his tongue, the envy as ripe as ever. 'Gotta be his. There isn't another one like it in the Cities.'

'So what's he doing here?'

'Beats me. Buying flowers?'

Neither one of them had seen Marty Pullman since he'd left the force a year ago, a few months after his wife had died. Not that they'd known him that well even when they were all carrying the same badge. In Minneapolis, Homicide and Narcotics didn't mix nearly as often as they did on TV. It was just that once you saw Marty, you weren't likely to forget him. He still had the wrestler's physique that had taken him to State in high school. Short, bowlegs, massive chest and arms, and dark eyes that had looked haunted even before they were. They'd called him Gorilla back when he'd still had a sense of humor, but those days were long gone.

The big glass door of the greenhouse opened, and Pullman walked out to meet them.

'Man,' Gino said under his breath. 'Looks like he lost about fifty pounds.'

'Hell of a year for him,' Magozzi said, and then Marty was there, shaking their hands, his expression as sober as ever.

'Magozzi, Gino, good to see you.'

'What the hell, Pullman?' Gino pumped his hand. 'You take up gardening, or did you join up again and nobody told me?'

Marty blew a long, shaky breath out through puffed cheeks. He looked like he was teetering on the edge of something. 'The man who was shot was my father-in-law, Gino.'

'Oh shit.' Gino's face fell. 'He was Hannah's dad? Oh man, I'm sorry. Shit.'

'Forget it. You had no way of knowing. Listen, you don't have much of a scene here.'

Magozzi heard the quaver in his voice, and decided to hold off on the sympathy until the man was strong enough to accept it. 'So we heard,' he said, pulling out a pocket notebook and a pen. 'Anybody else here this morning besides you and the funeral director?'

'A couple of the employees – I sent them home, but told them to stay put, that you'd be checking in with them before the day was out. I blocked off where Lily said she found Morey with my car, but that's about the best I could do.'

'We appreciate it, Marty,' Magozzi said, wishing he could walk away from this one. Lily Gilbert had lost her daughter one year, her husband the next. Magozzi didn't know how you survived that kind of double tragedy, and asking her the questions he had to ask suddenly seemed like an appalling act of cruelty. 'You think your mother-in-law will be able to talk to us?'

Marty managed a half smile. 'She's not falling apart, if that's what you mean. Lily doesn't do that.' He glanced toward the main greenhouse. 'She's in there. I tried to get her to go to the house – it's on the back of the lot, behind all the greenhouses – but that's not about to happen until they take Morey away. ME's on the way, right?'

Magozzi nodded. 'He'll do a little on-site before they move him. I don't think you want her around for that.'

'Hell, no, I don't. But Lily will be wherever she wants to be. That's just the way she is.' He sucked air in through his teeth. 'There's something else.'

Magozzi and Gino waited quietly.

'After she got him inside, she washed him. Shaved him. Changed his clothes. He's lying in there on one of the plant tables all decked out in his funeral suit.'

Gino closed his eyes briefly, trying to hold his temper in check. 'That's not good, Marty.'

'Tell me about it.'

'I mean, her son-in-law was a cop. She had to know she was destroying evidence.'

'She's damn near blind, Gino. Can't even get a

driver's license anymore. Says she never saw any blood. I'm guessing the rain washed it away before she got out here. He caught it in the head, small caliber right behind the left temple, and he's got this great head of thick white hair . . . hell, even I had to look for it and I knew it was there.'

'Okay.' Gino nodded, letting it go for the moment.

Magozzi made a note to have the crime scene techs collect the clothes the dead man had been wearing when he was shot. 'Anything you can think of that might help us out here?' he asked.

Marty's laugh was short and bitter. 'You mean like who'd want to kill him? Sure. Look for somebody who'd pop Mother Teresa. He was a good man, Magozzi. Maybe even a great one.'

The air in the greenhouse was hot and swampy, laden with the scent of wet earth and vegetation. Long tables filled with plants were lined up in two rows, leaving a narrow central aisle – it looked like every other greenhouse Magozzi'd ever been in, except for the front table, which held a corpse in a black suit instead of potted flowers.

Even dead and laid out for viewing, Morey Gilbert was still a formidable presence. Very tall, very well-muscled, and better dressed than Magozzi had ever been in his life.

Two young bike cops fidgeted near the body, trying to pretend it wasn't there.

'Where are they?' Marty asked them.

'Your mother-in-law took the old gentleman back there, sir.' One of the bike patrols tipped his head toward a door in the back wall.

'What's back there, Marty?' Magozzi asked.

'The potting shed, a couple more greenhouses. Lily probably wanted Sol out of here for a while. He was pretty shook up.'

'Sol?'

'He's the funeral director who called it in, but he was also Morey's best friend. This is a tough one for him. Hang on, I'll get them.'

Gino waited until Marty was out of earshot before whispering to Magozzi. 'Her husband is dead, and she's consoling the funeral director? That's a little ass-backwards, isn't it?'

Magozzi shrugged. 'Maybe that's how she holds it together, by taking care of other people.'

'Maybe. Or maybe she didn't like her husband very much.'

They walked over to the front table to take a closer look at the dead man before the family came back. Gino used a pen to lift the white hair, exposing the bullet hole. 'Tiny. I suppose you could miss it if you were half blind, but I don't know.' He looked up at the bike patrols. 'You guys can take off now if you want. We got it covered. Send copies of your reports up to Homicide.'

'Yes, sir, thank you.'

Magozzi was looking at Morey Gilbert's face, seeing a person instead of a corpse, starting to form the kind of bond that always linked him to victims. 'He's got a nice face, Gino. And he was eighty-four, still running his own business, taking care of his family. Who'd want to kill an old man like this?'

Gino shrugged. 'Maybe an old woman.'

'You're just pissed because she moved the body.'

'I'm *suspicious* because she moved the body. I'm pissed because you made me come here in short pants.'

They both took a step away from the table when the back door opened and Marty came through with his little geriatric entourage, led by a tiny, wiry old woman with silver hair cropped close to her head. She wore a long-sleeved white blouse under child-sized bib overalls, and thick glasses magnified her dark eyes, making her look a little like Yoda.

A tough Yoda, Magozzi decided as she drew closer. There was no sign that she'd been crying, no surrender to despair, or to age, for that matter, in the straight backbone or squared shoulders. She was barely five feet and probably never saw ninety on a bathroom scale, but she looked like she could roll over Cleveland.

The elderly man who followed in her wake was a different story. Grief was weighing him down, pulling at his puffy, red eyes and a mouth that trembled.

Magozzi thought it was interesting that Marty reached out as if to touch the old woman's arm, but pulled back at the last minute. Apparently not a touchy-feely relationship. 'Detectives Magozzi and Rolseth, this is my mother-in-law, Lily Gilbert, and this is Sol Biederman.'

Lily Gilbert stepped up to the table and laid a hand on her dead husband's chest. 'And this is Morey,' she said, frowning at Marty as if he'd been rude to exclude his father-in-law from the introductions, simply because he was dead.

'Marty tells us your husband was a wonderful man, Mrs Gilbert,' Magozzi said. 'I can't imagine what a terrible loss this must be for your family. And for you, too, Mr Biederman,' he added, because tears were running freely down the old man's face now.

Lily was staring at Magozzi intently. 'I know you. You were all over the news last fall for that Monkeewrench thing. I saw more of you than I did of my own family.' She gave Marty a pointed look, which he studiously ignored. 'So, you have questions, am I right?'

'If you think you're up to it, yes.'

Apparently she was not only up to it; she decided to skip the questions and go straight to the answers. 'All right. So this is what happened. I got up at six-thirty, just like I always do, made some coffee, came out to the greenhouse, and there was Morey, lying in the rain. Marty thinks I should have left his father-in-law outside with the rain falling in his eyes; left him there so strangers could come and see his mouth filling with water.'

'Jesus, Lily.'

'But this is not how families take care of each other. So I brought him inside, made him presentable, called Sol, and then I called Marty, who hasn't answered his phone in six months.'

'Lily, it was a crime scene,' Marty said tiredly.

'And I should know this? Am I a policeman? I called a policeman, but he didn't answer his phone.'

Marty closed his eyes, and Magozzi had the feeling he'd been closing his eyes to this woman for a long time. 'I'm not a policeman anymore, Lily.'

Magozzi had an immediate flashback to a day almost a year gone, when he'd passed Detective Martin Pullman as he went out the front doors of City Hall, carrying his career in a cardboard box, looking like he'd been run over by a truck. 'You'll be back, Detective,' Magozzi had said, because he didn't know what else to say to a man who had lost so much, and worse yet, he didn't understand a man who could walk away so easily from a job he loved. Marty had smiled, just a little. 'I'm not a detective anymore, Magozzi.'

Magozzi shifted back to the present in time to hear Gino asking the usual litany: Was anything missing? Any sign of a break-in? Did Morey Gilbert have any enemies, any unusual business dealings?

'"Unusual business dealings?"' Lily snapped. 'What's that supposed to mean? You think we're growing marijuana in the back greenhouse or something? Running a white slavery ring? What?'

Gino had never responded very well to sarcasm, and his face started to turn red. They'd dealt with their share of grieving relatives over the years, and Gino did okay with the ones who fell apart. They tore him up, and he suffered for a long time afterwards, but at least he knew how to respond to them. People were supposed to fall apart when a relative died. That fit in with Gino's image of life and death and love and family, and made it easy for him to be softspoken, gentle, as comforting as a cop could be in such a situation. But the angry ones who lashed out, or the stoic ones who kept their feelings close to the vest, always threw him into a tailspin, and Lily Gilbert seemed to be a combination of the two.

'Excuse me, Mrs Gilbert,' he interrupted gently, eliciting an eye roll from Gino. 'Would it be too difficult for you to take me outside and show me where you found your husband? Maybe walk me through it, step-by-step, while Gino talks to your friend Sol? We can get through this faster, then.'

The reminder of finding her husband's body brought the first sign of weakness to her eyes. Just a flicker, but it was there.

'I'm really sorry to have to ask you to do this. If it's too hard, we don't have to do it right now.'

Her gaze sharpened immediately. 'Of course we have to do it now, Detective. Now is all we have.' She marched toward the door, a little old soldier focusing on the mission, so she didn't have to think of anything else. Magozzi hurried to open it for her.

'Wait just a minute.' Marty frowned. 'Where's Jack, Lily? Why isn't he here yet?'

'Jack who?'

'Damnit, Lily, don't tell me you didn't call him.'

She was out the door before he finished.

'Shit.'

'Who's Jack?' Magozzi asked, still holding the door.

'Jack Gilbert. Her son. They haven't talked in a long time, but Jesus, his father just died. I gotta call him.'

While Marty went to the checkout counter and started punching numbers into the phone, Gino walked over to Magozzi and said under his breath, 'Listen, while you're out there talking to the old lady, why don't you ask her how a ninety-pound peanut managed to drag over two hundred pounds of dead weight all the way in here, then heft it onto that table.'

'Gee, Mr Detective, thanks for the tip.'

'Glad to help.'

'You don't like her much, do you?'

'Hey, I like her fine, except for the fact that she's got a personality like ground glass.'

'Huh. She never mentioned your outfit. I'd say that was a kindness.'

'This is the deal. I'm thinking, How the hell did she move him? So I answer myself: Gee, maybe she didn't. Maybe she shot him in here, and just said he was killed outside so we'd think we didn't have a crime scene.'

Magozzi thought about that for a minute. 'Interesting. Devious. I like the way you think.'

'Thank you.'

Magozzi opened the door to go outside. 'But she didn't do it.'

'Damnit, Leo, you don't know that.'

'Yeah. I do.'